The Ratcatcher
By

Alfred Gerald Davison

Published by:
Marlab Media
Enghavevej 9A
7800 Skive
Denmark
www.marlab.dk/ratcatcher.htm

First Edition

ISBN 978-87-993990-4-8

Copyright © 2011 Alfred Gerald Davison

Cover and layout:
Alfred Gerald Davison

Dedicated to my good friend

Col. Juras Abromavichius

Killed by a car bomb in Kaunas, Lithuania

Happy Trails Juras !

Jack Bell had never really liked the winter. He had been forced to walk to school on cold winter mornings, wearing short trousers and thin nylon socks. Sometimes the wind would chill him to the bone while he stood waiting for the bus. When it was really bad, he would take off his school cap and stand in line with it clutched to his knees to keep them warm. That had been many years ago. Nowadays he didn't have to wear a school uniform, but his hatred of winter remained. The worst was the slipping and sliding on icy pavements; scraping the ice off the windscreen of the car in the parking lot on early mornings; hearing the wind howl down the chimney and watching the snow build up on the window ledge. He hated drinking morning coffee with only the lights of the town to break the monotony of the darkness. He hated driving through the streets in the evening, ever fearful that a pedestrian would suddenly appear from behind a corporation bus. He hated being alone. It made him feel like death, like his life was totally empty and valueless. The photographs in their frames on the living room walls looked down upon him and jeered. When he looked back, their eyes were empty, lifeless. He knew that when he looked away again they would shake their heads in wonder. When Jack entered the room he always did so in a hurry, hoping to catch them at it. So far he had not had luck on his side, but he knew that one day... Jack you see was a man of limited social awareness. He did not go to evening classes in porcelain painting, origami, or folk dancing like most of the others at the bank. He did not have hobbies like stamp collecting, or bridge. The theatre held no interest for him and neither did the cinema. In fact there was only one thing that could really light a fire under Jack. Eavesdropping.

This was a side of Jack that nobody really knew. Not even his dear, departed mother, god rest her soul. Doris Bell had spent the last three years of her life in the front bedroom of the house on Forbeck Road. Doris' stroke a couple of years before had left her too ill to move about. Or at least she said so. Jack had never really believed her. As far as he could see, it was just an excuse she had invented to keep him from leaving home, to make him feel guilty every time he mentioned going somewhere for a holiday. Jack had the back room next to hers, the one overlooking the back garden. One night in December, two years back, she had had a bad turn in the middle of the night. Jack had been on his way to the toilet when he heard a gurgling sound and put his head around the door. The yellow light from the sodium street lamp outside lit up the room with a kind of ghostly glare. Doris was having a fit on the bed, writhing and bubbling at the mouth. Jack hurried down the stairs and called the doctor. It was ages before he came, an hour at least, and by that time Doris had fainted. When the doctor finally got there, he looked like something the cat had dragged in. Jack showed him up the stairs. Half an hour later, Doris was on her way to hospital, and Jack was closing the front door behind the doctor.

Jack got a real shock that time. For the first time in his thirty-two year old life, he became aware of a fear of being alone. This was something new to Jack, the thought that maybe Doris wasn't just making it up. Maybe she really was ill! Everything he had ever done had been planned, not by his father James, who had run off and left the two of them alone twenty years ago, but by Doris. Who was it that had him sent to a boarding school until he was eighteen? Who was it that got him a job at the bank where her cousin was manager, when he came home again? Who was it that got her brother Arnold, the taxi driver, to make sure he turned up for work on time every day for the next five years? The only reason Arnold had stopped was because some young hooligans had stolen his taxi after a football match, and he had not been insured against theft. Arnold had always been a cheapskate.

By then though, Jack was thoroughly and completely brainwashed. He had never missed a day in the fourteen years he had worked at the Provincial. Jack got so scared at the thought of having to fend for himself, that he went down to Whites' Market the next day and bought a baby watcher. He spent most of the day installing one end in his mothers room, another station in his own room, and another in the living room downstairs, just under his mothers room at the front of the house. He put one in the kitchen, one in the bathroom on the first floor, one in the toilet through the kitchen door. Actually, it was the first time in his life he had had real fun. He did not have the tools he needed to connect the wires and drill the holes in the wall, so he drove the mini down to Union Street, to the Red Radio Shop. The manager of the shop was an Irishman, Sam MacAteer. He had taken over running the place twenty years before when the owner, Bob, had died, leaving a widow. She still owned the place, but did not take part in business activities any more. Now Sam was a clever man, and not what you might call a sneaky man. He could tell right away that Jack did not know one end of a soldering iron from the other, so he sold Jack a book about electronics, amplifiers, microphones, tape recorders and stuff like that, along with a good portion of tools. Jack did not know that so many tools existed, but bought them anyway. Sam was a good salesman. He was convinced that Jack would benefit from the deal.

So away went Jack. He finished installing the baby watcher and tried it out by putting the transistor radio next to it and turning it on low. It worked. With the volume turned up, and the telly on normal, he could hear what was going on all over the house. This was probably the first real victory that Jack had ever secured for himself, without interference from anybody else. No wonder he was hooked.

Six months after his mother had gone to her final resting-place at Ryhope cemetery, her room looked like the space centre at NASA. It was full of all kinds of tape recorders, amplifiers, microphones and other gadgets. Jack had bought or built everything in the book he had bought from the Red Radio Shop. All his spare time and cash went into this room, every evening and every weekend, because Jack did not go out at all with his work-mates. When the bank closed, and the others stood around chatting, Jack quietly put on his grey mohair overcoat, took his briefcase, and left through the back door. He always stopped to make sure that it locked behind him. Jack was conscientious. Then without further ado he started the mini, drove carefully down the back lane, right onto Joseph Street, right again onto Bridge Street and crossed the river. He would have to cross the river again at the Queen Alexander Bridge, but Jack liked the name of the bridge so that didn't matter at all. He never could wait to get home.

Monday evening, while driving home through the snow, caught behind a corporation bus on Fawcett Street, Jack had a sudden, strange, and very exciting idea. By the time he reached the house and parked the car in the front garden, the idea had become a crazy plan. Jack had decided to bug the bank. Now why would he do that? You may ask. Well, it may be because Jack always had the feeling that the others talked about him after he was gone. He did not know that the others really did not care enough about him to talk about him. Anyway, on Friday, Jack turned up for work as usual. When lunch break came, he sat to eat at his desk, as usual. When nobody was looking, Jack fixed the microphone he had bought, to the underside of his desk where nobody would notice. He checked to see that the coast was still clear, and felt like the hero of a spy film on the telly. Then he slid the radio transmitter into his drawer and pushed it all the way to the back. Wanda Levinson, one of the cashiers, came by, so Jack pulled a random piece of paper out of the drawer, closed it slowly, and began reading. Wanda did not seem to notice anything. Jack dropped his pen, and rolled it under the desk with his right foot. While retrieving it, he connected the transmitter to the microphone.

Before leaving that evening, Jack turned on the transmitter. It was voice activated, and the mains socket in the floor just under his desk provided all the power needed. The transmitter had a range of five miles, which was enough to reach Jacks' house. He had tested it already, in Backhouse Park, by hiding it in the bushes by the gents' toilet. Later, it occurred to him that that had been a little risky, because there was only room for two in the toilet, and some men being what they are....

Jack did not rush home. He didn't need to, because he had already set up the receiver and tape recorder to start recording when the transmitter started sending. Anyway, the traffic was bloody murder as usual, and the last snow fall had been so violent that it was all he could do to keep the mini from jumping by itself into the tracks left by the busses and lorries.

Jack was disappointed when he played back the tape. The machinery had worked, but all his work mates were saying was idle chitchat. Not one single word was said about Jack. Anyway, that night, when Jack went to bed in his room at the back of the house, he was happy. It worked, and that was enough. Sooner or later someone would fall into the trap.

Saturday was cloudy, and there was still a lot of snow in the garden, so Jack decided to stay in bed and watch some morning television. At nine o'clock, the cartoons started. Jack loved to watch cartoons, especially Daffy Duck. It was not that what Daffy did was particularly funny. No, it was more like Daffy was the kind of loudmouthed extrovert who was always trying to get ahead at everyone else's expense, and always ended up being smashed, or chopped to bits, or squashed under a sixteen ton weight. Jack always experienced a true sense of relief and pleasure whenever Daffy got what was coming to him. Then, after Daffy, came a repeat of an episode from a series about a boy and a dolphin in Australia. Jack loved that dolphin as if it was his very own. He always ended up crying when he watched the series. It restored his faith in people to see that humans and animals could get along together. But it reminded him too that he was alone in the world, left to fend for him self in a world as big as the ocean, without any friends to care for him. When the tears got to be too much, he climbed out of bed, went downstairs and made him self a cup of hot, sweet tea.

There was a noise at the front door. Jack peeked through a crack he made in the venetian blinds. The postman was on his way down the short flight of concrete stairs leading from the front door to the garden gate. He was sorting letters. His bag looked heavy. Jack put his cup on the coffee table in front of the sofa, making sure that he found a coaster to put it on. His mother had taught him that. He went to the front door. There was a letter lying face down on the mat. He picked it up and turned it over. It was from the bank. "Strange..." he thought and opened it. The letter was signed by the managing director and was quite brief.

"Due to the present economic situation in the banking world and in Provincial Bank in particular, we find ourselves forced to take unpleasant measures in order to assure the survival of the company. We have therefore decided to make a thirty- percent reduction in staff. We have chosen the staff members at random, and regret therefore to inform you that your services are no longer needed at the bank. Your long service with us requires two months notice to be given. We will therefore continue to pay your salary for the next two months, but release you herewith from your work, in order to give you time to seek other employment. Good luck for the future."

That was it. No thank you for fourteen years of service. No discussion. No reprieve. No future. Upstairs, Daffy Duck was squealing as a buzz saw sawed him in half. Jack went into the living room, put the letter into the envelope and placed it in the brass letter rack on the mantle. He took his tea and went upstairs to restore his faith in mankind.

After the ten o'clock news, there was the weather report. Charles Buffin stood before the weather chart and pointed out the lows and highs. He drew up cold fronts and occlouded fronts and stuck magnetic rain clouds onto the board behind him. Jack was completely unaware of the approaching storm. He had fallen asleep again half way through the news. His cup lay on its side on the floor and there was a puddle where the last remains had spilled out. The television blared to an unattentive audience in number six Forbeck Road.

The storm broke over the town at one o'clock on Sunday morning. Its' coming was reported by newspapers and empty polystyrene scampi cartons which rose from the pavements and cobbles, and began moving around with minds of their own. The streets of the town centre were empty, except for a couple and a group of partygoers walking home after the last bus. A taxi stopped by the pavement outside Woolworths on Fawcett Street. The couple ran from the shelter of the doorway towards the car. The man had his coat collar turned up and held closed by a hand as he reached to open the door of the car. The woman was carrying a folded umbrella. The door slammed shut behind them and the taxi pulled slowly away towards the bridge as the first of a new fall of hail began to beat an angry tattoo on the pavement and store windows.

At two thirty, a grey Grenada turned the corner into Joseph Street, splashing slush onto the pavement. Its dipped headlamps picked out the ornamental front of the old post office a hundred yards away at the end of the street through the hail. It moved slowly along the street, windshield wipers batting hail aside, until it had passed Joplings store. Then it turned left into the alley and kept going, flanked on both sides by the crumbling brickwork of Victorian walls, its exhaust sputtering.

The Grenada stopped in the parking lot of the Provincial Bank and two men got out. One was wrapped tight in a heavy overcoat with collars pulled up around his ears. The other wore a dark duffle coat with the hood up. Two other cars were parked there, a white Rover and a blue Ford Thames van. The Grenada passenger put one hand on the hood of the Rover. It was still warm.

The two men approached the back door of the Provincial Bank. The driver pressed the bell and peered into the fisheye lens. A minute later, the bolt was drawn and the door opened. The two men went inside and the door closed quietly behind them. The alley was now both dark and empty. Inside, they stamped the cold out of their feet, took off their shoes so as not to drag slush up the stairs, and hung their coats on pegs attached to the wall.

Computers are marvellous things. Fifty years ago, accounts were held in reams and reams of papers with shabby edges, on shelves that were kept tidy by an army of bookkeepers. Nowadays, the same amount of information can be held in a very small space. So the shelves have gone. Metal fireproof boxes with thick doors, containing row upon row of small plastic biscuits each enclosing a thin sheet of magnetic material have replaced them. In the past, bookkeepers' desks contained neat piles of papers, a mug holding pens and pencils, and a mechanical calculator. Now the desks are clean and empty except for a small, square screen and a keyboard. Even the bookkeepers have changed. At the end of the war, bookkeepers were middle-aged men in grey suits, long overcoats and Trilby hats. They walked to work each morning with bent backs and a briefcase and walked home again in the evening in the same manner. Computers have changed all that. Now the bookkeepers are striving young technocrats in expensive clothes. They don't sit at home in the evening pondering over a game of whist or a jigsaw puzzle. They go to discos and dance technocratic dances to technocratic music. Some members of that generation though are much more dangerous than others. The ones to watch out for are the youngsters who not only use and understand, but also love the computers they have at their disposal. For them, breaking codes and gaining unauthorised access is like a game of chess, a pitting of wits with invisible programmers on the other end of a modem link. They are the hackers.

Hacking can take many forms. It can vary from the simple breaking of a protective code in computer games, to planting of virus in defence computers. When you mix a computer, a modem, and a clever young man of twenty-two years old together, in a quiet building in the middle of the night, then anything can happen.

"Come on then Brian... what's taking so long?" The tall, thin man with round rimmed glasses was becoming impatient.

Brian Wallis, twenty-two, skinny, spotty, and with glasses, looked up from the screen.

"Take it easy Black. Go and get yourself some coffee or something, you're making me nervous and when I get nervous I can't think straight!"

The tall thin man shrugged and turned away. He did not at all like it when Brian talked to him like that. But there really was not a whole lot he could do about it. On the other side of the room, by the front window looking down upon the empty street, another young man was sitting. He had just lit a cigarette when the tall thin man turned towards him. The tall thin man walked quickly across the room, pulled the cigarette violently out from between the young mans lips, and dropped it into the cup of tea placed on the window ledge.

"I told you Peter, no smoking! Do I have to repeat myself? He hissed, close to Peter's ear.

"You know better than anyone that smoking isn't allowed up here, so if you smoke, then they'll be able to smell it when they come to work in the morning. We don't want them to know we've been here now, do we?"

The anger and nervousness in the tall thin mans' voice told Peter Lennox that it was best to agree, so he did so without hesitation. This kind of work was new to Peter. He was not used to crawling around in empty buildings in the middle of the night, keeping a lookout for coppers. But the group needed him Brian had said. He was the only one who could get them into the bank at the weekend. It had taken nerve indeed to 'borrow' the key to the back door from the manager's desk. Now he was here. Outside in the street, the snow was falling heavily, and slanting almost horizontally as it blew past the window. Brian hadn't said that there would be foreigners involved though. Peter didn't know where they were from. He hadn't asked and they hadn't offered any information, but they spoke English with a heavy accent, probably continental, perhaps German. So the whole thing had become international. Maybe he would get to travel abroad along with Brian and Billy and the others, if they found him useful. Footsteps sounded on the stairs and Peter turned his head. The light from a torch in the corridor outside the office swept briefly past the opaque glass window above the door. It lit up the white ceiling in the office for a moment and cast the darkened strip-lights dangling on the end of thin steel wires into shadow. The torch was shut off just before the door opened. Brian Wallis noticed nothing. He was bent over the keyboard, caught in the dim glare from the screen and the desk lamp placed strategically to light up the keys without shedding too much light on the rest of the room. A man entered the room, and the tall thin man went out, taking the torch from the fourth man without a murmur as he went. He closed the door behind him and light footsteps sounded on the stairs. The fourth man was also tall and thin, but wore no glasses. His hair was close-cropped just like the tall thin mans'. He wore a black duffel coat with the hood back. His shoes were flat, with thick rubber soles and no laces. He stopped briefly beside Brian, looked at the screen without understanding what he saw, and went across to the window.

"Hi Erik. Everything alright?" Peter asked and got a nodded reply from Erik, who was busy peeking through a slit he made in the venetian blinds.

"How are you holding up Peter?" Erik asked, without looking at the youngster.

Peter hesitated for a long time. Erik was all right; at least he was easier to talk to than Black.

"Well, it's all new to me so I'm a bit nervous. I keep thinking the cops are going to bust in here at any minute!"

Erik let the blind fall back into place with a slight plastic crackling sound. In the eerie glare from the desk where Brian was working, he looked down at Peter and placed a hand on his shoulder. Erik smiled a crooked smile, and a glint of gold sparkled briefly from his partially open mouth.

"Not to worry. If we keep all the lights off and don't make too much noise, they'll never know we're here. Besides, who wants to walk about the streets in this weather? Any policemen coming up this way will be in a car. They'll see nothing. In any case, Black's downstairs on watch by the back door so we'll get enough warning should anything go wrong".

Peter nodded. He felt more comfortable being with Erik than with Black. Brian was all right though. Well, he was from Newcastle wasn't he! Black was obviously the leader, maybe that was why he was so touchy.

"How long have you been in the group Peter?"

"About a month. I met Brian in the Central over on Bridge Street a couple of months back. He plays dominoes for the Democratic Club and they were playing away to our team. I beat him in the finals. Anyway, we got talking after the match and he told me about the group. They sounded like they were a great bunch of lads, and I had nothing better to do, so I went to a couple of the meetings and then joined up."

Erik nodded. In the minutes that followed, there were no sounds except for the quiet and rapid clicking of the keyboard. This suddenly stopped, and Brian said in a low whisper,

"I'm in! ".

Erik crossed quickly to the desk, turned halfway across the room towards Peter, who was getting up, and said,

"Stay there. Keep a sharp look out. We'll be finished in a couple of minutes".

Peter obeyed and turned towards the window. It won't be long now, he thought, and peeked through a slit in the blinds.

Erik pulled up a chair and sat down next to Brian.

"We've just passed the front door and entered the lobby" Said Brian. "Now I'll feed in the password and let's see what happens next."

He typed a short sentence and the screen went blank for a moment, only to come back with an account sheet belonging to a large international shipping company. Brian smiled with glee.

"How much do you want me to move?" He said to Erik.

Erik reached into the right hand pocket of his duffle coat and brought out a small pocket book bound in light brown leather and embossed with a cobble stone pattern. He pushed the book into the light and flipped though some pages; missed the one he wanted, came back, then forward again through the book, and finally settled on a page.

"Two million, three hundred thousand" He said.

Yes computers and glasnost are wonderful things. In the twinkling of an eye, you can move two million dollars from a bank account half way across the world, and put it into another bank account in Lithuania with no questions asked. No faces for bank personnel to recognise, no problems crossing borders and going through customs. The money just disappears from one account and appears in another. The money just disappears.

The transfer was complete. Brian shut down the link and carefully erased all the messages and files the work had left lying around inside the computer, whilst Erik moved silently around the room, removing the plastic cups they had brought with them and checking that everything was in place. When he was finished, Brian turned off the machine. The only sound in the room was the receding whine of the blower running down to a full stop and the rustle of papers as Brian collected together all the notes he had made during the last two hours and put them in a plastic bag. He did not take off the surgical gloves he had worn the whole time. They still had to get out of the building. When everything had been cleaned up and returned to normal, Brian and Peter followed Erik out of the office. Peter locked the door behind them and put the key in his pocket as they descended the stairs to the rear hall.

At the bottom of the stairs they met Black, who was ready to go. He handed the torch to Peter, who opened both locks in the back door. Black held the door open with his foot while Erik and Brian put on their shoes. Not wide, just wide enough to prevent it closing while Peter walked round the stairs, along the corridor, into the main office. By now Peter was feeling fine. The job was over. He could relax. Nobody in the bank would ever know that they had been there and that he had let them in. He opened the top right-hand drawer of the manager's desk all the way out and placed the key where he had found it. Peter closed the drawer and left the office. He returned to the back door. Black was saying to Brian;

"We'll meet you at one o'clock outside the Democratic. Your turn to pay for the beer."

Brian nodded and slipped out of the back door. He disappeared into the snow between them and the parking lot. They waited until the blue Ford Thames van had been gone for two minutes. Nobody said anything. They just stood with their backs against the wall in the dark, until Black turned to Peter and whispered,

"Your turn Peter, see you later!"

Black didn't seem so annoyed now. Peter slipped out and felt the wind grab the collar of his jacket and bite deep into the tips of his nose and ears. It was a good thing the heating in the bank was turned off at the weekend, he thought, or coming out of the warmth into the cold would have been even harder. He crossed the back lane to the parking lot, dug the key to his fathers Rover from his overcoat and opened the door. The clock in the dashboard showed four thirty as he drove down the alley and turned right into Joseph Street. Free! He was elated.

Erik and Black closed the door behind them immediately the Rover turned the corner and hurried across the lane to the Grenada. The engine started immediately and they too drove down the lane and turned right into Joseph Street.

The snow had not eased up at all, and the wind was still howling around the corners, throwing up flurries here and there as it played.

The footsteps and tyre tracks in the lane were already beginning to fill in. Within an hour it would be impossible to see when they had been made.

The Rover drove up Fawcett Street, continued on across the new traffic system on Bridge Street and crossed the bridge at the green light. Fifty yards behind, at the limit of visibility in the driving snow the Grenada drove in the same direction. As the Grenada crossed the river, Black, who was sitting in the passenger seat, looked left. Through the white haze the bright floodlights of Pickersgill's shipyard hung like remote blazing suns, with no connection to the ground. Snow was building up on the windscreen in the places where the wipers could not reach. Up front, the Rover turned right at the bus station on the corner of Roker Avenue. Erik looked across at Black.

"He's taking the Roker Road. We'll take the Fullwell Road. Step on it Erik, we have to get to Marsden first!" Said Black.

The Grenada took the roundabout by the old police station, swung left again by the bowling hall, and accelerated up the hill towards the mill at the top of the Fullwell Road. When it got there, it swung round the big roundabout, its rear end sliding in the slush and snow, and accelerated again down the hill towards the coast. Black was hanging on to the strap above the door. Erik saw nothing but the road ahead, what there was to see of it that is. The Rover slowed down for the Marsden roundabout and Peter checked both ways before pulling out to go around it. The tape was on, and Dolly Parton was singing about Applejack. As the Rover straightened out after the roundabout, a brief flash of grey against white to the left attracted Peter's attention. He managed to turn his head just in time to see two pairs of headlights bearing down on him.

The Grenada rammed the Rover in the left side, just behind the passenger seat. Metal grated on metal. The passenger side window of the Rover burst, sending glass shrapnel flying across the face of the driver as the door folded. Peter had not been wearing a seatbelt. He felt the first shock of the impact, mostly down his left leg, then everything went black. The Grenada shuddered. Its two occupants held on for their lives, fastened tightly by their seatbelts. Locked together in a mortal grip, both cars continued on across the traffic island in the centre of the road, across the far pavement and into the metal balustrade. For a moment, the Rover seemed to hang on the edge of the cliff, contemplating the rocks below. Through the remains of the windscreen, the driver could be seen slouched over the wheel, blood spurting from the front of his face. The Grenada kept pushing. The rear wheels were having trouble keeping their grip on the slippery surface. Slowly, agonisingly, the flimsy metal tubing of the balustrade gave way and the Rover toppled ever so stately over the edge and disappeared. The sound it made hitting the rocks forty feet below was washed away in the roaring of the waves and the howling of the wind.

The Grenada's engine stopped and its lights went out. Black and Erik climbed out, shaken. For a few seconds they stood peering down into the blackness below, trying to make out details they knew were there somewhere, but that they were not able to see. Both men turned as if on the same signal, and ran towards the Roker Hotel. The road was still completely empty.

Five minutes later, two men walked round the corner of the Roker Hotel. One was dressed in a heavy overcoat with the collars turned up to keep out the cold. The other was dressed in a duffle coat with the hood up. They climbed into a brown Simca and drove it away. The bellboy had just been up to a guest with headache pills when the engine started. He glanced out of the lobby window as the Simca left the parking lot, and wondered briefly who would be out and about at five o'clock in the morning in weather like this, then forgot it again.

You know how it is when the phone in the hall rings and you're in a deep sleep after a hard night on the bottle? Bill Lennox did, because that's the way it was that Monday morning. He lay in a heap on the bed, more unconscious than asleep, with the sheets piled up on the floor and a bucket beside the headboard. He always did that when he went on the binge, except for one time when he had not had the energy. Funnily enough, that was the only time he had ever thrown up! He tried to wave it away, but the phone just kept ringing, and ringing, and ringing. He turned on his stomach and was crawling out of bed onto the floor when it stopped. So he rolled over on his back and went back to sleep again, with his torso on the floor, arms splayed out, and his legs up on the bed.

Round about noon, he came to himself again, and got up on his feet. He was still dizzy, and felt sick at the least movement. He took two steps toward the living room, stopped for a breather at the foot of the bed while leaning on the bedpost, pulled himself together, and stumbled on until he passed through the blue bathroom door. He decided not to look in the mirror. He knew by experience what he would see, so he fell straight into the shower, pulled the curtain closed and turned on the water. The shower was thermostatically controlled. It was always set to body temperature so as to save on the heating bill. It still took him by surprise though. He gasped as the water hit his body, and his headache got suddenly worse, then he relaxed and let it pour down over his head, over his body, over his feet, washing away the sins of the night before. There were headache pills on the shelf just above the washbasin. He decided to take two when he was finished in the shower. Fifteen minutes later while he was shaving, the doorbell rang.

Lennox wrapped a towel around his torso and stepped out of the bathroom onto the landing. Through the square opaque glass window in the front door at the bottom of the stairs he could see two figures, one tall, wearing something that resembled a policeman's helmet, and the other slightly shorter and without headgear. He went down the stairs and opened the door. The shorter man reached into the inside pocket of his overcoat and pulled out an identity card that named him as sergeant Frederick Hawkins and had a photo that seemed to match as far as blurred vision could make out. The wind was biting cold.

"Come in quick and close the door, I'm freezing my balls off!"

Bill said and hurried back up the stairs. The two men stepped into the hall and closed the door behind them. Bill started putting his clothes on. They watched him from the bottom of the stairs.

"What can I do for you gentlemen?" He asked loudly.

"Are you Mister William Lennox?" The shorter man in the civilian clothes asked.

"Yes I am, Sergeant Hawkins. What's this about?"

He pulled on his trousers and started stuffing the denim shirt into them. His back ached, so it was not easy.

"Do you have a son named Peter Lennox?"

Bill stiffened. They had his attention now. He looked over the railing, suddenly sober again.

"Yes, I do. What's he been up to?"

"I am afraid I have some bad news for you mister Lennox. Your son was involved in a car accident on the coast road early this morning. I am sorry to have to inform you that he is dead. We would like you to come down to the infirmary to identify him."

To DS Hawkins Bill Lennox seemed too cool a customer. He had so far shown no sign of emotion at all. Hawkins decided to consider it a sign of shock, though the usual signs were not there to be seen.

"Let me finish getting dressed and I'll be right with you."

Bill Lennox said. He was not in shock. He was in fact quite surprised that Peter had been killed in a car accident. He was always driving too fast, that was true, but he was good at it and had never been involved in even a minor scrape. Lennox walked down the stairs, passed the policemen without a word and went into the living room. On the mantle just above the gas fireplace was a framed photograph of himself with Sara, Peter and Alexander. He picked it up and looked deep into their eyes. Sara's eyes said nothing. They had said nothing ever since the divorce and perhaps even long before that. Both policemen entered the living room. Lennox put the photo down and turned around.

"How did it happen?" He asked while pulling on the sweater he had taken with him.

"As far as we can make out, another vehicle skidded into him in the early hours of this morning on the Marsden Road. Your son went over the cliff. He was dead when we got there. I must warn you mister Lennox, that he is not a pretty sight."

Bill did not seem to care. He said nothing, just brushed past them into the hall and started to pull on his wellingtons and seaman's jacket.

"What about the people in the other car?"

"They must have panicked and run off. At any rate, they were gone when we got there. We're checking on the vehicle registration. It's only a question of time before we find the driver."

"Yes, unless it's stolen."

Sergeant Hawkins ignored the comment.

"Do you know how your son came to be driving on the coast road at that time of the morning?"

Bill Lennox shook his head.

"I am afraid not sergeant, though I must say that it does not really surprise me. I work abroad a lot and his mother and I were divorced a while ago. I had a standing agreement with Peter that he could use the car while I was away, and sometimes while I was home if he asked first, on the condition that he looked after it, paid for repairs etc."

He stood up and seemed ready to go, so they left and Bill slammed the door shut behind him. When they were in the police car and heading down the road past Thompson's Park, Sergeant Hawkins asked,

"Did he ask to borrow the car this weekend, mister Lennox?"

"Yes, I had a chat with him Friday night in the Central. I told him I wouldn't need the car this weekend and that he could use it if he needed it. Why?"

The sergeant shrugged. Once again it occurred to him that Lennox seemed remarkably cool. Lennox was not really listening for the answer. He was looking out of the window, at people on the pavement. But perhaps he was really looking inwards rather than outwards. What is wrong with me? I should feel something. I mean it is my own son lying dead out there. Why don't I? But to be honest, I really don't feel anything at all so why pretend to myself that I do? Sad isn't it – that life has done this to me? "Just for the record mister Lennox."

Monday morning was not the same as usual in the Provincial Bank. Some faces were missing, faces that had never been missing before. The employees were standing around talking about it when the manager arrived and went into his office. He put down his briefcase on the desk, hung his hat and overcoat on the silent waiter in the corner behind the door. Then he went back to his desk and took a written statement from the top drawer. On his way out of the office, Chapman stopped to check the setting of his tie. Looking at his reflection in the mirror, it suddenly occurred to him that he had grown much older this past weekend. His hair seemed thinner and more grey than usual. His face too seemed more wrinkled than it had a right to be at sixty years of age. The suit sat well though, and the subtly striped grey tie was as straight as the big hand on the clock in the background that said eight thirty. He went out into the main office.

When Chapman had finished explaining the situation in the bank and the redundancies that had taken place over the weekend to everyone, they went about their business. He knew that there would be mutterings and speculation in the corners for the rest of the week, but hoped it would soon pass. On the way back to his office he called to one of the junior clerks.

"Oh, Mira."

Everyone stopped in mid stride and looked around. Mira Ainsley seemed scared. Chapman knew they were all very nervous now.

"Yes Mister Chapman?"

"Go around the desks of the people on this list," he handed her the typewritten list," and clean them out please. Put all personal belongings in a pile on the left-hand side of each desk, and all bank papers and property in a pile on the right hand side. Fetch me when you have finished." She looked relieved.

"Yes Mister Chapman."

Fifteen minutes later, much quicker than expected, Mira knocked on Chapman's door.

"Come in."

He was reading the credit report on Watkins Haulage Company, which was open on his desk. She stepped inside. Chapman waved to her to wait a moment. When he had signed the loan documents, he carefully closed the file, screwed the two halves of his pen together, and placed it on top. Then he looked up at Mira. She seemed excited about something.

"I found something very odd out here mister Chapman. Would you come and look at it please?"

"What is it Mira?"

"I don't really know. It looks like some kind of microphone."

Now some might say that Chapman overreacted to what he saw by calling the police station on Gilbridge Avenue. Some may even say that the police overreacted by getting a warrant to search Jack Bells' house for the proceeds of what they suspected was a case of industrial espionage. But whatever they say, at eleven thirty that Monday morning, a police car pulled up outside number Six Forbeck Road, and two very large uniformed policemen got out.

Forbeck Road was accustomed to being visited by the police. The street was totally dilapidated. A burned out car stood at the end of the road furthest up the hill. Half the garden fences were either completely broken, or had been flattened by the hooligans that lived in numbers seven, nine and eleven. Car tyres, newspapers and broken bottles lying strewn around. Loose dogs poking their noses into spilled litter and flitting from house to house looking like lean, hungry wolves with their tails between their legs and their ribs showing.

One policeman knocked at the front door while the other went through the arch joining number six to number eight, round to the back door. Nobody answered, so they broke in through the back door after ten minutes wait. Nobody paid any attention to the sound they made as they broke the back door window. The sound of breaking glass was an everyday occurrence in these parts. The woman in number ten was hanging out her laundry on the washing line. She looked briefly over the line, saw the back of the last of the two policemen disappear through the back door of number six, then went back to her work.

When Jack Bell returned from his shopping at one o'clock, he got the shock of his life. Two police cars were parked outside his front door, which was open. When he got inside, carrying his two plastic Safeway shopping bags, he found four policemen waiting for him. They did not waste any time. They told him they had confiscated all his equipment and that he was under arrest for industrial espionage. It was not until they got Jack to the station that he woke up to the reality of the situation. When they asked him why he had bugged the bank, all he could do was laugh. When they asked him to describe how he had bugged the bank, he laughed. When they told him he could get five years in prison for this, Jack fell off his chair in stitches. So they called the psychiatrist and put Jack in a cell to calm down. But for Jack, sitting on the cot bolted to the wall and the floor in the detention room, the future looked bright. You see Jack had suddenly realised that his winter ordeal was finally over, that his loneliness was finally over. For Jack, the prospect of prison was not a threat; it was more of a miracle, an escape from having to look after himself. All he could do was look at the wall, clasp his hands between his knees, and giggle.

After identifying the remains of his son, Bill Lennox was driven over to police headquarters on Gilbridge Avenue to make a formal statement. Sergeant Hawkins was right. Peter had not looked a pretty sight. It had been difficult to make a positive identification. Had it not been for the scar on the right side of his abdomen, where his appendix had been removed at the age of four, and the ingrown toenail on his left foot, even Bill might not have been able to identify him.

"When and where did you last see your son alive mister Lennox?"

Constable Martins sat on the other side of the small desk, in a very long and narrow room that looked just like an interrogation room Bill Lennox had once been in Palermo. Martins was typing up his statement with one finger of each hand. Bill Lennox looked up at the ceiling. A fly was buzzing around the light bulb. Strange to see a fly this time of year, he thought.

"Friday night, outside the Central on Bridge Street."

He answered. Martins typed it word for word. Outside in the corridor, two big policemen were half carrying some giggling lunatic off to somewhere. Lennox could hear him through the open door, laughing and saying something about a bank and jail in a high-pitched whining voice. Martins did not pay any attention to it.

"Do you know the whereabouts of your sons' mother?"

"No, I am afraid I don't. We did not get on well together, so she left. I don't know where she went, and I never thought to ask Peter if he knew. I can imagine her being somewhere in the town though; most of her family lives here. Her mother lives over at Plains Farm."

"Can you remember her mothers' address?"

"Sure. Its either twenty or twenty two, Premier Road."

"Do you know any of your sons' friends mister Lennox?"

"No, not really. I work abroad most of the time and don't get home that often. That's why the marriage broke up I suppose. Peter never introduced me to any of his friends. I don't even know if he had any."

Bill Lennox was looking past Martins. From up here on the third floor he could see the Vaux brewery across the street. There was smoke coming out of the brick chimney and a smell of fermented hops through the open window. A span of heavy, grey shire horses was standing outside the main gate, hooked up to an old-fashioned bright red wagon loaded with modern stainless steel casks. Vaux was one of the few remaining breweries in the country that still had shire horses. They regularly won equestrian competitions with their teams. Had Colonel Vaux been alive today, he would have been proud of his handy work.

"I suppose all this makes me sound like somebody who couldn't care less about his family."

He said, almost to himself. Martins looked up from the typewriter and stopped typing. He turned to Lennox and offered him a cigarette from a packet he took from his shirt pocket. Lennox declined.

"No thanks, I don't smoke". He said, and lied.

"Well, to be honest mister Lennox, it does give that impression, but then again, indifference to ones' family is no crime. Me though, I like to see my wife and kids."

"Yes, so did I in the beginning. But as the years went by and the work got harder, I just seemed to get lost somewhere. Working in my line of business is a bit like the drug habit. Once you're hooked everything else takes second place. Suddenly nothing seemed to matter any more."

"My Uncle Jack was a sailor during the war. He got torpedoed on the royal mail liner Asturius when they were coming back from New York. How old are you mister Lennox?"

"I was forty three last birthday. Getting on a bit you might say."

"I wouldn't say that. But then again, I'm nearly forty myself, so perhaps that's why. Well, that's all for now mister Lennox. Where can we reach you if we need to talk to you again?"

"I'm not expecting to ship out for a month or so yet, so you'll probably find me at home, down the Central, someplace like that."

"Fine. Well, do you want somebody to drive you home?"

Lennox stood up and started to button his coat.

"No thanks. I'll have a walk around the town and get a bite to eat somewhere. I need a bit of fresh air after last night." Then he said as an afterthought "..and this morning."

The sun was shining when Lennox stepped out of the police station lobby. He stood on the top of the steps leading down to the street and gazed across the new roundabout towards Carter Street and the shopping centre. To his right, people were beginning to come out of the Londonderry. The wind had dropped while he had been inside. The traffic was heavy to and from the roundabout. It still seemed strange to him that he felt nothing more about Peters' death than he did. More by instinct than need, Lennox turned up the collar of his coat and walked down the steps. There was a rumbling in the pit of his stomach that would not go away and he could smell fish and chips.

After eating at Carricks, by the bus station, Lennox took a walk through the shopping centre that filled almost the whole town centre. When he was young, before the skyscrapers appeared, this place had been a maze of small streets behind the old town hall. Dirty streets, with dirty kids playing in them. Now all that was gone. The town centre had been torn down. Skyscrapers with twenty floors were built, and the three new streets full of bright, modern, high-priced shops that replaced the old maze were now covered by a high glass and steel roof. There was even a private security service walking around among the shops as if they owned the place. The town centre had been sold to big money. Fortunes were being made in there every day. But the kids were still dirty, and in the mean time the town had lost what little character it had ever had. Now you could burn the whole lot down and nobody would ever miss it.

The darkness arrived at five o'clock. All the streetlights were lit, and people were being asked to leave the shopping centre. They were closing. Just imagine, being thrown out of your own town centre! Lennox watched the doors close from the doorway of the newspaper shop on Carter Street. He felt a sudden chill, as if someone had walked over his grave. Time to go home.

The lights were off when he got back to his house in Victor Court, on the north bank of the river. Some kids were playing football in the street. Others were having a snowball fight. All of them were yelling. Lennox put the key in the lock and turned it. He had to put his foot against the bottom of the door and push, while pulling on the handle at the same time. It always got stuck in the winter. Something to do with the damp. When he got inside, the place seemed cold and desolate in a way it never had before. He took off his coat and hung it on the banister. Then he sat on the bottom stair and pulled off his wellingtons. They were wet from the snow so he put them in the corner behind the door and went into the kitchen to dry his hands and put the kettle on. When the kettle was on, he went back into the hall and turned on the light. Then he walked past the kitchen door and into the living room. When he turned on the light there, three pairs of eyes blinked.

"Good evening William. Nice to see you again."

Lennox was surprised, but tried not to show it. George Green, from the London office, was sitting in his black overcoat, in the only armchair where the springs did not stick out. His bowler was on the three-legged stool beside him. Green seemed to have sunk into the armchair. That was not surprising though. It had already been worn out when Lennox bought it at the jumble sale nearly a year ago. On the other side of the room, facing the one big window in the living room sat Avon Wailes, Greens' minder this year on business trips. Lennox nodded to Wailes, who returned the nod with a smile. The big man was always happy.

"Evening George. Glad you let yourself in. It's cold as buggery outside. I've just put the kettle on. Do you want a cuppa'?" George Green had never, ever been here before. Why now?

"No thank you." Said Green. "Yes please." Said Wailes at the same time.

Green glared at him, but Wailes ignored the sour look.

"No milk or sugar Bill."

Lennox nodded and went into the kitchen. He opened the hatch connecting the kitchen to the living room, and started getting the cups ready.

"To what do I owe the pleasure, George?"

"Oh, I am up here to check out the security arrangements for the queen's visit next month. I heard about your son Peter at Gilbridge Avenue police station, so I thought that I'd drop in and offer my condolences."

Lennox had noticed that Green still had his gloves on, so he obviously was not planning to stay long. He smiled to himself - I hope the lops get him! The kettle started to boil. Lennox turned off the gas and poured water into two shabby mugs. There was a Lipton's tea bag in each.

"Well, thanks very much George. Dumb kid got himself into an accident and went off the cliff at Marsden. I always told him to drive carefully, but he never would take any notice of his elders."

"Just like someone we know, what Avon?"

Wailes smiled politely and nodded. A football hit the window. Nobody said anything or took any notice. Lennox came into the room with two steaming mugs of tea. He handed one to Wailes.

"Well, that was all there was to it George." He sipped his tea and burned his lower lip.

"Well, perhaps it may seem that way to you right now, but I rather imagine that there is a deeper meaning hidden somewhere, if you know just where to look."

"What do you mean by that George? If you know something that I don't, then don't keep it to yourself."

Green twisted the small, dark moustache hanging on his upper lip. He loved fishing, and when the fish was Bill Lennox, he loved it even more. His grey eyes flashed.

"Well, I'm not certain, but I think your son may have been involved in something or other. While I was visiting the police station, I overheard something about the Provincial Bank being bugged. That's where your son worked isn't it?"

"Yes. At least he did the last time I asked him."

"Well then. I had a chat with the chief constable. I told him that you might be interested in listening to those tapes. Are you?"

Green eased himself upright and tried to prevent himself from slipping back into the hole in the middle of the armchair by supporting his weight on his elbows. He felt like a bit of a fool. It was not at all a pleasant feeling.

Bill Lennox had been George Greens' minder. He could read Green like a book, or rather, like a nursery rhyme. Green always reminded Lennox of Humpty Dumpty, who sat on the wall watching all the kings men go by. When he fell off that wall, all the kings' men could not put him together again. But as far as Lennox could see, Humpty Dumpty was cemented in place and would stay that way until the wall crumbled around him. There was absolutely no danger whatsoever of him falling off.

"I'll drop by and check them out tomorrow morning."

Lennox said over the rim of his mug. Green smiled heavily, obviously pleased with himself. Lennox' mug looked dirty and disgusting.

"Splendid William!"

He got up to leave, and brushed the back of his fine overcoat. Then he took his hat. Avon Wailes put down the mug on the window ledge and stood up. Wailes was big, much bigger than Lennox. He filled the room from floor to ceiling, and had to bend to get through the living room door as he followed Green out into the hall. Once outside, Green turned and said,

"Oh, by the way William. I hope I'm not intruding on your grief. This is probably not the right moment to talk about work, but after you have heard the tapes, please telephone me. I will be staying at the Palatine Hotel until Wednesday evening."

He did not wait for a reply, just put on his bowler and turned away. Wailes shook Lennox' hand.

"Sorry about your kid Bill! See ya'." Then off he went after Green.

"See ya'" said Lennox to an empty street.

It was beginning to snow again, so he went inside and locked the door.

At seven o'clock on Tuesday evening, Bill Lennox parked his Land Rover by the abandoned Catholic church behind the multi-storey car park and got out. The snow had stopped falling and everything was quiet. No wind at all. It was cold too. He was wearing a black duffle coat and his jeans were pushed down into his wellingtons. The thick woollen socks he had on were rolled over to stop snow from creeping inside. His head was bare. Across the street from where he had parked, a row of street lamps was lit, but there were none on his side. Lennox crossed to the opposite side and walked past the car rental company. He checked for traffic before crossing to the Palatine Hotel. It was not often that he came to the Palatine, although the bar was well known as the place to go if you were between the ages of thirty-five and eighty. There was a juke box in the bar that only held mouldy oldies. All the women who visited the Palatine bar and lounge did so in groups dressed to kill with make-up and perfume. Not exactly his style. Lennox liked the Londonderry. The Londonderry was more old-fashioned. The bar furniture had not been changed since the place was built in eighteen ninety. There was no sawdust on the floor, but it always felt like there should be when you walked in. The women who went there wore no war paint. Lennox walked past the entrance to the bar and lounge and went up the stairs to the reception on the first floor. You could still hear the noise from the jukebox downstairs. The reception desk was unattended. He walked along the corridor and turned right by the shared bathroom and shower. A few steps further on and then right again. George Greens' door was marked number seventeen. Lennox knocked and went in without waiting to be asked.

George was standing by the window, with his back to the door, looking through a crack he had made in the heavy brocade curtains. He had his overcoat on. On the single bed just around the corner where the shower had been installed, lay his suitcase. Greens' bowler, gloves and umbrella lay on top. The light at the head end of the bed was on and Avon Wailes was sitting in the armchair just under it, reading a book, with his glasses half way down his nose. He looked up as Lennox entered, and relaxed his grip on the King Cobra revolver in his lap. Lennox wondered when Wailes had begun to wear reading glasses. He had never noticed him wearing them before. Wailes noticed his interest.

"Don't you dare tell anybody I wear glasses Bill! They'll take the piss out of me."

"Don't worry about it Avon. My lips are sealed. I see that you've still got the Colt."

"Nothing like a Colt Bill. You can keep all that Smith and Wesson stuff for my sake. I never could get a Smith and Wesson to sit in my hand the same way twice running. You still got that model three oh' nine?" Lennox shook his head and crossed himself religiously.

"Nope. It went to the eternal armorer just outside Gib last spring. I went over to the enemy Avon. Bought myself a Glock instead." Wailes sneered.

"Never thought I'd see the day you went over to plastic, Bill. A real shame...."

"When you two are quite finished, I'd like to conclude my business here. Wailes, keep watch outside."

Green intervened. Wailes closed his book, which had the Palatine Hotel stamp across the front cover and stood up. He put the book on the bedside table, shut off the light over the headboard, dropped the colt magnum into the shoulder holster under his left arm, took off his glasses and folded them before putting them in his top pocket. Then he buttoned his jacket and left the room without saying another word. Even in the half darkness from the lamp on the desk by the window, Lennox could see that he was peeved. George Green did not seem to care one way or the other.

"Well, William. I take it you've been over to listen to the tapes. What was your impression."

Lennox sat down in the chair beside the desk and stretched out. His wellingtons were still wet and left a puddle on the floor.

"You were right George. Peter was into something a bit too rough for him to handle. Bearing that in mind, I'd say that his death may not have been an accident at all."

Green turned to face him. His hands were clasped behind his back.

"My sentiments entirely, William. That is why I am going to ask you to take on a little job that may give you the opportunity to put things right again."

Lennox folded his hands across his stomach and looked at Green without expression.

"I don't feel any need to get even for anything George. Peter got himself into a mess he couldn't get out of. That's all there is to it."

"Well, I'm going to ask you to take the job anyway. Let me tell you a little story."

The little story lasted until midnight. Green said he had been called back to London at short notice, so he left by the side door of the hotel. Lennox left fifteen minutes later. In the inside pocket of his coat was a passport in the name of Richard Brown and a company credit card. He stood for a long time looking at nothing in particular. The street was empty, still, and cold.

Chapter Two – Crossing the Styx

The ferry from Harwich to Esbjerg sails three times a week in the winter period. Brown found himself in a rusty old blue Morris thousand, in a queue of only forty or so vehicles waiting to be checked in on the quay. It was Friday evening, just after teatime. Most of the rust on the Morris was invisible, being under the rubber mats on the floor. How it had ever passed the last M.O.T. test was impossible to guess at. Outside the weather was still cold and windy. Inside wasn't much warmer because the Morris's heating was on the blink. It was out of the wind though, and since the wind was increasing in strength that was no small thing. Snowflakes had stopped melting against the hood some time ago and were beginning to solidify into a crisp, white blanket. Brown rubbed his hands together, then cupped them and blew on the fingertips. His breath made seeing anything through the windows almost impossible. The collar of his old donkey jacket was turned up and all the buttons except the one that was missing at the bottom were fastened. His toes felt like ice despite the thermal soles and the woollen socks and walking boots he had on. The window partially open. Brown turned on the radio again for the hundredth time in a row. It still didn't work, so there was really nothing to do at all but turn it off again and feel the cold, and hear the wind howling like a banshee against the gap in the car window. He started to doze.

Brown woke up when the engine of the car in front started. He sat up, still half-asleep, pulled the choke and turned the key in the ignition. The Morris started first time. By now the taillights of the car in front were disappearing through a gap in the fence. He pulled a dirty handkerchief out of his pocket and wiped the inside of the windscreen clear of dew. A man with an orange vest and a radio was waving him on, so he put the Morris into gear and slipped the clutch. The cars behind him started moving too. Like a long, fat anaconda they wormed their way through the gate, turned right up the quay, moving under the passenger loading tunnel that hung propped up on thick steel stilts, feeding a few passengers into the side of the ferry. The queue stopped at a signal from another man with an orange vest and a radio. The cars were allowed to move forward in groups of three. There was a momentary delay on the loading ramp while the officer in charge took Brown's boarding pass and decided which side of the ferry to put the Morris on, then it rattled up the loading ramp and was on board. Brown parked the car between two truck trailers with blue tarpaulins and a haulage company logo, and felt very small when he got out. He set the Morris in reverse gear; heaved on the handbrake; took the overnight bag from the back seat; locked up and went upstairs into the warmth.

There was no urgent need to look around. All Brown felt that he needed was some sleep, some warmth, some food and some more sleep. So he went to the cabin he expected to be sharing with three others, two flights down from the reception desk at the other end of the ship. Number two hundred and seven. A stewardess was standing against the wall in the corridor. Brown put her age at around twenty-five. She had long, naturally blonde hair and a blue uniform. She seemed a little bored. There was nobody else in the corridor.

"Which cabin sir?"

Brown showed her his passenger slip and wondered how she decided which country a passenger came from. Maybe he would ask her later when he had had a chance to warm up.

"It's just round the corner to your right and two doors up on the left."

"Thank you. Good night."

Brown said. He felt like he wanted to be friendly, but did not have the energy.

"Good night to you too sir." She replied.

When Brown got to the cabin there was nobody else there. Four keys were hanging just inside the door and the four bunks were empty. There were no suitcases either. The main lights were off. The only light was from a small bulb in the ceiling just over the entrance. He left the lights that way and stowed his bag under the bottom bunk to the right of the door. Brown visited the toilet, got undressed in the dark and put his clothes on the chair beside his bunk. When he climbed into bed, naked, the fresh linen sheets felt quite cold.

Avon Wailes did not like driving for George Green at all, and he was sure that George had noticed by now. George liked being driven in the Austin though and Wailes liked driving it, so the trips they took together usually went well enough as long as nobody said anything. Wailes came from a small town called Crook, in Durham County. As a youngster he had often hitchhiked down the A1 in the summer. Not that London was anywhere for a youngster to go, being a chaos of traffic and streets, but it was the trip that fascinated him. You saw everything on the old A1. It did not all flash by your car window somewhere on the other side of a slower car you are overtaking. There was always something to look at and always people to meet. The grass went all the way up to the edge of the road in most places. He liked driving past Scotch Corner in those days. There used to be a transport cafe there, in a little-used lane on the other side of the roundabout from the Scotch Corner Hotel, where you could get a mug of tea and a bacon, sausage and egg breakfast for under a pound. There was never any trouble getting a lift from there, and lorry drivers knew how to have a laugh - not like those toffee-nosed sods that stopped at the hotel restaurant. Those were the days - he thought as they drove past the Scotch Corner hotel at one o'clock in the morning, under the stark glare from the lamps on the roundabout, heading south towards The Smoke.

When he checked the rear view mirror just after Scotch Corner, Wailes could see that George Green was sitting reading something or other in the dimmed light of the rear reading lamp. Good, as long at he's busy he doesn't have time to make conversation. The lights at the roundabout disappeared behind them and everything went dark again. The Austin was moving along at eighty, but even so they were passed once in a while by somebody clocking at least a hundred. It reminded Wailes of the Triumph sports car he had done his first drive to London in. He had left Durham City at one in the morning, in the middle of a July heat wave, with the top open, the stars above, the sound of the engine and the stereo belting out Brenda Lee. Unconsciously, he leaned back in his seat, straightening his arms.

"Oh Wailes, I'd like you to drop me off at Catterick Camp. I've arranged with Squadron Leader Henderson to give me a lift back to the office. You don't mind driving the car back to London alone do you?" Wailes' bubble burst.

"Not at all sir. Will you be going by helicopter?"

"Yes. Noisy, smelly things, but they do get the job done and I am in rather a hurry. When do you expect we'll be there?"

"About thirty minutes sir."

"Fine."

Wailes was pleased with the prospect of driving the rest of the way alone. He liked driving in the dark, turning up the radio and opening the window. Although spring was still a way off and there were patches of snow on the road, it was not so bad as to completely remove the pleasure of an open window, not as long as you shut it again after fifteen minutes.

After a while, the Austin approached the roundabout at the entrance to the village of Catterick. Wailes turned left into the village and the approach road to Catterick camps' main gate. Five minutes later the Austin stopped at the guardhouse. The main gate was closed. There was a light on behind the big glass window of the guardhouse, and a couple of spotlights illuminating the gate from the tops of poles on each side of it. A soldier sat on the other side of the window reading a newspaper and pretending not to see the car as it pulled up outside the gate. Wailes got out and went up to the gate. He pressed the bell button. The soldier put on his hat and came out.

"What can I do for you, sir?" He asked sourly. It was warmer inside than out and he didn't really feel like getting cold at this time in the morning because some stranger couldn't find his way.

Wailes took out his identity card and the soldier flashed a light on it. He said.

" What is the purpose of your visit sir?"

"I have a passenger for a special flight to London. Please inform Squadron Leader Henderson that we have arrived, and open the gate so we can come in. I don't like sitting out here on the open road at this time in the morning."

"Just a second sir. I'll have to check."

The soldier wasn't impressed by the identity card, and anyway, if he had to be out and about then why shouldn't a couple of civilians? He went inside and called the officer of the watch. Lieutenant Davis was asleep on the couch in the rear of the guardhouse and didn't take too kindly to being awakened at two o'clock in the morning. It was to his credit though, that when he heard Private Johnson's report, he came very quickly awake.

"Let them in Johnson. I don't like having them sitting out there in the open. Tell the driver to park just round the back here... Go on then man!"

Johnson seemed a bit slow, but then he had been on duty all night and hadn't had a chance to catch his usual forty winks because the lieutenant had taken his place instead.

Wailes dropped George Green off behind the guardhouse and drove off again. As the main gate closed, he could see Green and a young officer step into a short Land Rover and drive towards the main building. Then he turned out of the village, left around the roundabout, and drove south, alone and comfortable. He lit a cigarette and spent a few pleasant moments thinking about what Laila would be doing at this time of night.

Wailes was married to a girl from Malaya. She was small, brown and apparently very frail. But what there was of her was made from steel wire, impossible to break. Wailes didn't have a ring on his finger though. He contended that it got in the way of his revolver when using the left hand, and anyway, only those that knew him should know that he was married - it was best that way. They lived in the small house in Crook where Wailes had been born. It lay about two hundred yards from the fish and chip shop his mother and father used to run. The shop was sold after his father died of a heart attack.

Laila had learned to accept that Wailes worked at odd hours and in odd places, and couldn't always manage to get home at weekends. She never asked about his work. Malayan women are like that. Mind your own business and take the goodies when they drop on your doorstep. Wailes carried a photograph of her in his wallet. Behind her and her mother was a tropical rain forest. On the back was written "To Wailes, from Laila. Ranjid". Ranjid is a small fishing village about a hundred miles north of Kuala Lipis, on the road to

Tanah Merah. Every Friday, all year round, a broken down old freighter, the "Lapis" arrives from Cambodia at Ranjid. Its' cargo is poppy seeds. Once, many years ago, it had also carried a wounded and sick passenger, Avon Wailes.

After twenty hours of boredom, beer in the disco and breakfast in the restaurant, the ferry docked at Esbjerg. Brown drove the Morris down the loading ramp. The sun was out, though there was a cold wind blowing from the north. Patches of snow lay here and there in the customs holding area and along the dockside. The water looked cold and grey. If he hadn't known better, he would have sworn that he was still in England. Everything looked almost the same.

Brown showed his passport at the shed housing the immigration office. The official standing outside the door looked through the window and checked the photo against the face. There was no difference. He handed the passport back and waved Brown on. That was it. Long live the EEC, thought Brown as he drove out through the gate and up the road to the first traffic light. There was a big sign saying "Remember to drive on the right", by the side of the road.

At the first traffic light, Brown turned right. There was a sign saying that Copenhagen was in that direction, along the E20. But Brown was not bound for Copenhagen. He was bound for the city of Aarhus, in the northern part of the mainland, or Jutland as it is known. The road was easy enough to find once he was out of Esbjerg. Brown turned on the radio, and found a station playing music. The talking was all in Danish, but that didn't matter at all.

Esbjerg is a thriving sea town. It is the headquarters of all the companies associated with the North Sea oil industry in the Danish sector, as well as a large fishing port and one of only two places on the west coast from where ferries come and go. Outside Esbjerg and between towns there are long stretches of countryside, which are often ravaged by snow storms and freezing winter winds at this time of the year. The countryside looks flat and barren. Many of the smaller trees and bushes are bent, showing that the prevailing winds come from the west in the growing season. From Esbjerg, the E20 runs mostly eastwards, close by some small provincial towns and villages, until it comes to the town of Vejen. It circles the outskirts of the town, which is remarkable only in that there are no houses more that two stories high and continues east to meet the E45. Going north, the E20/E45 skirts the major industrial city of Kolding before splitting into two. The first part, again the E20, continues eastwards crossing the Little Belt bridge, the island of Fyn, the new Great Belt bridge connecting Nyborg to Korsør, on the island of Sjælland, and continues for one hundred and forty kilometres to Copenhagen. The second part, the E45, continues northwards, through the major industrial city of Vejle, past the city of Horsens, the town of Skanderborg, where tourists gather in droves in the summer, then on to Aarhus. Brown followed the E45 for another hour and a half, and arrived in Aarhus at five in the evening, an hour after sunset.

Turning right off the motorway at Viby Ringvej, and stopping at the traffic lights, Brown remembered the last time he had been here. He had been a student of the language many years ago. If he turned to the right here and continued on up the hill, he would pass the head office and printing facilities of one of the country's largest daily newspapers, the Jutland Post. If he went a little further he would come to the student housing complex, where he had lived for two years. The light changed to green and Brown turned the Morris left onto Skanderborgvej, past the Merkur Hotel and the shopping precinct, and on up the hill. It was just like being at home again. Just after the Marselisborg Hospital, there was Harald Jensens Place, where all the town buses met several times a day to exchange passengers. Most of the kids in the student facility travelled by bus, but Brown had always travelled by car. Not that he had been rich. He was just older than the rest, and had an employer back in England who picked up the tab if he kept it within reason, as the bookkeeper had told him before he had left the office the first time.

At Harald Jensens Place, the Morris turned left onto Søndre Ringgade. Nothing had changed, despite the years that had flown by. The car crossed the twisted spaghetti trails of the main railway lines at the Ringgade Bridge and kept on going, past the Greek cafe where Brown had often eaten Pita sandwiches, to the lights at the junction with Silkeborgvej. Once across the lights, the Morris continued slightly uphill, past the cemetery on the left, and the county hospital on the right - not a very pleasing prospect when you come to think of it - across the Viborgvej lights. Past the school on the left and after that the botanical gardens on the right, past the kiosk on the corner of Paludan Møllers Vej, where Brown had met his first Danish girlfriend, Inge. That had lasted until Brown had finished his studies and was called home. It had not been easy to end. Inge had wanted to follow him. These things are always a messy business. But there had really been no choice.

The car stopped at the lights on the corner of Vestre Ringgade and Langelandsgade. The ivy still grew up the tower of the university library. Langelandsgade still went to the right, down the hill past the garrison and on to the city centre, and to the left, into the quiet part of the street. The light changed and the Morris turned left. Brown parked in a small parking lot just round the corner in Taasingegade, across from the Christian bookshop, and got out. It was too cold to stand around and admire the view, and he was rather tired from the drive. He pulled his suitcase and bag from the back seat and locked the door. Round the corner again into Langelandsgade and he walked quickly up the street to number ten. A student hurried the other way down the street, pushing a bicycle with a bent front wheel. He was buried in a heavy, green, fur-lined Musk-Ox parka, of the kind that had been popular before thermal underwear and jackets had dropped sufficiently in price for people to afford them. The wind whistled up the street, playfully biting Brown in the nose and ears as it passed. He pushed open the door to number ten, then turned around and watched the student disappear down the street.

There were eight apartments in the building. In the hall there was a post box with each residents name on it. The one for the first floor right apartment said 'Brown'. He dragged his bags up the stairs and rang the doorbell.

When the door opened, a familiar slightly plumper face greeted him. Arne Jensen held out his hand in welcome. Brown took it willingly.

"Davs du gamle - hvordan går det?"

"Godt nok Arne. Kors, hvor er jeg glad for at være tilbage igen!"

Arne smiled. In all the years he had worked for the department, Brown had never known Jensen to actually grin. He had seen him smile, get drunk as a pig, get sick, get serious, but never seen him grin. He thought Jensen looked odd.

"Nice to know you haven't forgotten the language you old bugger!" Said Arne.

"Same to you!"

Brown replied and stepped inside. He dropped his bags beside the same old green commode in the hall. The door closed behind him.

"There's coffee in the pot".

"Thanks Arne, that's just what I need!"

Brown went into the kitchen, took a mug from the cupboard above the sink and poured himself a cup from the coffee machine. It was thick, and black and bitter, just like the Danish coffee he had grown first to love and then to hate. Drink too much of it and it will keep you awake at nights and make your heart bang like the skin of a big bass drum at one in the morning. But for now it tasted good. He knew he would be going over to tea within the week though.

Arne was waiting for him in the living room, sitting at the small table just beside the front window and looking out onto the street. The curtains were open as always, and Brown could see the double mirror perched on the end of an iron bracket just outside the window. This was another peculiar Danish institution. Many people, especially pensioners, had them installed so that they could watch what was going on in the street outside. Brown looked around the living room. It was furnished, but the old armchair was gone and the place had no sign whatsoever of the character he remembered it having in the old days. There were a few books on the shelf over the television. Otherwise, there were no paintings, or clothes strewn about, or typewriters or overturned wastepaper baskets like the last time he had been here.

"I see you cleaned the place up Arne."

"Yes, Birgitte and I moved out about half a year ago. We bought a house over in Risskov. The department needed a flat in a hurry, so they made us a good offer. They paid enough to enable us to put down a deposit on our own place. I still keep a key though, for emergencies only. It was a bit of a surprise really. They're normally very stingy."

Brown nodded. Arne continued.

"I was expecting a visit, because when I came by on Wednesday to check the place over and empty the mail box, the Mob from Copenhagen were here. They wouldn't tell me anything though. You know what they're like. How is Sarah?"

Brown took a seat at the table across from Arne.

"It went to hell and back between Sarah and me. We got divorced about eight months ago." Arne shook his head apologetically.

"The boys?"

"Alexander is still in school. Peter got himself killed last week."

"That's terrible! How come?"

"He got himself mixed up with a bank robbery. They did him in afterwards when they didn't need him any more. Pushed his car off the cliffs. There wasn't much left of him to identify, but it was him all right. How's yourself and Birgitte?"

"Well, I finally made Doctor, so now I am working at the county hospital and doing a bit of research into brain activity over at the faculty at the same time. I got a lot of money and computer gear from an American company just two months ago, so I'll be specialising a bit in computer models of the brain. Birgitte is now rector at the foreign language faculty of the university. She is a bit overworked right now, and will be off to Spain for a conference tomorrow, so she won't have time to visit you. She sends her love though."

"Thanks. Tell her I send her mine back."

"Will do. Look, I have to be off now, so I'll put you into the picture. Here are the keys to the flat. There's food and drink in the kitchen, and equipment in the top drawer of the commode in the bedroom. The alarm system code is AXZCDFG. If you change it, please remember to put it back in the system before you leave for good. Well, I hope it goes well for you, whatever it is. Take care of yourself. I had better be going. I promised to help Birgitte pack."

"That doesn't sound like the Arne I know."

"Well, it is a bit egotistical really. The faster she is finished and away, the faster I can have some peace and quiet to get on with my work."

They both stood up, almost at the same time.

"That sounds more like you. Take care old friend!"

"You too. Don't kill anybody I wouldn't! Call me any time if you need me."

The door closed behind Jensen and as Brown listened to the retreating step, he changed the security alarm code. A few moments later, in the rear bedroom, he opened the top drawer of the commode. There was a .38 Smith and Wesson revolver, a military service Neuhauser, nine-millimetre parabelum. Brown chose the Neuhauser, dropped the clip and partially slid back the breech. The clip was full and there was an extra round up the spout. He shut it again, pushed the clip home and placed the weapon on top of the commode. The drawer also contained a Sidekick shoulder holster - nice and comfortable but you needed a belt to wear it, so he let it lay. There was a set of keys to a Lada parked in the university car park. He decided to leave the keys at home. The car might come in handy later, or it might not. In the next two drawers there was enough ammunition and explosives to start a small war.

"Well, it looks like the game is set to begin" He said to his reflection in the mirror above the commode. His reflection stared back. It had a missing right upper incisor and a mole on the right side of its chin, just under the corner of its mouth and the tip of the droopy moustache. There were bags under its eyes and small cracks of blood in the whites. "Christ! You look tired old son. Why don't you get some sleep?" He said to himself and obeyed.

The bed felt comfortable, the continental quilt felt warm, the shadows thrown on the white walls and ceiling by the streetlights did not move. The security alarm was working, there was a loaded gun in the drawer, Carlsberg beer in the fridge and all the food he could need. Brown fell asleep with a smile on his lips, feeling ever so comfortable and free once again. This was real living, not the boozer and the fish and chip shop!

Chapter Three – All that glitters

It was Friday night and raining cats and dogs. Dick Brown stopped at a lay-by just south of Padborg. There was a toilet, three wooden benches bolted to concrete foundations, two recently emptied rubbish bins, and no cars. It was just what Brown hoped to find. His bladder was bursting.

Three small lamps lit the toilet area. It seemed to be reasonably clean. There was enough light to see by, so Brown stopped the Morris under the lights, turned off the engine and got out. After he had washed his hands, Brown stood in front of the mirror with his arms out-stretched. There was no shaking. That was a bit of a surprise really, because there should have been. It had been days now since his last real drink. He lowered his arms and went outside. The generator was on the blink. It was not making enough to recharge the battery, so the headlights were just faint yellow discs. Not enough to see by, but enough to attract the attention of the German motorway police if he did not fix it. Brown went round to the back of the car and opened the boot. The tool kit was a bit of a mess. The tools and bits and pieces were all jumbled up. There was a small voltmeter somewhere. He found it easily enough, but the wires were tangled up, like the Gordian knot. It's always like that. No matter how hard you try to pack them decently, they're always tangled up when you get them out again! It took him longer to undo than it had taken Alexander the Great; but then again, Alexander had not needed to use the bits afterwards. After about ten minutes Brown had found and fixed the problem. When it was done, he put the tools back into the tool kit, rolled it up again and dropped the roll into the boot. Let's hope that works, he said to himself, as he slammed the lid shut.

The engine started easily enough. He let it run for a few minutes, while he got a little uneasy shuteye in the drivers' seat. It felt great to close his eyes and drift off to the sound of the engine and the feel of the fresh air on his face through the partially open window. After a while, an auto camper pulled up alongside the building. A couple of small girls sprang out of the passenger door and hurried into the toilet. A fat woman in a short-armed blue blouse squeezed herself out of the drivers' seat and followed them. She watched him carefully as she went by. Brown sat up and checked his watch. He had been asleep for forty minutes. Time to get going again or he would not be there by dawn. The headlamps were working fine when he drove off, but the rain was still pouring down. He soon passed a sign saying "Hamburg 107 - 7 - Ausgang 500m". Brown turned right onto E7 at the next exit.

Gunther Hassenbach had always thought of himself as a good man, a man who was kind, honourable and dignified. That was why it felt so strange when he came to and found himself beating the young man about the head and shoulders. It was not the sound that the young man made that brought Gunther to himself, because he made none, being unconscious at the time. Gunther did not know what it was. All he knew was that suddenly, the lights went on in his brain and he could see again.

There was blood on his right hand. Gunther asked himself where that had come from, and in turning his head to look at his left hand, which held the young mans head by its long blonde hair, he could see that it came from the corner of the young mans mouth. He gasped and pulled his hands away from the battered face. The head fell back onto the pillow, and a very thin trickle of bright red blood appeared at the right nostril and began to move down across the high cheekbone and the sunken cheek. Gunther grabbed the towel that lay on the bed beside him and bent over to stem the flow.

Gunther began to think again. Here he was a married man with two children and a very precarious job, sitting naked and straddling an equally naked youth, in a hotel room. Where could he go from here? After a while, the blood stopped flowing and Gunther bent to listen for a heartbeat, fearing the worst. But Gunther was lucky this time. The young mans heart was beating just like it should. Gunther was pessimistic, elated and pessimistic again, all in the space of one breath, as he bent over and put his ear against Martins hairless chest. He had to listen again, just to make sure. Yes, Martin was still alive. Gunther decided to get up and take a shower. When he got off the bed and stood up, his legs were shaking and his knees were like jelly. Martin lay there, his eyes closed, his mouth open. Gunther decided to turn Martin over on his side, just in case. He folded the towel and put it under Martins head, to catch any blood that might drip. It would be foolish to leave signs of violence on the pillow. Although it was Martin who had rented the room, Gunther could not be sure that he had not been seen entering it earlier that evening.

On his way out of the hotel, Gunther stopped in the lobby to check the street outside. He wanted to make sure that nobody had seen him, although standing there among the potted plants was just as conspicuous and probably equally dangerous. So he turned up the collar of his grey overcoat, pulled down the brim of his hat as if expecting a cold wind to blow outside, and went through the revolving door into the street. Nothing unusual happened. Kreuterstrasse was the same as usual. The occasional car rolled either up or down the hill going to or from the city centre. A taxi pulled up outside the hotel and the driver flipped his "For Hire" sign up so that it lit green and yellow. Then he pulled out a book and started reading. Gunther watched from the darkened doorway of a tobacconist's shop a short distance away. Two young girls came out of the hotel. They were giggling about something or other. The blonde was dressed in an ultra-short, black leather skirt and a black leather jacket with chains on it. The dark-haired girl was dressed in a long white evening gown and had a feather boa draped around her neck. She wore elbow length white gloves. The taxi driver put away his book when the blonde bent over forwards and knocked on the kerb side window. Gunther watched the black leather skirt ride all the way up the blondes' thigh. It left no impression on him. The taxi drove off down the hill past Gunther with both girls in the back seat. When they were gone and the street was quiet again, Gunther left the shadows and walked quickly towards the city centre.

He had not gone far, however, when a voice whispered to him,

"Wieh Getz Gunther?"

Gunther stopped in his tracks and turned around, although he felt like he should just run away as fast as he possibly could. A man stood in the doorway just beside him. The stranger wore a donkey jacket and a cap. Gunther felt a lump in his throat and swallowed. He heard himself asking,

"Who are you? What do you want?"

The man stepped out of the shadows. Gunther did not recognise him.

"Let's walk Gunther." The stranger took Gunthers elbow. Gunther began to pull back.

"Don't make a fuss Gunther. Or I may have to tell your wife and your employer about Martin. " Gunther felt himself becoming pale.

"I don't know what you're talking about. I don't know any Martin..." He exclaimed. The stranger was unabated.

"Now Gunther, be reasonable. If you had hit Martin one more time then we might have been talking about murder right now, instead of just a little episode in what I hope will be a long and fruitful life."

Now Gunther was in a state of complete shock.

"I don't know any Martin....".

"Oh, I think you do. Come on. Don't worry about it. As long as you do exactly what I tell you then nobody will ever know what happened."

Gunther followed. It occurred to him that the stranger had somehow been watching and listening to what happened in the hotel room. The curtains had been closed, so it could not have from across the street. Martin must have been in on it somehow. Gunther was glad that he had not hit Martin harder than he had. How many others knew? The stranger spoke German with a heavy English accent. What was going on?

"I want you to do something for me Gunther", said Brown. "If you do it right, then I'll make sure you receive the video film we took."

"A video film? How did you manage to ..."

"That doesn't matter Gunther. What matters is that you'll get the only copy when you've done what I ask you. This is not blackmail Gunther. I am really not interested in money, or in your sex life, so I won't be keeping copies for future use. What I am interested in is inside information."

Brown stopped outside a cellar pub 'Der Grosse Alpenhause', "Let's go in here and have a beer, I'm thirsty with all this talking."

They went down the stairs, and through the heavy wooden door. The bar was empty. Brown bought two beers and they went to the back of the pub, finding a table beside the door into the back yard. It was warm. Brown opened his donkey jacket, but didn't take it off. Instead, he took off his cap and placed it on the table. Gunther hadn't noticed the heat. After a sip of his beer, Gunther had regained a little self-confidence. It was as if his return to the shadows strengthened him. When he put the heavy glass down with a dull thud on the beer mat, he said.

"What is it you want to know?"

"That's better Gunther. Now we're doing business! Your employer is one Herr Jürgen Moltke, P4's top headhunter. I need to know Herr Moltke's itinerary for the next fourteen days. Do you think you can arrange that Gunther?" The tone in Brown's voice was slow and threatening.

"Why do you want to know?" Gunther asked. He was nervous again.

"Does it matter?"

"If anything happens to him they will suspect me immediately. After all, only three people know Herr Moltkes' itinerary, and I am one of them. I don't think I could take the pressure they will bring to bear on me in the interrogation room."

"You're probably right Gunther. I won't try to tell you that there isn't a danger of that. However, consider what will happen if the video turns up at your employers house and you are not there to receive it."

"Alright, alright. I didn't say I wouldn't do it. I only said that it is risky. What happens if I get caught? Will you still send the video to Herr Moltke?"

"Don't get caught Gunther, you wouldn't like the consequences. Look, all you have to do is drop a copy of Moltkes' meeting plan for the next fourteen days into a left luggage box at the Hauptbahnhof. Here is one of the keys."

Brown handed Gunther the key under the table. Gunther looked around the room before putting it into the left pocket of his overcoat. He drank his beer.

"One more thing Gunther. Don't lose the key. If the list is not in the box by seven o'clock tomorrow night, then the deal is off."

Gunther nearly choked.

"That's too early! I'll never get hold of it by then!"

Brown stood up slowly and got ready to leave. He fastened his donkey jacket again and pulled on his cap. Then he drained the contents of his glass and said,

"Seven o'clock tomorrow night Gunther."

"Not so fast. When will I get the video?"

"When I have had a chance to talk to Herr Moltke privately and not before. I need to be sure that your information is genuine. I will leave it in the same left luggage box. Don't worry so much. If you do it right, then you'll be all right. Might I suggest though, that you stop beating up young boys in hotel rooms? It is only a question of time before someone less understanding and friendly than I, uses it against you. Who knows, maybe even somebody in P4!"

Gunther said nothing. Brown left by the back door. He smiled to himself as he shut the door behind him quietly. He never intended to return the video to Gunther, but that was because there was no video.

At seven o'clock the following night, the traffic outside the Hauptbahnhof was limited to the comings and goings of taxis, buses and the occasional car. It is always that way on a Wednesday evening. Seven o'clock is the magical hour between work and play. It was too late in the evening for the bees to be working and too early for them to be out on the town. Brown was out on the town though. He was standing leaning against the Morris in a darkened alley between the main building and the goods terminal, with his arms folded, waiting for something to happen. Behind him was an iron gate with a huge padlock on it. In front of him were the parking lot and the street. After a while, a young man, about twenty years of age, with long blonde hair, came out of the main building, through the swing doors. He was wearing faded denims with the knees torn, an equally faded denim jacket, and dirty white sneakers.

Martin was carrying a brown envelope. His left eye was bruised, and there was bruising over his right cheekbone. Brown got in and started the car without revving it. Martin walked across the parking lot and stopped at the bus stop. Brown watched him for a couple of minutes. Nobody followed him. Brown stopped the car at the bus stop. He leaned out of the window and exchanged one brown envelope for another, then drove off down Adenauerallee towards Berliner Tor. The traffic was light. Just after the intersection of Adenaueralle with Lindenplatz Brown crossed the intersection and turned left up Stiftstrasse.

Brown stopped the Morris at the intersection of Stiftstrasse and Alexanderstrasse. When he looked back there was no sign that he had been followed. So Brown continued up Stiftstrasse to Rostockerstrasse, where he had to turn either left or right. He turned left, then right on Schmilinskystrasse, passed the church of St. Marian and the Haus des Kunsthandwerks on the left, and straight ahead to An der Alster. Her he turned left and followed the curvature of Lake Ausenalster until he passed the Atlantic jetty where the tourist ferry was just laying to with another load of passengers. Brown had now almost come full circle. He followed the main road right to Kennedy Brücke, but instead of crossing it; he manoeuvred the Morris into the verge. The inside light did not work, so he got out of the car but left the engine running, and checked again that nobody was following. He was still alone, except for the traffic. Brown tore open the envelope in the light from the lamps lining the bridge. The list seemed genuine enough. It consisted of fourteen pages in standard A5 format, each a photocopy of a single page of a hand-written diary. Most of the names and places seemed to have an official significance. Visit to the TV tower, central law court and Davidwache police station. There was one interesting thing though, a visit to Museum for Völkerkunde on Friday at eight in the evening. Völkerkunde can be translated in two ways, one innocent and the other less innocent. Brown chose to believe that the less innocent was the most likely. The museum is in Rotherbaum, on the north side of the city, and is a very large building in typical gothic style. Brown folded the sheaf of papers and pushed them into the inside pocket of his coat, then he got in the car and crossed the Kennedy Brücke. At Mittelweg he turned right. Traffic was reasonably heavy now. It was eight o'clock already. Brown turned left on Heimweg and stopped on the grass verge. He could see by the green and white sign at the entrance to the museum that it closed at seven in the evening on Friday. So if Moltke was having a meeting there at eight then it had to be reasonably clandestine. The little street was quiet; the lawn mowed perfectly, the bushes few, and clipped all nice and neat. The front of the museum was well lit by four strategically placed floodlights, and there were many shadows both to the left and right of the extremities of the building. No lights were on in the building at the moment. There was a slight breeze, which rustled the bushes not quite enough to drown the traffic noise in the background. Brown rolled down the drivers' side window, pulled a pack of cigarettes from the breast pocket of his jacket and lit one. It really was a nice evening. While he relaxed, he noted that the bushes on the left-hand side of the drive were thicker than the rest, and big enough to hide both himself and the car from anyone walking up the path to the museum at night. It was strange that they had not been cut as well as the others. Brown shrugged; perhaps they had not managed to get around to it yet. There was no sign of clippings on the lawn, though perhaps professional gardeners would always clean up after them at the end of the day. The only thing Brown knew about plants was that the roots went down and the branches up. Well, you can't know everything, and even if you did, then everybody would think you were lying, or being a big head, he said to himself. Friday night it would have to be then! Brown dropped the remains of the cigarette out of the window, rolled it up, and drove across town. Now he was tired, and his bed at the Hotel Europäischer Hof on Kirchenallee was calling loudly.

Brown was not tired at eight o'clock in the morning. He went downstairs to the dining room for breakfast, dressed in a rumpled grey suit that looked like it had been slept in for a week. The dining room was full of salesmen in similar suits. Nobody paid any attention, apart from the waitress serving coffee in her black dress and clean, white apron. She jotted down the number on his room key, which lay on the equally clean and white tablecloth. Brown asked for tea. The coffee here was too strong too. The tea came, and went, as did the yoghurt with müesli and the buttered rolls with cheese that he picked up from the self-service table in the centre of the room. Continental breakfasts do not give very much energy, but they are easily digestible. Brown patted his stomach as if satisfied and decided what to do next. He got up from the breakfast table, trying not to scrape his chair as he did so. Then he left the restaurant after dropping the room key off at the reception desk on the way out. There is a souvenir kiosk in the hotel lobby. They sell newspapers, cigarettes, that kind of stuff, and one or two amusing items. Brown bought a phone card.

Outside, the sky was overcast, although there were faint signs of light blue showing through the grey. It was going to be a reasonably chilly morning though. The morning rush hour was over long ago. Now the street was busy with people going about their business. Down the street wasone of the very few phone booths remaining in Berlin. Brown stepped into it and pulled out the card.

After a while, the phone at the other end was lifted, and a voice said,

"Zvei funf drei acht. Bitte?"

"How's things my Bavarian baboon?" There was a short pause.

"Ah, my Scottish colleague! Fine, fine, how about you?"

"I'm still not Scottish!"

"And I am still not Bavarian!"

"I'd just like to remind you of our appointment for this morning. I know what a busy man you are."

"Well, I am rather busy at the minute, but I'll be there on time. Where are you calling from?"

"Hotel Europäischer Hof. "

"Okay. Then you can do me a favour. My daughter wants me to get her one of those green frogs with flashing eyes they sell over there. All the kids in her class are running around with them and she's driving me crazy asking for one. Would you pick one up for me?"

"No problem"

"I'll pick you up outside the Red Diamond Club as we agreed."

"Okay, see you in a bit then."

The Red Diamond club is not what might be considered a respectable club, being on the Reberbahn. It does have one or two advantages though, the biggest of them being that the booths are soundproofed, so that their neighbours cannot hear the moans and groans of the occupants during the video show. Brown knew the place well, having been there several times. Today though, he did not go in. He stood outside on the pavement, by the hamburger and würst stand, chewing on a lightly done Brockwürst and freshly made sauerkraut. Sauerkraut that is fresh tastes fantastic, but some of the rubbish that you can buy in cans in German supermarkets is exactly that! He was halfway though the würst when a dark blue Mercedes trundled slowly around the corner and pulled up alongside the kerb. The rear window rolled down a little and a finger beckoned. Brown got in and the driver headed towards Barmbek. Horst Ritter said hello as he rolled up the window separating him from the driver. He dispensed with the formalities.

"How did it go then?"

"You were right. Hassenbach is an informer." Brown handed him the itinerary. Horst unfolded it and read it. He seemed pleased.

"Okay. Thomas, drive anywhere you please. I'll let you know when we've decided where to go." Horst said into the intercom. Thomas nodded.

"Well, my friend. It seems that you have fulfilled your part of the bargain. Now it is time for us to fulfil ours. Where do you want the assassination attempt to take place?".

Jürgen Moltke was a very careful man by nature, so that evening, before leaving for his meeting at the Museum for Völkerkunde; he got his bulletproof vest out of the closet. Frau Moltke helped him to put it on. She paid particular attention to the location of the ceramic trauma plates in front and back. Frau Moltke was an expert in this matter, because she never allowed Jürgen to do it himself. Sometimes he felt that she was getting him ready for the grave. Jürgen held up his arms so that she could button the cuffs of the starched, white shirt. Perhaps this ritual did Marianne some good, he thought. It must be a pain to see your husband go out of the door and never know if he would come back alive. Tonight would really test Mariannes' strength of character. He opened his mouth to say something, but she reached out to fasten the button at his collar, pushing his chin up in the process, so he dropped the subject. She chose a purple bow tie. Jürgen hated bow ties, but Marianne told him it made him look even more distinguished, so he smiled the smile of a martyr and bowed his head so that she could reach around his neck to tie it. No modern elastic or Velcro here. Marianne was a stickler for procedure. It occurred to Jürgen that the knights of old were dressed in this way by their squires before combat. Jürgen stood looking at the portrait of his great, great, grandfather Wilhelm, with his handlebar moustache, uniform adorned with medals, and spiked helmet. Perhaps you know what is going to happen tonight! He thought. Wilhelm hid not answer, even though his portrait looked so lifelike that he could have been expected to say something. Marianne brought his overcoat, the long, dark blue one - his favourite. Jürgen held his arms out behind him and she helped him on with it. When she was finished buttoning the overcoat, Marianne took two steps back and passed a critical eye over him. There was a piece of fluff on his lapel. She took one quick step forward and brushed it away with the back of a hand. Jürgen gripped her arms in to her sides, and kissed her gently on the forehead. Then he let her go. She smiled. Not one word had passed between them.

"Take care Jürgen." She said, then she turned on her heel and left the room. He could hear her climbing the stairs, and knew that she would be going to her sewing room. Without ritual, life had no meaning for Marianne. The grandfather clock in the corner by the living room window said six-thirty. A car pulled up outside. Jürgen Moltke went to the door.

On the way to the museum, Moltke asked his driver if there were any problems with the car. Gunther Hassenbach half turned. He felt nervous. But then, two days had passed and nothing had happened, so why should it happen now? Come to think of it, he always felt nervous, thought Gunther. Perhaps this nervous state had started about the same time as he had discovered a new side to himself. Perhaps this nightmare will end soon. He wished he could wake up and find that the whole affair had been just a figment of his imagination.

"No sir, everything is perfect."

Herr Moltke always asked the same question. It had become a part of the accepted daily routine. Outside, a light rain was falling. Moltke watched a single drop slide backward down the side window. The windshield wiper started to sweep backwards and forwards once in a while, automatically.

After about half an hour, the Mercedes turned left onto Heimweg. It parked by the kerb, immediately behind a carbon copy. Three men got out of the car in front. They were all dressed in grey business suits. They all had crew cuts. If Gunther had not known each of them as well as he did, he would have sworn that they were carbon copies of one another. One of the men walked quickly up to the front of the museum, another went behind Moltkes' car and stood looking back down Heimweg. The third stood in the cover of the bushes to the left on the other side of the road, and fixed his gaze up the street. Now is the moment of truth! Thought Moltke. Gunther got out of the drivers' side and walked around the front of the Mercedes to open the kerb side passenger door. Moltke stepped out. He stood for a moment, feeling the small drops of rain water on his head, and adjusting his clothing, then he pulled up the collar of his overcoat and stepped onto the path leading up to the museum. Moltke had not gone more than a few steps, and Gunther was in the process of closing the car door, when a small calibre rifle shot rang out across the open lawn. Moltke fell, seemed to try to get up again, then fell again and lay quit still. Gunther stood spellbound by the side of the Mercedes. The door was not even shut yet. He had not been looking when it happened. His attention had been fixed on the hole in the bodywork into which he was pushing the door. That was why he saw Karl, who was standing behind Moltkes Mercedes, turn around and spread his legs, the left foot forwards, forming a T with the right leg. Karl was carrying a silenced MP5. Gunther noticed the muzzle turning towards him, and began to turn his head to see what Karl was aiming at. So he never saw the muzzle flashes, or heard the chatter of the bullets hitting the Mercedes and his body.

A car hidden behind some bushes a few meters ahead started with a roar. The bodyguard standing on the left raised his MP5 and began firing as the car started from the bushes with no lights, and charged up the street. Brake lights flashed momentarily as the vehicle turned right at the corner of Heimweg and Rothenbaum. They lost the sound of the engine in the low rumbling of the trucks on the main road. Hans came running down the path from the museum. He was carrying a press camera. He turned Moltke over carefully. The body lay with arms splayed out. Hans took four photographs, two of Moltke, and two of Gunther, whose bullet-riddled body lay alongside the Mercedes, half in the gutter between the wheels. A few moments later, an ambulance came down Heimweg from Rothenbaum, with siren blazing and blue lights flashing. It stopped beside the two Mercedes.

The inside of the ambulance was dark when the rear doors were opened. The two-man crew took stock of the situation, loaded Moltke onto a stretcher and pushed it into the ambulance. Then one of them laid an open body bag out on the pavement beside Gunther Hassenback and they rolled the corpse onto it. One of the orderlies zipped up the bag. The two men lifted the stretcher and pushed it into the ambulance. The driver started around to the front while the other man locked the rear door securely. The ambulance left, this time with no lights or siren. The three bodyguards began looking for shell casings in the street, and putting them into their pockets.

In the back of the ambulance, the light went on, revealing a strange scene. Moltke sat up on the stretcher and began to take off his overcoat. Marianne was there, sitting with her back to the drivers' partition, as did Horst Ritter. Gunther Hassenback was still zipped up in his plastic bag, and would stay that way, almost all the way to his grave.

Jürgen Moltke looked first at Marianne. She seemed totally unaffected by the affair. Moltke was proud of her.

"Are you all right, Jürgen?" She asked.

"Jawohl mein schatz! No damage whatsoever, apart from the grass stains on my favourite overcoat."

Marianne smiled. That was Jürgen in a nutshell. She was glad to know him, but glad too that they had no children, because the world really could not afford too many Jürgen Moltkes! Nor

Marianne Rosenbaums for that matter! She lit two cigarettes, and handed one to Jürgen. There was silence for a moment, while all three of them looked at the plastic bag on the opposite side of the ambulance. As if coming out of a trance, Moltke suddenly said,

"I've known Gunther for four years. He has passed every security check. Who would have guessed that he would turn out to be a serious threat to the department?" Then, turning to Horst Ritter, "If it turns out you are wrong Horst...."

"I am not wrong Jürgen, Martin is an old acquaintance, who has worked on and off for us the last couple of years, in minor roles, and our English colleague found it very easy to get your itinerary from Gunther. If Gunther had been the man he should have been, then he should have told us all about it. My only worry is what other information Gunther has leaked and to who! It's not that I'm condemning Gunther for being homosexual. But allowing himself to be blackmailed? Anyway, this way he will have done us all a favour."

"Yes, and our English friend?"

"He is well on his way north by now."

"I don't envy him", said Moltke, and continued, "he is stepping into the lions den."

"A bit like Daniel." Said Marianne quietly. The two men looked at her, and Moltke smiled.

"Just like Daniel!" and continued, turning towards Ritter,

"Maybe its time we banged a few heads together Horst. Take care of that will you?"

"Yes Jürgen" said Ritter. "Otherwise, everything is going according to plan. When we get to the hospital the doctor on duty will sign Gunthers' death certificate. We will call his wife and ask her to come over and identify him. You will be kept in the hospital for a few days under heavy guard, until you are fully recovered. Gunthers' body will be removed to the chaple at nine in the morning. The chapel surveillance team is in position already. Uwe has written the press release telling how close you came to being assassinated, and how your driver protected you with his body and got killed instead. Gunther will get a hero's burial and his wife will receive a widow's pension.

"And in a few days, all this will be forgotten." Moltke whispered.

"Gunthers' wife won't forget that quickly. Nor will his children." Said Marianne. The two men said nothing for several seconds. What was there to say?

Ritter checked his watch.

Well, Jürgen, we are arriving at the hospital now."

"Take care of yourself Jürgen. As for Gunthers funeral, don't worry, I will play the part of the bereaved friend of the family as well as I possibly can." She looked across at the plastic bag. "It is a shame about Gunther. I really did like him. Strange how even I could be taken in!" Ritter helped Moltke out of the heavy coat, and into another.

Next morning the Deutche Zeitung brought a photograph of Moltke on the second page, under the heading "Attempted assassination of diplomat". The photograph showed Moltke lying on the lawn outside the Museum für Völkerkunde. There was a photograph of Gunther Hassenbach, lying in the street, bullet-riddled, and a long and detailed text of how it had happened. The story went all over the world, courtesy of the press bureau and appeared in many newspapers. It reached many men in many places. Among these men was Colonel Valentin Gregoriev in Kaliningrad.

Colonel Gregoriev dropped the newspaper and took another suck on the cigarette in his mouth. He did not feel any particular pleasure at reading this news, or any particular sadness, because he had never heard of Moltke. Gregoriev pressed a button on the intercom.

"Captain Chernenko can come in now!" He said impatiently, and did not wait for an answer. A few moments later the door opened and a captain entered. He closed the door behind him, turned to face Gregoriev, saluted, then stood at attention. Gregoriev looked him over carefully. He liked what he saw. A rugged jaw, well-trimmed hair and moustache, and a back like a ramrod. A good man to have around. He felt lucky to have Captain Chernenko as his brother-in-law.

"Sit, Chernenko!" He said curtly. Chernenko obeyed. Then he waited for Gregoriev to say something, which did not take long. Gregoriev was not a man to waste precious time or words. He often told himself that was why he would never make general. No compromise.

"Chernenko, I have a little job for you. I would like you to take a short trip to Lithuania. It will only take two days."

"I understand colonel! What is it you want me to do?"

"Some friends of ours have ordered some goods. I want to make absolutely sure that they get them, so I want you to take charge of the transport and hand-over personally."

"It will be my pleasure colonel. When am I to start this operation."

Gregoriev smiled. He had a sense of the theatrical, but perhaps that was because his father had been a wandering musician and his mother an actress from Georgia.

"Here are your orders."

He took a fat, sealed envelope from the right hand top drawer of his desk and handed it across to Chernenko, who put it immediately in the inside pocket of his jacket.

"One last thing Chernenko. You will only acknowledge communications from me personally. I will identify myself by the name - Sarafan. All other communications, orders and instructions must be ignored."

Chernenko smiled. He would have no trouble remembering this name. It was the name of his wife, Gregoriev's youngest sister.

"Of course colonel." He said, trying to hide the excitement in his voice. This was to be the first foreign mission he had ever undertaken. He felt proud.

"Good luck and goodbye!" Said Gregoriev and picked up the newspaper again. Chernenko knew that the conversation was over. He stood up, straightened his back, saluted, and left. Outside in the corridor he breathed a sigh of relief. At last his brother-in-law was beginning to trust him.

Chernenko walked down the corridor to the stairs leading to the ground floor. The walls of the corridor needed painting, he thought. For the first time in his career, he began to notice the dilapidation of the barracks, the nakedness of the concrete floors in the administration block, the lack of names on the doors leading onto the corridor. There was one large window high in the wall on the stair well. The window had bars on the outside. A soldier in a shabby uniform, the jacket open, showing a white T-shirt and braces underneath, was swabbing the bottom stairs with a mop. He did not even bother to stand to attention when Chernenko passed, and Chernenko did not even bother to chastise him for it. Times have changed, he thought as he stepped out into the sunlight and adjusted his cap. Only four years ago such behaviour would have been unthinkable. How low can a once-proud army sink? Why should it matter? Captain Orlov came by, his uniform looking a mess, no cap, and wearing sandles. In his mouth was a cigarette, which drooped as if it was about to fall out. Orlov is being sent home next week, Chernenko thought, to what? Unemployment in Kiev. No place to live. His wife has run off with a musician. Chernenko did not blame him for feeling and acting like a tramp. All the honest men go down the drain, he thought as he watched Orlov fall in through the door to the single officers quarters. Then he saw Gregoriev watching him from the first floor window of his office, straightened his back and walked off to his UAZ469, which was parked beside the petrol bowser.

Once in the jeep, Chernenko drove out through the main gate, which was open. The soldier sitting in the guardhouse looked up from a book and looked down again. Outside the gate, Chernenko turned right down the hill. At the bottom, the road turned sharp left. There was a dirt track, which continued on toward a forest of blocks of flats about a kilometre away. The dirt road was full of potholes. After a few minutes, Chernenko stopped the vehicle at the side of the road. He could no longer wait to look at his orders. He lit a Phoenix and threw the match out of the window. It fell in the dry dust. As he took the unmarked envelope out of his pocket, two dirty, shabby, children came by on bicycles they had made themselves. They made a sport of driving into and out of the biggest potholes. Chernenko watched them as they passed. When he was alone again, he opened the envelope and took out the papers it contained. There was a passport, in the name of Oleg Pavlov, an ethnic Russian from Estonia. The passport was stamped with Danish and Lithuanian visas. There were papers identifying Pavlov as an ordinary seaman. Chernenko grinned. He had never been on board a real ship in his life. There were five thousand Rubles earmarked for his own use. The envelope also contained a time schedule and instructions. Chernenko could see that he would not have time to drive home and tell Sarafan that he would be away for a few days. He turned the jeep around and headed for the Mikhail Lazny hospital. Imagine the feeling of freedom that comes with spring after having spent a long winter, locked in your house by deep, cold snowdrifts. That sense of relief was what Chernenko discovered on his drive across town. It was like a weight being lifted off his shoulders and his body being stretched high into the clouds. His ego was inflated almost to the point of exploding. Oh, the adventure of it all, he said to himself, and wandered off into a speculative dream.

Chapter Four – I am a mole, I am a mole…

Frederick Hammel was twenty-five, skinny, fair-haired, spotty and with thin framed glasses. His hair was not short, nor was it long. In fact it was rather ordinary. Frederick liked to wear a grey suit, a white shirt, and a tie. He felt that it made him look business-like, although in reality, his neck was so scrawny that it made his head look like it belonged to one of those little dogs with flashing eyes that flickered off and on in the rear window of cars back in the seventies. But Frederick possessed something that made people listen. It was not his voice, nor what he said, but there was a charisma in that young body that was just bursting to escape.

It was ten o'clock at night and the meeting was just over. Everyone had gone home but for Hammel, Jensen, Sieg, Erik and Black. The table at which they sat was at the far end of the meeting room from the door to the main street. The room was long and narrow. Svend Jensen had borrowed the key from the chairman of the radio amateur club that used the place, on the pretext that it was to be used to start a stamp collectors club. The cover had been good, because Svend knew that the chairman was not a collector, so the chances of him turning up on this one night were minimal. Fortunately, the chairman had had the flu for a couple of days when Svend had picked up the key that lunch time, so that was even better. All the lights were turned off, except for the single bulb hanging over the table where they sat.

"Anybody for burgers and cola?" Sieg asked. They seemed to think that was a good idea, so when he had taken their orders he left the club by the front door and went into the take away at the corner. When he had gone, Hammel shuffled some papers, found a blank page, and took out his stainless steel Parker. It made him feel better when he was able to write things down. He dropped the pen onto the blank sheet of paper and leaned back in the chair with his hands behind his neck.

"Well, there weren't all that many tonight, were there?" He said. Jensen, his right hand man, checked the list of names.

"Only six. Two of them have been to our meetings before. There were four new faces though. That's the price we pay for recruiting the way we do"

"Did you notice the old timer who sat at the back all on his own?" Black asked of nobody in particular.

"Yeah, English wasn't he?" Jensen answered.

"I think so. He sounded a bit like Tom McEwan." Black returned.

"That's right! I thought I recognised the accent. Christ that Tom McEwan's funny though. Did you see him on the telly last Monday?"

They all agreed that Tom McEwan was funny.

"Well, never mind the old-timer." Said Hammel, "As far as I could see, there was nothing special in the material. They seemed interested enough, but I think they were all two pennies short of a pound. What do you lot think? Did any of you see anything worth hanging onto?"

Jensen answered first. Black was stirring his coffee with a pencil. Hammel shook his head.

"No not really. It was a bit of a disappointing evening on the whole. But to change the subject, how long are we going to be staying here in town?"

Hammel leaned forward and picked up his Parker. Enough about the meeting, he was not really that interested in it anyway. The discussion was about to liven up, which was good, because so far he had been wasting his time. It was time to put the next stage of the plan into action. The other two noticed the gleam in his eye; a gleam that told them something was about to happen. Black stopped stirring the coffee and began licking the black drops off the red paint, slowly drawing the pencil across his tongue as if to underline some innermost thought.

"I've got something cooking, but let's wait until Frilev gets back. I don't want to have to repeat myself. Any more coffee in the thermos?" Hammel hated it when black did that. Doesn't he know that paint is poisonous? He asked himself, but not aloud.

Black lifted the thermos and shook it. It was empty. Hammel was pleased. He had stopped Black from licking the pencil. He did not want coffee anyway; it was made four hours ago and probably tasted like shit by now.

The door to the street opened and everybody looked briefly in that direction and away again. Frilev came in with a bulging plastic bag, closed the door behind him, locked it, and started walking towards them. Then he seemed to notice something on a seat at the back that caught his attention. He stopped and picked it up then continued. When he got to the table, he put the plastic bag down in the middle of it. They other three started to take their shares of the contents. Sieg sat down while reading the piece of paper he had found. It was a clipping from a three day old copy of Deutche Zeitung. There was a photograph of a man lying on a grass plane. The article was entitled "Assasination attempt in Hamburg."

"Look at this." He said, as he handed the clipping to Hammel and started poking about in the plastic bag to get at his burger, chips and cola.

Hammel put it on the table in front of him and read it while he stuffed hot chips into his mouth and washed them down with cold cola. There was a message written in English along the border of the clipping, in pencil. It wasn't completely legible. When he had finished reading the clipping, he shrugged, handed it to Jensen and kept munching. Then, quite suddenly, in the middle of slurping cola from the plastic cup it had come in, he stopped.

"Let me have that cutting again." He said.

The message in pencil said - one down, ten more to go! Hammel put the cutting aside. He reached out for a serviette and wiped his mouth and fingers carefully.

"You know, there's something interesting about that old timer at the back. I think we'd better have a chat with him."

"What for?" Jensen asked.

"Don't you know who Moltke is?"

"Can't say I do."

"Just think back to November, Svend. That time we visited Ingo in Hamburg." Hammel was suddenly being very patient. "He told us that the Garbo cell had just been blown, literally."

"Oh, yes... That's right! Their bus exploded on the way to Warsaw. Jesus, they were splattered all over the motorway!"

Black broke in, "Didn't Ingo say that the word was out that P4 had planted a bomb in the bus?"

"That's right." Said Hammel. "Moltke is chief of P4. Of course, this may mean nothing at all, but I think we'll have a chat with that guy anyway. Did you get his name and address?" Hammel sorted through the papers in front of him and stopped at the list of names.

"Brown. No address though. Did anybody talk to him at all?"

They all shook their heads.

"Then I guess we're going to have to find him the hard way. Black, get your lads together and find him."

"Do you want us to bring him along?" Black was excited at the possibility of finally seeing some action. The last week had been boring to say the least. The boys were beginning to get on each other's nerves again.

"No, just find out where he lives, then let me know. And Black.... Don't let your lads get out of hand. The last time they had to follow that journalist, I ended up having to take an unexpected holiday down south...."

"Well, Anders had had a bad day. His mother had just chucked him out, and..." Hammel was looking at the ceiling, so Black decided the time had come to shut up.

"I'll leave Anders out this time. Even though he's alright now." Hammel looked down again.

"Good. Now, listen up everybody. We're going into the gift and toy factory business."

Brown found what he was looking for in the Saturday morning paper. There was a phone number to call, so he rang from the flat on Langelandsgade. A woman answered. Her voice sounded mature, and soft. Brown asked if she spoke English, and when she said she did, Brown excused himself for not being able to speak Danish.

"That's alright. What can I do for you?"

"I have just arrived for a long holiday and a friend of mine told me you have a flat to rent. I was wondering if you've rented it already?"

"No, I haven't. It isn't a flat really, just a furnished room in my apartment on the third floor of the house. It's a bedroom with what we call a tea-kitchen. That's a hotplate for making coffee and stuff. Whoever rents the room will have the use of the living room, kitchen and the bathroom. The rent is three thousand a month, including heating."

"Sounds reasonable. I'd like to come over and look at it."

"Well, I'll be a home for the rest of the day. You can come on over at any time."

"Thank you, I will, just after lunch. By the way, congratulations on speaking English so well." There was a muffled sound on the phone. It sounded like a laugh.

"My ex husband was foreign-correspondent for a newspaper."

"I see. Well, I'll be dropping by later, bye for now."

"Cheerio then." The phone went dead.

Brown took a shower and shave. He did not want to look like a tramp when he turned up to look over the room. But he kept his duffle coat and walking boots on, so that he would not look too posh either. After all, he was not arriving in a Rolls. There was another advantage to the duffle coat. He could wear the shoulder holster and Neuhauser without drawing attention to himself. When he was ready, he packed a travelling bag with what he would most probably need and checked the mirror outside the front window. The street was empty, so he hurried out and locked the door. Then he walked down the three flights of stairs and went to the back door. The rear entrance to the house was down a short flight of stairs. Through the cellar where the other inhabitants stored bicycles and dried laundry on rainy days. Through another doorway and up another short flight of stairs into a totally enclosed courtyard with a garden about the size of a postage stamp. Just inside the front cellar door, the skirting board was loose. You could not see it because of the shadows, but Brown knew it was there. He bent down, and prised it away from the wall. Behind it was a small hole, about the size of a mouse hole. Brown stuffed the key to the flat into the hole and hammered the skirting board back into place with his fist. Then he left by the back door and crossed the garden to the house opposite, walked through its cellar and out the front door. Nobody saw him.

The traffic was a little heavy, because the shops closed at noon on Saturday. Most people were on their way into town to do the last weekend shopping. The Morris turned up Tåsingegade and right onto Randersvej. Then it crossed the traffic light at the junction of Randersvej and Nordre Ringgade. It followed Nørregade all the way down the hill to the docks, and a little street called Siberia. Brown turned the car right and followed the road past the dock for about five minutes until he came to Jægergårdsgade on the right. The rented room was in number forty-one, just around the corner. He parked the car by the right hand pavement. The road climbed upwards a little too steep so he put the Morris into first gear as well as pulling the handbrake. The handbrake had been a bit unreliable lately. The houses were similar in appearance to those on Langelandsgade. Five stories high, built in the twenties, dirty red brick. The stairs were the same, although the woodwork here was varnished instead of painted. Brown preferred the varnished version. On the third floor, there were two doors. One was marked Britta Nielsen and Tina Nielsen. Brown rang the doorbell.

There was a slight scurrying on the other side of the door. When it opened, a thin girl of about seventeen, with long, dark hair was standing there. She had on a white T-shirt and stonewashed jeans. Her feet were bare.

"I rang earlier about the room." Brown said. She understood English very well, although she was a little shy about speaking it. She called her mother.

Britta Nielsen and her daughter Tina were chips off the same block as far as facial build and height were concerned. Britta was about forty, with muscles you only get working out at a gym, aerobics, that kind of stuff, but without the same degree of diet control. She had a kind face and a tanned complexion. But whereas Tina had long dark hair, Britta was naturally blonde and had been to the hairdresser recently. Brown felt like a bit of a tramp in her presence.

"I'm Dick Brown." He said. She beckoned him in.

"Come in Mister Brown."

"Just call me Dick." He said as he passed over the threshold.

"I'm Britta." She said as she closed the door behind him.

"You can hang your coat here in the hall."

"I'll keep it on if you don't mind. I think I've got a bit of a cold coming on."

"That's alright."

Coffee was served in the living room overlooking the street. Tina left after exchanging a few niceties. She was taking her bike over to the bowling hall to meet some friends. They heard the front door slam. She was in a hurry.

"Do you take milk and sugar Dick?" Britta asked.

Brown shook his head.

"Neither thanks." Both of them were temporarily at a loss for words, so they drank their coffee in silence for a while. Britta thought it was a bit odd that Brown kept his coat on in the living room. He had said that he had a cold coming on, but the heat was on and there was at least twenty-five degrees in the room. After five minutes he still hadn't opened his coat, despite the fact that beads of sweat were dripping off his eyebrows.

"Perhaps I'd better show you around." She said suddenly. Brown nodded.

"Good idea."

The flat was not all that big. There were three rooms, all of them oddly shaped, not square like most places. All the doors led onto the hall, which was packed with coats and shoes at the end where the front door was, and had the door to the toilet/ bathroom at the other end. Although the flat was on the third floor, there was a narrow winding staircase leading down from the back room, past other similar doors. The back room was furnished, clean and the single window was open. Brown went across and looked out, down onto a courtyard typical of town houses. He opened the back door with some difficulty and looked down the stairs.

"The house was built for a merchants family about nineteen hundred and sixteen, " Britta said behind him. "The staircase was used by servants during their everyday comings and goings. Nobody uses it these days though. The door at the bottom has been painted over about a hundred times, and the handle has fallen off so you can't get in or out."

Brown closed the door. The hinges were not oiled, so they squeaked horribly. That was nice. Then they went into the kitchen. It was small and neat, everything in its place.

"Would you like a beer?" Britta asked.

"I don't mind if I do." Brown said. He had already decided that this was just what he needed.

"You don't mind if I call you Britta do you?" He asked. She grinned. It was a pleasant grin, full of life and vigour. A healthy grin from a healthy face. Brown felt something move in the cellar and ignored it.

"Good heavens no! Only the older generation use surnames these days."

"Well, Britta, I think this would suit me down to the ground. It's quiet, which is what I need, since my doctor back home says I've been working too hard.."

"What do you do for a living?" She asked.

"I'm a captain in the Merchant Navy. I travel around quite a bit, away from home most of the time. It seems I work too hard, and when I work too hard I drink too much, so I've had to go on the water wagon."

"Maybe I shouldn't have offered you a beer then." She said.

"Oh, no problem. Changing from whisky to beer is an important step in my detox programme, taking a long holiday is another. Once in a while my hands shake a bit, but that's getting rarer now, so it looks like I might be on the mend.

"When were you thinking of moving in?"

"This evening if I can. I have my gear at my friends' house, and I really don't want to be a burden on him longer than necessary. I'll pay in advance."

"Oh, never mind that, we'll talk about that later."

"I would prefer it Britta. I might suddenly decide to go back home, and I wouldn't want to leave you without having paid the rent."

"Oh, alright. It is normal here to pay three months in advance. Can you manage that?"

"Yes, no problem there. Fortunately I didn't drink up all my savings while I was at sea."

She laughed.

"You sound just like my ex husband. Foreign correspondents drink a lot too, I can tell you!"

She handed him a key to the front door.

That evening, Brown moved in. He did not hear Britta come home at midnight, take off her army boots and open the door to the back room where he was sleeping to check to see if he was there. She closed it again and went to bed.

At ten o'clock Monday morning, Brown was sitting at a window table in a restaurant on the corner of Park Alle, across from the main railway station, reading a copy of The Guardian he had bought at the neighbouring paper shop. His teacup was empty and there were crumbs on the plate where his cheese and ham sandwich had been.

The paper contained nothing of real interest, but it was nice to read something in English for a change. He was holding the paper up to catch the light from the window behind him, so he did not see the two young men enter through the street door at the other end. Both were reasonably tall, dressed in black leather jackets and trousers with zips here and there, punk-style. Both had shoulder length, dirty blonde hair. Both carried black motorcycle helmets with a blue lightning strike across the top. They looked like twins. Brown first noticed them when they each pulled up a chair at his table. Slowly, he folded the top half of the paper down and nodded to the two newcomers, then folded it up again. The game is afoot then! He thought. After a second or two, Mikael Mogensen said in English with a heavy Scandinavian accent that did not quite sound Danish,

"Is your name Brown?"

Brown folded the paper and placed it on the table. Both young men watched him closely.

"Yes, it is. Who are you?" Then he picked up his teacup and began to sip it. The tea was a little cold, and bitter. He managed to suppress a grimace.

"That isn't important mister Brown. What is important, is that you were at a meeting last week."

Brown seemed suddenly wary. They noticed it, which was of course his intention. He put the cup down onto the saucer with a deliberately heavy clank, just to underline his facial expression.

"What of it?" He asked.

Mikael's twin brother Jens lifted his hand.

"Nothing at all, Mister Brown, relax. It's just that our common friend mister Hammel would like to have a chat with you, if you can spare the time this evening."

Jens had the same heavy accent. There was a singing tone in it, so Brown decided that it must be Norwegian. He relaxed visibly and smiled crookedly.

"Certainly. I would be pleased to. Where and when?"

"Do you have a car?" Mikael asked.

"Yes, if you can call it that."

"Well then, meet us under the railway station clock at seven o'clock and we'll take you there."

Brown nodded, and without further ado the two got up and left. After they were gone, Brown got up, buttoned his double breasted seaman's jacket, rolled up the paper, stuck it under his left arm and left. As he passed by the window on his way up Park Allee, a waiter was flicking crumbs off his table with a towel.

Avon Wailes checked his watch. It was almost half past eight. He hated Monday mornings, especially when they were cold, dark and damp. This one was all of that, as well as being boring. It is not easy sitting on your backside in the back of a dark blue Transit for two hours in a row when you are as big as Wailes. He felt like his legs ended at the knees. He was alone in the van, and his watch was not due to end for another hour. The receiver had not uttered anything other than noise for the last half-hour, since the front door had closed and Paul Anderson's wife Anna had left for work at the hospital on her new, bright yellow bicycle. Wailes shivered, despite the fur-lined jacket. A light drizzle was falling. He could hear the faint crackling of it against the roof of the Transit. Two large droplets began to race each other down the one-way rear door window. A postman stopped outside number sixteen and pushed something through the letterbox then went on his way.

A door opened in the headphones. Wailes pressed the left one to his ear and listened intently. Footsteps moved across a floor. Another door opened and the footsteps began moving down the stairs. The feet had shoes on. Wailes could hear the click, clack of leather against the bare wooden steps on the other side of the door to number sixteen. Wailes reached across to the receiver and changed microphone to the one buried in the light switch by the front door. Paper was being torn. The letter was being opened. There were a few moments of silence, and the footsteps began moving up the stairs again, this time faster. That letter must have been important! Wailes thought, and changed to the microphone in the ceiling light fitting at the top of the stairs. The footsteps moved through the door to the living room. Wailes changed to the microphone in the television. Something was beginning to happen. Wailes could sense it. The chest of drawers that he knew was under the window immediately above the front door was being moved. It was heavy, and he could hear the scraping of its small, round wooden feet against the bare floorboards. There were no carpets in the house, because Anna suffered from asthma. A heavy thud and a very slight screeching sound as of metal against metal. A metal box of some kind was being opened. Paul Anderson appeared at the window for a moment, looking up and down the street. He looked at the Transit too, but it had been there since the phone man who had moved into number thirteen a month ago had come home at midnight. Then he disappeared back into the room. Wailes reached for the radio.

"Five-five this is two one. Over."

"Five-five. Over"

"Action. Over."

"Roger. Over and out."

Wailes put down the radio on the seat beside him. In number sixteen, footsteps were moving across the living room.

Anderson was prepared for this eventuality. Ever since he had moved in with Anna, he had known that the time would come when he would have to say goodbye in a hurry. The only surprise was that they had left him alone so long. He left the tin box open on top of the chest of drawers under the window. Anderson checked the safety on the pistol before lifting up his Icelandic sweater and pushing the weapon under his belt. He set the timer on the small black box to ten minutes, then took the key that had lain in the box alongside the pistol and crossed the living room into the kitchen. There he took a ball of string and the steps Anna used to reach the top shelves of the kitchen cupboards and went out on the landing at the top of the stairs. The entrance to the attic had not been used since he moved in. The cobweb where his pet, a big black spider, lived, had not been disturbed. Anderson tied one end of the ball of string to the steps and climbed them. The spider ran off across the ceiling when Anderson pushed open the trapdoor. The steps were just too short, so he had to pull himself up through the hole. It was not difficult though, because he was in good condition. The torch was where he had left it, but the batteries had leaked in the meantime and it did not work any more. He had two new ones in his pocket, so he changed them and when he could see again, he pulled the steps up through the hole and dropped the trapdoor into place. He walked across the ceiling to the far end of the house, taking care to stay on the beams and not to make any unnecessary noise. The house was pre-war, and terraced, not in any way remarkable or different from any of the thousands of terraced streets to be found in Manchester. The attic of each house was separated from the next by a single brick wall. But shortly after his arrival, Anderson had begun carefully removing bricks, one at a time. It was not difficult work, because the mortar used had been cheap. It had crumbled over the years, so he had been able to remove most of the bricks by hand without any heavy tools. Fortunately, nobody in the street seemed to use the attic for anything other than dust collection, so he had been able to carve a way down the entire length of the street in a short time.

As Anderson reached the attic entrance of the disused shop at the corner of the street, smoke began to appear at the window of number sixteen. Then, a few moments later, there was a bright flash as flames from the incendiary device he had left in the box caught the curtains and rushed upwards towards the ceiling.

Wailes saw the flame and grabbed the radio.

"Five-five, this is two-one. Over."

"Five-five. Over"

"He's torched the place. Call the fire brigade, I'm going in! Alex, come in through the back door!"

"Roger. Over and out."

Wailes was already out of the back door of the van and running across the street when a dark blue Ford Escort turned the corner with his backup in it. Fred James saw Wailes charging through the door to number sixteen, the smoke bellowing out through the opening where the door had been, and stood on the gas. The Escort screeched to a halt outside the house and the driver rushed inside.

At the corner of the street, Anderson peeked through the back door into the yard. Nobody was watching, so he went out and shut the door quietly behind him. The air was thick with the smell of smoke, and a black pall was rising from somewhere up the street.

Anderson opened the padlock on the coalhouse door and went inside. His motorbike, a Yamaha cross machine, stood just as he had left it. He put on the helmet, pushed the bike through the door into the back lane, and shut the back door behind him. The bike started first time and he drove up the back lane, passing number sixteen's green painted wooden door on the way. Smoke was filling the back lane now and he could hear the blare of a fire engine approaching, over the sound of the bike. There was only one thing he regretted.

"Sorry Anna!" He said aloud as he turned the corner and joined the traffic.

Wailes, James and Sanders were standing beside the van when the fire brigade arrived. James had moved the Escort. They watched the firemen rolling out their hose and unscrewing the cap of the fire hydrant half way up the street.

"Well, looks like he got away Wailes." Sanders said as he lit a cigarette. Wailes shrugged. He had had a good few lungs of smoke and his throat was burning.

"How he managed it I don't know. He must have had a rat hole somewhere. We'll have to go through the tape and try and make out what he was doing just before the fire started. Anyway, the whole thing was not a complete waste of time. I managed to get hold of the letter he got this morning. He was in so much of a hurry he'd left it on the coffee table. Probably thought the fire would destroy any evidence."

They climbed into the back of the van. Sanders rewound the tape and they listened intently. Outside, the fire brigade had everything under control and a police car had just arrived. The street was full of bystanders trying to get a good look. It was noisy, so they had to turn up the volume to be able to hear what was going on.

"He crosses the room and goes out into the kitchen." James commented. "What would he be looking for in the kitchen? Then he goes out onto the landing. He put something down."

Outside in the street, constable Harbin thought he heard noises coming from the back of a Ford Thames van parked across from number sixteen.

"He went up into the loft." Said Wailes. Now he had remembered what had been missing from the kitchen when he charged in, the steps. The other two looked at him.

"When we put the microphones in, I noticed that there was a small set of kitchen steps. Anna is small so she probably used them to reach the top shelves. They were gone when the fire started. I think he went out onto the landing, went up through the loft entrance, pulled the steps up after him and shut the trapdoor."

"Do you think his wife knows about him?"

"We'll find out soon enough." He reached for the microphone.

"Five-five, this is two-one. Over."

"Five-five. Over"

"The fire is under control. We'll be going to take a closer look in a minute or two. Pick up his wife and take her in for questioning. Better let Green in on the action."

"Roger. Over and out."

There was a heavy knock on the back door of the van. James opened it. A constable was outside asking them to come out of the van. James showed him his identity card. The constable nodded and left.

Half an hour later, the three men were standing in the back yard of the disused shop at the corner of the street. Sanders took his handkerchief and carefully dabbed it in the little pool of oil on the floor.

"Bit clean for a coalhouse." He commented. Nobody answered.

"Well, we now know that he left on some sort of moped, or motorbike. The boys in the lab might be able to tell us something about the bike from the oil sample. In the meantime there's nothing more to do here. Let's get back to the office and collect the threads a bit. I need a cup of tea." Wailes' throat was bone dry, and irritated by the fumes he had swallowed.

Anna Anderson was more than a bit surprised when two men turned up at the hospital laboratory and asked after her. Margaret, the lab chief, showed them to the room containing the blood analysing machine. She had asked what it was all about, but they had politely and firmly, refused to tell her anything about it. All they had said was that it was a routine investigation and that they would like to speak to Anna Anderson. Margaret was nosy. She liked to know what was going on in her domain. After she showed them into the room and shut the door, she stood for a moment trying to hear what was being said. Then nurse Patterson turned up and started asking about the results of some blood tests she had taken the day before, so Margaret had to leave it all behind and go back to the office together with the nurse.

"What's this all about?" Anna asked. Although she was standing, the two men towered over her by at least a foot. She felt like a pigmy standing beside two lampposts. One of the men was dressed in a dark suit. He looked very distinguished. The other had a sports jacket that obviously had not been pressed for a while. The dark-haired one had on a white shirt and a horrible brown tie that was not tied correctly. It looked like he had put it on in a hurry while on his way out the door somewhere. The brown-haired one with the cold, grey eyes and the aristocratic accent was apparently his superior. He was better dressed anyway.

"Well Mrs. Anderson. We have a few questions to ask about Paul Anderson, your husband. It will only take an hour or so, but I am afraid that I'll have to drag you away from your work in the meantime. I am loath to discuss the matter here in these surroundings."

Anna shuddered, as if somebody had just walked over her grave. Something has happened to Paul!

"Is Paul alright? He hasn't been in a accident or something?"

"Not as far as I know of Mrs. Anderson - may I call you Anna? Although you see Anna, Paul has disappeared and we really are very anxious to talk to him. Would you come with us please?"

"Where are you taking me? I'll have to let the lab chief know. She goes spare if we take time off without telling her."

"You can tell her that you are assisting Special Branch with their enquiries and that you will be back within the hour. Now, please

Anna, are you ready? The sooner we get this over with the sooner you will be able to return to your work."

They stopped at the office down the corridor while Anna Anderson told Margaret where they were going. They left the third floor by the elevator, walked out of the building through the main lobby and got into a waiting Ford Granada.

Anna Anderson had always imagined the offices of Special Branch to be modern, glass and concrete facilities with computers whirring away and people going about their business like bees in a hive. But then again, this was Manchester, so perhaps they always used the local police station for this kind of thing. At any rate, the room where she was sitting was very bare. The only furniture in the place was a small desk with a chair on each side, and a shelf with a tape recorder on it. She was all by herself in the room, and had been for some ten minutes by her wristwatch. The two men came in through the door, the tall aristocratic one first. On their way to the station, in the car, he had introduced himself as Superintendent Dawson. He had introduced the other man as Sergeant Liddle. They had seemed kind enough, though somewhat aloof. Dawson sat down across the table from Anna. She noticed that Liddle took up position by the door, leaning against the wall with his hands in his pockets and his sports jacket partially open. She noticed the butt of a revolver in a shoulder holster just under Liddle's left arm. Liddle noticed her stare, traced it to his open jacket, dropped the jacket in place and stood with his arms crossed on his chest. Several seconds passed before Anna could drag her gaze away.

"Well Anna, I hope you don't mind if I tape this conversation? I really am awful at keeping notes." Dawson said. Anna snapped back to reality and nodded her consent. Dawson set the tape in motion.

"Interview with Anna Anderson. Marble Road station, Manchester. March sixteenth. Twelve-fifteen hours. Superintendent Dawson and Sergeant Liddle attending." He said for the microphone in the centre of the table. Anne felt guilty already. It is always like that when you go into a police station. Even though you have done nothing wrong, there is always that sense of nagging guilt. She wondered if policemen felt it too. Maybe not, she thought, I don't feel particularly ill just because I work in a hospital.

"Just for the record Anna, will you tell me when and where you met Paul Anderson?"

"Are you going to tell me what this is all about?" She asked.

"Later Anna. For now I would like to have your honest answers to my questions. If I tell you what it is all about now, then that might cloud your judgement, or memory."

She could see then sense in that.

"Well, we met on a holiday cruise in the Baltic. It was the fourth of august, two years ago. Until Paul came on board, it had not been much of a holiday actually. The first two days at sea, I was seasick and stayed in my cabin most of the time. It was quite high up in the ship. The steward was kind enough to suggest that I move to another cabin down around the water line where things didn't move so much. It got better after that. Then the next two days I spent just laying about, reading a book. There weren't that many people on board. The night life was miserable."

"Where did Paul join the ship?"

"Helsinki. He told me later that he was a sales representative for a Finnish shoe company."

"Paul Anderson is not his real name is it?"

She giggled.

"No it isn't. But don't ask me to pronounce it properly. It goes something like Povl Savoleinen or at least something like that. He said that Anderson was a close approximation."

"I suppose that it is safe to assume that you got on well together?"

"We met for the first time the day after the ship sailed. There was a dance in the ballroom. I was bored. Paul came up and asked if I would like to dance. I said yes, and things went on from there."

"What happened when the cruise ended? Didn't you split up?"

"Yes, we did actually. We had had an enjoyable time together, but when the ship docked at Harwich again and I got off, I thought I'd seen the last of Paul. I was sorry about that really. Anyway, about two months later I got a phone call from him. He said his company had sent him to Manchester to open a shoe shop, and he wondered if I could help him find a place to stay. I did, and after a while we started seeing each other again."

"Did he actually start the shoe shop?"

"Well not really. As things turned out, after about a month of looking around, the company seemed to get cold feet..." She grinned at the pun. Dawson humoured her.

"They seemed to think that Manchester wasn't the place after all. They wanted him to move to Newcastle. Paul didn't want to go. To be honest, I didn't want him to go either. Anyway, he had a couple of phone calls from the company and after that he quit his job. It wasn't easy for him to find another one in the town, so after about two months, I suggested that he moved in with me to save on the rent, and help me with mine. We got married at the registry office in January last year."

"Those phone calls from his head office. Did you hear any of them?"

"Yes, but a fat lot of good that did me. They were in a foreign language. I'm not very good at languages. I suppose it was Finnish. At any rate, I didn't understand a word of it."

"Yes, Finnish is an awfully difficult language. Also for the Finns..." He chuckled. Then he signalled to Liddle.

"You are on a Linguaphone course aren't you?"

"Yes sir, but..." Dawson had his back to Anna. He winked. Liddle got the message to play along with anything he said.

"It wouldn't by any chance be Finnish?" Liddle looked genuinely surprised.

"How did you guess sir?"

"Intuition I suppose. Do you have your tapes at the station?"

"Yes sir, I practise during lunch break."

"That's a stroke of good luck then. Would you mind fetching them? I'd like Anna to listen a little and confirm that that was the language Paul was speaking on the phone."

"Yes sir. Right away." He left and closed the door behind him.

A few moments later, Liddle returned. He had with him a tape recorder and three tapes. He placed the tape recorder on the table and propped a tape into it. Anna recognised the language immediately.

"Yes, that sounds like what Paul was speaking."

"Thank you sergeant Liddle."

Liddle removed the tape recorder from the table. He took out the cassette and put it back into its plastic container. The label on the box said - Russian for Beginners. Liddle left again. When he came back, Dawson continued the interview.

"Has Paul had foreign visitors at all?"

Anna thought a while, then answered,

"No. In all the time he's been living with me there haven't been any foreign visitors. At least, not while I was at home. He never told me he was expecting anybody either."

"What about favourite haunts?"

"He often went down to the radio club. Once in a while he had a few drinks with the boys at the Grange. That was about it really."

"Radio club? Is Paul a radio amateur?"

"Yes. He told me he has been a radio amateur since he was fourteen years old. He had to leave his gear behind in Finland though when he came over here to work. He uses the radio gear down at the club."

"Where is this club?"

"I don't really know. Radio doesn't interest me. I'm more to gardening. My back yard isn't really a place where you can do much gardening, but it's all there is, so I use it as best I can."

There was a brief pause. Then Anna seemed to come to a decision.

"Don't you think that it's about time you told me what this is all about? I think I've answered all your questions."

Dawson, who had been playing around with his pencil for the last couple of minutes, let it fall onto the notepad on the desk. Then he leaned back in the chair.

"Well Anna, you've been most helpful, and yes, you've answered all my questions, so I'm going to let you in on the story. However, I'm going to ask you to keep silent about what you are about to hear. I also want you to promise me to call me at this station should Paul turn up again."

"Turn up, again?"

"Yes, he has disappeared completely and we believe he will probably not be returning, but just in case... You see Paul Anderson is wanted in Finland for counterfeiting. Interpol asked us to find him some time ago and it has taken us a while to do so. We went to your house this morning, but before we could catch him he set fire to the house. In the smoke and confusion he managed to escape."

"Set fire to the house?" Anna was shocked. Dawson held up a hand to calm her down.

"Don't worry about it. Our man called the fire brigade immediately. There's no damage at all apart from some smoke damage, and the living room curtain is destroyed. Otherwise everything seems ok."

Anna got up.

"Will you give me a lift home?"

Dawson got up after her.

"I'll get one of the constables to drive you. Once again, thanks for your help Anna. Sergeant Liddle, please get one of the constables to drive Anna home, then come back here."

"Yes sir." Said Liddle.

When he returned, he closed the door quietly behind him.

"That was good about the counterfeiting, sir. Where do you get them from?"

"I'm like the proverbial magician Liddle. I pull them out of the top hat at the tip of a wink."

"Where do we go from here sir?"

"Bring in Wailes. I want a first hand account of what went on over there. Oh, and get somebody to bring a very large cup of black coffee. God, I hate using interview rooms as offices!"

"Yes sir." Liddle left.

Chapter Five – They that go down to the sea

The sea was not very kind to Oleg Pavlov. It fact it was downright nasty. Only twelve hours out of Leningrad, the wind turned to the south-east and increased to force eight. Oleg had not had the energy for breakfast. He had started to get an uneasy feeling in the pit of his stomach even before the ship left the quayside. He stood at the starboard railing on the aft end and watched the previous evenings meal disappear into the wind and the driving rain. It was dark, except for the stern deck lights. He was glad for that. Nobody could see the green colour in his face. Or so he thought, but there were three faces with noses pressed against the galley window, and a grin ran from ear to ear on each one.

Eventually, when he had retched a dozen times more and still had brought nothing up, his stomach seemed to declare a truce. Only now could he feel the dizziness in his head. It was time to go and lie on his bunk again. Oleg stumbled through the aft deck entrance into the accommodation block and found his bed in the cabin three doors up on the port side.

The three faces at the galley window belonged to the fat cook Luvov, his assistant Ivanovich and Boris Oganov, the steward. When Pavlov came inside, the three of them sat down at the working mess table.

"Pay up Luvov and Ivanovich! That's fifty roubles each!"

The other two reluctantly dug into their pockets and passed the notes across to Oganov.

"You lucky bastard." Said Luvov, as he got up to pour three teas from the samovar bolted to the bulkhead.

"Well, you win some, you lose some." Oganov said with a smile, rolled up the notes and stuffed them into the top pocket of his dirty white jacket. "I said he would throw up eighteen times - and that's just what he did. Mind you, I thought that last one was his death rattle!"

They laughed, and Ivanovich made a passable impression of Pavlovs' last retch, which made them laugh even more. Then the door opened and they stopped suddenly, as if on a single command.

The first mate, Ivan Ljublin stood framed in the doorway, in his underpants. His face was grim.

"Now you three have had your fun, put a sock in it, I'm trying to get some sleep!"

"Yes sir!" They said in unison. The door crashed shut.

Luvov sat down again and handed out the tea. After a few seconds they began to grin again.

After a while, the bridge whistle blared. Ivanovich got up and pulled the whistle from the brass pipe. He put his ear to it.

"Bridge here. How about my tea and sandwiches? Or have you three fallen asleep over a vodka bottle again?"

"Coming right up sir!" Said Ivanovich and propped the whistle back into the pipe. "He wants his tea and sandwiches." He said to the other two.

"You'd better take them up then. I've made the sandwiches already, they're on a plate in the fridge. The tea's ready too. When you get back we'll get the cards out. I want to win my money back from Oganov!"

"Who said I'd be playing?" Oganov asked.

"Does that mean you're not interested?" Luvov asked.

"Never said that..... Oh alright! Ivanovich, get a move on, I want to prise some more money out of Luvov here."

Ivanovich took the plate with three sandwiches from the fridge and placed it on a battered metal tray. He added a clean cracked mug from the cupboard. When he left he was carrying the tray in his left hand, and the samovar was swinging by its handle from his right. Oganov opened the door for him on his way out.

There were three floors above deck in the accommodation block of the MV Alexander Sagieski. The ship heaved and rolled heavily as Ivanovich climbed the stairs to the bridge. But Ivanovich was an expert. He had tried this many times, sometimes in even harder weather. On the bridge deck, he passed the radio room, where the radio operator Pushkin the middle was sitting in his swivel chair, which was bolted to the deck. He was called Pushkin the middle, because his father and younger brother were on board as well.

Pushkin had his feet up on the desk and his headphones on. His head was forward on his chest. He was fast asleep. Ivanovich went by without waking him. It was just after midnight, and Pushkin would be on watch for another hour and a half. Ivanovich braced himself against the bulkhead and knocked on the bridge door with the tray in his left hand. A few moments later, the door opened and captain Gregoriev took the tray and the samovar. Ivanovich hurried back to the card game. On the way down, he checked his wallet to see how much he could risk losing.

Captain Gregoriev put the tray of sandwiches on the chart table and the samovar in the wooden receptacle on the bulkhead behind him. The black curtains separating the chart table from the rest of the bridge were closed, and a single, small white light bulb in the chartroom lamp provided all the light that was needed to read the charts. The chart on the table covered the Baltic Sea, between Leningrad and Klaipeda in Lithuania. Several crosses in pencil showed the progress of the Alexander Sagieski in the twelve hours she had been at sea on this trip. Gregoriev poured himself a mug of tea, and took a sandwich with him through the curtains.

The bridge was dark, as it should be to preserve night vision. The only lights were from the dimmed rudder indicator above the rotating window, and from the engine telegraph, which was on half ahead. Gregoriev hated to reduce speed, but in this case there was nothing for it. It was either reduce speed to half and get there or not get there at all. His cargo was too valuable to risk. At this rate it would take three days to get to Klaipeda.

The port side bridge wing door was closed. Rain hammered at it. There was a slight movement on the starboard wing. Gregoriev took a good bite of the sausage sandwich and went outside. Here on the lee side there was only the wind caused by the movement of the ship. It was still cold though.

"Go down Rastov. Get yourself a bite to eat and some hot tea. Send Pavlov up to take over the wing watch."

"Pavlov's sea-sick sir."

"Never mind that! He's not getting special attention on my ship, even if he is a good friend of my brother! Make sure he puts on some warm clothing and a good hat. I don't want him to die on me before we get to Klaipeda!"

"Yes sir! I'll treat him just like his mother would!" Rastov answered with a broad grin and disappeared down the lighter.

82

Gregoriev mumbled to himself when Rastov had gone - You don't know his mother like I do! Then he went inside to check the radar. They were lucky this trip. So far the radar had worked all the way.

"You look terrible Pavlov!" Rastov said when he had hauled Pavlov to his feet. Pavlov was shivering, but there was sweat on his forehead. He sat on the edge of the bunk and pulled on his trousers over the long-johns he was wearing.

"You'd better put on a good coat, and a scarf. It's cold as hell up there!" Rastov said. "Here - have a good swallow of this!"

Pavlov wasn't too keen on drinking tea, but it was hot and sweet, and after a few mouthfuls he started to feel just a little bit better. Rastov helped him on with the overcoat and scarf, and loaned Pavlov his woolly hat. He stuffed a thermos bottle of hot tea into the pocket of Pavlovs overcoat, and shoved him mildly through the door. Rastov was Pavlovs only real friend on the ship. It wasn't that Pavlov was a landlubber that got up their noses. Nor was it the fact that he was a good friend of the captains' brother in Leningrad. No, it was the fact that the ship had been re-routed at a moments notice just before sailing, and that there was only one key to the sealed container in the fore peak cargo area. The key was in Pavlovs possession. Everyone knew that, because he had it on a chain around his neck and he had not taken it off yet. The first mate had hinted to the chief engineer that there was something funny about that container. There were no transit papers and no inventory for its contents. The captain had also given orders that that particular container was to be discharged on arrival at Klaipeda. The ship carried no other cargo for Klaipeda. Rumours abounded. Everyone was keeping a close eye on Pavlov to see what he would do next.

Rastov went into his own cabin and shut the door. Pavlov went out onto the deck on the starboard side and struggled up the lighter to the bridge deck. He was still feeling giddy, but the fresh air helped a bit. When he reached the bridge, Gregoriev was standing with his back to the lighter, looking ahead through a pair of binoculars. The collar of his coat was pulled up around his ears, and he had well worn black leather gloves on. Pavlov came up alongside him and stopped at the forward windbreaker, his hands buried deep in his pockets. Gregoriev looked sideways at him, then returned to his binoculars.

"How's it going Pavlov?" He asked. His tone was rough.

"Alright Captain Gregoriev." Pavlov chattered through his teeth. Landlubbers! Thought Gregoriev. A pain in the ass!

"Well, a bit of fresh air will do you good. We've had to slow down because of the weather. We're on half speed now. If this keeps up then it will take us three days to get to Klaipeda. You'll have got your sea legs by then, don't worry. Look, you haven't tried this yet, so this is what you have to do. Stay right here until I tell you to do otherwise. Keep a lookout especially ahead, but also two points either side. You're looking for dark shapes in the water, or small lights, anything unusual. If things are small, or not made of metal, we sometimes cannot see them on the radar until it's too late. We don't want to run into a container washed overboard from another ship, do we?"

Pavlov shook his head. Dark shapes? There must be thousands of dark shapes out there on a night like this, how do you tell one from the other?

"What's a point captain?"

"A point, Pavlov, is eleven and one quarter degrees." Gregoriev said impatiently, and went inside. Pavlov was left alone to bemoan his fate and the injustices of life at sea.

By the time his watch was over, two hours later, and by the time the sun rose through the morning sea-mist, the wind had dropped almost to nothing, and Pavlov was almost feeling his good old self again. That morning at breakfast, he ate four sausages, three eggs, four pieces of bread, and had two large mugs of hot, sweet tea. After serving Pavlov his second breakfast, Oganov returned to the galley and paid Luvov twenty five roubles.

"You're right Luvov, he is definitely over being sick. You jammy bugger!" Luvov guffawed.
"You lose some, you win some Oganov!"

"Bring the tea!" Ljublin yelled from the mess.

"Coming right up sir!" Oganov yelled back, and got back to work serving breakfast.

Apart from Rastov, there were three other able seamen on board the Alexander Sagieski. At ten o'clock that morning they were gathered on the fore peak, with working gloves on and hammers and chisels in their hands. Pushkin the younger stopped for a breather. The others continued chipping away at the rust encrusted port anchor winch. It had been frozen in place for two months now and Ljublin had decided it was time to get it working again. Pushkin wiped the sweat off his brow with the back of a glove. In doing so, he caught a glance of Pavlov on the port bridge wing.

"How come Pavlov gets off with light duties?" He said to nobody in particular. Pushkin the older answered him without looking up from his work.

"Because he's a good friend of the captains' brother."

"Have you seen his hands?" Varasov asked, and continued without waiting for an answer, "I tell you Pjotr, they are not the hands of a man in the habit of doing manual labour. His eyes are strange too. If you ask me, he's KGB!"

"What would a KGB man be doing out here? No Alexei, I don't think so. On the other hand, many of the old KGB people are out of work these days. Maybe he's working for the Mafia, a lot of them do you know." Pushkin the older said.

"Maybe, maybe not." Varasov said, puffing on his rapidly dwindling cigarette. "But if they are Mafia, what would they be moving out of the country?"

As if on a single signal, they looked at each other.

"Money!" They said, in one voice.

Pushkin the younger got down on his knees again and began to chip rust. "I think it's about time to find out what he's got in that container!" The other two stopped a moment and looked at him, then continued working.

They worked for a few minutes, then stopped for a water break. One at a time, they filled their tin mugs from the water bottle they had brought with them. Then Varasov lit another cigarette and they stood with their backs against the prow railing of the ship. Their eyes were glued to the singular container in front of them.

"Maybe you're right son." Pushkin the older said suddenly, and lit a cigarette himself. "But the question is, how do we go about it without drawing attention to ourselves. The doors are facing the bridge, so anybody trying to get in will be seen right away.

"We could wait until one of us is on wing watch tonight. I don't trust Rastov, he's too friendly with Pavlov. Then the other two could sneak out and break open the padlock." Pushkin the younger suggested.

"There's only one drawback as far as I can see. They'll notice right away that the doors have been forced. It won't take them long to find out who did it, then we're in trouble. Whether Pavlov is Mafia or KGB, then he won't take kindly to the cat being let out of the bag." Pushkin the elder answered.

"Not unless we loosen the shackles at the same time." Varasov said quietly. The other two thought about it for a moment. It seemed a good plan. If the shackles were loosened just a little then the container would break free at the first serious wave. If it didn't pitch overboard, then the breaking open of the padlock might be attributed to the accident.

"Good thinking Varasov. Who's on watch around midnight?"

"Me." Said Varasov. "I'll be on until two in the morning."

"Alright then. Sergei and I will be on deck by the crane island at around midnight. When you're sure the coast is clear, light a cigarette and signal to us three times. When we're finished and back at the crane island, I'll light my pipe. In the meantime, Sergei, you can find a chance to hide a couple of crowbars down behind the crane winch."

"What about hiding them up here?"

"No. If Ljublin decides to come and check on our work, he'll have a fit at us leaving tools lying around. Then he might start wondering what we need crowbars for when we're rust chipping!"

"Alright."

That settled, they got back to work, this time with a vigour born of excitement at the coming nights activity. Pavlov watched the three seamen working on the fore peak and was glad that it wasn't him. It seemed too much like hard work for his taste. Now the sun was up, the engine was running at full speed ahead and the mist had disappeared, life did not seem that bad.

The day and the evening passed without any particular incident, other than the fact that Captain Gregoriev had worked out that they would be docking at Klaipeda late the following evening. The weather was reasonable for most of the day, which made the Pushkins and Varasov wonder whether or not they should abort their venture. Then round about the time of the evening meal, the tops of the waves began to turn white. Later still, foam began to blow off the tops. The wind was definitely getting up again. Everyone on the ship could feel it.

At ten o'clock, Pavlov was laying on his bunk sleeping with all his clothes on. His boots lay on the floor at the foot of the bunk. Pavlov awoke when his tin mug fell off the small table and rolled across the deck. It stopped just before it reached his bunk, and started to roll the other way. The ship was heaving. Every time she pitched forward into a hole behind a wave, the stern came out of the water and the engine speeded up. Then when she started up the next wave, the stern dug deep into the water at the bottom of the trough. The sudden load on the propeller caused the engine to brake quickly. When this happened, everything in the cabin shook like crazy. It seemed like the whole world rattled.

Pavlov got up and went to the porthole. He didn't bother to turn on the cabin lights, there was light enough slipping into the cabin from under the door. On the way, he stopped to pick up the mug and hung it on the hook just over his hand washbasin. He could not see anything outside, just blackness.

Pavlov turned around and went back to his bunk. He was not really tired at all, there was just nothing else to do. He turned on the light by the intercom on the bulkhead next to the bunk and checked his watch. It said five minutes to midnight. He turned off the light and lay down again. He could hear Luvovs' powerful laugh from somewhere down the corridor, and knew that the three of them were playing cards again. He turned over on his left side and faced the bulkhead. He felt uneasy. Perhaps it was the fact that this would be his last night on board. Tomorrow he would be ashore in Klaipeda. Yes, it must be that - he thought and closed his eyes.

At two minutes past midnight, Varasov reached the starboard bridge wing and opened the door. Captain Gregoriev had just taken over the watch from Ljublin. They were standing over the radar talking when Varasov came in. Both men looked up.

"Just checking in sir!" Vasarov said.

"Alright Vasarov." Gregoriev said and turned his attention back to the radar. Varasov went out again and closed the wing door after him. He did not know what to do. Ljublin should have gone down by now, but instead he was looking at the radar with the captain. Maybe there was something brewing. Vasarov decided to wait until Ljublin had disappeared before signalling the Pushkins.

Down on the deck, behind the cargo crane island, the Pushkins were waiting for Vasarovs' signal. It was cold, and the occasional wave swilling across the deck, made them glad that they had wellingtons on.

"Well, what do you make of it Ljublin?" Gregoriev asked.

"It beats me! You know, this radar never ceases to amaze me. In the two years I've sailed with this ship, I can't ever remember a trip when it worked all the way! What a useless piece of rubbish!"

"I agree with you there." Gregoriev said, and turned the range knob. Both faces seemed demonic in the shifting green glow from the screen.

"It seems to be working on the low ranges, but when we get up to the sixteen mile range, there's hardly any signal. We're getting sea clutter though." He said after a while.

"Yes. Maybe we should take a look at it after breakfast. I suppose there's no money in the till to get a repair man on board in Klaipeda?"

"You supposed right. Never mind, go on down Ljublin. We'll bang our heads together and see what we can do about it in the morning."

"Good night then." Ljublin said and left by the starboard wing door.

"Keep a good lookout tonight Varasov, the radar's on the blink again." Ljublin said to Varasov as he passed him. He did not notice

Varasovs' sigh of relief, both at the news that it was just the radar acting up again, as well as at the news that Ljublin himself was on his way down to his cabin.

Three minutes later, everything was as quiet as it could be on a night like this. Only the steady rumble of the ships engine broke the silence. It was a comforting sound. Varasov lit a cigarette in the lee of the wind breaker and stepped out again. He leaned on the forward railing. The wind made the cigarette flare wildly. When he was sure that Gregoriev was not anywhere in the vicinity, he held his hand for two seconds in front of the glowing tip, and removed it again. This he did three times in a row. Then he went back into the lee of the wind breaker. He hoped the Pushkins had seen the signal, but he did not know for sure, as it was too dark to see anything on the deck below.

The Pushkins had seen the signal. They began walking towards the prow of the ship, trying to look as though they were just enjoying an evening walk, although the crowbars up their sleeves would have been a give away had one of them had to try and bend an arm. Varasov leaned on the railing and tried to see what was going on deck, but could not. Then it occurred to him that that was probably the best thing that could happen. If he couldn't see anything then nobody else could either. He tried to relax, but the excitement made that difficult. So he moved to the aft end of the bridge wing and took a look out in that direction for a while. Varasov was just about to leave his new position, when the watertight door to the accommodation block at deck level, opened and light spilled out onto the starboard deck, over the side, and lit up a small piece of the grey waters of the Baltic. A figure stepped out and the door closed. But the figure had been framed in the light long enough for Varasov to see that it was Pavlov. Pavlov started walking forwards up the deck. Varasov followed him, moving along the railing and peering over, until Pavlov disappeared into the darkness ahead. Varasov did not know what to do. He was confused. They had not arranged any alarm signal so he had no way of warning them that Pavlov was on his way. Then a brief flicker of flame a little further along the deck told him that Pavlov had stopped to light a cigarette. The flame died, blackness again. Varasov hoped that the Pushkins were forewarned.

Sergei Pushkin broke open the seal on the container with the crowbar, then heaved up on the handle and swung open the door just enough to be able to squeeze in sideways. The hinges were rusty, but the noise they made was lost immediately in the sound of the bow breaking water below. Once Sergei was inside, Pushkin the elder closed the door and stepped back into the shadows.

When the door had closed behind him, Sergei lit the torch and shone it around. He found himself in a corridor between two piles of pallets, stacked to the height of the container. There was just enough room to walk between them. He shone the torch on a pallet to his left. The pallet was not made of wood, but of metal. It was shaped like a cage. The cage was full of clothes, not neatly arranged, just pressed in, as if the shipper really did not care whether or not they got damaged. Sergei grabbed hold of a sleeve he saw and pulled it out through a gap in the wires of the cage. It was made of a heavy, dark cloth. There were no buttons on it. Impatiently, he pushed the sleeve back inside and checked the pallets on top. It was the same story, so he went further in. There were three more pallets of the same kind, but the next row proved to be different. There were still wire cages, but when he flashed the torch on them, it turned out they contained boots.... heavy duty military boots of the kind he had worn when he had been a conscript in the Red Army. - Rubbish! He muttered and turned his attention to the other side of the gangway. There were no metal cages here, just wooden boxes, lots of them, piled up on wooden pallets and held fast there by steel wires and bottle screws. Sergei didn't need to open them to see what they contained. On the side of each one was a yellow hammer and sickle. Alongside that were some letters stencilled in black, they said 'AK74 - 50 pcs.'. It dawned on Sergei that there was no money to be found in here. This was in fact something that they would have been better off not knowing about!

Sergei turned to leave, but suddenly the door swung open and a shadow appeared in the hole, outlined by the mast head lights above the bridge, on the accommodation block at the other end of the ship. Sergei shut off the torch. It was Pavlov!

"What are you doing in here? I think you'd better come out and be quick about it!" Pavlov said threateningly. He was holding a Makarov in his right hand. It was pointing at his belly so Sergei didn't argue. He walked towards Pavlov. He still had the crowbar in his left hand. He kept it behind him, out of sight. He said nothing, because there was really nothing to say. It bothered him though that his father had not come to his assistance. Perhaps Pavlov had already done his father in. That must be the case, Sergei thought, because Pavlov would not have got this far if he hadn't! He tightened his grip on the crowbar. Just three paces more and Pavlov would get what was coming to him! Pavlov had made a mistake in stopping Sergei. He realised that when Sergei was just three paces away from him. It suddenly came to him that he had to find a quick solution to his problem or he had better watch his back for the rest of the trip, because with three Pushkins on board, and the crew on their side, if any harm came to Sergei then he might not make it to Klaipeda.

"Stop just there!" Pavlov barked. Sergei was about to go on. He started to take another step, but stopped in mid stride and pulled his foot back. Just one more step! Just one! But he lacked the courage to take it with the pistol pointing at him. Pavlov had found the solution to his problem. He could just shoot Sergei right there and dump the body overboard. No-one would ever know that he, Pavlov, had had a hand in it. There was only one problem - he had never shot anybody in cold blood in his life. Sergei Pushkin was standing alone and still before him, waiting. He had to do something, and do it now before anyone else turned up. It would be too late then! His finger tightened on the trigger. It had to be done!

Pavlov was no killer. He lacked the complete disregard for himself as well as others that is required in that profession. No, Pavlov was an officer. Had he been otherwise, he might have lived. Had he been the cold-hearted bastard that his chief was, he would have shot Sergei immediately he found him in the container, shut the door, put on one of the padlocks he had in his cabin, and forgotten all about it. But he didn't. Fortunately for Sergei. Pavlov heard a sudden movement close behind him, like the rustling of oilskins. He half turned. Pushkin the elders crowbar hit him on the side of the head. He dropped to his knees. Sergei leapt forward and cracked his skull. The sound of the dull thud was swept away in the wind and the crashing of the waves....

Pavlov died quickly. As he went down, the pistol fell out of his hand and skidded away across the deck. Sergei jumped across the body and started after it. Pushkin stopped him with a heavy hand.

"Forget it Sergei! Give me a hand, we'll dump him overboard!" Sergei obeyed and the two of them carried Pavlovs lifeless body to the railing and shoved it over. They went back to the container.

"Shut the door son. Let's get these bottle screws undone!" They worked like demons in a trance for the next ten minutes. It was dangerous work, because the ship heaved and pitched all the while, and neither wanted to be crushed or taken with it if it went overboard. The wind howled and foam sprayed across the fore deck. When it was done, they left quickly along the starboard side.

Varasov was nervous now. A few minutes ago he had seen the short flash of a torch quickly extinguished on the fore deck. Other than that there had been nothing. No sound, no light, nothing. He checked his watch in the light from yet another cigarette. Forty minutes had passed. They had agreed upon a half hour. He had not seen the flame from someone lighting a pipe by the crane island. How could he take the suspense? From somewhere ahead, there was a scraping sound, as of writhing metal on metal. The ship rolled. The sound got louder, and was accompanied by a sudden banging, again when the Alexander Sagieski rolled the other way. It suddenly occurred to Varasov that the container was loose! The Pushkins must be back then! He slid open the bridge wing door.

"Captain Gregoriev! I think something's broken loose on the fore deck! I can hear scraping and banging."

Gregoriev came out from behind the black curtains. He had a steaming mug of tea in his hand. He was in no hurry.

"Turn on the spotlight Varasov. Let's take a look!" He said as he stepped outside. Varasov did as he was told and turned on the big spot light perched in its cradle on the outermost tip of the bridge wing. He had to take off the canvas cover first. When he flipped the switch, the powerful beam lit up a patch of angry sea a kilometre off to starboard. Captain Gregoriev was now by the front railing, looking forward. Varasov turned the searchlight and bathed the front of the ship in a glaring white light. Everything seemed normal at first. Then the ship rolled to port, and the dark container on the fore deck began to move. As the roll deepened, the container picked up speed, until it smashed into the port anchor winch with a terrible crash. Gregoriev cursed vehemently and turned quickly back into the bridge without another word. Varasov kept the light beam on the fore deck. A moment after, the sound of the engine changed.

Gregoriev turned the ship around until its aft end was into the weather, and rang for dead slow on the engine telegraph. "Varasov!" He yelled. Varasov hurried into the wheelhouse. "Go down and wake the Pushkins, Rastov and Pavlov! Have them in the deck office in five minutes, then get back here!" Varasov disappeared down the port lighter. Gregoriev set the new course on the autopilot. Then he phoned Ljublin.

"What the hell!" Ljublin said. Gregoriev ignored the outburst.

"Pavlovs container has broken loose on the fore deck Ljublin. I've sent Varasov to muster the crew in the deck office. Get on down there and take charge!"

Ljublin mumbled something and dropped the phone.

Gregoriev went over to the radar, but it was still on the blink so he turned it off and went out to the port side spotlight. At the same time as Gregoriev reached the bridge wing and took over the spotlight, Ljublin was hurrying along the port side with the rest of the crew. But someone was missing. Gregoriev counted them again. Pavlov wasn't there.

"Didn't you wake Pavlov?" He said sharply to Varasov, who had just returned. Varasov shrugged and answered,

"He wasn't in his cabin. He might be up there already. I saw him walking that way about half an hour ago!"

Gregoriev accepted the explanation and turned his attention to the fore deck. He had his binoculars with him now, and followed Ljublin and the crews fight to get a wire over the container. It took half an hour to lash the container. Then Ljublin and his team came back. Varasov turned off the spotlight. Everything went suddenly black again. Calm returned to the Alexander Sagieski, at least on the surface.

Ljublin turned up on the bridge a short while later. He was wet, and tired and in a bad temper.

"The shackles had been loosened! Who the hell would do a thing like that?"

"Loosened?" Gregoriev said in disbelief and handed Ljublin a cup of hot tea. Ljublin took it and gulped a huge mouthful. Then he wiped his lips and moustache with the back of a hairy hand.

"Yes, the bottle screws had been screwed all the way out and the chains thrown off. They weren't broken. Did Varasov see anything?"

"He said he saw Pavlov walking up the deck about half an hour before it happened. Did you see Pavlov up there at all?" Ljublin shook his head.

"No, but I did find this on the way up there!" He pulled the Makarov from his right hand pocket and held it up with one finger through the trigger guard. "I think we'd better search the ship for Pavlov! Another thing. The seal on the container was broken. It could have happened by accident, but who knows?"

Gregoriev said nothing for a few moments, then seemed to come to a decision.

"No matter. If Pavlovs' gone overboard then he's lost. I'm not wasting time looking for him. We have a cargo to get through, and we've got to put Pavlovs' rampant secret container ashore without too much notice being taken. If we report him missing then there'll be questions. Questions that we don't want to have to answer! The quicker we get that thing off my ship, the happier I'll be!"

Ljublin nodded. He wasn't keen on leaving somebody to drown out there on a night like this, but it couldn't happen to a more deserving character than Pavlov. Ljublin had smelled Mafia and KGB and god knows what else, as soon as Pavlov had walked on board. He doubted if anyone other than his employers would miss him. Ljublin couldn't know it, but he was right. Pavlovs' wife was at this very minute teaching a young Red Army lieutenant the art of deep penetration.

Gregoriev turned the ship around again, ordered full speed ahead, and went back to his tea. Ljublin returned to his bunk and was asleep before his head hit the pillow, despite the laughing coming from the galley down the corridor. Varasov returned to his watch, and wished it was over so that he could find out what the Pushkins had seen in the container.

There was a heavy knock on the door of the interview room.

"Come in!" Dawson said curtly. The door opened. Avon Wailes stepped in and closed it purposefully behind him. Dawson stood up and stuck out his open hand across the table. Wailes took it. He liked Dawson. There was no nonsense with this man. Once you got past his apparently arrogant facade, he was a good man to work with.

"Nice to see you again Wailes. Take a seat."

When they were both seated again, he continued. "George Green suggested that I get you to give me a hand with the Paul Anderson case. He said a change was as good as a rest, and that you needed a rest from being his minder. He mentioned the word insubordination."

Wailes nodded. "Don't get me wrong sir, but working as George Green's minder isn't exactly my idea of adventure! Anyway, I was due to be relieved at the end of the month, so I doubt if it will cause him any anxiety."

"No, I suppose not. I heard you were on the scene when Anderson did his disappearing trick. Tell me about it."

"Nothing much to tell really. We were parked across the street, watching his place. I was on watch at the time. I saw smoke inside the flat and ran across the street. I had seen him at the window just a few minutes before, so I knew he should have been in there. Anyway, when I got inside, the place was full of smoke and Anderson had disappeared."

"Who was watching the back door?"

"Alex Sanders."

"When did he leave the back lane?"

"Just after I got inside. I called him on the radio and told him to come in through the back door and see if Anderson was anywhere around. He didn't see anybody on his way up."

"How did Anderson get away?"

"Through the loft. He had been well prepared, probably since the day he moved in. He had made holes through the joining walls to the other houses. There's an empty shop at the corner of the street. He had a motorbike parked in the coal shed in the back yard, and disappeared on that."

Dawson was silent for a moment. Wailes took out a pack of cigarettes and held them out across the table. Dawson waved them away.

"No thanks, go ahead yourself."

"Thank you sir. I'll open the window."

"Good man."

Wailes got up and opened the window. It was sunny outside, and still cold. You could almost feel the spring coming, though there were no signs of green on the trees anywhere yet. Wailes lit his cigarette. A couple of dirty kids were playing football in the street. A Northern bus stopped at the corner of the road and turned right. A taxi trundled past the row of single story miners cottages opposite, where an old man was stepping backwards out of a green door with his walking stick in his right hand. The taxi beeped his horn at the kids, but they didn't seem to notice. The old man walked up the street towards the shop at the corner.

"This letter you retrieved isn't much to go on."

"No, not much at all. Apart from the fact that it's written in English and the post mark is from Newcastle there really isn't anything."

"What do you make of the message - Shut the shoe shop. Your boss says it's time to go home."

Wailes went back to his seat and sat down across the table from Dawson.

"Well, I'd say his employers had some kind of special job for him and that whatever it was, it had a higher priority than whatever job he had here. I'd also say that whoever sent the letter was a middle man or contact of some kind."

"Yes. Indeed. By the way, why were you watching his house?"

Wailes became visibly thoughtful.

"A curious thing really. I came to work the Monday before last, and there was a P27 on my desk. It was an order to watch the house and place microphones etc. It was signed by George Green. I went over to George's office when he came in, and asked him what it was all about. To tell the truth, I was happy to be able to do something other than sitting around the office waiting for George to decide to drive somewhere. Anyway, to cut a long story short, George said that he had heard from a reliable contact at the Russian embassy that Anderson was worth watching. That was all - nothing else. Anyway, George got a bit upset when I asked him if he was serious about this. He said he was, and that I'd better get on with it. So I did. That's that really. I've put a copy of the P27 in the report."

"Yes, I know." Dawson lifted a brown envelope from his desk and let it fall back again without further comment. "Any idea where he might have gone?"

"None at all sir. We've had the ports and airports covered since he disappeared, but nothing so far. My guess is that he's slipped out already, probably within a couple of hours of his disappearing act. As to his destination, it's hard to tell. The only lead we've got is that the letter is from Newcastle."

Dawson heaved himself upright in his chair and stretched his arms. He massaged his left shoulder.

"Well, Avon, the reason you're here is that I need somebody with your experience to track down Paul Anderson. Since you have actually seen him, that only makes you more appropriate for the operation."

"What about the photos we sent over to the lab?"

"Ah, a sad story I am afraid. Somebody over at the photo lab spilled black coffee all over the negatives, in the dark room mind you, before any prints were taken! I need not tell you what I said to the lab chief - but never mind, the result is the same, the negatives have been destroyed. And for some strange reason, all the photographs of Anderson at the house have disappeared. He probably destroyed them or took them with him. So there are no photographs. Never mind. I want you to follow Paul Anderson's trail, wherever it leads. I want you to find out what he was doing here and report back to me personally at least once a day. I want to know why he was here, who sent him, why they want him to come back, and last but not least, where BACK is!"

Dawson pushed a brown envelope stuffed with papers across the desk towards Avon. "You can start by finding the amateur radio club that he frequented. Any questions? No? Then get on with it."

Wailes stubbed out his cigarette in the ash tray on the desk and stood up. Dawson stood up too. Although he was tall, Wailes was taller, and more rugged. They shook hands.

"By the way, Wailes. I'll be moving to a new office tomorrow. I don't know exactly where it will be yet, but I'll leave a message with the watch officer here for when you call. He'll let you know. Good luck!"

"Thank you sir!" Wailes said and left. He decided to call the wife. She was out, so he sent her a telegram instead. It said - Going hunting darling. See you when I get back. All my love. Avon.

Chapter Six – Back Room Boys

Brown was tired when he got back to his rented room. It was daylight, and a heavy fog was drifting up the street. It smelled of seaweed. His footsteps were heavy on the stairs and he had to lean on the banister to help himself up. When he reached the third floor, he stopped for a breather then took the door key from the inside pocket of his brown bomber jacket and opened the door.

The warmth inside hit him immediately and he started to sweat. Nobody was home. Brown was pleased about that, being too tired to answer any questions or have a sociable chat. He took off the jacket and hung it on a hook in the passage, took off his knitted woollen hat and pushed it wearily over the top. Then he took off his walking boots. It was a pain to bend over, and even harder to straighten up again. He had to lean against the wall.

"Christ, I'm beat!" He said aloud and eased himself upright again with the help of the radiator. He felt damp all over. Do you know that feeling when you really fancy a good, hot shower, but at the same time you're just too bloody tired to get it together and take one? Well, that's how Brown felt at that moment. He stood in the passage for a minute that seemed like an hour, looked through the door at his made up bed, then along the passage to the shower, then back again to the bed. Finally, he made up his mind and almost fell into the bedroom. Removing his shirt was hard, but finally it came off and fell onto the armchair. Taking off his trousers was harder, because he had to bend his knees to pull his feet up through the legs when they lay on the floor. But it was nigh on impossible to get up enough energy to take off his socks, so he kept them on, fell flat on his belly on the bed, made a failed attempt to pull the quilted cover over him, and fell asleep.

When Britta opened the front door an hour later, she immediately noticed Brown's boots in the middle of the passage. She picked up the shopping bags from the floor and went in. She did not close the door with her foot as usual, but went straight into the kitchen and put the bags on the table. Then she went out and closed the door. The door to Brown's room was half open, so she looked in on him. He was sound asleep on his back, with one leg dangling over the edge of the bed, and his naked right thigh sticking out from under the covers. His arms were splayed out and his head back, his mouth wide open. It looked pretty uncomfortable. Britta went in and lifted his leg back onto the bed, and in doing so two things happened. Firstly, she saw a long, white scar down the outside of his thigh. There were signs of stitches. Seventeen of them. It was an old scar. Secondly, touching his warm skin brought back fond memories of Gordon. Maybe she did hold on to Brown's leg just a little longer than necessary, but what the hell! It had been a long time, and she wasn't too old yet! She pulled the covers over his leg, and paid particular attention to tucking him in. Then she carefully lifted his head, so that his mouth shut, and pushed the pillow into a much better position under it. She went out into the passage and took off her coat. It was probably better to get on with something which could take her mind of Brown's thigh.

When Brown awoke, it felt like every muscle in his body ached. He rolled over carefully and looked at the bedside clock. It said four. By the light outside, it seemed like it was afternoon. He lay in that position for a few minutes with his eyes closed, until the smell of fresh coffee reached his nostrils. When he looked up, Britta stood in the doorway with a steaming mug of coffee. Brown noticed that his naked ass stuck out from under the covers. Britta didn't seem to mind.

"Thought you might like some coffee!" She said, and smiled.

"Oh, yes please! That's the best offer I've had these last two days! I think I'll get up though. I'll join you in the kitchen."

"Not the living room?"

"No thanks. I think my back's broke. I need to sit up straight for a while." He got up and got dressed. Britta turned and went into the kitchen.

When Brown came in, she was sitting at the table, looking out of the window into the street, and sipping coffee. He turned a chair around so that he could lean on the back and sipped some of his own. Britta turned to face him.

"You look like something the cat dragged in!"

"I feel like it too!"

"I hope you don't mind me asking, but what happened to you? Get in a fight or something?"

Brown took another swig of coffee and used it to think of what to tell her. "No, I met a couple of young guys a couple of days ago in a pub. It turned out they were going on a two day hike to the west coast and I was stupid enough to tell them I used to do a lot of walking. Well, they bet me a hundred kroner that I wouldn't make the trip, me being an old timer and all that. I couldn't let them get away with that, so I went with them!"

Britta smiled. "How did it go then?"

Brown reached into his pocket, took out two crumpled bank notes and put them in the middle of the table. "I bet them two hundred I'd be first home!"

Britta smiled again and shook her head slowly. Yes, it was Gordon all over again. Why is it I always get attracted to the leather-necks, the hard men, the ones who take up a challenge at the drop of a hat? Her body looked out of the window, but she was looking inside herself at the same time. Maybe that's because they are the ones who live! There was never a dull moment with Gordon. Oh yes, there were times when I hated him, for his stubbornness, his way of suddenly taking things into his own hands and forgetting agreements and appointments with me. But mostly I loved him for the fact that he made me feel very much alive.

"Just like my ex husband. No challenge is too great, no amount of money too small! He always wore his pride in his boots too." She said at the window, then realised that she was saying it aloud and turned suddenly. "Sorry, I was thinking aloud!"

Brown simply shrugged. "You're right, it was stupid. The whole of my body agrees with you! Anyway, it will probably be a couple of days before I can walk properly again. What have you been up to?" It was just like being married all over again. He wondered if he should mind his own business, but she answered,

"I've been on a first aid course, gun shot wounds, legs blown off and all that." She said it blandly, but Brown was suddenly genuinely interested.

"Gun shot wounds? That's heavy stuff isn't it? How come you're learning that kind of stuff?"

"Hadn't you noticed?"

"Noticed what?"

"I'm a squad leader in the National Guard." She said and sipped more coffee. It took Brown a second or two to recover from the shock though. He had thought that nothing could ever surprise him again, but that Britta was a sergeant in the national guard had done exactly that.

"Well, well, that does surprise me!" and then, not wanting to sound crude, "Pleasantly though, I must say. It sounds really interesting. Maybe you'd like to tell me more about it over a couple of beers down at the pub after I've had a shower?" Britta looked across at him, decided he was on the level, and said yes, she would love to, if she could decide which pub it would be.

General Rye was commander in chief of the Fredericia garrison which was surrounded by the German army in the war of 1864. A young lieutenant, Anker by name, became famous by leading a breakout from the besieged city, a breakout which turned the tide of the war and meant victory for the Danes later that year. They named a pub in Aarhus after General Rye. That was where Britta took Brown at seven o'clock that evening. It was a small place, built in what seemed to be an old shop. The windows had been painted and the whole thing had been tidied up, but when they went inside, Brown had the distinct feeling that there should have been sawdust on the floor.

Anyway, it was still a bit early and there was only three customers in the place. Britta picked out a spot by the window. There was a table with two chairs. She told Brown to take a seat while she got a couple of beers from the bar. He did so. It was evening, but outside was as bright as daylight because of the lights. Across the street there was a pizza take-away with a bunch of youths outside having an argument. They were all wearing hip-hop caps with the peaks turned backwards and oversize clothes. It used to be punks, and before them skinheads, and before them mods and rockers. Kids always have to find something they can identify with! Further up the street a crowd was pushing through the doors of a cinema. The pedestrian traffic was lively. There were no cars to be seen. Britta came over with the beer and put them down. She sat down across from him, with her back to the door.

"Skål" She said, lifting her glass.

"Yeah, cheers." Brown took a long swig. It was cold and light.

A couple of minutes passed without comment. A man in his mid thirties, with jeans and dirty long hair came in, looked around and went out again. Brown watched him through the window as he disappeared up the street.

"How long have you been in the National Guard?"

"About ten years. I started one time when Gordon was away on an assignment."

"Why?"

"Well, I wanted to be able to go with him once in a while, so I joined up to learn the ropes. Thought maybe I could help out."

"You said your ex husband was a foreign correspondent. What did he report on?"

Britta met his gaze. The waitress turned up, placed half a candle in a candle stick on the table and lit it. Then she left.

"He reported mostly on the war in Afghanistan. I did actually get to go with him on two occasions. The Russians weren't very happy about foreign journalists covering the war, so we had to slip across the border from Pakistan."

"Must have been a hair-raising experience!"

"Oh yes, you can say that again. Although mind you, the Muhajadin were both helpful and organised. They had the kind of spirit and vivacity that comes from living on the verge of death all the time. I found them pleasant enough to be with, but they could change at the drop of a hat. I felt a bit uncomfortable with them sometimes. Gordon loved it though, he was all over the place."

"What happened between you and Gordon then?"

"He went out there once too often, and didn't come back again. I got a note in very bad English from one of their leaders, saying that he had been killed by gunfire from a helicopter just after the group had ambushed a supply convoy outside Kabul. A couple of months after that the guerillas moved into the city. I got three rolls of unexposed film, his watch, his passport and his empty wallet in a package from Karachi. That was all."

"I'm sorry to hear that. It must have come as a shock."

Britta smiled, then grinned as if remembering something long forgotten. "Not really. What surprised me was that he lasted as long as he did. Whenever he was away, he wrote saying how much he missed home, Tina, me. But whenever he had been home for three weeks he started to get itchy feet. Then he would walk about like a lion in a cage for another week, then he would be off again. It was like a drug for him really, he was totally dependant on it, and on us. He just couldn't do without either."

"Gordon. That's a strange name for a Dane."

"He wasn't. He was English, like you, although he was from the south coast, Brighton. As far as I know he still has family over there, although it's been a couple of years since I last spoke to any of them.

"Seems you have a fancy for Englishmen." Brown said, and drained his glass.

"Some Englishmen." She said, looking him straight in the eye. Brown got the message alright, but didn't know whether or not to do anything about it just yet. There was so much to do.

"Fancy another - beer?" He asked.

"Yes please, I thought you'd never ask!"

When he returned with the beer he asked why she had stayed in the National Guard.

"I had got used to it. Besides that though, I'd made some friends and found it challenging. But enough about me. Tell me more about yourself. Are you married?"

"I used to be. I got divorced a while back. I have a son, or I should say that I had two, but one of them was killed in a car crash a couple of days before I came over here."

"Well then, it seems we've both got something to be sorry about! Skål!" Their glasses met over the candle for a moment.

"How did you get the scar on your leg?" She asked suddenly. Brown hesitated a moment, but decided to tell her the truth. Somehow it didn't feel right bullshitting Britta. Maybe that was because she'd been around a bit herself and seemed to have her heart in the right place. Well, maybe half the truth.

"I got into a knife fight with a crook a couple of years ago. I almost lost."

"Dick, I can see right through you. You're full of shit! I've answered your questions truthfully, now you answer mine that way. What really happened?"

"Oh, alright if you really want to know. It was almost the truth. I just left out that the guy was a KGB officer, that's all."

"Well, don't worry about it. I won't tell anybody. Now, I won't ask you who you really work for, but I could tell right off that you're no merchant navy man. I've been too close to too many of your kind for too long."

"What kind of work do you do?" Brown asked, changing the subject quickly.

"I'm unemployed at the moment. Mind you, that's not as bad as it sounds. I have lots to do. You won't find me moping about the house cleaning the same bits time and time again, not like some other women I know! My last job was as a secretary in a fitness club."

A young man in his twenties appeared in the door. He clapped her on the shoulder.

"Hej bedste, hvad laver du her?"

She clipped him across the ear, lightly. He grinned widely and pulled up a chair. Brown must have looked inquisitively at her because she continued in English.

"Dick, meet Walther. Walther, Dick." Walther suddenly became very polite and put out his hand. Brown shook it.

"Walther is one of my squad. When they're feeling particularly friendly, they call me grandma."

"And when she makes us walk too much we call her something much worse!" Walther said. He and Britta stuck out their tongues at one another. Then Walther got up.

"Well, I can see that I'm interrupting something. So I'll just take a walk up the street and see if I can find the others at the video shop."

"Are you having a party or something?" Britta asked.

"Not really, although it might end up that way. We're renting a film and having a couple of beers at my place. You can drop by later if you like."

"Thanks for the invitation." She said as Walther left. He waved a goodbye from the doorway and disappeared up the street, with his hands in his pockets.

"Grandma eh?" Brown said quietly.

"Don't you start too!"

They got on well together. About eight o'clock they left. The place was still pretty empty. They walked up the street towards the town centre and the shopping precinct. Britta stopped to look at some shoes in a shop window.

"I think the dark blue ones look quite nice, don't you?"

"Yes, they suit you fine!" Brown replied, and meant it.

She took him by the hand and they walked on. It had been years since Brown had held hands with anyone. In fact he'd forgotten when and was just a bit embarrassed to be seen doing it in a busy street. But none of the passers-by seemed to pay any attention to it. They came upon a Chinese restaurant. Isn't it strange how they all look the same, both from the outside and on the inside, and all have the same menu?

"Let's eat in here." Britta said. They went inside. They hung up their coats on pegs in the hall and were shown to a table in the corner by a young man who looked more Korean than Chinese. He was wearing wide black trousers and a white shirt with a red, fire-breathing dragon on the back. He disappeared immediately after handing them both the menu.

"Did I tell you that Tina has moved in with her boyfriend?" Britta said suddenly.

"No you didn't. I didn't even know she had one. How long have they been going together?"

"Oh, about a year. His name is Martin. He's a good lad. He's at college. He wants to be a mechanical engineer. He has a small college flat over in Viby. Tina says she'll be leaving most of her stuff at home, because his place is too small." They looked at each other across the table. Both of them knew what the end of the evening would bring. No words were needed to seal the pact. When they left the restaurant an hour and a half later, they were laughing at one of Brittas' jokes. She said,

"Let's go home and have some coffee and a brandy or two."

"That sounds fine to me!" Brown kissed her on the tip of her nose. Not a big kiss, just a touch, but oh what a fire it lit!. For the rest of the walk home, they went arm in arm. Britta seemed pleased. Brown felt like he was a fly wandering into a spiders' web, but he didn't mind one little bit.

The clock said it was three in the morning. The knocking on the front door told Black that somebody wanted to talk to him very badly indeed. He rolled back the quilt. The blonde he was sharing his bed with pulled the sheets up over her shoulder and rolled over on her side. Black rolled out of bed. He was naked. He pulled on his jeans and went to the door. The knocking stopped when he started on the latch. Erik was standing on the landing. Black turned around and went over to the small kitchen without a word. Erik came in and closed the door, just as the timer turned off the light in the corridor outside.

The flat was dark, although a street lamp outside the kitchen threw shadows on the wall. Erik sat down on one of the two chairs at the kitchen table. Black filled up the electric kettle and plugged it into a wall socket. He took two mugs from the cupboard over the sink, spooned instant coffee into both and sat down across from Erik. He put his feet up on the table and leaned back in the chair.

"What do you want Erik?"

"Hammel wants us."

Black yawned. He was dog tired too. The last couple of days had been hard on everybody.

"Couldn't he wait until tomorrow?"

"He said something's happened that means we have to change the plan. He wouldn't tell me what it was, but he rang me about an hour ago and asked me to come over and pick you up. We have to be at his place by four."

"Must be important. I'll get dressed. When the kettle boils make the coffee will you, I'm going nowhere before I've had a cup!"

Erik nodded and Black went back to the other room and got dressed in the dark. When he returned two minutes later, Erik had poured water into the mugs and was stirring the coffee in one of them. They drank their coffee without turning on the light and without a word. Then they left quickly, and went down the concrete stairs of the housing block and out through the front door into the parking lot. Black got into the drivers seat of a brown Simca. Erik climbed in the passenger seat and they left. Erik lit two cigarettes and handed one to Black.

"How did the trip go?" Erik asked when the turned onto Skanderborgvej. The streets were empty.

"That old man's a hard son of a bitch!"

"What happened?"

"Well, Mikael and Jens brought him over to Marselis woods. Anders and me had arranged to meet him down by the pavilion. It was pitch black when they got there. Anyway, we had a talk. I asked him if he wanted to join the group and he said he did. I told him that we had talked about it and that we had decided that he would be most useful in my squad. Then I said that I didn't really want him, because he was too old and couldn't make it swing with youngsters like us. I said that I'd been outvoted, and so here he was with a chance, but that we'd be watching him the whole way to make sure that he didn't cheat."

"What did he say when you gave him the map?"

"He didn't say anything. He just looked at it for a minute and said nothing. I was sure he would back out, but he didn't. After he'd looked at it, he just lit a cigarette and said - When do we start? - I said, now, then he said - I'll just lock the car then, I wouldn't want anybody to nick it while I'm away." They shook their heads.

"A cool customer eh? What do you make of him?"

"Ex pro. There's no doubt at all that he's ex special forces. Maybe even SAS. He didn't seem to give a shit! Anyway, when I told him to go, off he went through the woods, as if he was taking a Sunday stroll. Didn't seem in too much of a hurry."

"Did anybody catch him?"

"Oh yes. I'd told him he had forty eight hours to walk to Esbjerg and back, that I'd stationed the rest of the group at different places along the road that he would be taking, that they had orders to rough him up a bit if they caught him, and hold him for four hours. You know, I honestly didn't think he'd make it. I even bet him a hundred kroner that he wouldn't!"

"What did he say to that?"

"He bet me two hundred he would be back early!"

Erik laughed. "Did you take the bet?"

Black looked across at him. "Of course I did! Money for old rope I thought." He said the last part of the sentence with a slight scowl. Erik laughed again.

"You lost then! Well that's a turn up for the book!"

They had reached the traffic light at Harold Jensens Place. It went red as they got there so Black stopped the car. There was no cross traffic though. The streets were still empty. Black continued.

"Anders and Jens were waiting for him when he passed the Blue Market at Låsby. They saw him coming and hid in the bushes. When he came by they jumped him. It must have been one hell of a fight!"

"What happened?"

"Anders got a broken arm and Jens ran away. I shouldn't be surprised at Jens, he's always been a bit of a mothers boy. Anyway, when he came back to pick up his bike, Anders was going on about his arm. Jens brought him back. Anders said that the old man had bashed him over the arm with a piece of pipe. He must have picked it up along the road somewhere."

The light changed to green. The car started moving again. Erik threw his cigarette butt out of the window and rolled it up again.

"Did you send Anders over to the hospital then?"

"Yeps. They plastered his arm and sent him home."

"I'll drop in and see how he's doing later on."

"If you're going to play the good samaritan then you'd better drop in on Werner too. Our Mister Brown hit him across the shin with his piece of pipe outside the inn in Byrup!" Erik whistled,

"He doesn't give in does he?"

"No he doesn't. What worries me though is if he'll take orders. On top of that, I've got enough on my plate keeping Anders in check. If he takes to thinking about getting revenge on Brown, then it might get in the way of our work. I'll be keeping a close eye on both of them in the future. I'd be obliged if you would too."

Erik nodded. Black stopped the car outside Hammels' flat on Heiberg Street. The row of old, four storey houses formed a three sided square around a small green patch with a few trees and bushes and a couple of park benches. Hammel's flat was on the second floor, at the corner of the street. It was a big, open, Victorian style flat with large windows and a balcony from which you could look out across the park towards the harbour on the other side of the boulevard. It was austere. The floors were plain, unvarnished wood. There were four rooms, a kitchen and a bathroom. There was furniture, a desk and chair, and a mattress on the floor in the room with French windows leading out onto the balcony. The other rooms were empty. Hammel did not use the place very often. There was a back door leading out of the flat to a narrow, spiral staircase.

By some curious twist of fate, Hammel's flat was no more than five hundred metres from the flat where Dick Brown and Britta Nielsen were making love at that very moment.

Erik and Black climbed the darkened stairs as quietly as possible and pressed Hammels' doorbell. A moment later he let them in. He had been waiting behind the door since he saw the Simca pull up under the street lamp outside and both of them get out. When they were inside, he shut the door and went into the living room. He offered the two men a beer from a crate beside the mattress and took one himself. They opened them and went out onto the balcony. It was quite still outside. There was no wind, no fog, but a slight nip in the air. Spring was just around the corner.

"Skål!" Hammel said. They drank. "Well, it seems that we're going to have to change our original plan a bit. This is the situation. Our very important visitor is arriving as planned, by private plane at Tirstrup in about five hours. The idea was that we should have seen him safely across the border and hand him over to the Vulkan group. However, I got word a couple of hours ago that the Vulkan group has run into a spot of trouble with P4. Typical! It's probably because of the assassination attempt on Moltke. Any idea how Brown got hold of the hit list?"

Both Erik and Black shook their heads. Black said, "Well, we've been distributing them everywhere from the post box in Randers. We took some with us when we went to England. Maybe he got one from there?"

Hammel nodded. Yes, that must have been the case. "Hans phoned me and asked if we could escort our visitor all the way home. I said we could."

"Where is home?"

"Kaunas, Lithuania."

Erik and Black almost choked on their beer.

"You're kidding!"

"Do I look like I'm kidding?" Hammel asked.

"Alright, so you're not kidding! Isn't that asking a bit much? None of my lads are trained for this kind of job!"

"Are you saying you can't do it?"

Black thought about that a moment before answering.

"No, I'm not saying that. All I'm saying is that it might not be that easy. We not only have to deliver him to Kaunas, but we have to come back again, and if the Vulkan group is having problems, a bunch of strangers wouldn't have it any easier." Hammel put his arm around Blacks' shoulder.

"Don't worry about it. Firstly, Anders stays home. He won't be much use with a broken arm. You can take Brown with you instead, he's experienced enough..." Black attempted to say something, but Hammel insisted. "..I know you don't trust him yet, I know he's an old timer, and a stranger and a lot of other things - but you have to admit, he's the best damned soldier we've had around here for a long time, and he's got guts!"

Black nodded. That much was indeed true.

"Okay then, Anders stays. Brown goes. Mind you, if you find out he's up to something then you'll just have to get rid of him. I'll leave it up to you. Next, I've borrowed an old Volkswagen minibus from the publisher, along with the registration papers. You can use that for transport. I had the banker over about half an hour ago. There's money for the trip on my desk in a brown envelope. You've all got passports, and visas are not needed for Poland and Lithuania for those carrying EEC passports, so there's no trouble there. I've picked out the route you'll be following. So what could be easier? Any questions?"

"What happens when we get to Kaunas?"

"Well, when you get there, our V.I.P. knows the ropes. You'll make sure he gets to where he has to go and help him with whatever he has to do. You'll be taking the place of the Vulcan group. But remember, it is your responsibility to see that your lads get home safely. You'll be helping out, but the decision on when to leave and what to accept or not accept is yours. You'll be the man on the spot, so to speak. But don't come home right away. It may look suspicious if you leave the same day you arrive."

Black shook his head. They went inside and closed the windows and the blinds. Hammel switched on the light and spread three maps out on the floor. The maps of Germany and Poland were large, and the map of Lithuania small.

"You'll cross the border at Padborg. Then turn south east on the E7 to....."

It was more than an hour before Erik and Black left the flat. By that time Brown and Britta were both totally and blissfully unconscious. Black drove round the corner and wrote a note. Erik hurried up the stairs to Britta's flat on the third floor and pushed it under the door. When they drove off again, Black said,

"Let's get some sleep. I hate getting up in the middle of the night!"

Erik nodded in agreement. They drove back to Black's flat.

At eight o'clock Brown got up to make coffee. Britta was awake already. As he left the bedroom without getting dressed, she watched him go. When he got into the hall, he noticed the note that had been pushed under the door. He picked it up and went into the kitchen, where he poured water into the percolator, put coffee in the filter beneath the outlet, and turned on the machine. He opened the note and read it. Then he crumpled it up into a little ball and threw it into the waste bin under the kitchen sink. The percolator bubbled. He went back to bed and climbed under the sheets. But he wasn't interested in making love, Britta could tell that right away by the look on his face. He was far away, in another place and another time although his body was right there beside her. She had seen that look before, many times.

"What's the matter?" She asked. He pondered a moment but didn't answer. Maybe this was the break he had been waiting for. But he wouldn't be able to do the job without outside help. He could see that now. He found himself asking,

"You know when you said last light that you missed the excitement you got living with Gordon, and was bored with being unemployed? Did you really mean it?"

Her heart began to beat just a little bit faster. In the silence that ensued, the only sounds in the flat were the bubbling of the percolator and the muffled rumbling of a truck in low gear climbing the street.

"Yes, I really meant it. Why do you ask?"

"I need somebody to help me. It might be a little dangerous though, so I'd not mind at all if you didn't think you could do it."

"What is it about?"

Brown looked at her and kissed her gently on the forehead.

"Don't take offence, but I can only tell you that if you agree to help me out. Otherwise, it will be safer for both of us if you don't know too much."

Now she was both excited and wary at the same time. Then suddenly she sat up straight, pulled the bedclothes around her stomach, although she was completely naked, lifted her right hand and said solemnly,

"I swear I'll help you, as long as it's legal that is. There, how's that?"

Brown was looking at her breasts more than at her hand. They weren't the breasts of an inexperienced young girl, but of a mature woman, large and somewhat droopy. He heard himself saying,

"God, you're beautiful!" He meant it.

She laughed. In the kitchen, the percolator gave a last, throaty bubble and went quiet. Britta said, suddenly serious,

"Let's get up and you can tell me all about it over coffee."

"A good idea!"

They got out of bed and didn't bother straightening the sheets at all, or getting dressed. Brown went into the kitchen. He took two mugs from the cupboard and set them on the table beside the window, then poured coffee for them both. Britta came in as he put the pot back on the percolator. They sat down.

Tirstrup airport is surprisingly provincial for a city the size of Aarhus, and surprisingly far away, about an hour by car. Maybe that is because of the noise. Anyway, Black and Erik were there at the appointed time, waiting in the lounge and looking across the runway when the Lear jet landed and taxied up to the arrival entrance. There were no special preparations. The door opened, a man with a small suitcase came out, the door closed and the plane taxied back towards the runway. Erik had a piece of cardboard with the words "Mr. Smith" inscribed on it with a broad felt-tipped pen.

Paul Anderson noticed the sign and went across to the two young men. Black stuck out his hand and said,

"Welcome to Denmark Mister Smith. I hope you had a nice trip."

"Comfortable enough thank you."

"The car is waiting outside. I'll take your bag." Erik said. Smith shook his head.

"No thanks, I like to keep it on me!"

They left. Only four people saw them go. An odd-job man who was sweeping the floor; a passenger in a long overcoat on his way in through the swing doors; the driver of a taxi parked outside. He looked up from his book when they came out, and looked away again when they walked round the back of his car and crossed towards the parking lot. Then there was the woman in the passenger seat of a brown Toyota parked about fifty metres behind the taxi. She was busy lighting a cigarette when they came out.

The minibus was waiting in the parking lot. Mikael Mogensen was behind the wheel. Brown was sitting in the back, along with Steen Hansen. Smith and Erik got in through the side passenger door. Black closed it with a clash from outside and got in the passenger seat. They left. As they drove out of the parking lot, Black turned around and said,

"We're on our way then! Steen, break open the beer, I'm parched."

There was general approval of the suggestion, and not a little whooping and joking. It was as if the pressure of waiting was being relieved. Smith took the beer Black offered him and swallowed half of it in one huge gulp. It was good to be among friends, no matter how temporary the condition.

Britta stopped the brown Toyota in the parking lot outside the D.I.Y market and walked the two hundred metres to the corner of the ring road and the road to Randers. The pedestrian light was green, so she crossed, and turned right up the Randers road. Just past the research buildings on the left hand side, is Tåsinge road. She turned left and followed it to its intersection with Langelandsgade. So far she had not been followed.

It took a couple of minutes to find the key to the flat, because the bulb in the cellar had blown. But she got it in the end, and climbed the stairs. She listened to the door for a few seconds. Light from the stair well window lit the lower part of the stairs. It was windy outside, and cold, that was why she was wearing a parka over her sweater, and woolly socks in her hiking boots. She pushed the doorbell several times and waited. There was no sound at all.

Britta put the key in the lock, but before turning it, she went through the sequence once again. When the door opened, she would have only ten seconds to key in the correct code on the panel behind the door, or the entire place would be filled with a mixture of smoke and tear gas and the alarms turned on. She turned the key, thought - it's now or never - and went in. The code was accepted and she closed the door. She did not turn on the lights, although the blinds were drawn and the flat was in darkness.

The flat was as Brown had described it. She lit the torch she had brought with her and looked around. It seemed very empty indeed in relation to her own flat, in fact completely without character of any kind. It was obviously not the kind of place someone willingly lived in for any length of time. She went into the bedroom and opened the drawers in the commode, one by one, starting at the bottom. When she found the revolver, Britta checked to see if it was loaded. It was. She pushed it into the inside pocket of her parka. She dropped five boxes of ammunition into her pocket. In the next drawer up there was money, lots and lots of it! She gasped at the bundles, and tried to count how much there was. As she fingered it, she thought how much she could do with it - and tax-free too! But there was no time to play around. She took fifty thousand, closed the drawer and went back into the living room. There was no sign of any watchers in the street. She went back into the bedroom. There were still too many shadows in the courtyard. It was difficult to see if anyone was hiding there. She had to take a chance! She checked the revolver once again and held it in her hand as she put it into her pocket. Until she was safely back in the car, she would not be letting it go. She was both excited, and elated. She had not felt such a surge of adrenaline in a long time! She wasn't nervous, or panicky, but she couldn't keep back a smile as she opened the front door and checked the stairs. While she was looking out, there was the sound of a door opening on the next floor up. Startled, she stepped back inside and shut the door quietly. She stood with her back to the wall behind the door and the revolver clenched in her hand as heavy steps approached. Then they receded down the stairs and there was an echoed bang as the front door crashed shut. She did not move for several seconds more. Then she opened the door again. This time there were no surprises. She coded the security system and closed the door behind her.

As Britta was putting the key to the flat back in the mouse hole in the cellar, two men were approaching her own apartment. Jens and Sieg reached her door and paused to catch their breath. Then Jens motioned silently to Sieg, who moved to the top of the stairs and stood with his back to the wall, out of range of the fish-eye lens in Brittas' door. Jens pressed the doorbell. There was no answer. He pressed it again. Still no answer. Sieg relaxed visibly. Jens pressed it again, this time more urgently. There was still no answer.

Sieg said, "What do we do now?"

Jens thought a moment.

"Hammel said we should go through Brown's gear, right?"

Sieg nodded,

"Well then, we'll just have to break the door down and mess up the place a bit. Maybe take the TV and the stereo to make it look like a burglary."

Sieg agreed and produced a crowbar from under his raincoat and pushed it into the jamb beside the lock, then he heaved with all the weight his body had. There was a splintering of wood, the jamb moved. Jens pushed the door with his shoulder while Sieg held the crowbar and the door opened. Jens almost fell into the hall and Sieg almost dropped the crowbar. The two men went inside and closed the door. Jens turned on the light, but Sieg hissed at him and he turned it off again. They moved through the flat, and found Brown's big suitcase under the bed in the rear bedroom. It has a DFDS label with his name on it. Sieg threw it onto the bed. It was locked, but the crowbar soon fixed that. Sieg turned the suitcase upside down and dropped the contents onto the quilt.

Both men rummaged about in Browns' belongings. There were no papers of any kind, no secret hiding places in the suitcase, nothing of any value at all, just clothes. They turned their attention to the commode, turned out all the drawers on the floor, checked for hidden letters taped to the underside of the drawers - nothing. They continued for about fifteen minutes, in the living room, in the other bedroom, in the hall. The place now looked a right mess! Then something happened that made them stop.

Light had appeared under the front door and there were heavy steps outside, two people were talking. One sounded like a girl. The other like a young man. They sounded perturbed, had probably seen the state of the door jamb and worked out that there had been, or was a break-in. Jens grabbed the crowbar. He and Sieg backed into Brown's bedroom. Sieg looked around for a way out and spotted the door in the corner leading to the back stairs. Jens got ready to bash anyone who came through that door over the head.

He changed his mind when Tina's boyfriend kicked in the front door. He was almost two meters tall, and a body builder who had been doing all the right exercises for a very, very long time. Martin stood framed in the doorway, ready for anything, but he did not go in just yet. Jens lost his courage immediately. Sieg had the door to the back stairs open now, and hissed at Jens, who turned and scuttled over the jumble of clothes and drawers on the floor, dropping his crowbar in the rush. Both men fled through the door and down the stairs. Martin rushed into the bedroom as the door closed. He almost fell over the crowbar. He picked it up and opened the door. The two fugitives had reached the bottom of the stairs by now. But there was no way out! The handle was missing and the door was impossible to move! The lights went on. Sieg turned to go back up the stairs, but the sight of Martin on the landing, holding the crowbar in one hand, and ominously letting it fall into his other palm, made him change his mind. Tina was on the phone talking to the police. She dropped the receiver into its cradle and came into the bedroom.

"They'll be here in a couple of minutes Martin. " She sat down on the bed and looked around. "What a mess! It's lucky we came back to pick up more of my things! What will mother say! Are they still there?"

Martin answered, talking sideways without taking his eyes off the two frightened rabbits in the trap at the bottom of the stairs, "They aren't going anywhere for a while yet".

Five minutes later, two armed policemen were pushing Jens and Sieg, both manacled, through the front door and out onto the street. Tina and Martin followed them.

"We'll be sending somebody round to take a statement from you both later this afternoon." Said one of the cops, as he folded Jens through the door of a police car. They drove off towards the town. Tina turned to Martin.

"Maybe we should stay until mother comes back."

Martin shook his head, "No, I don't think that will be necessary. They won't be coming back. Let's get your things and get going."

"I think we should at least call in the locksmith. Mother will go bonkers if she comes back and finds the front door open!"

"Alright then. You call the locksmith. I'll make some coffee, and we can clean the place up a bit while we're waiting."

Tina hugged him, and looked up as he caressed her. She felt like a china doll in the hands of a gorilla, and liked it.

"You're a darling Martin. And who knows what else we can get up to while we're waiting?"

Martin grinned broadly and clapped her on the backside. "Get up those stairs!"

Britta returned just as the locksmith was leaving. After what she had been through that morning, nothing could surprise her, she was still high. So she was not at all taken aback when she found Tina and Martin cleaning up the mess as she entered. Brittas underclothes were piled in a heap on the bed. Tina was folding them and putting them back in the drawers from where they had been taken, when Britta walked into the bedroom. She looked up, and was surprised to see that Britta did not even lift an eyelid, but just looked coolly around.

"What's happened?" Britta asked, standing in the doorway to the bedroom with her hands deep in the pockets of the parka and her boots wet from the rain that was now coming down more heavily outside.

"Come and sit down and I'll tell you all about it.

Tina told her the story as they both sat on the bed. Martin came in with coffee for all three of them and listened while Tina told her mother about Jens and Sieg. When she was finished, Britta said,

"It seems you're our hero Martin. Thanks!"

"That's all right Mrs. Nielsen, we just happened to be at the right place at the right time."

But Britta was already in another place and another time. Suddenly, she became aware of the danger they were all placing themselves in by staying here. Jens and Sieg had been taken into custody, but maybe they had friends, and what would those friends do when they didn't return? - We have to get out of here, and quickly! She stood up. The other two sensed her urgency.

"They may have friends who will come looking for them. Drop everything. We'll leave right away. Have you packed your things Tina?" Tina nodded. "Good. Help me pack a suitcase. I'm going to

122

take a holiday for a while. I don't know when I'll be back, but I'll let you know as soon as I can."

"That's a bit sudden isn't it mother? Where are you going? Does it have anything to do with this lot?"

"No, it doesn't. I've been planning it for the last week or so, it's just that this seems as good a time as any to start. As for where I'm going, do you remember that little place just north of Oporto where we spent the summer holiday just after your dad died? I'm going to stay down there a while." Then she seemed to stop and think for a second. She was, of Brown.

"Have either of you seen Dick? " She asked. They both shook their heads. "Well, he should be warned of what went on. I'll leave a note on the dresser in his room. Will you drop by after I've gone and check up on him?"

"Why not just leave Martins phone number and he can ring us when he gets' back?"

"Because the badies may come back and I don't want them to find out where you both live. If you just drop by and make sure he hasn't been bludgeoned in his sleep, that's a good girl." She didn't feel at all bad about telling fibs. She knew where Brown was, or at least where he should be. But the less Tina and Martin knew, the better it would be for themselves, and for her, and especially for Brown! Tina had seen that look in her mothers' eyes before, a long time ago, when she was a child and was being left with an aunt while her mother and father disappeared for a couple of months at a time.

"This reminds me of when dad was alive." She found herself saying to her shoes. Britta looked at her, pulled her daughters' head into her.

"I'll be back. Don't worry! Besides, Martin will look after you, won't you Martin? But for now, we really do have to get out of here!"

The front door crashed shut behind them minutes later.

But Britta was not going to Oporto, or anywhere else in Portugal for that matter, although she was going south, temporarily.

Chapter Seven - Bloodhounds

Avon Wailes stood at the main entrance to Newcastle Central Station and lit a cigarette. It was windy and wet outside. He felt like he needed to breathe fresh air, even though it was drawn through a filter together with smoke. The letter in his inside pocket was the only lead he had to go on. It was better than nothing, but not much better! He listened to the rain hammering on the line of taxis waiting outside and thought about the train journey he'd just had. Noisy kids running up and down the aisles, grannies needing help with suitcases big enough to take the Taj Mahal, yuppy businessmen, or rather businessboys, on their way to and from meetings, with their attache cases and their itty bitty mobile phones. God, what a relief it was to get off! The station clock said it was five past six. It was evening and the lights of the city were in full bloom. People bustled to and from work, some with shopping bags heading for busses that stopped outside, others with bate bags slung over their shoulders. Some had raincoats and see-through plastic rain hats. Others had duffle coats and caps. All had in common that they lowered their heads and looked down as they went.

Ten minutes passed. Wailes considered the possibility that his contact wouldn't turn up, and was working on the intricate details of a suitable punishment when a dark Cortina stopped by the curb. The door opened and the driver leaned across the passenger seat and whistled through the opening. It wasn't somebody Wailes knew. The man was waving to him, so he pulled the collar of his raincoat up around his shoulders, picked up his suitcase and approached the car. When he stuck his head inside, he could see that the back seat was empty. The driver was aged about twenty two. A fair-haired, freckled faced kid who looked like a yuppie dressed as he was in a sharp pin-striped suit with a light shirt and multicoloured tie. Wailes couldn't see what colours they were.

"Mister Wailes?" The kid asked.

"That's right, and who might you be?"

"John Watkins. I'm here to take you to your hotel."

"Well, John Watkins, do you mind opening the boot so I can stow my suitcase?"

Watkins wasn't much for stopping the engine and getting out in the rain, so he did it in a hurry, with the lapel of his jacket turned up although his round trip only lasted less than a minute. When he got back in the car, he wriggled in his seat as if to throw off the cold, put the key in the ignition, and turned on the engine again. Wailes got rid of the cigarette butt and got in the back. He seemed to fill the Cortina completely. He had to sit sideways with his feet in the leg room reserved for the other rear passenger. Watkins turned the car out of the drive and into Newcastle's bulging network of one-way streets. After a couple of minutes, he said,

"We reserved a room for you at the Novotel. It'll take us a bit to get there." Watkins had a Geordie accent tempered by time spent in the south, probably on the various courses and training sessions everybody had to go through down in London.

"Just as long as there's a shower and a bed, I'll be happy." Wailes said from the back seat. The rain that had wet his head was now beginning to roll down the back of his neck. He rubbed the area where his shirt collar was making the flesh raw.

"There is a shower and bath. There's a colour TV too."

"Well, I didn't come up here to watch TV" Wailes lit another cigarette. Watkins watched him in the rear view mirror.

"We don't allow smoking in the cars Mister Wailes."

Wailes ignored him, and blew smoke into the front of the car. "I hope you've arranged a car for me John Watkins." He said.

"I knew there was something I'd forgotten!" Watkins cursed himself.

"Yeps, doesn't surprise me at all. You forgot to turn up on time too."

"I'll fix it as soon as we get to the hotel."

"Don't put yourself out. I'll do it myself. What about the reception committee? When are they going to turn up?"

"I was told that the chief, Mister Brannon, and Ms Harris, our second in command, would be coming to see you at around nine. Mister Brannon said that you'd probably want a wash and a brush-up and a bite to eat as soon as you got in. He said to tell you they'd meet you in the lounge."

"Good. Suits me fine. How long before we get there?"

"We've just passed the Haymarket and the hotel's in Kenton. I'd say about fifteen minutes. Why didn't you want to stay at the County Thistle? It's just across the street from the station."

"Did your instructors ever tell you not to ask too many questions John Watkins?"

Watkins shut up immediately, he was getting tired of Wailes using his full name every time he addressed him, he felt nothing but antipathy for his back seat passenger. Wailes could see he had become tight-lipped through the rear view mirror. Watkins stayed quiet the rest of the way to the hotel, which sure enough was fifteen minutes later.

At ten minutes to nine, Wailes was sitting in an easy chair in the lounge, which was quite empty at the time. It was still a bit early for the tourist season, so most of the people he had seen in the restaurant were businessmen and women travelling to or from somewhere for some reason or other. There were only three people in the lounge. The waiter and a man and a woman sitting at the bar talking low about something or other. The man was about forty and half bald. He had a pint glass of dark brown ale, half empty, on the bar. He helped himself to peanuts from a bowl once in a while. The woman was about the same age, with long, dark hair and an aristocratic face. She smoked a cigarette and had a martini. The olive was still in the glass. The waiter turned up at Wailes' table, bringing Drambuie and hot coffee, just the ticket after a good meal of steak eggs and chips. He poured coffee from the stainless steel pot, noted the room number on the key that lay on the table and disappeared again. Wailes lit a cigarette and relaxed. You think better on a good meal. Think about what? Think about how to make the drip that was the letter Paul Anderson received into a river that would take him all the way to whatever it was that Anderson had been up to. While he was thinking about the letter, turning it this way and that in his head, when two shadows fell on the table. A moment later, two figures appeared in his field of vision and stopped. The man was about thirty, dressed just like John Watkins in a sharp grey, pin-striped suit of the kind you don't normally see around the streets of Newcastle. His shirt was a very faint blue with fine vertical traces of a slightly deeper blue thread. His tie was multicoloured with pastel greens and blues in an abstract pattern. His shoes were of classic Italian design. Dark grey leather with a pattern of holes stamped through the uppers, and leather soles. His face was young, a little flabby but not overly so, clean shaven. He reminded Wailes of a bank manager. The woman was dressed for business too, although she was more colourful. Her shoes were dark blue with flat heels and straps over the arches which were fastened by oxidised brass buckles. Her skirt was knee length, pleated in a way popular in the forties, navy blue. Her jacket was double breasted, navy with navy buttons. The blouse was a lighter blue, and she wore a cameo broach at the neck, ancient Greek style, light blue background and a chalk white vase motif. Her hair was long and red, and bound in a knot at the back. She too was aged about thirty.

"Mister Wailes?" The man said. Wailes eased himself upright.

"Yes. What can I do for you?"

The man held out a hand. "Mark Brannon." Wailes took the hand and shook it. Brannon had a grip, he squeezed just a little more than necessary. Wailes decided that that was because he felt just a tad inferior, as if he had something to prove. His accent was decidedly London. Wailes turned his attention to the woman.

"Eileen Harris." She put out her had and Wailes shook it, carefully and slowly. She hardly exerted any pressure at all, didn't bend the fingers in a grip but kept them straight. Maybe that was because her nails were well manicured and sharp. At any rate, Wailes noticed that they weren't painted at all. He also noted that she had an Irish accent tempered by several years spent in England.

"Take a seat." Wailes said. "Can I get you anything? Mark? You don't mind me calling you Mark do you? Just call me Avon."

Mark Brannon did not mind. At least he said he didn't and ordered coffee.

"What about you Eileen? You don't mind me calling you Eileen do you?"

She said she didn't and ordered tea. Wailes whistled after the waiter. In the almost empty lounge it was a sound fit to awake the dead. Wailes didn't care at all that the man and woman looked across the room at him. With the other two seated and Wailes standing, they felt very small indeed, which only increased Brannon's urgency to get on with the business at hand. Eileen did not mind feeling small at all, she was used to it, being about three inches smaller than most of the men

128

in the office. The waiter started across the lounge and Wailes sat down. When the waiter had taken their orders and disappeared again, Brannon said,

"Well Avon, let's get down to business." Wailes nodded and sipped the hot coffee, then washed his mouth with Drambuie, a potent combination that makes you think your mouth has exploded. It sets fire to every taste bud you have, even the ones you don't know about.

"We received a telex from Dawson telling us the purpose of your visit, and instructions to help you in any way we can. What exactly do you have in mind?"

"Well, firstly I'll need an assistant. Preferably somebody who knows the area very well indeed, doesn't dress like a yuppie on parade, and doesn't mind getting his hands dirty. Got anybody in mind?"

"John Watkins, the one who picked you up at the station." Eileen said. Wailes almost choked on his coffee. "I see you don't think much of that suggestion. Why not?"

"John Watkins. First he turns up late, then he forgets to order the car, thirdly he doesn't smoke, and last but not least he certainly fits my description of a yuppie on parade. What more do you need."

"Well, don't take John Watkins at face value. The suit was my idea. In fact that's why he was late. He had to borrow one from the stores. Normally he turns up for work dressed in jeans, a sailor jacket and hiking boots. We thought that was unsuitable for picking up a VIP like yourself so I made him change."

Eileen said. The waiter arrived with the coffee and tea. They remained silent until he was half way back to the bar. The man and woman were getting ready to leave. He was helping her on with her overcoat. He had his on already.

"Apart from that," Eileen continued, "he knows the area like the back of his hand, and in any case he's the only one we can spare at the minute."

"Well, in that case I'll just have to make do won't I? Mark, do you mind giving him a call and asking him to come over right away?"

"Yes, ok, just a second."

He pulled a micro telephone from his inside pocket, punched a number, waited a couple of seconds and when the phone was answered, he said,

"John, would you mind coming inside. We're in the lounge."

He put the phone away.

"He's our driver for tonight too." He said.

John Watkins arrived and sat down. He did not feel particularly comfortable, anybody could see that. Eileen said,

"John, while Mister Wailes is here you will be working with him as his assistant."

He seemed to shrink in his chair.

"My pleasure mister Wailes." He said.

Ever heard of The Icelandic Wool Company? Not many have. Not even customers, because they don't do business in the wool trade any more. The company was founded by two friends in eighteen eighty seven and has premises in a dockside building on the north side of the Tyne, just a couple of hundred yards down river from the Tyne Bridge. The building was quite new when the company moved in. It is well suited to the wool trade, being five stories high and consisting as it does mainly of spacious storage facilities intermingled with postage stamp size tally offices scattered here and there. The top floor, in under the roof, has been converted by the successors of the founders of the company over the years for various uses. First it was accommodation for the owners. One of the partners, a bachelor who was partial to Jamaican rum - having sailed the West Indies at one time as a chief mate - died ten years later. The other continued to live in the attic, only now he had a wife and three kids. They were glad to have the extra space. That lasted until after the turn of the century, when there was so much money in the wool trade that the family moved to a fine house in Jesmond. The attic was converted to accommodation for company workers, who paid rent of course. Now the same space housed soundproof and radio-dead conference rooms without telephones or cables of any kind, and with portable battery powered lighting and propane gas heating. The floor below had been converted into inconspicuously modern open office space. The rest of the building was remarkably empty.

There were a few comings and goings in the main office that morning, but it didn't amount to all that much traffic. In the corner beside the lift, Wailes and Watkins were sitting at a desk, or rather Wailes was sitting at it and Watkins was sitting on a corner of it with a note pad and a biro. Eileen had been right about Watkins dress habits.

"Okay, let's go through it one more time to see if we've missed anything." Wailes said.

"Well, we know Paul Anderson is not his real name. According to his wife, his name is Finnish. We know he has spoken Russian on the phone, so there is a possibility that he used a false Finnish name. He keeps the name Paul in both cases, so maybe his real name is Paul or some derivative of it. We know he joined the Winston Churchill in Helsinki. The Churchill starts these Baltic cruises in North Shields, so he had to have come into Britain through the Tyne. He turns up in Manchester a couple of months later with an excuse that the company wants him to start a shoe shop and a story that he doesn't want to move to Newcastle. The question is, where was he in those couple of months? Did he continue on the cruise and go back to Helsinki? Did he stay in Newcastle? Why the move to Manchester? Why doesn't he want to go to Newcastle? We know he is a radio amateur and that he's good at Morse Code. The RSGB club in Manchester confirms that. We know he rides a motorbike, or at least knows how to, although the lab couldn't tell from the oil sample what kind of bike it was other than that it was Japanese. How did they find that out?"

"Japanese motorbike engines are apparently made of a different set of alloys than European motorbike engines. The lab found microscopic bits of metal in the oil. Go on."

"Interesting. Anyway, his car was still parked in the street outside the house after his disappearance, and as of yesterday nobody has turned up to collect it. His wife doesn't have a drivers license so she doesn't use it. It's been bugged with a microphone and a location beacon. So unless he dumped the bike somewhere and used another means of transport, then he's used or is using the bike. As far as the letter is concerned, there's nothing at all remarkable about the paper or the envelope, so we'll get nothing out of them. The letter was printed on an old fasahioned matrix printer, so whoever sent it probably has access to a computer. The address on the envelope was written by hand. It seems he's still taking orders from his boss, because he left when he was told to, so the story about him quitting was a lie. We know he has, or had a contact in the Newcastle area since the letter came from here, and that the contact communicates with these bosses, wherever they might be. Is this contact also a foreigner? That's it."

"It seems like a lot when you read it aloud, but it's not really. Anyway, I can't think of anything we've missed out. If we have, then it'll turn up later I suppose. "

Wailes drew a deep breath. Something was beginning to stir in the back of his mind. Something important. A missing piece of the jigsaw puzzle. It just wouldn't come out though.

"We know that Paul is a radio amateur, and we know that his contact can communicate with Paul's boss, so maybe his contact has radio equipment. If not then everything would have to happen by phone. If we can get a court order, then we can get BT to list all phone calls from the Newcastle area to foreign countries, but how big should this area be?"

Watkins was standing with his back to the window.

"It would have to include Sunderland at least, because that's only half an hour by car from here and Paul's contact could have driven here, posted the letter and left again. If we make a radius that includes Sunderland, South Shields and all that, we must be talking about at least two and a half million people. I don't know what percentage have phones, but there must be an awful lot."

"Yes indeed. Okay, if Paul's contact has access to a computer then he, or she may also have modem equipment and be able to communicate with these bosses in that way. Would there be any advantage to this?"

"My cousin Eddie has one. He told me once that it's a simple matter to code your transmissions, so even if somebody patched into your phone line they wouldn't be able to make neither head nor tail of it."

"Yes. We have to remember that Paul spoke Russian on the phone. Did he speak to someone outside the country or inside? If he spoke to someone inside, then why speak Russian unless the other party on the line was Russian? That would indicate a Russian network of some kind in the country, and not one which the Russian government is keen on."

"Why?"

132

"Because it was the Russian embassy that tipped us off about Paul in the first place. No, it only makes sense if Paul was speaking to someone outside the country. As far as his wife knows, he only received a couple of calls. She picked up the phone one time and the person on the other end asked for Paul. She said he sounded foreign and that it seemed that there was a delay on the line and that it was very poor, so everything points to Paul's Russian calls coming from outside the country, probably from somewhere in Russia itself, because the phone lines to Finland are not that poor. I don't know any Russian that trusts the telephone. If they were up to something then that makes the phone even more unlikely. No, the more I think about it, the more I'm convinced that Paul's contact and his bosses communicate over radio. They told me in Manchester that they only open club premises at night. What about here in Newcastle?"

"I don't know, but I can check. The radio club is probably in the phone book."

"Do that, later. I don't think that Paul's contact will use a club station though, because there'll be too many people about, and if they're busy then he may not be able to get on the club station at the right time. Paul's contact might be a member of a club though."

"I've got an idea." Watkins broke in.

"Let's hear it then." Wailes said and lit a cigarette.

"Paul's contact has access to a computer. He has access to radio equipment good enough to put him into contact with Russia without using the Internet at all. That would make him easily traceable. He may have modem equipment. All this points to Paul's contact having some degree of technical knowledge. Maybe he is a student!"

"Maybe. Where could a student get ..... "

Wailes stopped and sat up straight. He pointed a finger at Watkins, but didn't say anything. Many long seconds went by. Watkins could almost see the wheels rotating in Wailes' head. The finger didn't move. Ash from the cigarette in Wailes mouth fell onto the desk. He came awake suddenly. Watkins expected an exclamation, but Wailes didn't exclaim anything. He simply said,

"Bill Lennox." and dropped the cigarette into the ash tray.

"Who's Bill Lennox?" John asked.

"Get your ass into gear. We're off to Sunderland. You can drive. I'll tell you about it on the way."

They left in a hurry.

When they were in the car and crossing the Tyne Bridge, going south, Wailes was cautiously jubilant. He lit another cigarette. Watkins opened the driver side window. He hated the stink of cigarette smoke.

"Bill Lennox is one of us. His oldest son Peter was killed a couple of weeks ago. At first everybody thought that it had been an accident. But then it turned out that one of the people at the bank where Peter worked had bugged the place, just for fun. He taped something that might be interesting. Do you know Gilbridge Avenue police station?"

"Yes. I've been there loads of times."

The file on Peter had been moved from "Unsolved Accident" to "Unsolved Murder". Fortunately, the tapes were still there although they had been sealed with red tape and marked as secret in the meantime. Constable Fisher had left Wailes and Watkins alone in one of the interview rooms with the tapes. Wailes turned off the machine after the door closed behind Peter and Erik. He had been taking notes.

"Okay, this is what we have. There were four of them, including Peter. Two of them are foreigners and the kid on the computer is from the Newcastle area. He's obviously hacked into some computer or other, and transferred a couple of million dollars to a bank account somewhere else. Why do that? either to pay for something received, or for something about to be received. Peter says he met Brian at a dominoes match at the Democratic Club. Any idea where that is?"

"Yeah, on the north side of the river just by the Wear Bridge, left hand side. It's a club for working men, CIU affiliated. My dad was a member there. I've had a pint or two there myself. If Brian plays dominoes for the team then he should be easy to locate. Maybe he already has been located by the lads at the station her."

"We'll check it out. Anyway, Peter calls one of the foreigners Erik. Sounds like it might be German or Scandinavian."

"My girlfriend Gina works at the language faculty at the university in Newcastle. She's from Italy, but she must know somebody there who can find out where they came from if we can let her borrow the tape."

"Maybe the lads here have tried that too. That can be checked. No, I doubt it. The tapes were sealed and marked secret. It's unlikely that anybody in the station has listened to them since I was here last. We'll make a copy of the relevant parts of the tapes, and let your girlfriend borrow it. Brian calls the other one Black. Black sounds like a foreigner, but the name sounds English. Perhaps he is a foreigner with an English father. Well, the letter itself wasn't all that much to go on, but together with these tapes, it might be another matter. Go and check on things with the station sergeant, I'll wrap up here and meet you in the canteen, I'm dying for a cuppa'."

Traffic was light as a blue Ford Thames van turned the roundabout at the top of Grindon Lane and took a right up Pennywell Road, about a hundred yards up to the crumbling brick western wall of the Grindon Hall Hospital, where it turned left then left again. The van passed the pub on the left, and turned right up Portslade Road, took the second left and third right into Pickering Square. The sun was out and it was just after noon, but that didn't make Pickering Square look any better. It still looked like the dump it was. The van didn't seem out of place. It moved carefully up the lane behind the houses and the coal sheds, between broken bottles and bits of brick, to the end of the lane then turned left onto what should have been a green patch nestled among the houses, but what looked instead like a war zone. The van passed a Toyota, or what was left of it. It had been stripped of wheels and doors and set alight earlier in the week. All that was left was a burned out, blackened ruin. The grass too was littered with bits of bottle and brick and old tin cans. It was uneven, with pot-holes that the kids used for building bonfires on Guy Fawkes day. There were no kids about today though, they were at school, or at least those who weren't playing truant were. The van picked its way over the lumps and bumps and stopped outside number twenty nine. An olive green Volkswagen LT35 was already parked there.

Brian Wallis got out. The woman who lived in number thirty stuck her head round the open curtains to see who it was, then disappeared again. Nobody appeared at any of the other windows. Brian went round the little brick wall separating the green patch from the pavement in front of the houses, and went up the couple of steps to the door of number twenty nine. He pushed the doorbell and went in without waiting for an answer. He took his jacket off and hung it on a peg in the narrow hall. The house was typical of post-war council houses. A hall going straight from the front door to the little kitchen at the back, and half filled on the left by a flight of stairs going up to the bedrooms and bathroom on the first floor. A door to the right just inside the front door, leading to the living room, where the telly was on. There was a bit of carpet in the hall and some squares of carpet on the stairs. Otherwise the floor was covered by grey linoleum with random coloured spots. The walls were painted a horrible shade of pastel pink. The woodwork had been painted white at some time or other. Brian walked down the hall into the kitchen. There was nobody about, but the kettle was on and there were three mugs with tea bags in them standing on the itty bitty kitchen working surface beside the old fashioned electric cooker. Wallis took another mug off a hook on the wall, planted it beside the others and dropped a tea bag into it. Then he went into the living room by way of the little dining room at the back.

Billy Thomson, Bob Wood and Doug Trotter were sitting on the sofa opposite the gas fire, watching the television. Brian parked himself in the easy chair with its back to the dining room. Nobody had uttered a word yet. The atmosphere in the living room was heavy, forboding, watchful, and all the other adjectives you can think of that matches a situation like this. They were all waiting for something. The whistle on the kettle started to scream its head off in the kitchen. Doug got up and went out. The sofa was overloaded. You could hear the springs breath a sigh of relief when Doug got up. The others didn't budge. When he came back, Doug was carrying four steaming mugs of tea and the tea-bags had disappeared. He put them down on the mat in front of the fire and sat down again. Each took his own mug. Still nobody had said anything. All eyes were glued on the television.

When the intro music for the local news started, the tension in the atmosphere increased markedly. You could almost hear the static crackle and jump between them.

"Here is the one o'clock news, read by Ian Blyth. Wearside police are anxious to interview a Newcastle man, Brian Wallis, in connection with last months' break in at the Provincial Bank in Sunderland. Wallis is described as being aged twenty two, five feet seven inches tall, thin with short black hair, pale complexion with spots, and wears wire-framed glasses. If anyone knows the whereabouts of Brian Wallis, call Wearside police on this number - oh nine one, three seven six five, four nine two. All information will be treated in the strictest confidence. The rail strike planned to start on Monday has been called off ....."

Billy Thomson got up and turned off the television. Then, standing with his back to the window, he said to nobody in particular,

"We've got to get out of here before things start getting hot." Bob, Doug and Brian agreed with him. "Bobby and Dougy. You two get the camping gear packed into the van. When you've done that, pack all the tools and other stuff we might need as well. Don't pack the guns and ammo away though, we might need them before we're finished here. Just get them out and put them on the kitchen table so we know where they are. Brian, you go round and close all the curtains. Then you can give me a hand to dismantle the gear in the back bedroom and get it ready for moving. When it's ready for moving, we'll bring it downstairs into the living room. Bob and Doug can give us a hand to load it in the VW when they're finished."

"I'll have to let our Beryl know that I'll be disappearing for a bit, she'll go spare if I don't." Doug said suddenly. "But we can't risk leaving a note. If the fuzz turn up before she gets it, there'll be hell to pay."

"Never mind Dougy. Our Beryl will be glad to get rid of us for a couple of weeks. If we told her about it in time she'd probably tell us to take the kids with us!"

Bob said. He was Doug's brother in law and Beryl's brother.

"Just drop her a note saying you'll be in touch - nothing else. She'll get the picture."

"Okay, do that when the van's packed Doug."

Billy said. He checked his watch. Like the jacket he was wearing, it had been bought in an army surplus shop.

"Right. Let's see if we can be ready to roll in fifteen minutes." There was a sudden scramble.

That much activity in a place like this is bound to attract attention, which indeed it did. Not only from the woman in number thirty, but from the other neighbours on that side of the square. Suddenly a couple of scruffy kids appeared on the steps of number twenty, then the couple in number twenty two started cleaning the front windows, something they had not done since Christmas. Bob and Doug paid no attention though, they were too busy going into the house empty handed and coming out again with sleeping bags and tents and cooking gear and camouflaged bags with camouflaged clothes in them, and boots and shovels. They emptied the cupboard under the stairs of everything it contained, and stuffed it all into the back of the Thames van. When they were finished, they sat on the doorsteps and lit cigarettes. One of the kids, a boy of about five, came running up and asked what they were doing. Doug said they were going on a camping holiday with their mates. The boy ran back up the street and talked to the man in number twenty two, who was trying to look busy polishing the door knob, even though it was plastic.

Brian and Billy dismantled the radio and computer gear and packed it in the cardboard boxes that had been standing in the corner of the back bedroom since the last time they moved.

"What do we do about the aerial?" Brian asked as they dropped the various connecting cables into the last cardboard box.

"We'll leave it. We've got what we need to make a new one when we get to the cottage. Okay, let's get this lot downstairs."

He grabbed the box with the radio and went down into the living room. On his way down, he noticed Bob and Doug sitting on the steps with their backs to the door. The front door was open.

"Finished already?" Doug half turned and nodded. "Give us a hand with this lot then, and shut the front door."

They came in and closed the door, then tramped up the stairs. Billy lit the torch he had in his pocket and went into the cupboard under the stairs. There was a loose floorboard in the darkest and innermost corner. He prised it up with his pocket knife and pulled out six parcels wrapped in linen and stuffed into plastic bags. He had to get down on his knees and poke about in the hole with his left arm to find the four waterproof boxes of ammunition, then drag them out. Meanwhile footsteps sounded up and down the stairs over his head as the others moved the back bedroom equipment into the living room. When he had everything out of the hole, Billy banged the floorboard back into place and went into the living room. Doug was just putting a box down on the floor. The other two were there too.

"Got everything? Right. The tricky bit is to get this lot outside and into the van without attracting too much attention. Bob and Doug, you take the VW round the back. Park it right outside the back door with the side door open. When you've done that, come back round the front and start messing about with the engine on the Thames. Brian and me will wait a couple of minutes then start loading the gear. I'll let you know when we've finished. Off you go."

They did as Billy said they should, and it worked. So none of the neighbours actually saw that the VW was being loaded, and with what. They were too busy watching Bob and Doug trying to get the Thames going. It seemed they never would. But ten minutes later there was a knock on the front window from inside the house, and suddenly the engine seemed to want to start. Doug climbed in the driver's side and Bob got in the other. They drove back up the green patch the way the Thames had come when it arrived. Meanwhile Billy had dropped the latch on the front door, written the words - Gone camping Beryl, back in a couple of weeks - on a used envelope, and scooted out the back door and into the VW. He slid the side door shut with a slam and the VW left with Brian at the wheel as the Thames came round the corner at the end of the back lane. That was it. They were on their way.

"What the hell were you thinking about?"

Wailes wasn't at all happy. Watkins stood on the other side of the desk with his hands deep in his trousers pocket and his face as red as a beetroot. That was partially in anger. Everybody in the office looked at him. Most looked away again, but there were one or two who kept looking. He could feel their eyes boring into the back of his neck.

"The tapes had been sealed and marked, so nobody at the station had investigated them further! I thought the press would be able to help us find him. He hasn't been to the club for some time, and nobody knows his address."

Wailes shook his head and looked down at the table. What a bloody mess! The bloody sorcerer's apprentice strikes again! He took his head in his hands. looking into the blackness of his palms helped reduce his blood pressure. Cut off from the world around him for just a few moments, he felt the anger begin to subside. When he looked up again, he said, more calmly.

"Look. If Wallis or one of his mates has seen that broadcast, or heard the radio news he'll be over the hills and far away by the time we get his address, assuming of course that somebody comes forward. And why should they? You know this place better than I do. How will they react?"

Watkins took one hand out of his pocket and massaged his right ear lobe. He always did that when he was nervous, Wailes had observed.

"Well, his friends and family will certainly not rat on him to the police. That much is for sure. Mind you, there's that much back-biting among neighbours in this part of the world, that we might get lucky on that score. I'd say there was a fifty-fifty chance we got his address that way."

"Sit down! I hate looking up to people!"

Wailes said curtly. Watkins pulled up the nearest chair and sat down. Wailes continued when he had done so.

"Alright, it's too late to do anything about it. We have to continue as if nothing has happened. But I'm telling you now, the next time you do something like this, I'll have your guts for garters! You understand me?"

"Yes."

"Yes what?"

"Yes sir!" Watkins replied.

"Good, then let's pick up where we left off! I want you to make a copy of the sections of bank tape where the two foreigners are talking and take them over to your girlfriend. See if she can identify the accent. But don't tell her anything other than you want to know which country the two men come from. When you've done that, come straight back here. In the meantime, I'm going to check with records in Swansea to see if Brian has a drivers' licence, and with the home office to see if he has a passport."

"We're still don't know that Brian Wallis ever met Paul Anderson." Watkins said.

"That's right, but we know that a very large sum of money was moved by Brian Wallis from some account or other to some other account. Somebody must be missing money somewhere, and there's a feeling in the pit of my stomach that says we're on the right track! At any rate, after I've had a chat with Swansea and Whitehall, I'm going over to the Provincial Bank for a chat with the manager. You got any questions?"

Watkins shook his head. His brain had gone into hibernation. He just couldn't remember where the tape recorder was, but he wasn't about to ask Wailes that!

"Good, then get on with it."

Watkins got up and left. It was my own stupid fault! He thought to himself. I should have checked with him before ringing the radio and TV. people. Why on earth did I go and do something stupid like that? Not thinking again. Sometimes I seem to have my brains where my ass is! He walked into the equipment room on the other side of the lift, hunting for the tape recorder. Wailes was lifting the phone off the hook and flipping the pages of the little, brown phone book on his desk.

Brian Wallis didn't have a passport, but he did have a drivers' licence, although the address was two years old.

"Harry - have you got a minute?" Wailes called out across the office. Harry Seaton, middle-aged, bald and wearing horn-rimmed glasses, came across as Wailes was pulling on his overcoat.

"What can I do for you?"

Wailes handed him a slip of paper with Wallis' name and the address from his drivers' licence. Seaton looked at it. "Will you get one of your lads to look this place up and find out where he his ? I've got another appointment."

"Sure thing. This is a Felling address, so it won't take more than half an hour to check it out. Do you want to wait until you come back to hear the news?"

"Yes, I'll be back in a couple of hours anyway. Thanks a lot."

"No problem. Better put your hat and scarf on, it's getting cold outside again."

"Thanks mother." Wailes said. Seaton grinned and went back to his desk.

Chapter Eight – Coming Up for Air

"What's your plan of action then?" Dawson asked.

Wailes was standing in a telephone booth in the lobby of his hotel. There was a phone in his room, but you never know who's listening to hotel room phones, or cell phones for that matter. Wailes still had his overcoat and scarf on. He had just come in.

"Well, when the lads have done their bit, I'll have to take it from there. I'm damned sure that when we crack this group, we'll find out where Anderson went and maybe even why. In any case, if the group has scarpered to a hide-out somewhere it may take a while to find them. When we do find them, who knows what might happen. Any news from the home front?"

"None at all I'm afraid. We're at a standstill down here until you get a breakthrough. Oh yes, George Green sends his regards. He also told me to tell you that, quote – E,lvis has left the building - unquote. Make any sense?"

"Yes indeed. It's nothing special. He promised to keep me posted on the whereabouts of an old mate of mine. One of ours."

"Ah, I see." There was a long pause. Dawson didn't see, nor did he believe it. Wailes knew that irritated the man. "Anyway, keep me posted. That's all for now."

When Wailes left the phone booth he went into the restaurant. He took off his overcoat and scarf and hung them on the dumb waiter by the door. The head waiter, a small, dark-haired woman in her thirties in a tight white blouse and black skirt, came towards him. She had a black butterfly tie just under her chin and carried a menu folder in red leather, which was actually plastic, under her left arm.

"Table for one please Maria. Not by the window if that's possible. I don't feel like looking at the world much today."

She smiled and showed him to a table in the centre of the restaurant, in front of one of the supporting pillars. On the way, she said, "I know what you mean. Spring is keeping us waiting a long time this year isn't it?"

"Yes indeed. We need a bit of sunshine and fresh air."

Wailes sat down with his back to the pillar. This table suited him fine. From here he could keep an eye on the entrance and didn't need to have one in the back of his head. While he was stretching the napkin out across his knees, he was thinking about Bill Lennox, about the Provincial Bank in Sunderland, and most of all, about Brian Wallis.

The A69 from Newcastle goes west, following the north bank of the river Tyne through Hexham, which for centuries has been a place for the education of priests, and Haltwhistle, until the river turns south just before Greenhead. The A69 then continues on to Carlisle and the Solway Firth, on England's west coast. A few miles after the road passes through Hexham, and Haydon Bridge, there is Bardon Mill. Bardon Mill is high in the hills. From here three minor roads go off to the north. Two of these join shortly after, to the road going to the small town of Once Brewed, and crosses Hadrian's Wall going towards Steel Rigg. This is dangerous country to be caught out in when unprepared for the ravages of weather. The names alone tell you that. Names like Spy Rigg, Sighty Cragg and Black Knowle. Old names from the days when a name meant something, before the time of the bard and his "what's in a name" mentality. The hills are bare on both sides of what remains of the second Roman wall built to keep the unruly Picts out of Roman England, two thousand years ago. There are cottages here and there, cottages of stone mainly stolen from the wall after the assimilation of the Roman armies into Northern English culture. These cottages are few and far between, their inhabitants living mainly from hardy hill sheep, which are the only farm animals capable of surviving the winters and living off the stiff hill grass. You can see for miles here, when the craggs and hills don't get in the way, and when the clouds are not so heavy with rain that they scrape across the hillsides, round the walls of the buildings and over the roads on their way from the Atlantic Ocean to the east coast.

One such cloud was at this very moment moving around the walls of an algae-clad stone farmhouse huddled in the shade of the summit of Round Top, one thousand and sixty five feet above sea level. There was a ramshackle, weather-beaten wood and stone barn beside the house. The two buildings stood wall to wall. Inside the barn was an olive green VW LT35, parked close to the barn wall, and a blue Ford Thames van. There was condensation on both. They had not been there very long. Sports bags, boots, cardboard boxes and other stuff lay in a heap in the back of the VW. The Ford van was empty. A single light was on in the ground floor room just to the left of the dilapidated green front door of the house. Although the window was well covered by some heavy material, very small slivers of light escaped from the corners when the material moved in the draughts through the window frame. The first floor was hidden from ground level by the black mass of the rain cloud. The gravel and dirt path leading to the single track road that passed as the highway to Bewcastle, fourteen miles to the west as the crow flies, was only visible for the first few yards.

Billy Thomson, Bob Wood, Doug Trotter and Brian Wallis were sitting around an old wooden table in the living room. There were tea mugs and the remains of chocolate biscuits and cheese and onion sandwiches on the table. The fire was lit. Once in a while smoke came back down the chimney and bellowed up towards the ceiling. Nobody took any notice. Otherwise the living room was bare of ordinary furniture, although there was an old black and white valve television set standing in the corner. It was off. Four foam rubber mattresses with sleeping bags on them were laid out in an unruly row in half-light, along the wall opposite the front window, which was temporarily covered by a heavy grey - or was it just dirty? - flannel sheet. The short wave radio station had been set up on a small table with wobbly legs in the corner beside the front window. It too was off. The four sat at the table in the middle of the room, immediately under the light bulb without a lamp shade that was fed with electricity by two wires which were held up out of harms way by hooks screwed into the ceiling. The wires disappeared through the top of the door into the hall. A camping gas stove with three burners stood beside the fire-place. One of the burners was lit and a kettle was on it. The petrol generator that supplied light, and power for the radio and television, was humming merrily to itself in the kitchen. Brian had just filled it with petrol again, so there was a distinct smell of the stuff in the hall. The rest of the house was empty. The reason was simple. The roof leaked, the upstairs windows were all broken, most of the floorboards had been torn up to seal the windows and doors, and the stairs had rotted away. The first floor was completely unusable. Under the stairs there was a shoddy mess where the toilet had been before somebody had smashed it a long time ago, so now they had to use a hole they had dug in the corner of the barn. Not that it was bad, but the toilet paper hanging on the six-inch nail driven into the wall beside the hole was almost always damp. The kitchen was a shambles. All the furniture and fittings had been removed, although for some strange reason the water supply had not been cut off. That was why they had chosen this place as their hideout. With the water supply intact, and power provided by their own generator, they had what they needed to survive in reasonable, though somewhat cramped, comfort. All the windows and doors had been boarded up when the house had been abandoned, although it had not taken long to prise the planks off the front door and living room window with the crow-bar. Bob and Doug had used a sledge hammer to knock a hole in the side of the house and the barn the first time the four of them had been up here for the weekend. It was possible to slide the side door of the VW back and get in without being exposed. A fox always has two entrances to its burrow. This was the foxes way out.

Bob Wood got up and brought the kettle back to the table. He poured water into all four mugs, put the kettle back on the gas stove and turned off the burner. Billy Thomson had already flopped tea-bags into the boiling hot water.

"There's been no mention of anything on the telly or the radio. I wonder what's going on ?"

Doug Trotter said more to himself than anybody else, as he dunked the tea-bag up and down in the mug a couple of times then pulled it out and dropped it into the ash tray.

Billy Thomson nodded thoughtfully.

"You're right about one thing Doug. We need to be able to find out what's going on back in the town. It's no use just sitting here waiting for somebody to come creepin' down the path. We need to be one step ahead of them. The question is...how? The nearest phone box is fifteen miles away, so we can't call our Allison. None of our families have short wave radio, so we can't use that either. We can't use the cell-phone or they might find us, even if we use a new SIM card."

There was a long, drawn-out silence. Then Bob said,

"Just a minute. My cousin Paul has a short wave radio. You know Paul, one of the Barns' boys ?"

Brian Wallis muttered

"I know George, and Allan and Michael. I knew they had a brother Paul, but I never met him. Are you sure he has a short-wave ?"

"Yea, dead sure. I remember my aunt Nita complaining about him being up all night on the radio a couple of years back."

"Is he to be trusted? " Billy asked.

"No problem. Paul comes from a good family. His brothers were prof burglars! He won't get mixed up in anything fishy himself, but he knows how to do the family a favour, and how to keep his mouth shut when the fuzz is around."

"Okay, here's the plan then.." Billy said.

"Tomorrow Bob and Brian take the Thames down into Bewcastle. You can do the shopping while you're at it. Then Bob rings his cousin Paul.. You do have the phone number, don't you ?"

Bob patted the breast pocket of the shirt he had on under the army surplus sweater.

"Right here."

Billy nodded and continued.

"When you call Paul, get him to check Doug's place to see if there's been any activity, then put Brian and him together so they can work out the technical details radio-wise. We need to be able to talk to him at least once a day. Brian, you tell him we'll leave the station on all the time, so's he can get in touch with us whenever anything happens. Work out some kind of code you can use to check that it really is him we're talking to."

"One thing Billy. Somebody might recognise Brian in Bewcastle." Dougy pointed out.

"Yes, but that's a risk we'll have to take, because none of us knows enough about radio to be able to set up the link. Anyway, Brian can stay in the van until just before they have to make the phone call. You can pretend to read the paper Brian. When that's done, come back here. Make sure you're not followed Bob. And make sure nobody sees you turning down here."

"That goes without saying. I'm not daft you know! I didn't spend eight years in the bloody army for nothing!"

"Alright, keep your shirt on. I was only saying it, that's all. Anyway, anybody got any questions?"

The others shook their heads. Billy checked his watch then turned to check the sheet of paper pinned to the wall behind the door. It was the watch rosta.

"Okay, it's now eleven o'clock. I've got the watch from twelve to two tonight, so I won't bother turning in. Bob, you're on... ?"

"Two to four."

"Four to six." Dougy said, and yawned.

"Six to eight."

Brian stated. It looked as if he too was ready to hit the sack.

"Okay lads, get some sleep."

Chairs scraped on the bare wooden floor as Brian and Doug got up and went across to their sleeping bags. Bob said,

"Get the cards out Bill, I'll get us a couple of beers from the van and we can have a game. Got any cigs on you? "

Billy pulled a packet of Woodbines from a pocket, took one himself and handed them across the table.

While Bob Wood was crawling through the hole into the VW and reaching out for two bottles of Newcastle Brown Ale, the van carrying Brown and the others was standing in a queue five miles long on the Polish side of the border with Lithuania, just east of the small town of Suwalki. The border post wasn't shown on any of the European maps, although the town was. But it was shown on the Lithuanian map Black had with him. There was only one other border crossing available, ninety kilometres to the west. Smith had told them that that crossing was reserved for military vehicles and that they wouldn't be able to cross there. It was two in the morning and the border was closed for the day. It was also bitterly cold. An icy wind whipped around the mini bus, bringing sharp crystals of ice from the nearby fields with it. How people can sleep in a Lada filled with carpets and petrol cans, under circumstances like these is impossible to believe. But they did. The people in the car behind the mini bus were freezing despite three thick coats and a woollen blanket, because petrol was too expensive to waste by running the engine to keep up the heat. The cold didn't bother those in the mini bus though. They had a Webasto heater installed and it was working overtime. At fifteen cents a litre the petrol prices did not bother them. The mini bus was too small to let them all sleep at once, so they took it in turn to sleep stretched out in the back on top of the luggage.

Black and Erik were laid out, sleeping as best they could. Brown and Smith were half asleep in the front. The others were trying to get some sleep in their seats. There was a long wait ahead of them. The border crossing did not open until nine in the morning. Smith had told them it would take two hours to cross and that he knew the ropes, so they could just leave it up to him. Black had said they would do just that.

"Where are you from Brown? " Smith suddenly said in the darkness and the depth of the fake fur collar of his overcoat. Brown was glad of the chance to get to know Smith better.

"Just south of Newcastle. What about you ?"

"Kaunas."

"You're going home then?"

"Yes. It will be good to speak my own language again, talk to my old friends, and my family."

"I know what you mean. I used to be a sailor in the Merchant Navy. I lived abroad for sixteen years off and on, until my dad died. It was then I started to think that it was time to move back home... Strange really. I hadn't missed the place at all while he was alive. Your dad still around?"

"Yes. He's a funny old man. In nineteen forty, when he was nineteen, he enlisted in the Wehrmacht, you know. He got to be a Lieutenant." Smith fell silent for a moment. He didn't know why, but suddenly, sitting here on the border, in the middle of the night, waiting for sunrise and the sight of home, he felt like talking. "In nineteen forty two he was taken prisoner by the Red Army and sent to a Gulag on Novaya Zemlya."

"I was never much good at geography in school. Where's that?"

"Siberia, north of the Arctic Circle. He was there for thirteen years, until the General Amnesty when Stalin died."

"He must be a big man to have survived that long in the Gulag!"

"No, quite the opposite really. He's about five foot five and not at all the strongest of men. But I believe that what there is of him is made of steel wire. You know, when Lithuania got her independence, he took the bus from Kaunas to Vilnius and volunteered for the Army again."

"Wow, how old must he have been? Seventy odd? Did they let him in?"

Smith smiled at the thought of the old man walking into the new Minister of Defence's office in Vilnius and demanding to be signed up.

"Not only did they let him in, they gave him his old rank back and made him second in command in Kaunas. As far as I know, he still is, although it's more than two years since I last heard from him."

"I hope you don't mind me saying it, but isn't he a bit old for the job?"

"Oh, I don't mind at all. There's an awful lot of younger men who would agree with you. In a way you're right. But in another way it's a good thing that men like him are still around. He knows what war means. He knows what carnage and devastation are. He will never forgive the Red Army for causing the death of his comrades in Gulag! And I don't blame him. The Red Army deprived me of my father for the first thirteen years of my life. Then, when they gave him back to me, they made it very difficult for us to make a living by honest means. You know, all through my school years, the teachers and other parents, and even my class mates, were always treating us like second class citizens because of my father's record. The sly remarks, the inquisition every time he or my mother tried to get a job, the concrete blocks of flats where we were packed like sardines together with other - criminal - elements!"

The wind had died down. The howling as it passed by the cracks around the doors of the minibus had stopped. Brown bent his head and looked through the side window. The clouds were beginning to part, and the moon was beginning to appear from behind them. Now it would really get cold. He sat up straight again, and reached for his cigarettes. He handed the pack to Smith, who took one.

"Sounds to me like you've got an axe to grind. Be careful, sometimes the axe you're grinding for others cuts off your own hand!"

Smith laughed. There was movement in the back of the minibus. It died down again.

"You sound like a Lithuanian Brown! That's just the kind of thing my father would say. So wise at such a young age. How can that be ?"

"Well, I guess I've had my grudges in my time. It's cost me a friend or two, a wife and two kids."

"I'm sorry to hear that. I had a son once too. He's dead now. So is his mother" Smith crossed himself. In the yellow light from the lighter and the cold blue light of the moon on the hood of the minibus, the movement seemed almost mystical. For the first time since they met, Brown realised that Smith was a religious man of sorts.

"How did that happen?" The lighter went out, leaving two cigarette ends glowing in the half light. Now shapes were visible inside the minibus, and Brown could see Smith's shadow moving so that his back was against the door.

"One night we held up a Russian meat truck outside Klaipeda. My son Povl and I were in a car just behind the truck. A cousin of mine, Juri, and his neighbour Boris, were in another car with the rear window removed. Boris was in the back seat with a machine gun. Juri passed us, passed the truck, and when they got in front of the truck, Boris fired into the air. The truck stopped, we all stopped. Juri and Povl jumped out of the cars. The driver of the truck started climbing down. Everything was going exactly according to plan. But the driver was armed, and not afraid to use his weapon. He shot Povl through the head and wounded Juri. Boris got scared, jumped out of the car and ran into the woods. I got scared and backed down the road as fast as I could."

"You got scared? I can't believe that. You don't strike me as the kind of man who gets scared easily."

"I was a family father in those days. My cowardice during the hold-up plagued me so much that I changed. Today I wouldn't hesitate to shoot it out. Apart from that, my wife Ingrida never forgave me for taking Povl along. She went crazy. One day, when I came back from doing business in the gypsy market outside Vilnius, I found her hanging by one of my belts from the banister in the apartment block we lived in. The neighbours were all standing around on the ground floor just looking up at her hanging there. Nobody had tried to cut her down. After the funeral, I moved to a friends' summer house. Since then I have worked for him."

A conspiracy of devils indeed. There was more movement in the back of the mini-bus. Brown turned and said in a loud voice,

"Your time is up lads. It's our turn to get some sleep now. Wakey wakey!"

Erik and Black took over the front seat. Smith and Brown clambered into the back and lay down on top of the luggage. Smith turned over, pulled the collar of his jacket up around his ears and went to sleep. Brown didn't. Mafia and nazis', what could they possibly have in common?

A passing drunk rambled into the side of the van. Smith woke with a start, sat up straight and looked around like a hunted animal suddenly alert. It was daylight outside. Small wisps of steam were coming out of the windows of cars parked in front and behind. There was a heavy mist, laden with icy crystals, moving slowly around the van. Brown was still asleep, with his face down in the luggage and his coat pulled all the way up over his head. The two in the front were fast asleep, with their heads rolled backwards, mouths gaping. Mogensen and Hansen, who occupied the two seats on the right, were the same way. It would have been so easy to slit their throats. Smith resisted the temptation. It was going to be hot today. He could tell by the smell, and the way the crystals melted in his nostrils. The heater had gone out. He shivered, slid on his backside across the luggage, turned the handle on the rear door, and got out. He left the door open.

Smith lit a cigarette, and coughed violently when the smoke hit his lungs. - I really have to give these up! - he murmured to himself. His overcoat sat unevenly, and the cold got through to the skin of his stomach there where his shirt and sweater had crept up during the night. He adjusted his clothing and went for a walk up the line of cars towards the border post.

The line from the van to the border post was about two kilometres long. On the way there, Smith noticed that people in the cars and busses were beginning to move about again. Everybody looked shabby. Many were coughing. One or two were lighting small spirit stoves to make hot, sweet tea. He passed a tourist bus from Berlin. It was the only vehicle still completely still. There was a smell of gin and vodka and old, wet cigarettes in the air around it. That's one way to keep out the cold - he thought, and hammered on the side of the bus a few times as he passed, just for fun. He enjoyed disturbing tourists.

When Smith got to the front of the line of vehicles, the office was just opening. It was eight o'clock. There were a few eager beavers already forming a queue in front of the rolled up window. A customs and immigration official was checking lazily through their papers. She didn't seem to have any particular desire to shorten the wait. Smith dug into the inside pocket of his overcoat and pulled out the groups' passports. They had entrusted him with them the night before. He pushed his way to the front, not hurriedly but in a way which left no doubt as to his intolerance of nonsense. There was of course a bit of an outcry from the others, but a jolt here and an ugly grimace there smoothed the way somewhat. When he got to the window, the official waved him to the back of the queue again, and refused to glance at the bunch of passports he had pushed through the window at her. Using his thumb, he slid a ten dollar bill out from under the pile of passports, and pushed it in again. All the while, he was explaining that he was bringing tourists into the country and that they were good for business and shouldn't be treated with disrespect. She shrugged, stamped the passports, and returned them to him through the window, minus the ten dollar bill. Smith pushed his way back through the queue, which was becoming more chaotic and disorganised by the minute. He crossed to the entry gate and presented the passports to the soldier from the Lithuanian Border Guard. The soldier counted the passports, and wrote the number six on a small slip of paper, which he handed to Smith together with the passports. He hadn't checked the photographs or details, just the rubber stamp from the office with the rolled up window.

Smith walked back up the line of vehicles to the van, and climbed in the back door. Everyone was awake.

"Well, the passports are stamped and we are clear to cross when the border opens in about half an hour. I'd better drive." Then he lit another cigarette, and coughed violently again.

At quarter past nine, the first vehicle was waved through the border post. An hour later, the blue minibus trundled through. The border crossing was not just a simple post. Heavy construction gear was moving about, digging, scraping, spraying with water, rolling. It looked as though they were widening the road, making parking spaces, and lots of other stuff. Getting the place ready to meet the onrush of tourists and goods that were expected to begin crossing the border soon. The minibus stopped at the first post, where a soldier checked the slip of paper with the number six written on it. They were all there. He wrote a number six just under the first one and waved the minibus on. The road ahead consisted of a sand and gravel path with deep pot holes in it from the innumerable heavy trucks and busses that had passed that way previously. The path wound in and around the bulldozers and workers and sheds. After ten minutes of slow driving, the minibus came to the next post. There were two soldiers there. One of them took the small slip of paper, checked that there were two sixes on it, checked that there were six people in the minibus, then waved them across with a smile.

"Welcome to Lithuania" - Smith said.

Now he was smiling. It was good to be home again.

"Open a beer somebody, I'm parched!" Brown said.

Everybody seemed pleased that the end of the journey was in sight.

As the minibus turned the last corner of the sandy slalom route onto a road with tarmac, Brown noticed that all the phone wires on the line of telegraph poles approaching the border had been cut. He counted the number of lines. There were sixteen. Only one was in place. The others hung like lianas in an African jungle from the poles. It was plain to see that huge pieces had been removed from them. The picture was the same for the next thirty miles along the road to Kaunas.

At noon the minibus stopped at a lay-by overlooking the city. Mogensen and Erik cooked up a pot of stew, which they all ate along with the bread they had bought in Suwalki. Not much was said. Each was buried in his own private thoughts. They left when a truck with Danish plates on and 'Portugal - Estonia' written on the side arrived. The driver came across for a chat while they were packing in a hurry. Black kept him talking for a couple of minutes, until Smith signalled that it was time to leave.

The sun was high, and hot. The road was dusty and Svend Jensen was tired. He had been on the road for the last fourteen hours. In Europe he had been forced to limit his driving to eleven hours a day, but out here there were no rules. He took a walk around the lay-by, which in truth was no bigger than a postage stamp with a wooden shelter at one end and an overfull waste basket beside it. It was too hot to be outside in the sun, especially since the rig had air-conditioning. But sitting on his behind for long hours made his feet a bit numb. As the minibus left the lay-by, his gaze followed it for a hundred metres or so. Wierd people. Not very sociable at all! Didn't look much like tourists. He opened the fridge under the belly of the truck tractor, and took out a Piwo. It was cold, and tasted good. He walked around a bit more, then lit a cigarette and sat in the shade of the shelter a bit. The cigarette was almost finished, when a green Fiat Uno drove by. There was a blonde woman behind the wheel. Svend noticed that the car had Danish plates on. This country's getting too crowded! He muttered to himself, and wandered off back to the truck.

Kaunas is a big, sprawling city of three hundred thousand inhabitants, the second largest city in Lithuania. It lies at the junction of the rivers Neris and Nemunas, at a place where Swedish Vikings fought a last stand battle against a Lithuanian and Polish army in the ninth century. From the residential area on top of the hill on the south side of the river, you can look out across a town with lots of trees, the occasional industrial chimneys, church spires and the red-brick fortress from the fourteenth century. The minibus didn't stop. It drove down the steep hill towards the narrow iron bridge at the bottom. A bus crossed the bridge from the Pergales Krantine boulevard which follows the north side river Nemunas, going east. The bus turned in to the bus stop at the bottom of the hill. A ZIL truck in army green, with the hammer and sickle on the drivers door painted over, followed the bus until it stopped, then turned left and began to climb the hill with its load. As the truck and the mini-bus passed each other about a third of the way up, everyone in the minibus held his nose. The air was thick with heavy diesel smoke. The sound of the two engines almost in synchronisation, caused a deep rumble to reverberate throughout the minibus. It lasted for a few seconds, until there was enough distance and traffic between them, then it was gone again. Traffic was reasonably heavy.

Smith turned the minibus onto the bridge. It had a tarmac surface, broken up in places so that the iron girders and railway sleepers that were the foundation of the road, were easily visible. Everyone in the minibus held on to something. They were glad that the minibus had good springs. There is a small, cobble-stoned parking lot on the left at the north end of the bridge, surrounded by ancient brick buildings with ornate masterpieces of brickwork decorating their walls. A pale yellow police car with a wide blue stripe down its side and the word "Policija" written in white on blue was parked there, in the centre of the entrance. Two policemen were standing in front of it, watching the traffic with arms folded across their chests.

The minibus turned right at the north side of the bridge and followed the Pergales Krantine. After five minutes drive, among the hurried city traffic and weaving taxis, it turned left on Gedimino and slowed. As they turned the corner, Smith said,

"Keep your eyes open to the left. This street is very important to us."

The minibus trundled up the street. Brown, who was sitting in the passenger street, noticed a building further up on the left with a flag hanging from a pole outside. The flag was red, green and yellow horizontally striped. As they passed, he noted that it had a huge double gate into a courtyard of some kind. The snout of a Russian BTR70P, six-wheel drive armoured car with a fourteen and a half millimetre machine-gun was just visible through the gate. To the right of the double gate was an ordinary door. Then they were past. A few yards further on, Gedimino crossed Griunvaldo Gate and a hundred yards or so beyond that, A.Puskino Street. All the space between the two, on the left, was occupied by a huge white building in three stories with an ornate, pillared entrance. The building was speckled with antennas. In the courtyard there were garage facilities. A Russian soldier was washing a UAZ jeep. The minibus did not change speed until it stopped to cross A.Puskino Street. After they had crossed the street and Kaslucio Boulevard, Smith stopped the minibus at the church square that marked the entrance to the wide pedestrian boulevard Laisves Aleja. Smith turned off the engine and turned in his seat.

"The first building was the old German embassy from before the war. Later it became the conscription centre for the Red Army, and now it is the headquarters of the Lithuanian Army in Kaunas. The second building is the headquarters of the Red Army in Kaunas. It will soon be empty. Perhaps the building will be turned over to the Lithuanian Army for its headquarters within the next couple of months. If you look directly across the square, at the left hand corner, you will see a modern three story building with glass doors among the others there. That is the courthouse. There is a small door to the right. That is the rear entrance to the police station. The main entrance is just around the corner. You see, there are a couple of policemen standing around just outside it. We will be coming to this street very often. Please remember its' name."

Without waiting for comments, he started the engine again, turned the minibus around and drove down the street. When they reached Kaslucio Boulevard they turned right and joined the traffic going towards the city centre. There was no talking in the minibus, everyone was looking out of the windows, watching the buildings go by, looking at the people getting on and off the busses and tram cars, some with shopping bags, some with briefcases. They were soaking up the atmosphere. Smith was too. He was smelling the air, watching the traffic and looking around to see if there was anyone he knew among the crowds. Kaslucio, right on Pergales Krantine again and back towards the bridge. There was a fire station at the corner as they turned right, with a small open space in front of the doors. It had room for four fire trucks. Two were out front being washed as they passed. Smith turned the minibus right up Birstorio Street when the traffic light changed to green, then right again at the change of the light on Sv.Gertrudos Street. Brown could see all the way up Laisves Aleja to the church at the far end from here. It was a wide boulevard, with a very long double line of lime trees all along its length. Both sides of the boulevard were full of shops of various kinds. People walked up and down, mainly under the lime trees, which would soon be green with fresh leaves. Under the trees there were benches to sit on. The minibus swung left and Brown noted that they were on Savanoriu Boulevard, heading north.

"We've just passed the main shopping area. In another half hour or so we'll be at our temporary destination." Smith said.

Savanoriu Boulevard cuts through Kaunas like a deep abdominal slash from throat to navel. They followed it for ten minutes, past a night club on the left, houses, boarded-up shops, hotels, small cheap eating places, drunks rolling in the gutters, angry taxi-drivers. There were pot-holes, obstacles, traffic lights that didn't work, and some that did. Finally they crossed the last traffic light and passed a petrol station on the other side of the road.

"First petrol station we've seen!" Black said from the back.

"It's one of three. We'll be passing another in a few minutes." Smith said over his shoulder. He was signalling for a turn to the right up the ramp to the main road between Klaipeda and Vilnius.

"Only three petrol stations in a city this size? Christ, the queues must be enormous!" Mogensen was flabbergasted.

"The Russians could control the flow of fuel better that way! Keeps people in their places." Brown said. Smith nodded. It certainly had made it difficult to move around if you were an honest citizen. It hadn't slowed the Black Market down though. On the contrary, it was a bit like Prohibition in America in the twenties.

"Where are we going now?" Erik asked. They had just left the city and were driving east along a road comparable to those in the rest of Europe.

"Towards Marijampole. We take a turn-off about twenty kilometres from here." Smith answered.

"No, I meant our temporary destination." Erik said. He lifted his feet as Hansen rummaged around in the cardboard box where they kept the beer, and started handing them out as he found them.

"You'll be staying in a summer house just on the outskirts of Marijampole for a couple of days, until the last arrangements are settled. We took over a part of the summer house area a year and a half ago and put up fences around it. That way we don't get disturbed. There are guards, but don't worry about them, they are there to make sure our competitors don't make life sour for us. Mind you, you'll all have to stay inside the wire until I get back. Please don't try to get out. The guards are armed and they shoot to kill."

"Where will you be?" Brown asked, while lighting a cigarette. Black handed him an opened beer. He threw the match out of the window and took it. Smith looked across at him. Black handed him a beer too.

"I'll be off to see my family for a couple of days, and to check that everything is okay. Just relax a while, you'll all need to acclimatise to my country. There's food, beer, western cigarettes, films, games and a swimming pool, everything you need for a good holiday."

"What about women?" Mogensen asked.

"Not yet." Smith said. "You're going to be isolated a bit until everything has settled and you've had a bit of instruction in what to do and what not to do. We're very organised here, you know. Your instructor will turn up in a couple of days. He's an ex Red Army major. He's never had contact with westerners before so he'll probably get a bit of a culture shock when he meets you lot."

He sipped his beer and overtook a truck loaded with steel pipes. They were laughing in the back of the minibus. Brown was quiet. Smith noticed. He liked Brown.

The minibus followed the main road for twenty minutes, past the sign saying "Minsk 600" and two outdoor barbecues in the woods bordering the road. Then it turned right up a ramp. Smith checked both ways for traffic. A truck passed, then an old man on a moped, with the ear flaps of his headgear flapping in the wind. When the road was clear, Smith stepped on the gas. About half a mile up the road the minibus passed another petrol station on the right, and a station selling Butane gas from a long row of pumps. The gas station was full of Ladas and the queues were long. The petrol station was empty. Ten minutes later the minibus slowed and stopped outside a gap in a high hedge. There was a large white cross by the entrance. Two old women were sitting on a bench to the right of the entrance, with empty shopping bags on their laps. There was a bus stop sign beside the bench. The minibus turned into the entrance.

Brown noticed that the gardens were immaculate. All the plants and bushes and trees were beginning to don their spring colours. The whole place seemed to be coming alive. A teenage girl and a young man were painting the facade of a hut, in a deep red. The boards skirting the roof overhang had already been painted yellow. In another allotment, a thick set man lay on the grass under a flagpole bearing the Lithuanian flag. He was very red in the face and there was an empty vodka bottle by his side on the grass. Further on, a fat woman with a headscarf was hanging out washing on a line between some apple trees. Brown realised that the vast majority of the trees inside the allotment area were fruit trees of one kind or another. It was obvious that the allotment area was huge by the number of paths that the minibus crossed and the number of summer houses visible up each path. The minibus turned left after five minutes. It followed the path in a swing to the right, then stopped in a gully between two very high hedges. In the silence that followed the shutting off of the engine, Brown thought he heard the howling of dogs some way off. Then the sound of kids playing somewhere closer by. Smith got out.

"Welcome to your new home boys." He said with a smile and slammed the door shut.

Chapter Nine – Cat on a hot tin roof

"I'm bored stiff!"

"I know how you feel Bob. You know what I'm going to do when this is all over and the heat's off? I'm going to go to Blackpool, find a bird to shack up with, and have a good summer on the Golden Mile!"

"You couldn't afford it Brian. A week after you got there you'd have to hack into somebody's computer to get more money. Knowing you, though, that would probably be the most interesting part of the holiday! Blackpool's not a bad place to be in the summer though. I've got a cousin over there, Joan Fisher. She married one of the Smarts' boys."

"You've got family all over the place! How do you keep track of them all? I don't even know where my parents are!"

The Thames van stopped at a T-junction. It's signal was flashing for a left turn. There was no traffic at all. The sky was still black with the rain that was coming down by the bucket full. The windscreen wipers were going at full speed and still couldn't manage to keep the windscreen clear. Bob turned the van left and was a bit too quick to release the clutch pedal, so the gears ground some as he changed from third into top.

"That's easy Brian. I have all their names and addresses written down in a little black book. Once in a while I drop by to see how things are going, keep in touch so to speak. I stay a few days then bugger off to the next one. That way they don't have me long enough to get tired of me. Cheap way of living if you don't mind having to bum a pint and a fag now and then!"

At the sound of the word 'fag', Brian lit two cigarettes and handed one to Bob, who took it willingly. The speedometer on the Thames showed twenty miles an hour. The rain was coming down so hard now that visibility was down to just a few yards. Bob leaned over the wheel and looked up at the clouds through the windscreen. There was no trace of a hole. The Thames was the only car on the road. The tyres were getting a bit bald too, so there was no sense in rushing things. He sat back and enjoyed the cigarette.

"How long have you known Billy?" Brian asked between drags. Bob didn't take the cigarette from the corner of his mouth when he answered.

"Billy? Let's see. I'm thirty five and I met Billy when I was in the Army Cadets. It must be about twenty two years ago. Mind you, we lost track of one another in the Army. I went into the Armoured Corps and Billy went off to Germany with some unit or other. I can't remember which one. I do remember that he was commander of a Saracen doing intelligence patrols along the border to East Germany, though."

"Where did you go?"

"I was shuttled between Stratford on Avon and Northern Ireland for the next four years. All told, I did two and a half years in Ireland. Did I ever tell you I was shot twice ?"

Brian nodded, Bob had told him at least a dozen times, and on one occasion had shown him the scars left by the bullet wound just above his right knee, and the one through the neck muscle on the left side of his head, just below the ear.

"Did I ever tell you how I got the one below the knee?"

Bob didn't wait for an answer. There was nothing much to do anyway before they got to town, so he decided to tell it again, whether or not Brian had heard it before. Brian had.

"Well here I was sitting in the back of a Pig - that's a Humber Pig to the uninitiated. There was me, Harry Baldwin, George Shakesbye and John Parkin. We were supposed to be dropped off by the Falls Road. Ted Williams was driving and Fred Johnson was in the passenger seat. We come to this zebra crossing and there was this lass walking over. Wearing a mini-skirt she was. You could see all the way up her leg, even from the back! Fred whistled at her, but she couldn't hear him because the shields were down. What does he do, the daft bastard? He lifts up the shield and shouts something about taking her round the back lane after dark! Mind you, I wouldn't have minded doing that myself. I mean, we'd been there two months and there was no time off for good behaviour, not around there at any rate! She stopped on the curb and when she turned around, Fred must have thought his lucky day had come. It hadn't though. She had a gun, and shot him right between the eyes. What a mess! His brains were splattered all over the place, and the bullet went bouncing around inside the Pig like it was a ping pong ball. Hit me in the bloody leg!"

"What happened to the girl?" Brian tried to sound interested, although he'd heard this story at least a dozen times.

"She ran off into a house. We jumped out the back and chased her through these peoples' living room." He started to chuckle, as if this was the best part of the story. "Christ you should have seen them! They were watching the telly and drinking their tea when we kicked in the front door and stomped all over the furniture with our size nines. I swear they hadn't budged an inch when we went out the back way! John Parkin saw her running down the back lane. He got her in the heart. It was a good shot, but a shame that. She was a great looking bint! I asked him why he didn't shoot her in the leg or something, and he said he was scared to look at her legs - if he had they would have put him off his aim." Bob started to giggle, almost girlishly.

"Well, anyway, when I got out of the Army I just kicked about a bit. Hitch-hiked down to London a few times, went on the binge, stuff like that. One day, I was having a kip on the grass just under the statue of Jack Crawford in Mowbray Park, when along comes Billy. He'd just got de-mobbed and had no place to go. Anyway, I took him over to our Allison's place on Toward Road. She put him up for a few days. Well, it turned out to be more than that didn't it? Bill and our Allison got married! That was a turn up for the book, I'll tell you. What about you? How long have you known Bill?"

"About a year. I met him when I was playing dominoes at the Democratic Club on Bridge Street."

"I know the place. My old man used to go there when I was a kid. I didn't know Bill went there though. Not his style, I would have thought!"

"Now that I know him, I'd say you were right. Anyway, he was sitting beside the table with a pint in his hand, watching the game. I lost and got up to go get myself a drink, and he got up at the same time. We bumped into each other and he spilt his pint on both of us. I thought he was going to give me the blame and punch me out. I mean he's bigger than me isn't he ? Anyway, he said it was his fault and that he'd buy me a pint. He got a couple of pints and we sat in the corner, by the big window behind the door and had a chat."

"Billy's got the gift of the gab hasn't he? I bet you thought you'd known him all your life inside half an hour ?"

"Something like that. Yeps, Billy has the gift of the gab alright! He asked me over to the house when the club shut, said he had some whisky. I suppose that was because I'd told him that I was living on my own in a bedsit over at Park Place East."

"You know, there's something I've been meaning to ask you Brian. How come a bright lad like you didn't go to university or something? You could have had a good job, earned loads of money and stuff like that, instead of poking about out here on a day like this."

Brian shook his head and laughed.

"I guess I just didn't have the right snooty parents Bob. No, orphanage kids don't go to university, we only go to the school of hard knocks. Besides, I've taught myself everything I know about computers and radio. I doubt that I'd be able to sit in the same classrooms as them peuky bastards that go to universities, without throwing up! Arrogant sods think they own the place."

"Maybe they do." Bob said, half in jest.

Brian looked across at him.

"That's real deep for you Bob!"

They started to laugh. The cigarette end fell out of Bobs' mouth and onto the floor. He stamped it out.

The first traffic light in Bewcastle was just a couple of yards ahead when Bob saw it through the rain and braked. The light was red. A container lorry passed by their noses, going south. A couple of minutes went by. No other traffic showed itself. The light changed to green and the Thames crossed over the junction.

"Now to find a phone box. "

Brian said, rolled down the window, threw the burned out cigarette stub out, and rolled up the window again. The collar of his jacket on the side of the window was already wet. When the Thames reached the town square, it was void of all pedestrians. The shops were open, but nobody was moving on the street at all. Hardly surprising under the circumstances. The best place to be was curled up in front of a warm coal fire, with a cold lager and a thriller on the telly. There were one or two cars parked around the cobbled square. There was a phone box by the sandstone monument in the middle. It was one of those old fashioned red ones the Post Office used to have years ago.

It was empty. Bob stopped the Thames right beside it and Brian jumped out. He opened the door of the phone box and stepped in. It was dry there, and the phone hadn't been vandalised. Bob drove off across the square towards the bakers' shop.

"Is Paul at home? "

"I'll just have a look. Who wants him?"

The voice on the other end was that of a middle-aged woman.

"It's Brian. I'm a mate of his cousin Bob."

"Bobby? I haven't seen him for ages. Next time you see him, tell him I haven't forgotten he owes me twenty quid! Anyway, I'll see if our Paul is upstairs."

She put the phone down. Brian could hear her footsteps retreating across the room, the squeaking of a rusty door hinge, and her shout of, - Paul, you're wanted on the phone! - A few seconds passed, then the same voice called, - Somebody called Brian. He says he's a mate of our Bobby. Get up and answer it, you lazy bugger! - Another few seconds. The same steps approached again and the phone was picked up.

"He'll be down in a minute. Hang on son."

The phone was put down again. Brian dug deep into his pockets, and pushed another twenty pence into the phone. Five minutes seem like a long time when you're waiting for somebody to come to the phone. That's just like the old adage says - a watched kettle never boils - Brian had put another ten pence piece into the phone before new footsteps approached and the phone was picked up.

"Hello, it's Paul. Who's that?"

The voice sounded young, and very sleepy indeed.

"Hi Paul, we don't know each other. My name is Brian Wallis, I'm a mate of Bob Wood and Billy Thomson. Can we talk?"

"Sure. No problem, what do you want?"

"Bob said you're a radio amateur. Do you have eighty metre equipment? Good, what about a scrambler? Perfect! Billy asked me to arrange a sched with you. We're up here in deepest darkest Northumberland and need some help. I'll not say any more on the phone. What about thirty-six-seventy in about an hour? Great. Thanks a lot Paul!"

Brian put the phone down. - That should do for now -.

The rain was pouring down outside the phone box, and Bob hadn't come back with the car yet, so Brian just stood there and kept a lookout for a pair of headlights approaching the box. He got the shock of his life when somebody knocked on the side window, and almost jumped out of his skin. When he turned around, he saw that the face of a man was pressed against the glass. The man was wrapped in a raincoat, and had pulled it up over his head to keep the rain off. He was making signs as if he wanted to come in. Brian made signs in return to say that he was staying there, so the man pulled open the door to the booth and stepped inside with him.

Detective Sergeant Simmons was actually on holiday with the wife and kids. Bewcastle was his home town, so he'd been down to his old local pub, the Bear and Dog, for a pint or two. Well, it had actually turned out to be three or four, since there were a few people there he hadn't seen since he moved to Newcastle fifteen years ago. The time had gone quicker than he thought, and he hadn't been able to get a taxi, so there was nothing else to do but call the wife and ask her to come and pick him up. He didn't mind sharing the phone box with the kid. Mind you, the kid didn't look at all happy to be sharing the phone box with him! He put ten pence in the box, picked up the phone and rang.

"Hi sweetheart. I've just come out of the pub and couldn't get a taxi. I think this bloody rain is keeping them all busy. Do you mind coming down to pick me up? Okay, I'm standing in the phone box by the monument just across from the pub. Five minutes? That'll be fine. See you in a bit then."

He put the phone down and turned around to face the door.

"You waiting for somebody as well?"

He asked the kid, who was squeezed between him and the inside of the phone box.

"My brother. He's doing the shopping and he'll be back in a minute."

Two headlights approached the phone box. Simmons knew it was too soon for the wife, so it was probably the kids' brother coming to get him. A Ford Tames van pulled up just outside the phone box and the door was opened from the inside. Simmons couldn't see the driver. Simmons held the door of the phone box open and the kid squeezed by, out the door and straight into the van. The door of the van closed and it drove off around the monument, disappearing into the solid curtain of rain. Simmons held the door open a bit, until the lights of the van had disappeared, then closed it again. There was something familiar about that kid, and the Thames van!

"Did you get hold of Paul then ?"

Bob asked as the van left the square.

"Yes, everything is set."

Brian relaxed back into the seat. It was beginning to get cold, and the rain and darkness was getting on his nerves. He wished it was summer, with green leaves and light evenings. Bob noticed that his passenger shivered, and turned on the heater. After a while, Brian said,

"You and Billy know each other well then."

Bob looked across at him for a second, then away again.

"Yes. Mind you, it came as a bit of a surprise when Billy told me he was starting his own private army - Billy's Privateers he called it. I thought it was a great idea. At least it relieves the boredom. We were having a natter over a cup of tea at our Allison's one weekend when he came out with it. Allison was out doing the shopping. Billy asked me not to tell her. He wanted to keep it quiet. Clever enough. If the fuzz come looking for him, Allison wouldn't be able to tell them anything. Anyway, before you know it, Billy, Dougy, Charley and me went out camping up on Hadrians' Wall one weekend. That's where it all started really. I was bored stiff until Billy came up with the idea."

"Who's Charley ? I haven't met him."

The Thames van reached the traffic light, which was on green, and continued on out of town, still going at a snails' pace. The street was still empty. A taxi cab passed, going the other way. It looked like a motor-boat with its front tyres kicking up a bow wave, and its wake washing across the street. The pavement was invisible, submerged.

"Charley got killed. That's why there was room for you in the group. Charley was a good mate. He was bloody good with radios and stuff like that, although he was useless with a gun. He couldn't hit a barn door from ten feet away with a shotgun. His death was stupid really. He got pissed one night at the Ship Inn down the East End. The barman called a taxi. When it came, it was going the other way and stopped on the other side of the road. Charley being as pissed as a newt, went to cross the street, and got run over by a number nine bus. There wasn't much of him left to bury, and what there was didn't look a pretty sight. Bloody bus dragged him half way up the road before it stopped, leaving bits of him all over the place. Good thing he was an orphan, and had no family."

"Shame...What made you lot pick me ?"

"Ask Billy, he's the one who found you."

They fell into a silence that lasted for most of the trip back to the cottage.

"Want a mug of tea Dougy? I'm putting the kettle on."

Billy Thomson stopped looking out of the crack in the dirty sheet that served as a curtain across the front window and let the sheet fall back into place. He turned to face the room. Dougy was sitting at the table with a cigarette in his mouth and a Heckler and Koch MP5 dismantled on an oily rag on the table. He looked up.

"Don't mind if I do, Billy. Just the ticket, that is!"

Billy went across to the gas stove. Dougy continued polishing the sub-machine gun. He rubbed the dirty handkerchief in his hand along the slits in the breech block then dropped the rag on the table. Then he picked up a can of gun oil and sprayed a little on the block. He watched the drops of oil roll down the shiny metal, then around, as he rotated the breech block in the air. Ash fell from the cigarette onto the table and flew into a thousand tiny pieces. Dougy picked up the handkerchief again and smeared the oil out over the surface of the part.

"You'll wear it away if you keep polishing it like that Dougy. "

Dougy smiled, took the cigarette butt from his mouth and stubbed it out in the ash tray. Then he started to assemble the MP5.

"How long before Bob and Brian get back ?"

He asked. Billy checked his watch.

"About half an hour or so. It shouldn't take that much longer, but you never know in weather like this. The road can get flooded in no time. Mind you, it keeps the other traffic off the road, so the chances of them getting picked up, or followed is minimal."

The kettle had started to boil. Billy made the tea. He was suddenly reminded of the observation post he had shared with George Dobson outside the small German town of Schackenburg, at the junction of the Elbe and Aland rivers. The post had been established in the attic of an empty house, overlooking the barbed wire wall separating the Bundesrepublik from the DDR. Doing service there was the pits. Long hours taking turns looking across the wire at nothing in particular, intermingled with long hours of sleep, cards, tea, boredom of the worst kind. It is at times like these that a man begins to think of how things are put together. When you've been doing that kind of work long enough, you start to invent small games to play with yourself, just to break the monotony. Games like - will that soldier on the bicycle on the other side of the wire stop to look at you through his binoculars before he gets to the third telegraph pole from where he is now. Sometimes you won, sometimes you lost. Billy had won so often that it had made him believe that he was gifted with foresight, which as a matter of fact he was.

Bill was an intelligent man, with just one minor flaw - he hated darkies! His worst enemy was the Enoch Powell who had suggested letting the darkies, the Pakistanis, and the Indians, and them from Jamaica into the country. His hero was the Enoch Powell who had changed his mind and ranted about sending them all home. Anybody could make a mistake. Bill had forgiven Enoch his big mistake.

It wasn't that you couldn't use darkies for anything at all! He was just convinced that they should be kept down in the mud where they belonged. He had been saving his money for a long holiday in South Africa when Mandella took over. The night that happened, Bill had gone down to the gasthof and drunk himself silly with his holiday money. Everybody in the gasthof had drunk themselves silly on Bills bill as well. He was a big hero in the town after that night, at least for a while, until they found out he was broke again.

It was while he was coming too on a park bench in the rain, that Bill had hatched his plan to start his own private army when he got home after that tour of duty. From then on, Bill was a man with a purpose although nobody could see the change that had taken place inside him. He did his job, and on his time off he nosed around after the places where others with his frame of mind met. That's when he had run into Uli, of the Viking Group, and his mate Hammel.

Hot water splashed on Billy's sneakers and made him jump. He straightened and went across to the table. Dougy was pushing in the locking pins that hold the telescopic butt of the MP5 to the receiver. The gun was assembled. Dougy stroked it lightly with the oily rag. Billy put the mug of tea on the table and sat down across from Dougy.

"I wonder what our Beryl's doing now !"

Dougy said as he lay the MP5 down on the dirty rag and wrapped it up. He sipped his tea. Nobody said anything.

"Probably watching Crossroads on the telly."

Billy said after a while. Dougy's alright - he thought, though the only reason he's here is because Bob's in with us. If Bob ever left the group, it's certain that Dougy would leave with him. The question is - how is Dougy in a firefight ? Bob I can trust. He knows his business, the same as me. Brian won't do any fighting, he's already made that clear, but Dougy is an unknown factor and I don't like unknown factors. They make me nervous. But there's no doubt about the fact that he likes guns!

Dougy took the next rolled-up parcel and unwrapped a Colt forty-five, model nineteen eleven. It looked brand new and unused. He started to disassemble it. Billy watched him for a few seconds, until there was a brief gurgle from the generator in the kitchen and the lights dimmed for a second or two before picking up again. Then he got up and went to fill the tank with petrol. Dougy will be alright. He handles the guns as if he was a pro. Likes the feel of them, you can tell that by the way he rubs 'em down with oil. He'll be alright. Billy filled the generator. The rain was still coming down in buckets, cascading down the stairs and dripping off the landing and through the holes in the kitchen ceiling. There had been thunder earlier, but now there wasn't. The clouds were too thick and the rain too intense.

Dougy got up and peeked through the gap in the sheet at the sound of tyres on the gravel path. He had the MP5 in his right hand. It was alright. It was the Thames returning from its trip into Bewcastle. The van turned into the barn and the engine stopped. The only sound there was to hear was the hammering of the rain on the window pane. Doug dropped the sheet into place, went back to the table, sat down and drank his tea. Two minutes later, Billy, Bob and Brian came into the front room. Bob was rubbing his hands as if they were cold. Brian had his collar turned up around his ears and was carrying two shopping bags. Both were wet.

"How did it go ?"

Doug asked. Brian put the bags down in the corner beside the sleeping bags. Bob was warming his hands over the gas stove.

"Great. No problems. I have a sched with Paul in about ...twenty minutes. Let's have a cuppa'."

Bob was already putting the kettle on. Brian took off his coat and hung it on a nail behind the door.

Paul turned up on the right frequency at the right time. With the scrambler, they could hold a private conversation without anyone listening. He agreed to keep them informed of events, and said that he'd go on a visit to Beryl's immediately, which in fact, he did.

Albert Simmons wasn't due to go back to work for another week, so there was plenty of time to relax, put his feet up and watch the telly. He'd already forgotten about the kid in the phone box and the blue Ford Thames van. He fell asleep on the sofa in front of the fire. The wife and kids had gone to bed when he woke up. The china clock on the mantle said one o'clock. The fire had gone out and there was just noise on the screen. His back ached. His head ached. In fact, he was aching all over. Simmons swung his feet from the arm of the sofa and placed them on the floor. The wife had removed his shoes. That was good. Then using the back of the sofa as leverage, he sat up and rested for a second or two afterwards. He got up and went across to switch off the telly. Isn't it strange how the mind works? Noise is noise, and the little specks of white on grey on the television screen were no more than that, just random specks of noise. But something must have triggered his memory, because suddenly he knew the name of the kid in the phone box. Brian Wallis. Simmons was still aching when he went slowly out into the hall and shut the living room door quietly after him. He turned on the light by the switch just inside the front door with its' stained glass window. The light wasn't strong, being totally enclosed in one of those Chinese lantern type shades, but he had to blink anyway. He picked up the phone and called the duty sergeant in Newcastle.

"Stan ? It's Albert. How's things ?.... Yes, I know I'm on holiday, but listen. You know that kid Brian Wallis ? Yes, that's the one, skinny kid with spots. Well I saw him this afternoon in Bewcastle...... Yes, of course I'm sure! We were standing in a phone box together for five minutes. I'd just come out of the pub. It was bucketing down so I went to call the wife to come and pick me up. The kid was already standing in the phone box. He said he was waiting for his brother...... He was picked up by a Thames van. I'm not sure about the colour, the light being what it was and all that, could have been brown, or blue, something like that...... Good. I'll be off to bed then...... Good night to you too Stan."

Simmons put down the phone, switched off the hall light, and climbed the stairs to bed in complete darkness. The rain that had been hammering on the windows all day, had begun to let up just a teeny little bit.

When Avon Wailes came to work at the usual time, eight o'clock in the morning, the rain had stopped and patches of blue were beginning to appear in the clouds. He parked the Escort in the cellar of the Icelandic Wool Company and took the lift up to the office. Everything seemed normal. Harry Seaton was already at his desk over in the opposite corner, sorting through the messages that had come in during the night. Nobody else was in yet. Wailes hung his scarf on the peg, and his overcoat as well, straightened his suit, and sat down at his desk. It was completely clear. While he was in the process of deciding what to do next, Harry Seaton's chair scraped. Wailes looked up as Seaton came over to him. He had a slip of paper in his left hand, and was reading it while holding on to his horn-rimmed glasses with the other hand.

"I think this one might be yours Avon."

He handed it over and turned away again without waiting for an answer. The lift started working. When it stopped again and the door opened, Watkins stepped out into the office. Wailes was reading the note and answered Watkins call of 'good morning'.

"You're just in time John. Don't bother hanging your coat up, we're going out again. Read this."

Wailes got up and put on his overcoat and scarf again. Watkins read the note.

"Detective Sergeant Simmons reports seeing Brian Wallis in Bewcastle late last night. Wallis was picked up by a Thames van of unknown colour, driven by somebody who Wallis claimed was his brother. Simmons talked to Wallis for more than five minutes in a public phone box."

He looked up.

"Now that's what I call a positive sighting. Where are we going?"

He put the note in his inside pocket.

"Bewcastle."

Wailes said, then shouted across the office to Harry Seaton,

"Harry, do me a favour and get in touch with this Simmons character. Tell him I'm coming up to see him right away. Let me have his address as soon as you get it."

Seaton waved. As Wailes and Watkins stepped into the elevator, he was picking up the phone.

Traffic in Newcastle was heavy. The rush hour was on. When the Escort was out of town and heading west, Watkins asked,

"What's the plan of action?"

"We'll check out this Simmons character first. If I'm convinced that his sighting is genuine, we'll set up a control centre at the local nick and operate from there. Our best bet is to find the van, or somebody who's seen it close enough to give a description of the driver. We'll have to check out all the Thames vans in the vicinity, just to rule them out. Wallis claimed that his brother was picking him up. Maybe his brother lives somewhere in Bewcastle. It's a possibility we'll have to look into...."

The phone rang. It was Seaton, with Simmons' address. Watkins wrote it down.

It was easy enough to find number thirty two Saint Aidans Avenue in Bewcastle. Simmons opened the front door to the two visitors.

"Let's see some ID..."

He said, and checked both cards carefully before letting them in. He showed them into the living room. The fire was on, and there was a tea-pot with a flowered cosy covering it, on the small table in front of the sofa. There was a football game on the television. Simmons went across to the set and turned it off.

"Have a seat."

He said to Wailes and Watkins, who both accepted the offer. Wailes sat on one end of the sofa and Watkins took the armchair across the fireplace from the television. Simmons sat down and poured himself some tea. He offered a mug to the other two, who accepted. Simmons dropped two sugar lumps into his and stirred.

"What can I do for you two gents?"

He asked. Wailes noticed that he did not take milk with his tea.

"We got the message you sent to the duty sergeant at Newcastle last night. I'm in charge of this particular investigation, so I thought I'd come over and take a look at the place."

"I've got no problem with that. After your man rang and told me you were coming, I started to think a bit more about the van. I didn't see that much of it, but as far as I remember, it came from across the opposite side of the square from the phone box."

"I see. Were the shops open?"

"Yes, all the lights were on and it was too early to shut. Mind you, there were no customers as far as I could see. The whole square was empty, what with the rain bucketing down and all."

"I take it you didn't see the driver at all."

"Not at all. The only thing I saw was an arm opening the passenger door from the inside. I didn't even see if it was a man or a woman. It could have been anybody."

There was a sudden crack in the fire. A piece of flint in the coal. A burning ember hopped out and fell onto the hearth. It lay there, smouldering. Simmons got up, took the brass-handled tongs from a polished brass coal scuttle to the right of the fireplace and threw the ember back into the fire. He dropped the tongs back into the scuttle and sat down on the sofa again.

"Mind you, I have just remembered that Wallis said that his brother was doing the shopping. Maybe one of the shopkeepers can give a description."

172

"Do you know Bewcastle well?"

Watkins asked.

"You might say that. I was born and brought up here. I like it here, but there's no work, so I ended up moving to Newcastle."

"Would you mind working for me while we're here ? We need somebody like you to help us out. Your local knowledge will be invaluable."

Wailes said. Simmons pondered a few moments, sipping his tea in silence.

"You'd have to clear it with my boss first. If he says it's okay then it's okay with me. Mind you, I've still got another week's holiday left. The wife'll kill me for sure if I just give it up."

"We'll arrange for you to have the missing time, plus an extra week as compensation when the job's done. How about that?"

"Alright then. It's a deal."

"Can I borrow your phone?"

"Go right ahead."

Wailes rang the chief constables' office from the phone in the hall. When he put the phone down again and came back into the living room, he said,

"Welcome aboard Albert. Our first job is to go down to the local nick and set up headquarters. You must know the way, so why don't you lead on ?"

The police station in Bewcastle turned out to be a bit on the small side. Not that it was tiny, but as the locals say, there was just enough room to swing a cat. Wailes' headquarters turned out to be a back room on the first floor of the three storey red brick station, over-looking the coal yard. Everyone at the station was helpful though, which was a bit unexpected. Normally, when the big city boys move in, these one-horse stations get a bit upset. That wasn't the case in Bewcastle. They welcomed the excitement, and the fact that the matter was one of national security and involved a big-shot like Wailes only made the event even more interesting.

By lunch time Wailes, Watkins and Simmons were scouring the shops around the town square, looking for anyone who could give a description of the driver of the car that had picked up Brian Wallis the previous night. They hit the jackpot in Smith's the bakers.

"He was about as tall as my husband, that's about five foot eight. He was about thirty'ish. Looked a bit rough if you ask me. Unshaven. Partly bald on top. Oh yes, he had a widows peak, real definite, and his teeth were all to hell."

"What do you mean, all to hell?" Simmons enquired.

"Well, you know, all rotting like. Probably too much smoking and drinkin' if you ask me. Come to think of it he was a bit smelly as well, damp like, as if he'd been living rough!"

"What makes you say that?"

"My old man does that once in a while. Disappears for a couple of days at a time he does. When he comes back I know he's been drinking and sleeping rough. Always comes home sober though, and after a couple of days he's right as rain again!"

"Do you remember the colour of his hair, Mrs. Smith?" Simmons asked.

"Kind of a mousy brown, thin-like. He talked with a Sunderland accent."

"We'd like to send a photo-fit expert down to have a word with you. Will you have the time this afternoon about two?"

She thought about it for a moment.

"If we can do it in the back here, then that'll be alright. I haven't got the time to leave the shop."

"No problem. We'll be sending officer Richards over."

Simmons left the shop. Wailes and Watkins were standing outside. Wailes was leaning against a lamppost looking bored with the whole thing. Then again, they had been to about eight or nine shops before the bakers' and nobody had been able to give a description.

"We struck it lucky boss. As soon as we get back to the office, I'll get Sam Richards to come over. We should have a photo-fit picture of the driver in a couple of hours."

"Good. Let's go then, I need a cuppa' anyway."

They got into the borrowed Panda and drove back to the station.

True to Albert Simmons prediction, the photo-fit picture arrived at half past two. Nobody recognised the picture, so it was sent over to Newcastle by fax. Newcastle said that if the driver of the Thames had a record, that they would be able to identify him within two hours, but at seven o'clock that evening, there had still been no answer. Wailes decided to call it a day.

"Right Albert, we'll be off. You can just as well get off home yourself. I've told the inspector that you'll be running our part of the show until further notice. You'll be operating from here. You've got the phone number in Newcastle where we can be reached, so contact me as soon as anything breaks. Otherwise, there's no need for Watkins and I to hang around here."

Wailes and Watkins started for the door.

"Goodnight then."

Simmons said to their backs. Wailes waved without turning around.

Bob Wood did have a record, although it wasn't really criminal. Bob, you see liked to drink beer. When he drank beer, he couldn't stop until all the money he had had burned a hole in the bottom of his pocket. That doesn't normally give a man a record, but in Bob's case it had. You see, one day in June a few years ago, Bob had been a bit thirsty. After all, it was hot and sunny. So he had stopped the tank-transporter outside the Bell and Whistle in Alcester, eight miles west of Stratford on Avon, and went in for a pint. It was two hours before he came out again, and he had certainly put away more than one in the meantime. He was taking the Centurion on the transporter to Worcester, from where he would proceed west, through Leominster towards the training ground in West Wales. It wasn't normal to have just one transporter on the road without an escort, that was why he had taken advantage of the chance to have a pint. A centurion had broken down, again, on the training grounds. A replacement was being sent and the one that was broken down was to be picked up and brought back to the workshops. The MP's had been too busy to provide an escort, so he had been given orders to carry on without them.

About thirty five minutes after coming out of the pub, the transporter crossed the M5 connecting Birmingham to Bristol. By then the beer had taken its toll and Bob was a bit dizzy. So dizzy in fact that he drove the transporter into the ditch on the other side of the bridge over the motorway. The ditch was steep and the transporter travelling quite fast, so the Centurion rolled off the flat-bed, down the embankment, and landed upside down - on a police car. Fortunately for the two policemen, they had already left the vehicle and were talking to the driver of a car they had stopped for speeding, when their own car was squashed flat. They climbed the embankment in a hurry and rushed to the cab of the transporter, thinking the fact that the driver was slouched over the wheel meant that he had been injured. He hadn't. He was just very drunk.

That little incident had cost Bob six months in an army prison, not one of the nicest places to be. But the accident was soon going to cost Bob more than that, because the police station at Newcastle was able to retrieve his name, and the name of his next of kin, his sister Beryl, married name Trotter.

"Good work Albert. Stay where you are for the time being. In the meantime, we'll see what we can dig up about Bob Wood and his sister Beryl. I'll be in touch."

Wailes put the phone down. Watkins was sitting on the corner of the table.

"Now it looks like we're finally getting somewhere! Get on to Swansea. Check on Bob Wood's drivers license. In the mean time, I'll check out the records office in Sunderland. If he or his sister has an address there, then we should be able to find them."

"Before I do that, I'll check the phone book. "Watkins said.

Wailes looked at him, intensely at first. Just the heat of the chase and the smell of the fox's blood, he decided.

"Good idea, John. You do that. I'll hang about a bit to see what you get your hands on. In the meantime, I think I'll have a cuppa'."

Watkins smiled. It was about time the old man began to pay attention to his ideas, and not just fob them off as bits of nonsense. -

Now where's that Sunderland phone book? Maybe Harry has it lying around somewhere - he thought and got up to check.

There were literally hundreds of Woods' in the Sunderland phone book, although only eleven of them had christian names starting with a B. There were fifty four with the initial R. There were fourteen Trotters'.

Wailes said. "Start phoning them and see what happens. Use the other phone, I'll be needing this one in a couple of minutes." No sooner had he said that, when the phone on the desk rang. Wailes picked it up, said hello, paused, then handed the phone to Watkins.

"It's for you." He said and grimaced. Watkins took the phone.

"Hi Gina, how are things going?..... You have? When?..... That's good news. I have to go now, but I'll call you later.... Well, I was thinking we could go to the pictures later tonight.. Fine, I'll pick you up at eight. Bye."

He put the phone down.

"What was that all about?"

"That was Gina. The tapes we sent her? She says she has positively identified the accents of Black and Erik as Scandinavian, probably Danish or Norwegian."

Wailes sat up straight.

"Good girl! When you see her, tell her I'll buy her a drink next time we meet!"

Another piece of the jigsaw puzzle had turned up. As yet though, there were too many pieces missing to be able to tell what the picture was. What was strange though, was how many times Denmark had come into his life this last month. Some thing big was going on, and his nose was telling him that he was getting close to whatever it was. There was only one thing to do right now though, sit tight and continue with the footwork. Watkins went over to the other desk and started phoning. Wailes changed his mind about ringing from the phone on his desk, put on his overcoat and scarf, and went out. He went as far as the phone box on the corner, and called Dawson.

"What's going on Wailes?"

Wailes gave him a brief report on the situation.

"Strange, isn't it, how many times Denmark has cropped up in this story?"

"My sentiments exactly sir."

"You don't suppose that this might have anything to do with your, excuse the expression, old friend? He's over there somewhere, isn't he?"

"I hadn't considered that possibility sir. That's the problem with swimming around in the mud, you sometimes forget to look up at the sky. I would say there might be a connection, although what that connection might be, I have yet to find out. Anyway, I'm sure we're very close to the people who helped Anderson escape the country. That's our number one priority at this point in time."

"True. Anyway, keep me informed Wailes - and keep up the good work."

"Yes sir. Thank you sir."

Wailes put the phone down and returned to the office. Beryl Trotter didn't answer the phone when it rang, and neither did two other Trotters'. The others who did answer the phone, were crossed off the list of suspects. There was only one thing to do, go round the three addresses and check with the neighbours. Wailes decided to let Watkins do the leg work. After all, his jeans and red-black chequered woodsman's shirt and his accent gave him enough camouflage to get close without arousing too much suspicion.

The first Trotter had returned home from her job at the shipyard by the time Watkins got there. She didn't have a brother. At least that's what she claimed. Watkins crossed her off the list and drove over to Pickering Square. When he knocked on the door, there was no answer. But the neighbour in the next house up was peeking inquisitively through the curtains, trying not to be seen, so he went over there and rang the doorbell. A woman in her seventies opened the door. Watkins smiled. She looked nervous.

"Excuse me missus, but I'm looking for our Bobby. You haven't seen him around have you?"

"Haven't seen him for more than a week, since him and Dougy and Billy buggered off together. What do you want him for?"

"Well, I'm his cousin Pat. I've been working up in Scotland the last couple of years, but now I'm back for a holiday. My mother told me that our Beryl was living over here and that Bob was stoppin' with 'er. Who's this Billy and Dougy then? Never 'eard of them."

The old woman was suddenly suspicious. Still, if he's been away, there's probably lots of stuff he doesn't know about. She brightened up.

"Come in and 'ave a cuppa' son. It'll be a couple of hours before Beryl gets back. She's working at the Bingo Hall now ya' know! Making tea and cakes in the caf ' I think she said."

Watkins went in and shut the front door behind him. The old woman - Mrs. Gray she said her name was - was already standing by the kitchen sink filling the electric kettle with water. Watkins sat down in the flowered sofa, across from the gas fire. Funny how these places all look the same - he thought. A gas fire in the middle of one wall, a television to one side, normally the side closest to the window so you could watch the telly and see who was coming at the same time. Opposite the gas fire, there was always a sofa, and it was always flowered. Then the ubiquitous armchair on the other side of the fire from the telly. One or two simple ornaments on the mantle-piece, a flash of fake brass here and there, a little coffee table with the Sunderland Echo laid out on it in the middle of the room, right under the single lamp in its shade dangling from the ceiling. Always the same scene.

Mrs. Gray came back with a small tin tray painted with a scene from the Indian Mutiny. On it were an old Brown Betty, and two mugs stained brown by years of tea drinking. There was a small crystal sugar bowl with a few sugar cubes in it, and a cup with milk. She put the tray on the coffee table. She didn't bother moving the newspaper. Watkins poured himself a cuppa' without waiting for an invitation, as is the custom in these parts. He didn't wait for Mrs. Gray to start the conversation. She'd only ask him questions about himself.

"You were going to tell me about Dougy and Billy."

"Was I ?" –

She asked absent-mindedly. The mug stopped just before it reached her mouth.

"Oh yes."

She put the mug down on the mantle.

"Beryl got married to Dougy Trotter two years ago, just before they came to live here. Nice lad, Dougy. Always out of work, but then again who isn't in these parts? Billy Thomson is a mate of your Bobby's. As far as I know, they were in the army together."

"Has Dougy ever been in the army?"

"Not as far as I know. Mind you, he did a stretch in Durham jail for burglary before he met your Beryl. He told me that himself last Christmas at the party they had at their house. He was a bit plastered that night, I can tell you. Chucked a Brown Ale bottle at Beryl for no reason at all. Mind you, she chucked it back at him. Hit him in the belly it did. Big softie!"

"Our Bob wrote to me that he had bought a van. That surprised me that did. He's not really the kind to save his pennies."

"You're right about that. Yes, he bought a little blue one. Don't ask me what kind it was though, cos' I don't know anything about cars at all. Billy has a van as well. They used to run about in it a lot before Bobby got his. They were all over the place, campin' and stuff like that. I'm surprised you didn't see them up in Scotland!"

"Big place is Scotland." Watkins said.

"Aye, that it is, that it is. You like your tea?"

Watkins drank what was left in the mug.

"Aye, I did, Mrs. Gray. But look, I don't think I'll bother waiting for Beryl. I'll do away over to my mothers'. When you see Beryl, tell her I'll drop by later. Thanks for the tea."

Watkins got up off the sofa. Mrs. Gray heaved herself up with the help of the arm chair and her walking stick. She showed him to the door.

"Tara then son. I'll tell your Beryl you were here. Oh by the way, I almost forgot. There was another lad with them the day they buggered off. I've seen him around here before. Brian I think his name is."

Watkins waved goodbye and left.

Beryl Trotter knew something was wrong when Maggie Gray told her that her cousin Pat had been on a visit from Scotland. She thanked the old woman for the message and took the bus over to Paul's place. She didn't have a cousin called Pat.

Wailes summed up the story when Watkins was finished with his report. They were sitting in the lounge of Wailes' hotel, having a beer, buried in comfy armchairs - without flowers on.

"Alright, let's see what we have. Bob Wood and Billy Thomson are army buddies. Bob's sister Beryl is married to one Dougy Trotter, who did time in Durham jail for burglary. They disappear in two vans, one of them blue, together with someone called Brian, at around the same time Brian Wallis disappears. Brian Wallis is known to have had contact with Peter Lennox, son of my old mate Bill Lennox, who is at present on some assignment or other across the North Sea. Brian is also known to have had contact with two men who speak English with Danish or Norwegian accents, Erik and Black. Peter gets killed in a faked car accident, possibly by Erik and Black. Brian Wallis is a computer expert of some kind. He's clever enough to hack into a computer using the computer at the bank where Peter Lennox works as a clerk, and move a large sum of money from one account to another. Days after his disappearance, Brian Wallis is seen in Bewcastle. He is picked up from a phone box by a Ford Thames van supposedly driven by his brother. Beryl Trotter is still living at home and going to work as normal. In the mean time a foreigner calling himself Paul Anderson is called back to wherever he came from by a mysterious letter written in Russian and posted in Newcastle. Anderson has been under surveillance for some time on special orders, issued on the basis of a note from somebody at the Russian Embassy in London. Anderson is living in Manchester with a woman..... Your turn with question hour, I think." Wailes sipped his beer.

"One. Anderson is a radio amateur. We have to assume that he has a contact in the vicinity of Newcastle who sends him the message to return. Why not use amateur radio for the contact? Why have a contact at all?" Watkins asked. Wailes leaned back in the chair and thought about that one for a moment. Then he said,

"Anderson has to be mobile. If he wasn't and had radio equipment, he would have to register his radio equipment with the authorities, or risk being caught as a pirate radio station. The contact is obviously in a position to contact Anderson's masters without drawing attention to himself. Short wave antennas are quite large. They take up lots of space. The neighbours would notice if there was a short wave antenna in the yard. Try and find out if there is, or has ever been, short wave antennas in Beryl Trotters' back yard. If there is, then the connection between Paul Anderson and the Trotters' house is looking better."

Watkins wrote in his notebook. He looked up when he was finished. I have to admit that I like playing the quiz master - he thought.

"Why write the note in Russian? Is the contact Russian?"

"I don't think so. I saw the note. It was poorly written. There is a possibility that the contact didn't know what he was passing on. That's logical too. If I was the boss, I wouldn't want just anybody to be able to read the stuff I was sending. I'd be careful enough to pick someone who I was sure didn't know my language. I mean, all he has to do is write down what he receives and put it in an envelope to a forwarding address. Anderson must know the address of his contact to be able to make it work. Anderson scarpers just after receiving the note. Brian Wallis and his mates scarper when they see on the telly that Brian is wanted.... That could be a coincidence. Next question."

"If Erik and Black did away with Peter Lennox, why didn't they do away with Brian Wallis as well? Then there would be no witnesses at all!"

"That's a very good question, John. The only reason I can see for them not doing so, is that he's needed again. There is also the possibility that Brian is a member of a group which is helping the foreigners with whatever they have going on. They wouldn't be very popular with their friends if they harmed him. Besides, if he is known to them as a member of a sympathetic group, they'd know he would keep his mouth shut.... Mine's dry. Want another?" Watkins nodded. Wailes signalled for the waitress. She came right away and he ordered two more pints.

"Next question. Where did Bob Wood and Billy Thomson do army service? Can we get hold of their army records?"

"I'll call a man who can do that in the morning. My guess is that they did service in Germany."

"Why?" Watkins asked, surprised at the assumption.

"Because Germany borders up to Denmark, and Denmark keeps cropping up in this story. Let's change the subject. How does Dougy Trotter fit into this? Dougy is married to Bobs' sister, but that doesn't mean that Bob and Billy have to take him along does it? Since they are taking him along then he must have some value to them. We know Dougy has done time in Durham jail. We know he does burglary. What else does he do?"

"Maybe we can check with Durham Jail and find out who he had contact with while he was inside. That might tell us something."

"Good idea John. You do that......Thanks a lot"

The waitress had arrived with the beer. She bent over and put them on the coffee table. Watkins noted her cleavage, and the small amulet dangling from a silver chain, pressed by her bosom against the inside of the white blouse she was wearing. Her fingers were long and thin, with carefully manicured nails. On her left wrist was a ladies wristwatch with a silver buckle. He noticed that the watch said quarter to eight. She stood upright and left. Watkins followed her with his eyes. Quarter to eight, there was something special about that time..... bugger! I'm supposed to pick up Gina at eight! She'll murder me if I'm late.

"Sorry, I've got to go! I had almost forgotten that I promised to pick up Gina at eight and take her to the pictures."

"Go on then and don't forget to say thanks from me. Don't worry about the beer, I'll clear that away before I leave."

"Thanks. See you in the morning!"

"Don't be late! We've got a lot to do tomorrow!"

Wailes said loudly to Watkins' back. Watkins waved back without turning around, and without stopping to put on his overcoat. Wailes sat back and drank his beer slowly. There were still many questions to be asked and the night was still young.

"The more I think about it, the more I'm convinced that all the members of this little group are playing a major role in what is going on."

Wailes turned away from the window and faced the room. Watkins was sitting beside the door, with his arms resting on the back of the chair. Albert Simmons was sitting on the corner of the desk, with a mug of tea in his hand. A flip-over stood in the corner. Wailes went over to it, screwed the cap off the red pen and drew a small circle with a question mark inside in the centre of the paper.

"This is the plot. The only thing we know about the plot is the way in which it interacts with people and things outside. After all, a plot without action or connections is no plot at all. Okay, connected to this plot we have four known people, Bob Wood, Doug Trotter, Brian Wallis and Billy Thomson. Lets call them A, B, C and D." He wrote their names and tags in the upper right hand corner of the flip-over and drew four small circles, each with a letter in it, and connected them to the circle in the middle with an unbroken line.

"Then we have a possible connection, Paul Anderson. Let's call him E."

He added Anderson's name to the list and connected his small circle to the centre circle with a dotted line.

"Let's take them one at a time and see what we now know for sure."

He turned the page on the flip-over and wrote - Doug Trotter in the upper left hand corner.

"John, the latest news please."

Watkins stood up, went over to the flip-over, took the pen from Wailes, who then sat down in Watkins chair.

"Right. The latest news on Doug Trotter is that he did six months for burglary in Durham jail two years ago. While he was there, he was in the same cell block as Ben Avery the narcotics smuggler, Harry Rawlings the bank robber, George Porter the arsonist, Allan Smythe the forger, Terry Samuels, who was the armorer for an east London gang who tried to take over gambling operations in Newcastle a couple of years ago. There was a number of small fish in the cell block too."

Watkins wrote the names on the flip-over as he said them.

"Doug is married to Beryl Wood, Bob Wood's sister."

"Was he married to her before he went inside and did he have a criminal record before the burglary bit ?" Simmons asked.

"Yes, he's been married to Beryl for four years. Before the burglary charge he had a clean sheet, hadn't even had a parking ticket. What are you getting at Albert."

"Just a thought. Maybe his being done on a burglary charge was arranged so that he could get in touch with one, or even more of the professions he did time with."

"That's possible."

Watkins turned the flip-over back to the first page, and wrote Narcotics, Banks, Arson, Forgery, Guns, on the list of names, gave each a letter and put each letter in a small circle attached by an unbroken line to Doug Trotters' letter. Then he wrote Beryl Wood, connected Doug Trotters' letter and Beryl Woods' letter to Bob Woods' letter with an unbroken line. Everybody looked at it without a word, until Wailes said,

"I think you may be right Albert. Go on John."

Watkins turned the pages of the flip-over to the next empty page and wrote Bob Wood in the upper left hand corner.

"I got Bob Wood's military record this morning. He did time in a military prison two years ago for drunken driving. Other than that, he did a short stretch for beating up an officer in a pub brawl, and another stretch for driving a tank under the influence. It seems Bob likes his drink, and when he drinks too much he gets violent." He wrote - Bob likes drink, gets violent -on the flip-over.

"He did eight years in the Armoured Corps, two and a half in Northern Ireland. He was wounded twice, received the Northern Ireland Service Medal. When he came out, he had various jobs as a security guard, but couldn't really settle down. A year and a half ago, he came into contact with the National Front. We know that, because he was arrested along with a lot of other NF supporters at a rally by Greys' Monument last summer. They smashed a few windows, made a general nuisance of themselves, that kind of stuff."

He wrote - Irish medal, eight years army, security guard and NF on the flip-over.

"We also know that Bob has a drivers license, and that he bought himself a blue Ford Thames van three months ago from the used car salesman at the Wheatsheaf corner, on the north side of the

Sunderland Bridge. I've got the registration number written down in the file."

He wrote - Blue Ford Thames - on the flip-over then turned to a new page and wrote Billy Thomson in the upper left hand corner.

"I got Billy Thomson's army records this morning as well. We guessed right when we said that he was in around the same time as Bob Wood. Billy did eight years as well, although the two weren't in the same unit. Billy was with a recon unit in West Germany for three years, driving Saracen armoured cars along the Berlin Wall, and get this.... He was arrested once in a pub brawl in Schackenburg, or something like that. It seems he and a bunch of German neo-nazis were throwing some Turks out into the street and kicking them around a bit. The owner called the police. Billy was locked up overnight then released to his unit. He was in close arrest for a week, then sent back to work."

He wrote - Army, Berlin Wall, Pub-brawl, Neo-nazis - on the flip-over, then turned back to the front page and joined Billy Thomson's letter to Bob Woods' letter with an unbroken line. Then he joined Billy Thomson's and Brian Wallis' letters to Beryl Wood's letter with unbroken lines.

"The connection between Billy, Brian and Beryl is because the neighbour, Mrs. Gray, told me that Billy had left Beryl and Dougy's place along with Dougy, Bob and Brian. So Beryl Wood certainly knows all four of them well."

"Maybe she knows where they go when they disappear."

Simmons said, and slurped his tea again. Watkins hated that sound, but the idea was good enough. Wailes said nothing, but nodded agreement.

"Right Albert, that's worth looking into! Okay, now we have two foreigners, Black and Erik, of whom we know absolutely nothing except that they take part in an operation at the Provincial Bank in Sunderland, along with Brian Wallis and Peter Lennox. In fact, it seems that the foreigners lead the operation. So obviously there is a connection between Scandinavia and the Sunderland gang. Since Bob and Bill are closely connected to nazi organisations, I phoned our embassy in Denmark and had a chat with the ambassadors' assistant, Joan Higgs. I asked her about nazi organisations. I didn't know that Denmark is the only place in Europe where nazi organisations are legal! Do you know, they actually move around the streets openly over there! Must be something to do with the promiscuous society."

Wailes took over. Watkins sat on the window ledge after opening the window to let in a little fresh air. A bulldozer was moving around in the coal yard down below, pushing the huge mounds of coal around, sorting them into smaller piles, each with its own destination.

"Right. What we're looking at here is a big-time, European neo-nazi organisation. It's highly organised and international. Let's assume Bob Wood and Billy Thomson are old mates, even before they join the army. Bob ends up with the National Front. Billy gets involved with neo-nazis in Germany. Bob's brother-in-law, Doug Trotter, gets himself arrested so that he can make contact with criminal elements inside Durham jail. It's safe to assume that Doug is also a member of the gang, although whether or not he too is a member of the National Front is uncertain. The neo-nazis are getting organised and making contacts inside the criminal world. Contacts that give them expertise in the way of bank robbing, arson, forgery etc. It is also safe to assume that they have made contacts which will enable them to get hold of weapons, weapons which we know Bob and Bill are able to handle because of their army backgrounds. Bob was wounded twice, Billy patrolled the Berlin Wall, so again it's safe to assume that both of them have the will to use any weapons they have. Beryl knows all of them, perhaps she has even met or housed the two foreigners, Erik and Black. We'll have to take her in and find out what she knows. Whatever, when we find the gang, they are almost certainly armed and very dangerous, so we'd better tread carefully and take the anti-terror boys with us once we've located them. The next thing is Paul Anderson. I rang my old boss in London before I came to work this morning. He wouldn't say much, but everything points to Paul Anderson being a member of the Lithuanian Mafia."

Simmons and Watkins exchanged glances, and raised eyebrows. Wailes noticed, but didn't stop.

"I was also informed that Paul Anderson has left Denmark and returned to Lithuania, along with a small group. Two members of this group are our old friends, Black and Erik!"

Wailes wasn't normally the theatrical type, but occasionally he just couldn't resist the temptation to throw a hand-grenade into a conversation. Watkins sat up straight. Simmons put his mug on the table and stood up.

"So what we're looking at is the Lithuanian Mafia teaming up with European neo-nazis, who are very busy making contacts in the criminal world. That's over my head! Maybe this should be a case for MI6, not three men in a back room of the Bewcastle police station! You don't mind if I go out and pee, do you?"

"I would too, in your shoes. Go on then, we'll carry on."

Wailes said. Simmons left. Watkins got off his perch and came round Wailes. Both stood looking at the flip-over for a few seconds in silence. Then Wailes said,

"Destroy all the evidence here at the station John. We don't want leaks, and we don't want surprises. Do it right away, now. I'll ring Harry and get him to pick up Beryl Wood. I want to talk to her. Let me know as soon as you're finished - don't bother telling Simmons, we'll be limiting his role from now on."

"Yes, sir. Immediately."

"Good man." Said Wailes.

"Just one question. If some British nazis are teaming up with the Lithuanian Mafia, and the Mafia is getting contacts in the European criminal world, what are the nazis getting?"

Wailes looked down at him and said solemnly, "I think my old mate Bill Lennox knows the answer to that one! But for now we're going to have to cut this particular link."

Smith wasn't at all happy. Oh yes it had been good to visit his family, or what was left of it after all these years of wandering about. Yet another cousin had died, an aunt too, and his old school friend Yuri was lying in the hospital recovering from three bullet wounds he had received on the Klaipeda docks. The only positive things about the whole episode was that Yuri was still alive, and that the container had not been completely stripped of its contents. Yuri would be taken care of. The big problem was what to do about the arms and ammunition that had disappeared. Anyway, the new plan that had been devised and discussed in Alexandreiavich's living room over an open fire and Stolnichnaya had been initiated. There was no going back now, however unpopular they may become for the time being in the West.

Dick Brown, Erik, Black, Mogensen and Hansen were all laid out in the front room of the summer house when Smith returned. He parked the car among the bushes and pressed the bell on the gate. A thick-set man in his forties came round the corner of the house with a Kalashnikov automatic rifle slung over his shoulder, and a Doberman which was straining on the leash he held in his hand. When he saw that the man at the gate was Smith, he tied the dog to the water pipe with a tap on top, which was sticking up out of the ground by the corner of the house. He hurried across and opened the gate. Smith entered without saying a word. The man smiled and nodded to him as he walked by and entered the house through the veranda door. The place smelled heavily of beer and cigarettes. The five occupants were sprawled in the various positions in which they had fallen during last nights' party. Hansen was curled up in a foetus position on the rug in front of the fireplace. Mogensen was lying face down under the table surrounded by empty beer bottles. Erik and Black were unconscious on the sofa. Dick Brown was draped over an armchair with his head back and his mouth open. There were food wrappers, cans, boxes all over the place. Don't they ever clean up? Smith asked himself, while he was hanging his rain-coat on a peg by the door. He picked up an empty beer can and shook it. Something solid rattled around inside. It was the ring-pull. Smith went around the house opening all the windows. There was absolutely no movement of air outside, so it was going to take some time to get rid of the stench. When he was finished, he boiled water, made coffee and sat down on the window ledge to drink some, with his feet up on the ledge too. Smith had been enjoying the view for a couple of minutes, when suddenly there was a flurry of activity outside. A big, red tomcat came round the corner at full speed and headed for the bushes by the main gate. Ten yards behind came the Doberman, trailing its lead, and barking loud enough to awake the dead. The guard was last. The tomcat shot through the space between two of the bars on the gate. The Doberman had to sit down to brake. It stuck its head through the space where the cat had gone through and kept on barking as loud as it could until the guard got hold of its leash and dragged it back into the garden. As he dragged it away, the dog kept looking around, hoping to catch another glimpse of the tomcat.

There were stirrings in the room. Brown was sitting up, and rubbing the back of his neck with his left hand. There was a deep furrow in the arm of the armchair. He had been laying like that a long time. Erik was yawning and stretching and making strange chewing grimaces. His mouth felt like the bottom of a budgies' cage. He shook Black, who awoke with a start, made to get up, then fell back again clutching his head. Mogensen was coming to himself among the bottles and Hansen had stopped clutching three empty beer bottles in to his chest and was getting ready to sit up. The five of them had one thing in common - they moaned, and coughed as if their lungs were about to split wide open.

Brown was the first to notice Smith sitting in the open window. He didn't say anything, but just waved a good morning at him. Smith laughed loudly and waved back. What a pitiful sight they all are! He thought. When he laughed, the others noticed him. Everyone except Mogensen was by now making his way to the coffee pot. Mogensen was hurrying to the toilet in the back.

It was warm outside, and dry. The morning dew had risen and gone its way long ago, so the leaves on the trees and bushes seemed to be dusty. Smith looked up. There were one or two wisps of stratocumulus, but the sky was predominantly blue and contained nothing which could suggest that it was going to rain that day. It was good to have survived another winter. It was good to witness the coming of another spring. A pair of blackbirds were building a nest in a tree opposite his window. He watched them fly off and bring back twigs. They didn't fly directly to the nest, but landed on a branch a few feet away, and surveyed the territory for a few moments before finally taking turns to deliver their load and fly off for another. Blackbirds are very clever birds - he thought.

"Morning Mr. Smith" Black said. Smith turned around, away from the tranquility of the garden. He got down from his perch and crossed the room to the armchair that was empty. All of the others, except for Brown, had already lit the first cigarette of the day. Mogensen had just poured himself coffee.

"Well gentlemen, I see you've been enjoying yourselves. That's the spirit!"

He looked slowly at each man in turn. Mogensen was leaning on the mantle, drinking his coffee and coughing. Hansen was sitting on the arm of the sofa. Black was standing behind the other armchair, where Brown was sitting comfortably, waiting. Erik was sitting in the middle of the sofa.

"I'm sorry about the delay in my return. It should have been two days, but turned out to be five. Things here are not as they should be, I'm afraid - so there has been a change of plan." The coughing stopped.

"It seems that the man who was arranging for our organisations' take-over of the ex-Russian garrison which we had intended to use as a base, has been shot dead in an ambush outside his home in Vilnius. We suspect that our competitors have discovered our plan and are attempting to spoil it. We will of course, replace this man eventually, but that may take several weeks. In the mean time, we are faced with having to make a quick decision. Do any of you have experience with navigating ships?"

Brown waited for someone else to say something, but when none of them answered, and it looked as though Smith was about to say something more, he said.

"I have. I sailed as a skipper on merchant vessels for three years. If the boat's good enough, and the engine runs okay, and the charts are in order, then I have no problem with that."

Black and Erik looked first at each other, and then at Brown.

"You're full of surprises, Dick!"

"Ain't I just ?"

"Alright. That is excellent."

Smith was genuinely pleased.

"And it solves our little problem. We have a coaster laying up in the docks at Klaipeda. You and our English friends have paid for a large shipment of weapons. These weapons are in our possession, in a container which is also waiting at the docks in Klaipeda. It is possible that our competitors will attempt to find these weapons and relieve us of them, so we must get these weapons on board and out of the country as soon as possible, today if we can! So I suggest that you all go and pack. I have to go into town and make the necessary arrangements for your trip. I'll be back in two hours, so be ready."

Smith left without saying another word. On his way out, he stopped just long enough to put on his rain-coat, even though it wasn't raining. In the doorway, he turned and beckoned to Brown, who got up, obviously painfully, and followed him outside. Smith closed the door. The two men walked towards the front gate.

Inside, it was some time before anyone said anything, they just stood and looked at each other and at the door which had closed behind Smith and Brown. Then Hansen said,

"Maybe they're trying to cheat us."

"Of what?" Black said, nonchalantly. "We're going to get weapons and so are our mates in England. I wonder what they are..... Ah, shit, it doesn't make any difference!"

Hansen looked across at Black, who had come around from the back of the armchair and was standing on the rug in front of the fireplace, with his arms folded.

"It's the first I've heard of us getting any weapons! How do you figure that one out? The English have paid for them already. Do you know how much they paid?"

Black smirked and felt proud of himself. "Yep....." He didn't complete the sentence, but waited a long while for the inquiry - "Well, how much?

"Two million dollars." He said. Everybody but Erik looked astounded. Steen Hansen whistled.

"Where did they get money like that? Not in the tea kitty that's for sure!"

"Me and Erik and a couple of lads in England robbed a bank about a month ago. What a holiday that turned out to be! It was a laugh. The money was to cover a container of arms and ammunition. Half of it for the English and the other half for us. Mikael, do me a favour and see what's going on outside. Let me know if you hear anything, and when Brown comes back."

Mogensen walked across to the partly open window, seated himself on the window ledge, and lit a cigarette. It sounded like Black didn't trust Brown. Brown and Smith were standing by the front gate, talking. The man and the dog were nowhere to be seen.

"Now I know the English have paid for their half of the weapons, but there's no reason why we shouldn't help ourselves to a few more of them on the way over there, is there?"

"Oh yes there is!"

Erik interjected.

"Hammel always keeps his promises. We should too, if we don't want to wake up in a dustbin one morning with our throats cut!"

"Scared Erik ?" Black asked

"Nope, just too clever to renege on a deal. Them lads in England did a good bit of work. If it hadn't been for them, we would never have got in and out without anybody being the wiser. If it hadn't been for Brian, we'd never have got into the computer. If it hadn't been for Beryl putting us up for a fortnight it would have cost us a fortune. Need any more convincing?"

Black dropped his guard and thrust his hands into his pockets. He looked straight at Erik.

"You're right Erik. We'd be letting our mates down if we cheated them out of what was rightfully theirs. Hammel wouldn't have anything to do with it either."

Then he turned to the others and said,

"Let's pack, this place is getting on my nerves!"

Black had not changed his attitude. As he was pushing clothes into his travelling bag in one of the back bedrooms, he was considering the future, a future without his good old mate Erik, and anyone else who got in the way before they reached home.

Just opposite the white cross there is a big textile factory. When the border of Lithuania with Russia closed, the flow of raw materials to Lithuania stopped. The Russians wanted money for their goods these days. Mind you, the flow of farm products the other way had also stopped, which meant that Lithuania, although poor and with a dilapidated, antiquated industrial sector, was largely able to feed itself. But there was no work at the textile factory. So it closed. The buildings fell into disrepair, the grass grew out of control except for two circles where a little, crooked old woman with a scarf kept two cows pegged. She came by every day to milk them, but for some reason or other the cows had given less milk the last five or six days. Still, there was enough for the family so there was no reason to complain.

The factory was completely empty. All the machinery and all the furniture had been removed. The doors were intact and so were the windows, although the latter were very dirty indeed, both inside and out. There were big chains with padlocks on all of the doors and iron bars outside the windows. The cellar windows were boarded up. Once in a while an armed guard came by to shake the chains and check that the windows had not been broken. He didn't have keys to the chains, so he never went in. Why should he? The place was empty.

Britta Nielsen was quite comfortable, considering the circumstances. She had an air mattress and a warm sleeping bag laid out just under the big window on the first floor, north face of the building, overlooking the cross. She had cooking gear, water in ten litre plastic bottles and a supply of milk just outside. She had a backpack filled with rations, a pair of binoculars and a Mini Maglite which she rarely used. She had money in her pockets. But most important of all, she had a loaded revolver for protection.

The most difficult part of this job was the boredom. Following the minibus across Germany, Poland and Lithuania, now that had been fun! Maybe one day I'll write my memoirs and tell all about it! No - that wouldn't do. Gordon, I wish you could see me now! She whispered to herself while looking up at the ceiling where the cables which had held factory lights dangled, empty. A finch landed on the window ledge outside. She lifted her head just over the edge and looked at it. After a few seconds, the bird hopped forward along the ledge. Britta noticed for the first time that there was a nest in the corner of the ledge where it met one of the concrete pillars. There were three very small and very blind chicks in it, waiting with their beaks open and upward. She watched them being fed for a while. It was sunny outside, although here on the north side of the building there was shade. It really couldn't be a better location for an observation post - Although I would like to know what's going on in there... She checked her log book. The last two entries said - eleven fifteen Smith arrives in minibus - and - eleven fifty Smith departs in minibus. She checked the entrance with the binoculars one more time. There was no movement out of the ordinary. She checked her wrist-watch. It said fourteen thirty. She checked the entrance again. While she was looking, the minibus arrived and drove in. Once inside, she could follow it for the first hundred yards or so, although it was partially obscured by hedges and fruit trees. She lost is as it turned the corner. Britta logged the event in her book. Perhaps something is about to happen. I'd better pack, just in case!

It took Britta just ten minutes to pack, although it was a feverishly active ten minutes during which she had to keep an eye on the entrance across the road. When she was finished, she dragged the backpack full of food across to the top of the stairs, making sure to keep low, and keeping her ears open for the sound of a car engine, any car engine. She came back for the water and the other backpack with clothes, but left the plastic bucket with milk. One last check of the entrance. An old woman with an empty shopping bag was coming down the path from inside. She checked her watch. It was the same old woman she'd seen come down the path at the same time every day these last five days. Britta hurried back to the top of the stairs. Three times she had to make the trip two flights down to the cellar. Three times she wondered both if it was worth the trouble and if she was going to be in time. But when she checked the entrance for one last time, there was still no activity.

Britta had parked the car in an alley just inside the summer house area, outside a summer house which had seemed empty and from where she could see the window on the first floor of the factory across the road. She had waited until dark, then sneaked over to the factory to check it out, carrying a crowbar and with the revolver in her pocket. There were six cellar windows on the south side of the building, away from the road. She had carefully prised off three boards from one of the windows, removed the nails, and nailed the three boards onto one of two pieces of wood she had found lying in the grass. Then she had crawled inside and pulled the makeshift door into the hole behind her, locking it in place with the second piece of wood. She guessed that her entry wouldn't be detected. She had guessed right, although the first night she hadn't slept at all well and had kept the revolver very close to hand. The second night had been alright. By then she knew that the guard didn't open the chains on the doors and didn't pay very close attention to the cellar windows.

All that had happened at night. But this was daylight. She thought once more about giving away her hiding place, decided there was nothing to do about it, and pushed open her secret door to the cellar. It really was sunny on this side of the house. She took a pair of sunglasses from the top pocket of her jacket and put them on.

The minibus left the summerhouse, and drove out onto the road to Marijampole, where it turned left. The floor was again filled with baggage. Smith was driving. Brown was sitting in the back, head on one side, looking out of the window. For a second he found himself wondering if Britta was still there. Then he forgot her again. After all, if she is there, then she'll have noticed we've pulled up our tent pegs and follow. If for some reason she's lost us, then she'll have turned around and headed for home. Either way, she'll be alright and so far I haven't needed her. I'll have to find a way to check whether or not she is still with me when we get to the boat.

"Want a beer ?"

Steen Hansen asked from the seat opposite.

"I don't mind if I do. Thanks Steen."

He took the bottle, drank deeply, and relaxed back into his chair. It was going to take a couple of hours to get to Klaipeda.

The minibus turned onto the down ramp going west, towards Klaipeda, and joined the light traffic going that way. Two minutes later, a green Fiat came down the same ramp, accelerated to get ahead of a truck, then tucked itself in behind a row of cars with lots of space between them. Britta Nielsen's hunch that something was about to happen had paid off. She lit a cigarette and felt very pleased with herself. Where are we off to now ? She said aloud to the car and got no reply.

There is an old saying that nothing feels as dead as a ship unused. The same thing may be said of Klaipeda harbour. It is a large port, with all the cranes, buildings, railroad tracks and cabins associated with a port of this size. In the past, Klaipeda was a major port of shipment for Russian freighters, but these days the traffic has shrunk to less than half of what it used to be. Large areas are as inert, abandoned, quiet as the grave. Thick tufts of rubbery grass push up through the dirty gravel along the railway lines. Rust is heavy on the tracks that the big cranes used to run on before history caught up with them.

The minibus stopped at the gateway and a short, plump, middle-aged man in a blue uniform with a very official-looking peaked cap, came out of the watch-house. Smith rolled down the window and said something. Then he pushed his papers through the gap. The man didn't bother looking at them. He just removed the ten dollar bill that lay under the bunch of papers he had received and pushed it quickly into his pocket. Then he handed the papers back to Smith, smiled, took two steps backward and waved the minibus in. As they drove through the gate, Brown looked back. A green Fiat stopped on the opposite side of the road. Brown noticed that the woman behind the wheel was a blonde. Christ - she impresses me that woman! You know what old son? She's the best thing on two legs you've seen in a long time. But how will she manage to get in? Paying the guard is no problem, but she doesn't speak the language. Whatever happens, she'll have to be on that boat along with the rest of us when we sail!

The minibus trundled over a couple of railway tracks and drove along the north side of the main quay. Smith had to be careful, because a freighter was loading huge rolls of paper and they lay here and there all along the quay. Three fork lift trucks were busy moving the rolls alongside the freighter and into a crane harness hanging from one of the ships' cranes. The funnel was cream, with a red band around the top and a yellow hammer and sickle painted in the middle of the band. Some hadn't bothered to change their insignia yet. A few stevedores were hanging around, some smoking, others sweeping the quay, nobody seemed very interested in what was happening. But then again, it is hard to be interested in manual labour when it only pays twenty dollars a month! Nobody was keen to work. As the minibus passed the bow of the ship, Brown noticed the name 'General Karbychev' painted in big, white letters on the black hull. The minibus drove on. There was no sign of the green Fiat. At the end of the quay, which was formed like a huge box with two entrances at one end, one on each side, Smith turned left. Everyone was looking out of the windows. Dick could see all the way up the length of the main dock. There were only two ships tied up alongside, one on each side of the dock. The minibus followed a gravel track that was obviously not used very often, by the grass and dandelions that grew up from between the cobbles. Then it turned left and bumped its way along a short stretch of rusting railway line until it came to an old, two-story, red-brick house on a wharf. To the left of the house, a ZIL truck with a large fuel tank mounted firmly on the chassis behind the cab, was parked. A thick, black rubber hose stuck out from the rear end and disappeared behind the building. Smith drove up to the building and parked behind the tanker. He stopped the engine and turned to the others.

"Stay here until I come back. I'm going to make sure everything is alright."

Then he got out and closed the door, leaving the key in the ignition. Black slid across into the drivers' seat. The tankers' engine was running. Dick guessed that it was bunkering whatever lay, out of sight on the other side of the building.

When Smith reappeared in the doorway of the building, he was accompanied by another man, who was wearing dirty overalls, a heavy jacket and a fur cap with flaps that dangled around his ears. The other man was pulling on a pair of working gloves. Smith and the stranger exchanged a few more words, then the stranger walked off and disappeared on the other side of the tanker. Smith approached the minibus and opened the passenger side door. First he looked across at Black, then down the length of the bus. All eyes were upon him. After a few seconds, he smiled broadly, and said..

"Everything is according to plan. The ship will be refuelled in a few minutes. Stay in the bus until the tanker leaves. When he's gone, move your things as quickly as possible into the office here. Leave the bus outside with the keys in the ignition. I'll be using it later. When you've got your gear stowed in the office, Dick, come aboard. I'll meet you in the captains quarters. Everybody else stays in the office until it gets dark. The less activity there is, the less attention we will draw to ourselves."

"If anyone was watching, they'd notice the tanker, and the hoses."

Hansen said. Smith scowled at him.

"Probably, but there's no reason to make things worse is there?"

Hansen shrugged and pulled a packet of cigarettes from the top pocket of his jacket. Not that he needed a smoke, but it was just as good an excuse as any to avoid Smiths' eyes. Brown, who was lying spread-eagled on the baggage in the back, turned to Black and said,

"Back the bus up to the door of the office. If you leave just enough room to open the back doors, we can move the gear in without anybody knowing any better."

Smith nodded approval, shut the door with a clang that reverberated around the thin metal structure, and strode off around the northern end of the building. Black started the engine and moved the bus into position. He wasn't at all happy that Brown was taking over. He scowled and crashed the gearbox. Once at sea, things might be different!

The inside of the office was dark, gloomy, and smelled of damp. What had, judging from the number of windows from the outside, seemed to be a long building with several rooms in it, turned out to be just three rooms. When they started moving the gear inside, Brown was in the forefront. He decided to have a look around while the others were busily unpacking the minibus.

All the windows had been painted over from the inside in the office section, where Brown was standing. There were four desks, all empty, a few kitchen chairs that seemed to have escaped from a jumble sale twenty years ago. Two of them had no back. The floor was bare and there were splashes of fluid in a trail from the door in the opposite wooden wall. There was also a collection of splashes by one of the desks. Brown went over to it and poked about in the ash tray with the little finger on his left hand. They weren't old ashes. There were about a dozen cigarette ends in the ash tray. They had been smoked recently. There was some fluid on the chair beside the desk. Brown touched the patch with the next finger on his left hand and lifted it up to his nostrils. It smelled of heavy fuel oil. So the bowser driver had been waiting here for some time for either Smith or the vessel to arrive. There was no sign of food wrappings, or tea cups, or even a place to get hot water for that matter. Brown rummaged around in the drawers and cupboards of the desk. There was nothing, not a single scrap of paper. He tried one of the others. Hansen watched him from a distance as he opened each of the three drawers in turn and closed them again.

"What are you looking for Dick?"

He asked. Brown looked up casually.

"Just wondering how often they use this place. There's no sign that they use it very often."

Hansen shrugged and went out the door again. Half a minute later, all the others, except for Smith, who still hadn't returned, came in. Black closed the door behind him. The room got dark, until Black turned on the light switch. There was still power, at least enough to feed the one single light bulb hanging in the middle of the ceiling. Brown was sitting on the corner of the desk just between the two exits. He lit a cigarette. Erik started looking around the room. Black was standing to one side of the door, leaned up against the wall, watching Brown.

Erik came back. "What do you think is going to happen now?"

He asked Brown in passing. Brown drew deep on the cigarette, then blew the smoke out through his nostrils before he answered. He was looking at Erik, but could see through the corner of one eye that Erik's question irritated Black. Everybody else was passive. It occurred to Brown that there was the tiniest bit of a rift appearing between Black and Erik, although it looked as though Erik didn't know it yet. With the right attention, maybe that rift could become a canyon.

"Well, when we've all settled in here, I'll go on board and have a chat with Smith, who I suppose will put me in the picture as far as the ship is concerned. He'll probably show me around and point out where things are. That'll take at least five or six hours. Then I'll check out the container we're shipping, and the rendezvous plans. By then it'll be dark, so I'll come and fetch you lot."

He dropped the cigarette end on the floor, stood up and stamped it out, making sure to rub it firmly into the wood with the toe of his right foot.

"Just one thing though."

He said demonstratively,

"Once we leave this port, and until our journey is completed, there's only one captain on board, and that's me! Anybody got anything against that?"

He looked directly at Black. Everyone else saw that he did. Black saw that he did. Black was furious, and showed it, but he didn't say anything at all, nor did he make any movement. He remained against the wall by the entrance. Brown let his gaze rest on Black for just a moment longer, then let it wander over to Erik, by which time it had softened considerably. Erik was glad that Brown liked him, which was apparent from the way he looked. He was happy not to receive a glare like that which Black had been on the receiving end of. Erik had known all along that Black didn't trust Brown, after all, he had made no secret of the matter, although it was difficult to see at which point in their acquaintance Blacks mistrust had turned to hate.

None of the others had any objections. They looked at each other and nodded. It was decided then, Brown was the boss, at least during the sea voyage. Suddenly there was silence outside the office building. For the first time since their arrival, the tanker pumps had stopped. Bunkering was completed. Brown checked his watch. The few minutes Smith had promised had become more than an hour. He hoped there would be enough fuel on board for the journey home without stops. The driver of the tanker uncoupled the thick rubber hose from the filler goose-neck in the scuppers of the Professor Petrov and lowered it to the quayside using the hose derrick welded to the deck close by. The gangplank was wobbly, and rattled heavily as he hurried down, with both hands on the railing and short strides that more resembled hops than paces. When he had uncoupled the wire from the bolt hole in the big steel flange at the end of the hose, he retreated quickly to the tanker and started the engine again. After he had done that, he came round to the rear of the vehicle and started pulling the hose back and over its reel. It was manual work, and dirty, but he was a heavy man and obviously accustomed to it. No more than three minutes elapsed before the tanker was trundling back across the dockyard, on its way to the front gate. He hadn't bothered reeling in the wire from the crane derrick. There was no time.

A couple of minutes later, Brown left the office through the rear door, the one facing the quayside, and got a look at the Professor Petrov for the first time in his life.

"What a bloody rust-bucket!"

He murmured aloud to himself. He looked around. Nobody was in sight. The whole dock area was completely deserted. Then Brown started walking up the quayside to the bows of the coaster, on a tour of inspection of the hull that lasted until he had seen enough to convince him that just keeping her afloat until she reached England was going to be a major undertaking. This must surely be her last trip. He doubted very much that she would be able to make the trip back, but then again, who would crew her if she was going to? Perhaps some other bunch of idiots who are wheeling and dealing!

The Professor Petrov had indeed seen much better days. Ninety meters long at the waterline and fifteen meters across, she drew three meters at the bow and five meters at the stern, showing that she was unloaded and as yet had taken in no ballast. There were no visible holes in the hull, although there were several places where the metal skin looked decidedly thin and battered, one where it looked as though she had hit a concrete bollard at some point in time. It was difficult to tell when that could have been, because the sea corrodes unpainted steel surprisingly rapidly, and there was almost no paint left on the hull at all. The rudder seemed intact, and thick smudges of grease had issued from the rudder bearing. That at least was one consolation. The ship was held to the quayside by four moorings of old, heavy rope, the foremost going up the quayside from the bow cleat, while another came back down the quay in the opposite direction to another bollard. The rear springs were carried out in roughly the same manner, although in the reverse direction. There were no rat-plates on the ropes. Whoever had laid her to had not wasted time on niceties, and didn't consider the risk that those who were to sail her on the next leg of the trip might get bitten by rats as being very important.

Brown went on board. There were three cargo wells on deck, as well as the usual windlasses and two small cranes of the type used to load and unload pallets and nets containing general cargo. A sign on the side of one of them said 'Max 10 tons'. The container was not visible, so Brown assumed that it was probably in one of the cargo wells. It must be small for one of those cranes to be able to handle it. Hardly worth the price they paid, although if you count the price of the vessel and the bunkers, well, maybe you could come up to that level. All three cargo wells were battened down with wooden hatches covered by very heavy green tarpaulins with hammers and sickles painted on them in yellow. Ex-military stock tarpaulins. They too were in poor condition, holes here and there, especially around the iron rings where the fastening ropes were attached. It was obvious that they would fly off at the least sight of a big wave, and with the removal of the tarpaulins, the wooden slats that the hatch covers were comprised of, would fly off too. The Professor Petrov would not live very long after that happened. Brown climbed the lighter to the bridge two floors above the main deck. He noted that there was only one lifeboat and no life-rafts at all on the port side, the side which was laid to the quay. He walked around the back of the wheelhouse to the starboard side. No lifeboats or rafts. The Professor Petrov had enough lifeboat capability for Browns' little group, but only just, and only if it was in order. Brown decided that immediately they put to sea, he would have a closer look at the lifeboat, which was just as well, because when he eventually got round to it, it turned out that the rudder had to be repaired, the little inboard engine didn't work, and half the oars were missing.

Brown expected the worst when he entered the bridge, and got it. The wheel was intact, and the rudder indicator moved when he turned it, so that was okay. There were charts of the Baltic and North Sea, suitable for getting them where they were going. The VHF radio seemed to work. The navigation light panel behind the chart table seemed to work, although he went outside onto the bridge wing and looked up at the mast just to make sure. There were only two things missing. The radar, which had been removed, leaving only a piece of wave-guide dangling through the deck head and a foundation plate, and the auto pilot, which didn't seem to work at all. This was certainly going to be a heavy trip if all the steering had to be done by hand. None of the others knew how to steer, so they would have to be taught immediately, before the ship left port!

Brown left the bridge and went down the lighter. He found the captains' cabin easily. It was the one with the open door and the muffled sound of a local radio station coming out of it. Smith was there when he entered, having a nap on the sofa bolted to the bulkhead, using his raincoat as a pillow. There was half a bottle of Stolichnaya on the coffee table beside the sofa, and three dirty glasses turned upside down. Brown turned two of them the right way up, unscrewed the cap on the bottle, and poured two good measures. Smith awoke at the sound of the first gurgle, and sat up, heavily. Brown sat down in the chair across from Smith, with a glass in his hand.

"Have a good nap?" He asked pleasantly.

Smith rubbed his fingers through his hair. He did look a bit tired.

"Yes thank you. Have you had a good look around?"

He swigged his vodka, like a true vodka drinker should, and banged the glass down on the table as if calling for more.

"Just around the deck and the bridge. I haven't been down into the engine room yet."

"Don't bother. If you do that you'll not want to put to sea. You realise of course that we're not expecting to see the Professor Petrov again?"

"What do you mean by that?"

"Well, that rather depends on you, my friend. Let's face it Brown, you are different from the others. I saw that the second I clapped eyes on you. Oh, not just because of your age. I mean, you and I are cast from the same mould, or as you British would say - like two peas in a pod. The others with you are just children."

"Dangerous children." Brown said.

Smith laughed, and poured more vodka into his glass. Brown hadn't downed half of his as yet.

"Yes, surely, but just as dangerous to themselves as they are to others. You, on the other hand are not so. May I ask you a personal question?"

"Go right ahead."

"How did you ever get mixed up with these people?"

"Boredom I guess. My marriage went to hell while I was at sea. I have two sons. The eldest got killed in a car crash. I drank a lot, didn't know what to do with myself. Got kind of lost you might say. Then I saw a documentary about neo-nazis in Denmark on the telly. Did you know that Denmark is the only place where it is legal to be a nazi?"

Smith nodded. He did indeed. Brown didn't wait for more of a reply.

"Well, it surprised me. I'd never been to Denmark before, so I bought myself an old Morris in Newcastle and took a trip over there to find out for myself. It wasn't easy, because I don't speak the language, and didn't know who to ask, but the holiday was good anyway. One night I was sitting in a pub and three or four skinheads came in and started handing out leaflets. I got one of them, eventually got invited to one of their meetings, and bingo...and that's it really."

Smith was attentive.

"Ah, the greatest incentive to action that has ever existed... boredom. How many of us are in the same boat!"

He chuckled at the obvious pun he had made up on the spur of the moment, and swallowed a huge gulp of vodka. Then he sat back in the sofa and put both arms up on the back rest.

"Dick, I won't insult you by beating around the bush any longer. I have an offer to make to you, an offer which will make you a reasonably wealthy man. But I want you to keep this offer to yourself, whether or not you accept it. Will you do that?"

Brown hesitated for just long enough to show that he was wary, but not so long that Smith would get the impression that he wasn't really interested. Then he said.

"Yes, I'll keep it to myself. Let's hear your offer."

Smith took his arms down from the back rest, lifted his left knee, placing his left foot on the sofa, and clasped his hands around the knee. He was trying to appear relaxed.

"Firstly a very short story indeed. I had to return from England because of this container of arms and ammunition. An old friend, and my closest superior in the organisation was badly wounded by our enemies while the container was being landed just here on this very dockside. My chief requested my return to take over his post until he recovers and is well enough to continue his duties, which he will eventually do. However, this has forced me to start a clean-up campaign locally, and I would be rather pleased to get this cargo under way so that no further mishap can befall it. That would not be good for business."

"I can see your problem.... By the way, if you don't mind me asking, what ARE you looking for in England?"

"What are we looking for? We wish to expand our traditional operations into Europe. We are at this time heavily involved in obtaining high-class, very expensive cars and transporting them here, for shipment and sale throughout the Baltic, Poland and Russia. There is much money in this business. We are also moving gold and other precious metals, as well as diamonds, emeralds etc. You would also be surprised as to how much money can be made from the transport of genuine Russian caviar, which it is illegal for 'civilians' to export. On the whole we have many business operations."

"What about narcotics?"

"Yes, those too."

Smith was quite bland.

"They are, after all, just another commodity needed by some hungry, desperate people somewhere. A product like any other, to be produced, and sold at the highest price the market can afford. Do you have any particular affection for narcotics?"

Brown shook his head.

"Never touch the stuff. I'm not keen on it being offered to kids under the age of ten, but other than that, no, I can't say as I am either for or against it."

Smith smiled.

"My sentiments exactly, just another commodity. Anyway, as you can probably imagine, finding the right people for our network is rather difficult. We must therefore rely on locals with contacts in the right circles. There are two problems with that. Firstly, locals always believe that they can outsmart a foreigner on their patch, which indeed they often can. Secondly, they normally require payment of a kind not always possible for us to obtain at short notice... cash. I do hope I'm not boring you?"

"No, not at all, I'm all ears. "

Brown had emptied his glass. He took a packet of cigarettes from the top pocket of his jacket, took one, handed the packet across to Smith, who gladly accepted, and lit. Then he unscrewed the cap of the vodka bottle again and poured both him and Smith a drink. When he put the bottle on the table again, it was empty.

"Good. Well, finally I met a representative of a very small group, mostly ex-British Army, in the vicinity of Newcastle. This group did not want cash, they wanted arms and ammunition. Some crazy idea about starting a private army and getting rid of all coloured people in Great Britain by other than peaceful means. Anyway, that's their business. This came as a welcome break for us. We have no problems at all getting arms and ammunition. They, on the other hand have the contacts we need in the underworld, and will indeed perhaps also come in handy as enforcers one day when the time comes to put our own plan into action. There was an agreement of terms and a plan was set into action. Then they added more items to their shopping list, anti-tank missiles, laser ranging and night vision systems, stuff like that. This wasn't part of the agreement, but I told them that they could get all the extra items, and that we would arrange the transport and delivery to any place of their choice on the East Coat of Great Britain, if they paid for them in advance by transfer to our own bank in Kaunas. They did."

"But how do the Danes fit into all of this?"

"Nowhere really. They were merely my link to England, and as such are presently more of a pain in a certain place than they are anything else. You see, although the nazi party is legal in Denmark, the police intelligence network is also very efficient indeed. I doubt if any of your comrades are even aware that their headquarters has been bugged for the last several months."

Brown didn't ask how Smith knew that. He was obviously part of a very well informed network. Smith planted both feet firmly on the deck and stood up. He walked towards the cabin door, and back again, as if speculating about something. Brown waited patiently. Smith said suddenly,

"My first problem is that this shipment must reach its destination soon, in order to maintain the best of relations with our friends in England. The second problem is that because of the efficiency of the police intelligence squad, we are in the process of reducing Denmark to the position of a half-way house, so to speak. A place where one can stop off in relative safety during shipping operations. Our operation there is to be a purely Estonian one - no Danes involved - and on a very small scale indeed."

Brown looked up at him, dragged deeply on his cigarette and blew smoke through his nostrils. Then he shook his head and said without any sign of emotion at all.

"Seems to me then, that you've got at least five too many witnesses...!"

Inwardly Smith applauded. Outwardly, he tried to look very solemn indeed. The applause showed through though.

"Not exactly Dick - four too many witnesses. That's where you come in."

Smith sat down opposite Brown again.

"Firstly, I want you to make sure that the container gets to its destination...."

"Which is ?"

"I don't know. I left a chart of the Northumberland coast up on the chart table, with your destination marked by a red circle. You will be contacted again by radio when you are at that reference. Once you arrive there, stay until you receive further orders. You must somehow manage to get the Danes off the ship before you receive your orders. I don't want them to be on board when the delivery is made."

"That's not going to be easy. There are four of them and I'm not armed. On top of that, It'll be a hell of a job to sail the ship to its final destination on my own. I won't be able to dock her at all unless some of those friends of yours can come aboard and help me."

"I appreciate that. I really do. And to make it as easy as I possibly can, I have a couple of things for you. Let me call them - going away presents -"

Smith reached in under the sofa and pulled out an ancient sports bag. He dropped it on the coffee table. It looked heavy and sounded heavy when it hit the wood. He leaned over the bag and unzipped it. He put a hand inside, and when it came out, it held an AK74 assault carbine with a folded stock. There was no magazine attached. He placed it on the table beside the bag and delved inside again, this time with both hands. He came up with a handful of grenades, then a handful of magazines, then three unopened boxes of ammunition for the AK.

Brown whistled lightly .

"There's enough there to start a small war!"

Smith smiled.

"Yes indeed, and to make the war worth fighting, this is yours."

208

He showed Brown the other contents of the bag. Brown put in a hand and pulled out a wad of twenty pound notes. There were fifty of them in it. He looked into the bag, then looked up.

"How much is in there?"

"Thirty thousand pounds. The first of two equal instalments. You will receive the other after you have delivered the ship to her final destination, without the Danes."

Brown looked closely at a randomly chosen note from the middle of the wad he was holding. The light in the cabin had faded. It was almost dark. But he could still see that the note was genuine. Smith laughed. A hoarse laugh. He was genuinely amused.

"You're right. Counterfeiting is another of our operations. But you, my friend will not be cheated. You see, if you carry out this mission well, and survive to take delivery of the second half of your payment, then we shall come to see a lot of each other in the future. That is, of course, unless you don't like that idea."

Brown looked down into the sports bag again . Then he said.

"I like that idea very much indeed. You've got a deal Smith."

"You can call me Povl, now that we're partners."

Smith stuck out his hand and Brown took it. Afterwards, he dropped the money back into the bag along with the arsenal of weapons on the coffee table and pushed it across to Smith, who took it and gently slid it back under the sofa. When he looked up again, Brown asked,

"When do we leave?"

"Any time you like. You're the captain." Smith stood up, put on his rain coat and went to the cabin door. He turned in the doorway and said,

"Bon voyage Captain Brown - and good luck to us."

Then he was gone. Brown was still seated in the chair across from the sofa as the gangplank rattled to Smiths retreating footsteps. It was only after Smith had gone that Brown realised that he hadn't yet seen the container or inspected its contents.

"Oh, well, never mind we'll have time for that at sea!"

He said to an empty cabin. But for now, there was one more important thing to be done before bringing the others on board.

Chapter Elleven – Travelling Light

Billy Thomson sat on the front door step and smoked another cigarette. It was pitch black outside, with only thousands of stars overhead to give any light at all. It's only when you get away from the lights of town and buildings that you really begin to notice just how many stars there are, and how little all the troubles of this grain of sand we call earth really matter in the scheme of things. But moments like these are short. Just one headlight from one passing car is enough to swamp out thousands of tiny, distant pin-pricks at one fell swoop. It was just a little chilly, enough to make Billy put on a sweater before he stepped outside to get a breath of fresh air and just a moments' peace and quiet. The others were playing cards as usual on the other side of the curtain, in the living room. Billy got up and walked up the path towards the road, the cigarette end a bobbing red prick in the dark. It didn't matter that a car came by once in a while, because the front of the house was hidden from headlamps by the curve in the path and a copse of fur trees right on the corner. They must have been put there on purpose - he thought. Maybe the previous owners didn't want to be disturbed at night in their bedroom by people coming around the hill. He stopped among the trees and leaned with his back against one until the cigarette was finished.

They had been there a week now, and apart from the message they got from Paul two days ago putting them wise to the police visit to Beryl's place, they had heard nothing either on the radio or the TV. They didn't get the newspapers. It was too risky going into Bewcastle to get one, and too little to be gained by it. But somewhere out there, the cops had to be doing something... It would sure be nice to know what! A helicopter had over flown the house that afternoon. They had all rushed to their defensive positions inside the house and the barn. The danger had passed as quickly as it had come upon them, but it was not before more than an hour had passed before they began to relax again. Maybe the strain of uncertainty was getting to them all. Billy decided that it was about time to review their travel plans again. That would at least occupy some of the time and take their minds off the waiting for a bit. He dropped the cigarette and stubbed it out, then he walked back through the trees with his hands buried in his pockets and his shoulders drawn unconsciously up around his ears. It was colder than he had imagined. His body knew it, but his brain was somewhere else, at least for the time being. It was home with Allison in a nice, warm bed.

Billy entered the barn and crawled through the hole in the side of the house. The passageway smelled damp. It was dark except for a thin sliver of light coming through the open door to the living room. As he approached the door with hardly disguised steps, the conversation on the other side stopped for a second. He pushed open the door and went in. He was looking down the muzzle of an MP5. It did not surprise him. They had been a bit edgy since Paul's message.

"I'm having a cuppa, it's bloody cold outside!"

He said nonchalantly and went over to the burner. Bob Wood let the MP5 fall lightly onto the table. The card game resumed with as much vigour as it had had when Billy had left it a half hour ago. When he had made himself a cup of tea with boiling water and a Lipton's tea-bag, he went across to the table and sat down. Bob and Brian were in the process of losing their last pennies to Doug, so the game did not last for very much longer. Doug put the cards away in the table drawer, then they all sat looking at each other in silence for several seconds. It was normally about this point that the arguments started. Billy decided to head them off at the pass.

"Maybe it's about time we reviewed our plans again. Anybody got anything against that?"

"Haven't we looked at them enough?"

Brian Wallis asked, leaning back in his chair with one arm over the back-rest and both legs stretched out under the table. Bob Wood looked across at him and grimaced. It was Brian's fault he had lost the last two quid in his pocket to Dougy!

"You're no soldier Brian, or you'd know you can never check your plans often enough! Good idea Bill, let's get the maps out!"

He said looking sideways at Billy. Doug said nothing. He was happy with the takings and had stuffed them in his pocket as quickly as he could when the game was over. He shrugged and got up to boil more water. Billy got up and went across to his mattress. He opened the rucksack that was standing by his pillow, took out a thick, brown envelope and came back to the table. Bob hung the MP5 from its sling over the back of his chair, while Billy was opening the envelope and taking out its contents. When he was finished, he put the envelope on the floor under his chair.

"I think we'll do it a bit differently tonight, just for a change. I'll ask questions about the plans and I'll pick somebody to answer. If you get the answer right, we go on. If one answer is wrong, we go over the whole thing again. A bit like twenty questions."

"What's that?" Brian asked.

"Before your time Brian. Anyway, first question. Where is our rendezvous point for the first leg of the trip? Dougy."

"The ferry terminal at Hull. We have to be there...."

"That's enough Doug." Billy broke in. "You don't want to spoil the others fun now do you? What day and time do we have to be there together? Brian."

"In four days time at three in the afternoon.

"Right. Bob, fill in your travel details for the leg to Hull."

Bob was lighting a cigarette. He finished, put the pack of cigarettes down on the table and the lighter on top of it. Then he said,

"At eight in the morning I drive the van to Hull via Durham City and Doncaster, making sure to keep to the small roads and to stick to the speed limits. I'll have the guns and ammo in the back, hidden under the mattresses, with all our rucksacks on top. If I get stopped for any reason, I say I'm taking my scout groups' gear to the camp-site just outside Hull. When I get to the area around the ferry landing, I nose around a bit to see if there's anything suspicious, extra police etc, that might get in our way. It'll be about ten thirty by the time I get there. At eleven, I phone Paul, who will be waiting at home for my call. He calls you on the radio and confirms that everything is okay at my end. Then I take my place in the ferry queue and wait."

"Good. What do we do then.... Brian."

"When I receive Paul's message that everything is okay with Bob, We dismantle the radio gear and pack it in the VW. We'll have already packed the rest of the gear, so that shouldn't take more than fifteen minutes. Then we leave for Hull, travelling over Newcastle and Sunderland, then down through Stockton to Hull. If everything goes according to plan, we'll join the ferry queue at about three o'clock."

"Yes. Dougy, what happens if Bob doesn't get in touch with Paul?"

"We pack up the radio and scarper. We find another place to hole up in, somewhere we know Bob doesn't know about, so he'll be free to tell the fuzz anything he likes."

"Alright, it sounds good so far. What do we do when we get off the ferry at Hoek-van-Holland. Bob"

"We team up outside the harbour and head for Frankfurt-am-oder. From there we cross the border to Poland and drive through Warsaw to the Lithuanian border. "

"Right. When we get up in that area there are two border crossings, Which one do we take Brian?"

"We take the one reserved for military traffic. There is a guard posted there. The guard will have been paid by our contact man to let us through. The contact man will meet us on the other side."

"How do we prove to the guard that we are the right people Doug?"

"We show him the hand sign that Anderson gave us, then we give him twenty dollars. If that's not enough, we kill 'im !"

"Well, it seems you know all the basic stuff alright. Now let's take a look at the training program they're going to put us through once we get there...."

"It's time for our sked Bill, can we wait until it's over?" Brian asked. Billy nodded and sipped more tea. It was cold. Doug said,

"Let's have a beer instead. I'm parched!" The others agreed. Dougy scraped his chair as he got up and disappeared through the doorway into the passage. Brian was already on the morse key.

The news was not good. When it was all over, Brian took off the headphones and dropped them onto the table. He read the message he had written down one more time, then he got up and came across to the others, leaving the note on the table. When he sat down in a chair, he felt very excited, and showed it. The others sensed it immediately.

"What is it Brian?"

"Bad news I'm afraid. The trip will have to be cancelled."

He loved throwing that into their midst. It was like throwing a live hand grenade into a dance hall. Brian wasn't normally like that, but for the last couple of days he had been plagued by the fact that Billy and Bob were running the show like a military exercise. This was his chance to get his own back!

"What for?"

Billy and Bob said in unison, looking at Brian. Dougy said nothing. He did show the slightest hint of a smile though. Which was not surprising, since he had never been keen on this part of the plan at all. Camping in the countryside was one thing, but trips to training camps run by ex-Russian soldiers was another. Dougy wasn't at all sure that he would have liked that part!

"This is a message from Anderson. It turns out that the Lithuanians have run into some trouble that makes it impossible to organise the training camp for at least three months. So he decided to ship out the stuff we paid for on a boat run by an Englishman, and with a bunch of Danes as her crew. Guess what? Two of them are our old mates Black and Erik! What do you think of that?"

Billy was sitting back in his chair, having a quick rethink. Bob was downing the last of his first beer. He had two more bottles on the table in front of him.

"Well, at least we know those two. What the fuck are we going to do now?.. Is there any more to the message?"

"Yes, the boat is a coaster called the Professor Petrov. Anderson says - you can keep her as repayment for this temporary setback - . According to him, she left very early this morning and should be arriving off the Northumberland coast on Wednesday morning. When she gets to the rendezvous point, we have to contact her on VHF and from then on in we're on our own until we hear from him again."

"Why not use the cell-phone ?", Dougy asked.

"Because they don't work outside twenty miles off the coast. Have you ever seen a cell-phone mast out there ?"

"Is there a coordinate for this rendezvous point?"

"No, and when we get it we'll need a sea chart of the area to be able to find out where exactly it is. And then we'll need a boat to get out to her. And what are we going to do with the bloody thing once we take over?"

Billy laughed.

"Well, for one thing we can user her as a hideout, and for another, if she's run by an Englishman then maybe he'll be able to skipper it for us, and thirdly, I can't think of a better way to start our little army than having a base as mobile as a coaster. I mean, think of it! We can turn up and disappear any time and any place we like."

Dougy moaned. "I get sea-sick on the Tyne Ferry!"

"There's pills for that Doug." Bob said.

Chapter Twelve – Ahoy !

"What are we going to do now?"

John Watkins asked, more to himself than to Avon Wailes, who was sitting out of sight behind him, with his feet up on the desk. John Watkins was standing by one of the huge, old fashioned windows with arched tops and peeling white paint, peering out across the river towards the south side. It was another cloudy day. A real drag of a day. And it had been like that for a while.

A dredger was slowly working its way down river. Watkins could see the figure of a man clearly in the powerful yellow lights along the river bank, standing on the wing of the bridge, with a white cup in his hand and his cap pushed back on his head. The man looked in through the open bridge wing door and waved an impatient hand at an invisible man. The he looked down river again and drained the mug. Wailes noticed that Watkins had his hands clasped behind his back and was twiddling his thumbs nervously.

"I've got no bloody idea. One things' for sure though, this waiting is getting on my friggin' nerves! Tell you what, let's get the reports from, say the last two weeks, spread them out on the big table over there, and look at them again. Maybe we'll see something we've missed. And even if we don't, it's still better that doing nothing!"

A chair scraped behind Watkins. He turned around and went over to the green steel filing cabinet just on the other side of the dumb waiter.

"Yeah - At least it'll give us something to do."

He said as he slid open the top drawer and began lifting scraps of paper out of the shoe-box that lay in the bottom.

"God, I hate shoe-boxes!" He burst out.

Wailes laughed. "Right now I can't imagine anything you don't hate!"

He said. Watkins nodded.

"Maybe you're right..." and slammed the drawer shut with a clash.

They went over to the big table in the middle of the room. Well, big table and big table. It was really a collection of desks pushed together to form a situation board. It was empty at the minute. Wailes made a point of removing all the documents from the table when they were out of the office. The office was empty at the moment. It was still only six in the morning and they hadn't been home that night.

"Alright, let's see what we've got once again. You pick a note, call out a word from it, and I'll see what I can remember. Correct me if I'm wrong, or miss something out. Okay?"

John Watkins nodded and turned the box upside down on the table. Wailes took off his jacket, rolled up his sleeves and tried to look like a man who meant business, which was difficult, since nothing worth investigating had happened for more than a week.

"We'll lay them out in chronological order as we work our way through them". Watkins had the first slip of paper ready.

"Motorbike."

"Right. That was Thursday last week. A fellow from Bewcastle was out riding his Norton. It broke down five miles east of the town, and while he was trying to get it going again, a blue Thames van came out of a side road, going like the clappers, and nearly knocked him down. He didn't get a look at the driver, and the plates were all covered with mud."

"The right rear brake light was smashed. Bits of yellow plastic were still in the frame."

"That's right. There was something about a dent in the right hand side too, just over the rear wheel well. It's amazing how some people have an eye for detail. Maybe you have to have one if you're going to mess around with antique motorbikes...."

"You'd be good at twenty questions!"

John Watkins exclaimed.

"Jesus, are they still playing that? I thought they've given that show up ages ago!"

"Not on your nelly! It's still popular up here you know!"

"Next one please. Animal, vegetable or mineral?"

"Animal - a black and white cat."

"Right. It got knocked down outside the Bulls' Head some time Thursday night after the pub shut. The owner of the pub heard brakes screeching on the cobble stones just outside, some kind of a thud, and when he looked out of the first floor window, his cat was lying dead in the street with its eyes hanging out. Must have been a shock!"

"It was. He was pretty pissed off when he rang the Bewcastle station at two in the morning. What time did the guy see the van?"

"Four in the afternoon."

"Hm. Either the van was parked somewhere between four and the time the cat got killed, or it was holed up in the vicinity. Never mind. Next one..."

The phone rang. Wailes went across to it and picked up the handset. He sat down on the corner of the desk. The voice at the other end was female. She didn't identify herself, but Wailes could tell that she was somewhere in her fifties or sixties. She spoke with a heavy Geordie accent.

"I'm not going to tell you who I am, so dinnit ask! But I saw your phone number on the telly a couple of days ago and I wrote it down, just in case. Are you this Watkins bloke?"

"No, but I know him, and I'll give him a message if you like. What's it about?"

"Well, you know that blue van you were looking for?"

She didn't wait for confirmation that he did, but continued without even stopping for breath. There was no doubt but that the quicker she could get off the phone, the happier she would be.

"It's been down here in the square at least twice this week. Been buying bread at the bakers just after opening time."

"Where's here?"

"Why, Bewcastle, where else?"

She was audibly put out that anyone could think that she referred to somewhere other than the town. Wailes guessed that she had lived there all her life.

"Alright, when was the last time you saw it....."

It was too late. Her nerves had failed and she had hung up the phone. Wailes dropped the receiver onto the hook and turned to John Watkins. He wasn't all that pleased by the report. They had had reports like this one coming in for more than four days now, but they still hadn't located the blue Ford van, despite numerous sorties by the local bobbies.

"Another anonymous sighting."

He said. Watkins shook his head.

"They always are." He commented. "What are we going to do about it?"

Suddenly Wailes had made up his mind.

"We're going to camp out in the square in Bewcastle and stay there until we get a sight of this bloody van that everybody but us seems to be seeing all over the place! That's what we're going to do! We'll pick up the Transit from the garage, drop by a sports shop on our way out of town and pick up a couple of sleeping bags. And we're not coming back until we've caught this bugger!"

Watkins liked the sound of it. All this brain work was going to his head! It was about time for some action!

"The Transits' Harry's"

He suddenly reminded himself, and Wailes. But there was no stopping Wailes now.

"Bugger Harry! I'll drop him a note saying we've borrowed it! Get your gear ready, we're off in ten minutes, after I've had a piss!"

He strode off towards the exit. Half way there he turned momentarily on his heel, pointed at the pile of papers on the table, and said

"And clean that bloody mess up!"

Watkins started stuffing the slips of paper unceremoniously back into the shoe box. The hunt was on, and the hunter was crying tally-ho, but where was the fox?

The foxes, all four of them, were in their lair, two of them sleeping blissfully, the other two, Bob and Doug, were standing by the window, with mugs in their hands. Bob was looking down into his half empty mug, which had thick, brown stains on the inside, all the way to the top, and lip marks all around the edge. The cup hadn't been washed for a week.

"If I drink any more tea I'm going to look like a bloody tea-bag soon!"

He threw the remnants out through the gap in the window and said,

"We've got to get out of here or I'll go bonkers! This waitin' around is getting on my bloody nerves! There's nowt' 'appenin!"

"You're right, Bob. It's the same here. Tell you what. We'll wake Brian and Dougy up, have a bit of breakfast, then work out what we're going to do. It'll be another week before the boat gets here, and we could do with finding somewhere else to hole up in. This place is getting on all our nerves, and if it keeps up it's only a matter of time before we start bashing each other about! What do you say?"

"Fine by me! I'll get them up. It's Dougy's turn to make the breakfast anyway."

Actually, Dougy was quite good at making bacon , eggs and sausages. Well, good and good. He didn't burn them to a cinder like the others did, and that was good enough for everyone. After breakfast, Brian took a walk outside to catch a breath of fresh air. The fog was lifting for the first time in two days, and it felt like a wind was beginning to stir the tiny drops of moisture hanging like a thick woollen blanket in the air. It was still chilly though. Spring was always late arriving here in the hills. He hurried back inside. The others were sitting by the table when he came in. Nobody bothered to look up or stir. They had grown apathetic. Their fire was going out and nobody had a poker. It was indeed time to get out of here. Brian sat down with the back of the chair towards the table and his arms resting on it.

"Alright, listen up everybody! We're getting out of here today!"

A sight of relief went around the table at Billy's words. It was like open country after a long, hot summer. One spark, and you've got a bush fire!

"Where are we going then Bill?"

Dougy asked.

"I don't know yet, but the boat doesn't get here for about another week, so wherever it is, it'll have to be out of sight. Any ideas?"

"I don't fancy holing up in another cottage in the hills. That's not exactly the kind of change I had in mind!"

Brian said, looking down at the table. Billy noticed how greasy his hair was. He looked around the table. They could all do with a hot shower and a brush up. They had to find a place somewhere near the coast so that they could meet the coaster when she arrived. But a description of the van had been circulating all over the county, and it would probably be recognised right off. The Thames had to be dumped! But what about all the gear? they would have to leave some of it behind.

"We'll have to leave the Thames here."

He said. The others looked at him questioningly.

"We've been using it to run around in, and its' description is all over the place by now. We'll have to leave some of the gear behind as well, but what do we do with it?"

Bob had an idea.

"We could fill the van up with the gear we don't need, drive it off somewhere and set the bloody thing alight! They'll probably find it right away, but if we do it right there'll be no evidence left. They won't be able to lift prints or track the van back to here. In the mean time we can bugger off in the VW."

"The ideas' good enough, but we'll have to follow the van in the VW to pick up whoever is driving it, and somebody might put two and two together. No, I think we're going to have to leave the van in the shed. That means we can't ever use this place as a hideout again, which is a shame, but there's nothing to do about it."

The others didn't think it was a shame - they'd been there long enough already, and none of them could contemplate ever coming back of his own free will.

"The big problem is the gear, deciding what to take and what not. We haven't got room for all four of us and all the gear in the VW." Bill continued.

Dougy and Brian hadn't said anything. Bob and Bill were the soldiers. As far as Brian was concerned, they knew what they were doing, so why interfere? Dougy was having an idea.

"What about pinching a boat?"

The other three said nothing. They were thinking about it. Dougy looked down at the floor and shrugged. But Billy liked the idea. That much was plain when he spoke again.

"Actually that's not a bad idea Dougy."

Dougy livened up. They actually liked one of his ideas!

Billy continued.

"We're going to need a boat anyway to get out to the coaster when she gets here. Until then we'll need a place to shack up, and if we nick a good motorboat with enough room for all of us and the gear on board, then we'll be safe enough at sea. A boat like that has berths and cooking gear and stuff, so we don't need to take our own. We can dump it somewhere."

"Yeah, in the shit-hole; then if they start digging around in there they'll get their hands all dirty, especially since my belly's been playing up the last couple of days!"

Said Bob. They grimaced, then started to laugh. It was the first time they had laughed in days. It felt good to hear themselves, and it didn't matter the least that what Bob had said wasn't all that funny... A laugh was a laugh anyway!

When they had quietened down again, and Dougy had got up off the floor and righted the chair, Billy said.

"We'll put all the stuff we don't need in the van, rig some kind of timer, and burn the whole place down, just like Bob suggested, only we'll burn the house down as well. Then we'll drive back to Newcastle in the VW, nick a big boat, dump the VW in the multi-storey car-park at the end of Gray Street, and piss off to sea without anybody being the wiser!"

"Why the multi-storey car-park?" Brian asked.

"Because we can leave it there for months before anybody notices. They've got a long-term section for people who take the metro over to the airport. We'll have to pay twenty quid deposit, but it's worth it to make sure nobody finds the VW."

"Have we got twenty quid?"

They rummaged around in their pockets and threw everything they had, apart from the ten quid Bob kept in his coat lining, and the twenty quid Billy kept in his, on the table. There was more than enough.

"Alright, let's get to it. Brian and Dougy, you two pick out the gear we'll be needing and start packing the VW. Bobby and me will put the other stuff in the van and rig some kind of delayed incendiary. It's half past six now. Let's see if we can be out of here before the postman comes by in two hours!"

When the post van drove by the lay-bye on top of Mill Hill, Henry Walsh, the postman, noticed the VW van parked in the lay-bye. He noticed the two men in blue overalls sitting in the front. There was a thermos bottle in the front window. One of the men had a mug in his hand and a cigarette in his mouth. The other was reading the Daily Mirror. He didn't think much more about it. Well, he wouldn't. Workmen always stopped there for a break in the mornings, and he was late anyway. The fog had gone and the sun was already showing its upper limb above the hill behind him. He turned the rear-view mirror down so that he wasn't being blinded any more, then looked out over the barrier, across the dale. It really was a beautiful morning. The top of Milky Cragg was alight with strips of yellow and green that stretched half way down its thinly vegetated side, until they melted into the rapidly sinking shadow. There were patches of ice here and there that glistened in the sun, like thousands of tiny mirrors. Other specks of white, not glossy, moved slowly here and there among small bushes that had been dehydrated by the icy winter winds and snows, trying to find a morsel of grass to eat. Yes, spring was certainly on its way... He felt pleased. He always did when spring arrived to chase the winter blues to somewhere where they could do no more harm until next Christmas. One or two wild flowers were already beginning to poke their heads above the browned grass by the verge. Most were yellow.

Henry stopped the van suddenly and got out. Yes, he had seen right. Across the dale, at the foot of Milky Cragg, there was a heavy, black smoke rising from a building that was on fire somewhere among the trees. An occasional flicker of yellow in the shadows told him the fire had a good hold. Henry turned around, leaned into the post van, and took out the cellular phone he kept in the glove compartment. He called the fire brigade.

Dougy and Brian were sitting in the back of the VW, which was facing west, with the side door open. They too were looking out across the dale, as were Bob and Billy, who had climbed out of the van, and were pretending to take a leak when a truck load of logs trundled past, on its way up the last quarter mile to the summit. The ground shook as it went by. Brian cursed. He was trying to hold the binoculars steady. Bob zipped his fly and lit a cigarette. There was no wind, so the smoke from the cottage fire just billowed up into the cold air, then flattened out into a pancake that spread thin across the dale below them.

"Fire's got a good hold."

Brian said. The others said nothing. They could see that for themselves. No, they were waiting for something else to happen, something more important than the fire. It happened. A pillar of black and yellow raised itself suddenly two hundred or more feet into the air. Along with it went something that resembled a wheel, glittering and blinking as it twirled upwards at tremendous speed. Bob grabbed the binoculars unceremoniously from Brian, who looked disappointed for a moment, but didn't want to lose sight of what was going on over there. Bob trained the binoculars on the column. He didn't care that he could be seen from the road. Yes, there were bits of differential, bits of scrap iron, an oil drum, something yellow that looked like the empty gas bottle they'd thrown in the back of the Thames. The flame had gone now, but the column of dirt and smoke and bits of flotsam and jetsam hung in the air as if they would hang there forever. Then came the sound of rolling thunder. It crawled up the hillside to where they were standing and washed over the VW like waves breaking upon the shore. It had taken almost eight seconds for the sound of the explosion to reach them from the other side of the dale.

By now the remnants of the barn and the Ford Thames were sinking rapidly back to earth. The column was already only half its former size. Bob handed the binoculars to Billy, who shook his head, and said.

"Nice job Bobby! Let's get the hell out of here."

They climbed back into the VW. Dougy slid the side door shut, then leaned back against the side of the van and said.

"Never seen an explosion before, have you?" His knees were still shaking.

"No, never. Christ it was amazing how high that shit went, wasn't it?"

They spent the next half hour discussing the destruction of the cottage, the barn and the Ford Thames van with everything in it, while the VW rattled and bumped its way over the summit and started down the other side, on its way to Newcastle, at a rapid, but legal, pace.

When Wailes and Watkins arrived at Bewcastle, they checked in at the local police station, just so that the bobbies there would know they were in the area. Wailes didn't want them turning up if somebody reported their van being parked in the square, with them in it, for too long. Sergeant Tim Andrews held the desk as duty officer. The white plastic clock on the wall behind him said it was ten thirty. In another half hour he could get along home. Wailes and Andrews came in. He recognised them from their previous visits and wished them good morning.

"Anything happening sarge?" Wailes asked.

"Been quiet all night, until about two hours ago. The postman driving the first delivery van reported a fire over by Milky Cragg. He called the fire brigade, who called us. They've been over there about an hour now."

"Anything special over there ? Factories and the like I mean."

"No, nothing at all. In fact I'm a bit surprised there was a fire over there. There's nowt there but a couple of broken down old farm houses and a shed or two where the sheep hole up when the weather gets bad, nothing that could catch alight by itself anyway."

Wailes ears pricked up.

"Any of your lads over there?"

He was obviously interested.

"No, not yet. The fire chief said he would give me a tinkle if there was anything out of the ordinary, and we're a bit understaffed, so I didn't bother sending anybody over to have a look."

"Do you mind if we mosey on over there and check it out?"

"No, not at all. By the way, why did you lads come here? Still looking for that Thames van?"

"Yes, we are. I'll drop in on the way back and let you know what's going on."

Wailes said over his shoulder. Watkins was already through the door and climbing into the van. They knew where Milky Cragg was. They had passed it on their way into Bewcastle. They had seen the two fire engines across the valley. There was no smoke, so they had assumed that the Fire Brigade was on some kind of exercise.

"What a bloody mess!"

The fire chief said. Wailes agreed. what had been some sort of a house was now just a blackened and charred ruin. The fire tender was still pumping water into it. The hose feeding the pump ran off somewhere among the bushes. The firemen were walking around, checking that the last bit of charcoal had stopped smouldering. Wailes was standing alongside the fire chief, close by what had been the front door of the house. The wall creaked and popped uneasily as the bricks cooled. There was a brief rumble and crash from the other side of the building. The fire chief listened for shouts. When none came, he relaxed visibly.

"We'll be finished here in a couple of minutes, then you can have it all to yourselves. Looking for anything in particular?"

"Just nosing about, that's all. We're looking for a blue Ford Thames van that should be somewhere in the area. Haven't seen anything have you?"

The fire chief shook his head, then said,

"Mind you, there's a crater just on the other side of the house that looks as if something exploded. It's very recent and probably connected with the fire."

"How can you tell?"

"No sign of snow or ice in it. If you look around among the trees and bushes you'll find bits of a car. There's bits inside the house, and big holes that could have been made by those bits going through the wall on that side. I didn't see any sign of colour at all. Whatever paint had been on it had been burned off by the time the explosion occurred. It is all a kind of yellowish grey. My guess is that there was a fire and whatever car was in the shed exploded during the fire. The fire started in the shed. We know that for sure. It spread to the house through a hole in the side wall. We found a couple of empty petrol cans that still smelled, so whoever set fire to the place did it on purpose."

"I think I'll nose about a bit."

Wailes said blandly and wandered off among the bushes.

There was no doubt about the fact that the car that had been in the shed was a van. They found enough bits of the jigsaw to be able to piece that together. After about two hours search, Watkins found an insignia from the rear of the van, two hundred yards away, by the stream the fire brigade had used as their water supply. There was now no doubt that the van had been a Ford Thames. They found no bits of registration number, which they assumed must have been removed prior to the fire, but they were able to identify part of the chassis number stamped into the remains of the engine compartment.

It seemed likely that they would eventually be able to trace the last owner of the vehicle, given time. Wailes decided to get some local assistance for that job on their return to Bewcastle.

It looked like they had retrieved all they could from the site. Watkins was wading through the remnants of the living room, leaving no stone unturned, when he came to the window. A blackened corner of a wooden table stuck out from under a pile of bricks and mortar. He was already dirty enough to have to take a shower and change clothes on their return to Bewcastle, so he decided to have a closer look at the table. When the bricks and mortar were removed, it turned out that the table was only burned at the corner he had seen. It appeared that part of the front wall and ceiling had fallen in early in the fire. The place was already rotten, so that was not only possible, but likely. Rubble had fallen onto the table. The legs had given way. They lay splayed out under more rubble. Watkins turned the remains of the table over and spotted the small slip of white paper immediately.

Wailes was in the remnants of the shed at the side of the house when he heard Watkins' shout. He left the mangled bits of metal he was messing about with, and walked quickly towards the front door. Watkins met him half way, red in the face and very excited indeed.

"Look what I found in the living room!"

He handed the paper to Wailes, who read it quickly. Watkins watched the expression on the big mans' face change. When Wailes looked up, he said, in a tone that belied his contentment,

"That's it John! This is the breakthrough we've been looking for. Where did you find this?"

Watkins pointed out the place. Wailes slapped him on the back.

"Damned good piece of work!"

Watkins was happy. They walked back to the van and headed for Bewcastle. Wailes folded the slip of paper containing the message that Brian Wallace had received from Lithuania, and put it in his inside pocket. The hounds had picked up the scent again, and were hungry for blood.

"I think we can stop looking for the van now, John." He said blandly.

"Do you believe in God and the Devil?" Britta asked, without looking away from the porthole. The sea was calm, and grey, and in the distance melted into the fog that drifted across the harbour. Dick Brown was standing next to her, occasionally taking a sip from the half empty whisky glass.

"No, I don't believe in either. What I believe in is the good and the evil that men and women do to each other. What about you?"

"Well, if you'd asked me that one before I met Gordon, I'd have had to say I belong to the nieve school of thought. Up until the age of about twenty five, I really and truly believed that I'd meet everyone I'd ever loved in heaven, including the dog I'd had that got run over by a car while we were away at a holiday camp one summer."

"And now?"

"Now things are different. I learned the value of life, at least my own life, in Afghanistan among the rebels. Strange how the closer you get to life, the further away heaven seems..."

"Not to me it doesn't."

"Oh?"

She looked at him, his gaze was still fixed on the fog. She could see the fire burning in the reflection of his eyes, and the lop-sided enigmatic grin on his face, in the reflection in the glass. His lips started to move.

"When I was a kid of eighteen, I had a pen pal, a girl....can't remember her name off hand now. Anyway, she lived on Malta, just outside Valetta. We had written to each other for about a year. I had a photo of her that I carried around in my pocket. She was good looking."

He drifted silently away into the past. Britta waited. He came back again after a little while.

"Anyway, one summer I decided to go and visit her, to find out what she was really like."

He laughed suddenly.

"It's amazing how far some people will go after pussy!.... Well, I only had five pounds seventeen shillings and six pence to my name - that's about sixty kroner in todays money. I was about to give up the idea, maybe just hitch-hike down to London and then come back, when my sister's boyfriend said - You'll be back tonight!"

He laughed again, but this time it was a different kind of laugh, more scornful in nature.

"Never mind, I'm getting away from the subject. I actually got as far as Syracuse in Sicily, but couldn't get a boat across to Malta, got picked up for vagrancy and was sent back home. The whole seance lasted less than fourteen days. Most of the time on that trip, I was alone. When I'm alone, I find that I think about all kinds of spiritual stuff. It's like the noise of every day living cuts me off from that part of myself, and I have to be away, and alone, to be able to rediscover it."

There was another pause, until the fog horn from the light at the harbour entrance died away again.

"Anyway, I came to some conclusions on that trip. Conclusions about me, my relationships with people, my relationship with death. Death is not the gateway to my heaven. I'm already in my heaven. Death comes to us all at some point in time, but to me, death will not be a relief from anxiety, uncertainty, pain, sorrow, and all the other things religious people connect with going to heaven. To me, this life has been a continuation of my last, and the death of this body will force me to be reborn again, to go through all the problems we humans go through, again, and to continue where I left off. Unless of course, I'm full of bullshit and haven't got the foggiest notion of what it's all about - which is, in reality, probably closer to the truth than anything...God, to think of myself going all that way under those conditions, at that age...!!"

He swilled whisky to save himself from a bout of nostalgia. The speed at which the action followed the words made the reason rather obvious.

"You don't like being nostalgic, do you?"

There was a long pause, then he turned his head toward her and said,

"Memories are alright. If I live long enough to get to be an old man, I'll be really glad I have them. But in the mean time, I live, and breath for the present, and the future, whatever it may bring, and the devil take the consequences!"

Britta laughed. "So you DO believe in the devil after all!"

Brown laughed with her, for a short while. Then, when it was over, he said,

"I'll be keeping you a secret from the others. You'll be my backup, just in case I need it. In the meantime, I want you to stay in your cabin. Keep your door locked and bolted at all times, and keep your revolver handy, just in case. Don't let anyone see light under the door, and keep as quiet as you can. I'll be bringing you food from time to time, whenever I can get the chance. I'll knock once, then slip a blank piece of paper under the door. When I'm gone, wrap a sweater or something around the intercom over there. Intercoms usually ring loud enough to wake the dead, and I want to be able to call you from the bridge without arousing anybody's suspicions."

"What about the others?"

"This boat has room for a crew of ten. I'm putting the other four up on the bridge deck. I'm taking the pilots cabin. It has only one door leading right onto the bridge, and no window, so I'll be able to lock it and get some real sleep without having to worry about keeping one eye open. The greaser's cabin here is the lowest on the ship. It'll be noisy when we put to sea in a couple of hours, and everything will rattle, but you'll soon get used to it, and you're as far off the beaten track as you can be on a boat."

"It's a good thing there's a washbasin and a toilet!"

Brown looked around. It was going to be difficult for her being cooped up in these nine square metres at the bottom of a ship at sea for the next week. But still, rather that than being cooped up in a coffin!

"It's not the Ritz, I'll give you that! Anything I can get you before I leave?"

"Yes. A kiss for luck."

"Hmm. I think I can manage that..."

After the door shut behind Brown, Britta began quietly stuffing one end of a thick, grey blanket into the crack between the top of the wooden door frame and the steel bulkhead. Brown's steps retreated up the lighter and were gone long before she was finished.

The weather report said that the fog would continue for the next three days, and that temperatures would lie around zero degrees Celcius, plus or minus three. Brown was pleased about that. It meant that the sea would be calm for the first leg of the trip to the Swedish coast, although the fog would make it necessary to have at least one other man on the bridge keeping a lookout, and getting in the way of his privacy. Still, there was nothing else for it. But there was a more pressing problem that he couldn't shrug off. Sooner or later, if all went well, he would face having to man the bridge almost alone, and without the auto pilot that wouldn't be an easy job. The auto pilot had to be fixed as quickly as possible. Hmm.. that'll kill two birds with one stone.

Black and Hansen were on the starboard bridge wing, looking down at the dirty dock water over the railing. Brown could hear the murmur of their voices through the half-open bridge wing door. Erik was standing on the other side of the chart table, prodding the chart that lay there with the pointy ends of a pair of brass dividers. It seemed like he was trying to work out how to use them. Mogensen was just lounging in the pilots chair, smoking a lazy cigarette and letting the ash drop on the deck by itself when it got too long. Brown decided it was time to get moving.

"Alright lads. Meeting right here behind the chart table. If we're lucky, we'll get this heap of shit on the way in an hour or so."

They came surprisingly quickly. It seemed that they too were anxious to get under way. When they were assembled, Brown said.

"Okay, we've a long way to go. I reckon that if all goes well we should be off the Northumberland coast in eight days. In the mean time we've got lots to do. The first thing is to get the engine running. I haven't been down in the engine room yet, so I'm going down there in a couple of minutes to see how I can get her started.

"Isn't there an ignition key or something?" Mogensen asked.

"There is on a motorboat, but not on something this big. The engine is too big to start by starter motor. It uses compressed air for starting, so I'll have to find out where the air and fuel valves are. Fortunately, there's always a manual control position on the engine itself, where it's possible to start and stop and set the engine speed, so I'll not have to waste time learning all the switches on the engine panel. In the mean time there's a job for everybody. Steen, you've just been promoted to ships cook. I want you to find out where the galley is - that's the kitchen - and brew up some tea and sandwiches. Smith said there were provisions on board, so take stock of them. We'll need to know if we've got enough to reach England - which I surely hope. Black - you and Michael are going to be the engineers. That means you'll have to keep an eye on the engine at all times. You can come with me when I go down to start the engine. I'll show you what to watch out for. Erik - you and me are going to do all the navigation, steering and watch-keeping on the Bridge, so you just stay here until we get back. Steen and Erik, you'll also have to handle the shore lines when we're ready to leave. I'll let you know what you have to do when we get that far. Any questions?"

There were none. That was fortunate, because Brown was wondering if they'd ever get off the quayside with such an inexperienced crew and such a rusty skipper, let alone this rust-bucket of a boat.

The hinges of the metal hatch to the engine room were well-greased. Obviously the route down from the accommodation deck to the bowels of the ship were well trodden. Brown turned the hatch locks at the top and sides and swung open the hatch hurriedly. It banged against the bulkhead with a crash that echoed up from the empty space at the bottom of the black hole that opened up in front of him. Brown started down the ladder into the engine room without further ado. It was impossible to see the bottom of the ladder. When he looked up, he could see the rectangle of grey light above, with Black's figure framed in it. Mogensen was already on the ladder and descending.

Brown's feet reached the deck. He turned around slowly, being careful not to tread somewhere he shouldn't in the darkness, took the torch from his pocket, the one that he'd brought with him from the bridge, and pressed the switch.

The light was sharp and white. It blinded him for a few seconds. By the time he was able to see properly again, Mogensen was just planting a foot on the deck behind him. "Wait here until I find the light switch. Watch out where you step, there's always a whole lot of things to fall over and break your neck on in a place like this..."

Brown said, and followed the beam of light from the torch until he came to what looked like a generator. The engine room was as silent as the grave, apart from the sound of his own heavy breathing, and Black's footsteps on the ladder somewhere behind him in the semidarkness.

Ghostly shapes and shadows danced a horrifying wild jig on all sides at every movement of the torch, as Brown looked around the generator and finally found a green switch that seemed to be a start button. He pressed it. There was a whirring sound, a coughing and spitting, and then the ear-splitting sound of the diesel engine coming to life a few seconds afterwards. Brown felt suddenly at home, here among the machinery, with the noise of an engine reverberating around the otherwise silent steel coffin. He stood for a few seconds, breathing in the sound, and the feeling, then went back the way he had come, to the electrical panel he had passed on the way to the generator. One of the instruments was now showing voltage. A quick check of the panel showed that the main circuit breaker was pulled. Brown pushed it back in. The whole engine room exploded into brightness.

"Let there be light!"

He shouted and started to laugh. The other two looked at him, then at each other. Mogensen shrugged and started off towards where Brown was standing. Black stayed where he was, and lit a cigarette. If anybody was going to get his hands dirty playing around down here, it wasn't him! He was thankful that Michael was there. Michael was good with motorbike engines, so they wouldn't be completely lost! - But you know? Maybe this isn't a bad gig after all! I mean, Erik and Brown are out of the way. Michael can be talked into just about anything. Steen shouldn't be too much of a problem. No, maybe this isn't a bad gig after all...! Black was thinking. He felt the sudden urge to smile, which made his face look all bruised and battered in the sharp flourescent lighting, and followed Mogensen.

The engine was an old Russian made three cylinder two stroke, the height of a two story house in middle suburbia, although it was much, much dirtier, and obviously not as well kept.

Brown found the flywheel housing at the rear end, and checked that the thick steel bar used to turn over the engine a little at a time wasn't still sitting in the locked position. It wasn't. Followed by Mogensen, who was watching every move he made, and Black, who looked as though he couldn't care less, he crossed the cat-walk over the rear thrust block and walked up the other side of the engine, that towered above the three of them, surrounded by two floors of catwalks, and looked like three giant industrial chimneys just waiting to pour out smoke. Brown found the manual operating position. The fuel gage said there was no fuel pressure. The air gage said that there was more than fifteen pounds of air in the starting air tanks.

"That should be enough for two or three start attempts, but we'll start the compressor anyway and while it's charging the tanks we can start the fuel pre-heater and the fuel pumps."

"Where do we do that?"

Brown looked around and spotted a green steel cabinet bolted to the bulkhead a few metres away.

"Maybe over there. Lets take a look"

The console proved to be the place to start the fuel pre-heater, the fuel pumps, and a whole lot of other things, among them the air compressor. Brown pressed the buttons, and was amazed that everything seemed to work as it should. The compressor started. The pre-heater started. The fuel pump didn't, but Brown knew that as soon as the pointer on the instrument measuring fuel temperature reached the thin red line half way around the scale, then the pumps could be started. By then they should be ready to start the engine. While they were waiting, Brown checked around. He found the intercom. It was immediately obvious that it didn't work, because the wires were dangling out of the box, and the loudspeaker was a complete mess. Brown took Mogensen and Black over to the manual control console at the base of the second cylinder and showed them how the engine telegraph worked, how to start and stop the engine, how to change its speed, and what gages to watch out for. By the time he was finished, the fuel temperature was up, the compressor had stopped pumping up the start air tanks and they were ready to start.

The engine started after three six second bursts of air. A deep rumble spread throughout the ship, and finally settled down to a rythmic thumping sound after several minutes. Brown became aware of feeling happy. The engine ran smoothly, Mogensen at least was an easy learner, the generator was working. It would be good to get under way. It suddenly occurred to him that within a very short time, he would be on his way home.... It seemed like it had been forever since he was having a pint down at the Central. But the Central was still a very long way off. A lot can happen in eight days at sea. He left Mogensen and Black in the engine room and returned to the bridge where he found Erik and Steen chatting over a plate of cheese and onion sandwiches and mugs of hot coffee. He let them talk. He was busy, going through a check list in his head, and working as he went.

Navigation lights - on. Horn - The throaty roar of the horn just above the bridge, stopped Steen and Erik's conversation in mid-sentence. Both looked around to see what Brown was doing, then continued again when the horn stopped. Erik waggled a little finger in his right ear. Engine telegraph. Brown rang for Stop and got an answer. It took more than a minute, but it came, and what was more, the engine actually stopped a short while after that! Rudder. The indicators seemed to work okay, but he got Steen to turn the wheel through its full range of movement, set Erik on the bridge wing to act as a go-between and went down onto the quayside to the aft end. The rudder moved as it should and didn't look like it might fall off. He boarded and climbed the lighter to the bridge. There was no reason to hold back now. Everything seemed to be well enough. When he got to the bridge, he said,

"This is it boys. Lets' get moving.! I want you both to go down on the quayside and heave the ropes off the bollards, but only when I tell you. To make things easy for all of us, we'll call them number one, two, three and four, with number one at the bow - that's the front end - of the boat. Can you manage that? "

"Yeah, sure. Sounds easy enough!"

Erik said. They left through the port bridge wing door. Brown followed them through the door and watched them descend to the quay side from the bridge wing. Erik went forward to the bow and Hansen went aft to the stern. Then Brown went inside and rang for start on the engine telegraph. This time it started right away. He kept an eye on the engine revolutions for a few seconds and when they didn't budge past the start line on the instrument he went outside.

Thirty minutes later, the Professor Petrov steamed out of Klaipeda harbour. Five men and a woman sailed with her. Only God knew how many, if any at all, would arrive at the English coast...But the fog horn at the harbour entrance must have known something, because it wailed for the ship long after she had disappeared into the mist....

Chapter Thirteen – A Can of Worms

The Professor Petrov's engine room was not the kind of place to hold a conversation. It was hot - so hot that Mogensen and Black had already stripped to the waist after an hour on watch. The smell of hot oil mixed with exhaust fumes permeated the air, making it difficult to breathe at the bottom of the engine well. Then there was the noise - an indescribable choir of thuds and bumps and rattles and teeth-jangling rumbling. All in all a hellhole. Black was stretched out on a torn-up cardboard box on one of the catwalks, with his head resting on his rolled-up jacket and a cigarette in his mouth that he took out from time to time. He didn't need to knock the ash off the end - the vibration was enough to do the job for him. Mogensen had just finished checking the exhaust gas temperature gages. Everything seemed to be running well enough. He wiped his hands with a cloth that was even dirtier than himself, one that he'd found hanging over one of the catwalk railings half an hour ago. Then he pulled a packet of cigarettes from his left side pocket and lit one. Time to have a look around.

There was really nothing that interesting about the engine room. It was full of pipes and wires and gages and small tanks speckled here and there up the flat steel walls, all the way to the reinforced engine-room roof that hung suspended high above the deck. There was a steel ladder with safety steel hoops around it welded to the bulkhead. The ladder went all the way up, past the topmost catwalk where the entrance to the engine room was, up to where the four-foot diameter exhaust pipes disappeared through the steel plate and into the funnel pipes. Mogensen climbed the ladder and followed the catwalk half way round the engine room until it ended suddenly. Above him was a hatch cover. A short ladder climbed the wall to it. The hatch was not at all well oiled. It took some work, and it was hot enough already inside the engine room. Mogensen hadn't realised he could sweat even more than he had done already. Finally, he managed to get the hatch open and climbed out onto the after deck. He went to the aft railing. It was still foggy, and cold, and he was still naked to the waste, but he just wanted to have a look see. The only light on the after deck was from a window in the accommodation, and a little from a lantern on the short steel pipe mast at the stern. Mogensen looked down. The sea was very calm indeed, not even a hint of white, although the water looked very cold and very grey - what he could see of it, that is - because it disappeared into the blackness a short distance behind the ship. The white froth of water churned up by the propeller seemed to run straight as a die behind her.

Mogensen turned towards the light in the accommodation block. He just had to have a look inside, although he was getting cold now and could feel a shiver coming on. He stood off to one side so as not to be too obvious and peeked in. Steen Hansen was making coffee and sandwiches and had his back to the window. Suddenly, Mogensen felt a bit peckish. He went back through the hatch and closed it behind him. There was still a shiver or two to go, but as he climbed down the ladder with the safety hoops, he started to warm up again. It felt much better than being outside....

On the catwalk below the entrance to the engine room and just above deck level, in fact the same one that Black was busy having a nap on, there was a hatch in the bulkhead. Mogensen opened it, and stepped out into a corridor. It was dark, but he found a light switch just outside the hatch and turned on the lights. He went through the hatchway into the corridor and shut the hatch behind him. His cigarette was suddenly finished. He hadn't even noticed that he'd smoked it, but isn't that always the way with cigarettes? He dropped the butt on the deck, and squashed it with the heel of his boot.

The corridor was quiet compared to the noise in the engine room, even though he could still hear it once his ears grew accustomed to the relative calm. It was a short corridor of steel bulkheads and deck head painted with something that had once upon a time been white. The colour had grown yellow over the years - not with sunlight, which obviously because of the lack of windows couldn't reach down here into the bowels of the vessel, but more because of smoke and fumes and dirty boots and hands. At the end there was a lighter going upwards. Mogensen walked to the end of the corridor and looked up. There were lights on up there, but he decided not to go any further in that direction. He turned around and surveyed the corridor behind him.

On the left there were two wooden doors to what looked like cabins. On the right, there was one cabin door, and further away a hatch resembling that to the engine room. Mogensen approached the first door on the left. There was a sign on it, but he couldn't read the language. He tried the handle. The door wouldn't open. He thought that maybe it was stuck and put his shoulder to it. It didn't budge. Mogensen decided to move on.

On the other side of the door, and the grey blanket draped across it, Britta lay fast asleep in the bunk, with the cabin lights off. She was tired, and had turned in early after reading a couple of chapters of a book by a female author with a hang to powerful, unscrupulous men, and weak-kneed women who never really managed to get over their upbringing. The book lay, open pages downward, on the small table bolted to the bulkhead beside the bunk. Beside it lay the loaded revolver. Neither Britta, nor Mogensen noticed the other - which was fortunate for both of them to say the least....

Mogensen tried the cabin door opposite. It opened easily enough and he found the light switch to the right of the doorframe, just where it should be. It was a small cabin, with bare walls and no mitigating features at all. At one end there was a table, bolted to the bulkhead just under a porthole that was painted so many times it would never be opened again. Beside that was a bunk. There was no mattress on the bunk, just the bare boards that were the top of the three drawers under the bunk. Mogensen didn't bother to check the drawers. It wasn't worth it. On the bulkhead beside the door where he was standing was a washbasin. That was it. There were no chairs, no cupboards, no decorations and no curtains. No sign of anything that might show that people had once lived here... Mogensen turned off the light, backed out of the cabin and shut the door. He tried the second cabin on the other side. It was almost the same story. Almost. The difference was that there was a mattress on the bunk, and about six chairs piled one on top of each other in the far corner. He shut the door again.

The hatch opened onto a long, narrow tunnel painted with the same yellowing colour as in the corridor, with dim lighting in the deck head. The end of the tunnel seemed to go nowhere. It stopped dead after about twenty yards, but since tunnels are normally there for a reason, Mogensen decided to take a look. He left the hatch open behind him and walked on. The place that had seemed to be the end of the tunnel turned out to be a dogleg. The tunnel had to apparently manoeuvre round something out of sight on the other side of the bulkhead. At the end of the tunnel was another hatchway. Mogensen turned the hatch locks and swung open the hatch open, away from him.

For the first few moments, all Mogensen could see was blackness, but the echoing of the rumbles of the ship, and the cold, damp smell of salt sea air told him that the space was big, very big. He stepped inside, and away from the hatch, so the light didn't blind him.

A large murky shape with straight sides and angular corners seemed to be waiting there in the gloom. Mogensen took a few tense steps toward it. He wished he had brought a flashlight. He relaxed when he got closer to the shape. By then his eyes had grown accustomed to the darkness. He could see that it was a container, held down to the deck by thick chains and bottle screws. He had found his way into the cargo hold. Mogensen went back to the engine room, closing the hatches as he went. Black was still asleep on the catwalk.

The Professor Petrov's main engine was actually placed in a well in the bottom of the engine room, with the bottom of the crankcase below deck level. Mogensen went down the metal lighter and walked around the crankcase on the bottom plates. There were three big inspection hatches on each side, and small sight-glasses beside each one. Mogensen wondered what the sight-glasses were for; stood looking at one for a while, decided he couldn't tell anyway, then went forward to the front of the engine. There were six factory lockers at the end, hidden away under the catwalk on the next floor up, close to that another lighter going upwards. Beside the lockers was a small workshop, with a few heavy tools, hammers and stuff, lying in net baskets welded to the bulkhead over the workshop bench. One of the lockers had a great, big padlock hanging loose on the door, with a key still in it. None of them were locked. Curious to see what was in them, Mogensen opened the first. It was empty. He shut the door and opened the next. A dirty boiler suit was hanging on the back of the door. A pair of oily boots lay in the bottom. They had no laces in them. The other lockers were empty. Mogensen went back up the lighter.

As he appeared from the space below deck, Black was sitting up, stretching, and Steen Hansen was on his way down the ladder with a cardboard box under his arm. In it there was a thermos of coffee and some cheese and onion sandwiches with slices of tomato and cucumber in them. Mogensen suggested that they eat in the cabin he had found in the corridor and the others agreed. All three left the engine room and took up temporary lodgings on the other side of the bulkhead to where Britta was just waking from sleep, disturbed by the sound of the engine, to which she was not yet accustomed.

"What's happening on the bridge?"

Black asked over the rim of his mug of coffee. He tried to pretend that the question was innocent, and congratulated himself when the others continued what they were doing without the least sign of a pause. Hansen shrugged, swallowed the mouthful of sandwich he had been chewing, and said..

"Erik was behind the wheel, steering, and Brown was sitting about on the floor under the steering column. He had a panel off and was messing about inside. I asked him what was going on, and he said that he was trying to fix the auto pilot."

There was a short silence, then Black said,

"I didn't know that it wasn't working.."

Hansen nodded.

"Erik told me when I was up with coffee just after we left harbour. He said that Brown had told him that he'd have to stay behind the wheel until he'd got it fixed, and that might be God knows when. Erik was real pissed off about it."

He continued to eat his sandwich. Mogensen said,

"I need a piss!" and got up.

He left the cabin and closed the door behind him. There was silence for a while then Black put his mug down on the table with a definitive clash. Hansen looked across the table at Black, who said,

"I don't trust Brown!"

Hansen grinned broadly.

"That's nothing new.." He said.

Black shrugged.

"Well, maybe not, but Brown's way out of our league in this game. I've been thinking about it, and it all seems just a bit too convenient that he turns up in Aarhus just before this caper. And I still haven't forgotten what happened in Marselisborg and the road to Esbjerg...."

Hansen nodded, neither had he.

The cabin door opened. Black and Hansen looked up as Mogensen stepped inside and closed it again. He sat down and slurped the last of the coffee from the mug. Black continued.

"Let's just take stock of the situation. Brown and Erik are on the bridge. You and me are down in the engine room, and Steen is all by himself in the galley, for most of the day. The auto pilot doesn't work, so Erik has to stand at the wheel, but Brown is working on getting it fixed. Let's just for the sake of argument say that Brown is up to something."

The other two looked at each other, then at Black....

"Alright, just for the sake of argument...."

They agreed that it was just for the sake of argument, although they were both equally aware the Black himself was probably up to no good. Everyone knew that Black hated Brown, maybe even enough to want to get rid of him.

"What makes you think he might be up to no good?" Mogensen asked.

"Well, let me put it bluntly. Why would a tough guy like Brown want to pitch in with a bunch of amateurs like us? We know what we're getting out of this mess of trouble. We're helping out our mates in England - people we have known for a long time - people we trust. But what about Brown - what's he getting out of this? Why hasn't he left us ages ago?"

"I don't know..Why?"

"I don't know either, but if he's not on the level, and expects to gain something from this, then the only thing worth his while aboard this boat is boxed up in a container in the cargo hold."

He smirked, as if he'd sussed the whole thing out and was one step ahead of the situation when all the others could do was tag along behind.

"What do you mean by that?"

Mogensen asked.

"Think about it.....What would a whole container of arms and ammo be worth on the black market in the west? Two million dollars? Three? Five? Whatever it is, then there's more for one man than there is for five!"

Black leaned back in his chair.

Mogensen and Hansen were silent. They just sat there, looking across at Black, who was now busily picking bits of crumbs off the table and popping them into his mouth. Hansen broke the silence.

"He'd have to get rid of all of us......"

"Right. And Erik's alone with him on the bridge, you're alone in the galley, and me and Mogensen are down here in the engine room!"

The gravity of the situation was beginning to dawn on Mogensen. Black leaned suddenly forward. He had them by the balls now!

"You see, Michael, that's what I'm getting at....Now, let's take this thing a bit further. If Brown intends to steal the cargo and get rid of us, he'll have to steer the ship by himself. He wouldn't be able to do that without the auto pilot, would he? I mean he's not going to let the bloody thing wander about on its own while he's making tea or taking a leak. All right. Let's give him the benefit of the doubt and say he's doing it to make life easy for both him and Erik - the effect's still the same though isn't it? With the auto pilot working, he wouldn't have to steer the ship by himself!"

Hansen flung up his hands into the air. He was beginning to believe Black, especially since he could see that Mogensen was already convinced.

"Alright, alright - Let's say what you're saying is true. He's still got to keep a lookout. Nobody can keep awake for as long as it takes to get to England!"

"Who says' we're going to England?" Black waited for the message to sink in.

"What if he has mates waiting somewhere here in the Baltic. Estonia, Latvia, Finland, Sweden, Germany..... I mean there's lots of places where he could have mates lying waiting for the container. And even if he hasn't, there's no saying that he's not prepared to take twice as long to get to England... But there's a third possibility, and one which we have to consider, even though it's not exactly my cup of tea..."

"What's that?" Mogensen asked.

"He could turn one of us against the others, use one of us as a helper. That way he wouldn't have to do everything himself would he?"

"Who? I wouldn't sell you out!"

Hansen stated nervously.

"I know, Steen."

Said Black.

"Who's the most logical choice?"

"Erik!"

Said Mogensen. Black nodded. Hansen looked relieved.

"That's right, our old mate Erik... It makes sense. Brown has been favouring Erik all the way here, fattening him up, while he's been pissing all over us! Erik's on the bridge, where Brown can brainwash him some more. Erik's learning how to steer the boat, keep a lookout. What else is he learning about? How easy would it be for Brown and Erik together to get the boat anywhere Brown wanted to go?... Simple! That's how easy it would be!"

"What can we do about it?"

Hansen asked. There was despair in his voice. Black smiled. He liked Hansen because he was a willing, social amoebe.

"Now that's a good question. If we're going to get out of this alive, we've got to get on top of the situation. We need to know what's happening on the bridge. You're the best man for the job Steen."

"You want me to spy on them?"

"I wouldn't exactly say spy. All I want you to do is begin spending a bit of time on the bridge. You've got the perfect excuse. You're the one who takes food and drink up to them, and you're otherwise alone in the galley. It's only natural you'd want to spend more time there where something is going on. And you come down here to the engine room with food and drink to us, so nobody on the bridge would be suspicious. You could keep us informed as to what was happening with no problem at all."

Hansen nodded. What Black had said was true. It made perfect sense at least.

"Piece of cake!"

He said, and smiled.

There was silence for a while. Then Black, looking worried, said,

"It's a shame we haven't got any weapons though. There's a whole container full in the hold and we're sitting here without so much as a revolver between us. The only way into the hold is through the hatch on deck, and either Brown or Erik will be keeping an eye on that!"

Mogensen smirked.

"No it isn't. Brown must have made a mistake when he was looking the ship over. I found another way into the hold."

The other two looked at him. Black looked as though he didn't believe it. Mogensen said,

"It's true. Do you want to see it?"

They both nodded. Mogensen got up from the table. They followed. Hansen left the cabin door open. Mogensen said,

"I'll just get a flashlight - it's pitch black in there!"

He disappeared into the engine room leaving the other two standing in the corridor for a couple of minutes. When he returned, he showed them the container.

"How are we going to get it open without anybody being any the wiser? That padlock looks like serious stuff. Do you think Brown has the key?"

Hansen asked as they stood looking at the doors of the container.

Black answered.

"I doubt if Smith would trust anybody with the key. Anyway, once it gets to England, it wouldn't matter if they had to cut open the lock to get it open. But if we cut it open, it'll be rather obvious, especially since we don't actually know whether or not Brown has already been down to check on it. I mean, he was alone on board for quite some time, wasn't he?"

"I think I know what to do!"

Mogensen retorted, and disappeared back into the corridor leading to the hold.

When he had gone, Black said to Hansen.

"I think you should go back to the galley Steen. If they call you from the bridge and you don't answer, Brown might get suspicious."

"I'm dying to have a look inside.....Can't I stay just a bit longer?"

"I think it's best you left now. But don't worry, we'll tell you all about it later on. You won't have missed a thing!"

Steen Hansen left through the rectangle of light in the bottom of the darkened hold. He still felt as though he was missing out on something.

Mogensen returned a few minutes later with a hacksaw, and a padlock that looked almost the same as the one keeping the container doors locked. Black asked, "Where did you find those?" Mogensen smiled in the dark. It was always good to surprise Black.

"I had a walk about the engine room while you were having a kip. I found these in the workshop! There's a key too, so we'll be able to come in and out whenever we want, without anyone else knowing anything about it."

He noticed that Hansen was missing. "Where's Steen?"

Black was rubbing his hands with glee. This was surely his lucky day!

"I sent him upstairs. The less he knows from now on, the better..."

Mogensen was surprised. Black could see it in the light from the flashlight reflected from the container.

"Don't worry, it's for his own protection, and ours! If Brown gets a whiff of what Steen is doing, he might be tempted to pump him for information. It's best for all of us if Steen can't tell Brown anything of real importance. It's more than enough that he knows how to get to the container below deck."

Mogensen shrugged. He was beginning to see Black in a new light. Perhaps it was time to stop trusting Black completely. Black put a hand on Mogensen's shoulder.

"Come on then! Let's get this thing open!"

Bob and Dougy were out walking along the promenade behind the South Shields marina. It was cold, and foggy. The ice particles in the air gave Dougy problems with his breathing. Bob had on a dark blue skiing Balaclava, keeping his ears, mouth and nose warm. Dougy said,

"I'm going to get one of them!"

Bobby laughed.

"You've been saying that for the last two years Dougy, and every time the spring comes around and the weather gets warm again, you forget all about it. I bought this four years ago, and I can tell you, I've been glad I did lots of times!"

Dougy lit a cigarette. The smoke was warm.

"We've been walking around here for the last hour, and we still haven't seen anything worth pinching! I wonder if Billy and Brian have found anything yet?"

"I don't think so. There they are on the other side of the marina. Can you see them? The two blokes just passing the container beside the harbour office?"

Dougy peered in the direction Bob was pointing. Two unidentifiable figures, barely visible through the fog, were standing by a yellow container just behind the fuel pump for filling up motor boats. Dougy nodded. They walked on.

There weren't that many boats about this time of year, and what there was, was small and showed no signs of having the right gear. There was something worth looking at a bit further ahead. Though it was difficult to see in the fog without jetty lights, half of which were out, it looked big at any rate.

The Sea Swan was a big motor cruiser. Forty three feet of cobalt blue glass-fibre hull, topped with a white glass fibre luxurious cabin and a poop deck with extra steering gear buried under a canvas cover. She was fitted with two short masts which bore radio and GPS antennae and an enclosed radar copula. She was tied up with her bows towards the jetty where Bob and Doug were standing. She seemed deserted. Bob took hold of the fore stay and stepped aboard. Dougy stayed on the jetty. The deck was teak. Bob walked up the starboard side. The cabin interior was mahogany, with small, polished brass simulated oil lamps dangling from gimbals bolted to the panels. A sofa in a U-shape with white leather cushions and a mahogany coffee table in the middle took up the aft end of the wheelhouse. He walked astern and climbed the couple of steps to the poop deck. He could see Dougy, lighting another cigarette, on the jetty. But more importantly, he could see the radar installed half way up the foremast, just as clearly. He came down on the port side and shone his flashlight into the cabin. There was a radar, a radio, an auto pilot, and a hole that went down into the inside of the ship. Bob turned off the flashlight and returned to the jetty.

"Just the thing, Dougy. Let's go fetch Bill and Brian."

Billy and Brian had not had any luck. Their side of the marina proved to be populated almost exclusively by small fishing cobbles. Billy checked his watch. It was half past two in the morning. If they hadn't found a boat and put to sea before five, then it was likely that people would start turning up. It would be too late then. They would have to get out of town and head north.

Bob and Dougy turned up.

"Found the perfect boat Billy. Just opposite here on the other side of the marina."

"Let's have a look at her then."

Billy said.

They walked back. After looking the boat over, Billy said.

"Nice boat - it'll do the trick nicely. Now for the next part of the plan. Brian, go and fetch the van. In the meantime we'd better look her over from the inside."

Brian disappeared. Billy climbed aboard the Sea Swan and went aft towards the wheelhouse door on the port side. He took a crowbar out from under his donkey jacket, inserted it into the space between the sliding door and the doorframe, just over the lock, and wrenched the door open. The lock itself popped out onto the deck. Billy pushed it over the side with a boot. It fell into the icy water with a definite, but muffled plop, and disappeared. Billy slid open the door and went inside. Bob and Dougy followed suit.

There were six berths on the boat, all the cooking gear they would need, charts in the chart holder just above the lighter up to the wheelhouse. Billy found the switchboard. Suddenly there was light on board. He switched off the flashlight and put it in his pocket. Bob opened the fridge and whistled.

"Hey, the fridge is full of beer!"

"It's like a dream come true..!" said Billy.

Dougy just threw himself on one of the berths and within seconds had dropped off to sleep. After a while, when Brian turned up with the van, Bob went to wake him up.

It took fifteen minutes to empty the van. Then Billy disappeared with it towards the multi-storey car park in Newcastle, on the north side of the river. Before he left, they agreed to pick him up from the jetty just below the bridge - which was of course, just a mere stone's throw from the very place where the two men who were looking for them had set up shop. Bob gave Dougy and Brian the job of stowing away the gear, while he rummaged around in the engine compartment below the wheelhouse floor and found a toolbox.

The engine control panel yielded to the biggest screwdriver in the toolbox, and Bob hot-wired the ignition switch. When he turned the power on, he could see that the fuel tank was half full. There should be enough to get them half way up the Scottish coast, but then they'd need more fuel - and the last of their money had disappeared with Billy towards the car park. Never mind - that's another problem for another time - Bob thought, and started the engine. When it had been running for a couple of minutes, Bob called Brian, who came up from below.

"Go up front and untie her Brian. When you've done that come back to the aft end. Dougy!...."

Dougy popped up through the hole..

"Come up and give us a hand."

Brian and Dougy hadn't tried anything like this before, but Bob had. When Brian had slipped the spring-loaded trosses holding the bows of the Sea Swan to the jetty and thrown them aboard, he came aft on the starboard side. Dougy was sent aft on the port side and Bob gently backed the boat out between the poles to which the aft end was tethered. He stopped the engine and gave a short burst forward to stop the boat with its aft end just sticking out between the poles. Brian and Dougy heaved the nooses at the ends of each of the aft tethers up over the poles. Bob started the engine again and eased the boat backwards. Dougy and Brian were on each side, keeping the boat from banging into the poles as she moved backwards, until the poles were no longer any danger. Then they came into the wheelhouse again and shut the doors. It was still cold inside - just as cold as outside, but they were out of the icy fog. They watched as Bob turned the Sea Swan around and headed for the entrance to the marina. Further up river, Billy was coming down the old stone stairs leading to the quayside below. The VW was tucked away safely. One or two pedestrians were walking around in the streets above, but the quay was empty. By quarter past three, Billy was on board and the Sea Swan was heading for the mouth of the river. When she was a couple of sea miles out, she turned north. There was some serious partying going on for the rest of the night. The stereo played heavy metal at fifty watts a channel, and the fridge door was almost never closed. There was no need now to keep quiet!

It was almost one in the morning by the time Dick Brown finally managed to get down to the cabin where Britta was in hiding. The auto pilot was working again. Erik, Black, Hansen and Mogensen had turned in. The engine was running smoothly. The fog had dispersed at last, moved on by a slight breeze from the east. There were no ships in sight. Brown stopped by the galley on the way down, found half a loaf in the bread locker, a jar of orange marmalade behind some jars of beetroot slices and mint jelly in the fridge and a couple of cans of Dutch lager in the second fridge. He put the lot into a plastic bag he found in a drawer - it was from a Polish supermarket - and went downstairs.

As Brown approached the cabin, he noticed several things almost immediately. The first was the smell of cigarette smoke in the corridor. The second was a cigarette butt on the deck just outside a hatch at the end of the corridor. The third and fourth were less obvious, but still noticeable. There were loose flakes of light paint lying on the deck just beside the second hatch, and what looked like a dirty shoe print among them. Brown hadn't noticed any of these things earlier on. He put down the plastic bag just outside Britta's cabin and went to have a look. He didn't touch the cigarette, but got down on his knees and smelled it. It had been smoked recently. Brown stood up and carefully opened the hatch behind him. It led to the engine room. He closed the hatch again, and turned his attention to the second hatch. Brown followed the tunnel into the hold. It came as a surprise to him that there was a way to get into the hold. It really was unfortunate that it was to be found just by the engine room, and Britta's cabin. He had brought a flashlight with him. The container showed no signs of having been tampered with. The lock was still in place. He left the hold and returned to the corridor, being careful not to step in the flakes of paint on the floor. Judging it to be prudent to check the other cabins, Brown stumbled on Black's meeting place with Mogensen and Hansen. There were three mugs on the table, three plates with crumbs, and three chairs. There were three more piled on top of each other in the corner. Brown closed the door. He went to Britta's door, knocked on it once, took a piece of plain white paper out of his back pocket, and pushed it in the crevice at the bottom of the door. After a few muffled sounds, the door opened partially and Brown entered sideways.

When the door closed behind Brown, and the grey blanket fell back into place, they greeted each other with a hug. Brown still had the plastic bag in his hand. Britta still had the loaded revolver in hers. Brown was the first to break off. He put the bag on the floor under the table, pulled out the two beers and pulled off the rings. They both took a hefty drink.

"We might have run into a spot of bother!"

He said. She nodded.

"I heard voices in the corridor a few hours ago. There was some moving about too. What is going on?"

"It seems that Black, Mogensen and Hansen have been holding a meeting just next door. I found the cups and chairs where they'd left them, and there were crumbs from cheese and onion sandwiches on the table. The cheese was fresh. It seems I made a mistake when I checked the ship over. There is in fact another way to get to the hold."

"From the deck?"

Brown shook his head - "No, from just across the corridor here. I think they must have been in to have a look. At least I found signs to that effect. I checked the container, though and it looks intact."

"Oops! That isn't good news."

"Nope, and to make matters worse, the hatch at the end of the corridor here connects directly with the engine room - which means that you can probably expect more meetings to be held on the other side of this bulkhead."

"Hmm. It might be an advantage if I could hear what they were talking about in there. Is there any possibility of that - I mean other than sitting all night with a glass up against the bulkhead and my ear on it...?"

"Off hand I'd say no. The dividing wall is steel. It would be something of a job to drill a hole in it, even if we had the drill and the bits we needed. On the other hand - there is the deck head. There's a space between decks, where cables and pipes are run."

"What, you mean crawl up there?"

"No, that wouldn't be possible - there's not enough room." Britta looked relieved.

"But if we took one of the panels down just over the table here, then we could get access to the space. The deck head in the next cabin wouldn't be any more than a few inches away. It might be possible to overhear what was being said."

"Well, it's worth a try - I could use a bit of excitement to liven up my day!"

"Let's do it then."

Brown pushed the book and cups aside. Britta put the cans of bear on the deck under the table, where they wouldn't get spilled. Brown climbed up on the table. It was secure enough, as it should be, since it was bolted to the bulkhead. There was not enough room for him to stand up, until he pushed hard on one of the panels in the deck head. It went up into the hole. He turned the panel on its side and passed it down to Britta.

"Don't put it aside up here. If it slides off somewhere you'll never catch it again!" He said - then stood up and shone the flashlight into the space in the direction of the next cabin. As it turned out, they were in luck. Over the washbasin in Britta's cabin, there was a lamp fixed to the ceiling. The switch was by the door. When he stood up in the space between decks, Brown noticed that the fitting for the light in the next cabin was missing. It occurred to him that the light had been missing in the next cabin when he had looked inside. So there was a round hole the size of the top of a teacup just over the washbasin. Brown signalled to Britta to hand him the panel. He pushed it up though the hole then dropped it in place, and got down from the table.

"We're in luck!" He said.

Britta picked up the two cans and handed one across to Brown, who continued without interruption.

"You see the lamp over the washbasin?" She nodded while sipping her beer. "Well, the one in the next cabin in missing, so there's a hole in the deck head. It should be possible to hear at least some of what goes on. Mind you'll have to turn off your lights before you open the panel. If they're on and the panel is missing, it may be possible for someone using the washbasin to see light. That would certainly make them suspicious."

"Ok. I've got a flashlight in my bag, so if I put a chair up on the table and keep the flashlight on my lap, I might be able to take notes."

"It's worth a try. You might not even need to put your head up in the spaces to hear. Only one thing. If you are discovered - don't hesitate to shoot! If you don't and they take you prisoner, who knows what might happen to both of us!"

"Don't worry, I can take care of myself!"

"Good, that's all I wanted to hear. One last thing - we should be off the Swedish coast in about twelve hours. We'll turn north west when we get there, and follow the coast until we're free of Sjælland."

"What part of the coast will we arrive at before changing course?"

"Ystad."

"I know it. A car ferry to Poland sails from there. Are we on schedule?"

"So far. We should be reaching Læsø the day after tomorrow, the Skaggerak the morning after that and then two days across the North Sea to Northumberland. We'll be there in five days if all goes well."

"Two days across the North Sea? The ferry normally makes it in twenty hours."

"The ferry does more than ten knots. Well, we might be there a bit earlier if the weather stays in the East."

"What's the weather report say?"

"Fresh breeze, showers, patches of fog here and there for the next twenty four hours. Not bad really, for the time of year."

"Yes, so far we've been lucky. Let's hope it stays that way...."

Brown got up to leave. "I'd better get back on the bridge. I'll be back as soon as I can. Keep your ears open."

"Take care. If anything happens to you while I'm down here - I'll be in real trouble!"

She showed him to the door and squeezed his hand just a little tighter than usual as he slipped though into the corridor. He returned the compliment.

"I'll be back later..."

He said, and disappeared. Britta closed the door and locked it. Looking at the table, she thought - maybe I'd better get things ready."

The bridge was still deserted when Brown returned. He took a look around in the corners and out on both wings, just to make sure. There were no lights to be seen at sea. Everything was as it should be. He settled down in the pilot's chair, and started thinking about the situation.

Down on the deck below the bridge, Erik was sleeping peacefully. The cabin lights were off. His door was locked and a chair was propped in under the handle to prevent it being turned.

He was totally unaware of the meeting going on in Blacks' cabin three doors away.

Black, Mogensen and Hansen were sitting around a table littered with sub-machine guns, handgrenades, pistols, rifles and bullets. Three empty sports bags lay thrown into a corner. They had just finished cleaning the weapons. There was a small can of oil and some dirty rags in the middle of the table. Mogensen was fondling a nine-millimetre Makarov. The other two were leaning back in their chairs. Hansen looked like he was about to fall asleep - well it was, after all, almost three o'clock in the morning.

"Okay, it's agreed then."

Black said blandly.

"We each take part of our weapons and stash them in our cabins. Steen takes the rest of his and stows them in the galley, and Michael and me take the rest of ours and stow them in the engine room." The others nodded. Black continued. "It's a good thing Steen overheard Brown and Erik talking about our course. If we can take over the boat when we get off Læsø, we can anchor her up and call the lads."

"Hammel's going to shit bricks when he hears about this!"

Hansen exclaimed. Black sneared.

"Hammel can go to hell! We've got a whole boat to mess about with, go anywhere we want with, and a container full of all the shit we could ever need. There's room on board for the rest of the gang. We're better off than we've ever been! Hammel might be good at planning, but he's not worth a shit when it comes to action - and now's the time for action!"

Mogensen looked up, first at Black, then at Hansen. He said quietly.

"I think he's right Steen. We've never been as strong as we are now! Once we've got Jens and the others on board, we can decide what to do. Anholt's a good place to anchor up for a few days, and Jens can bring the piggy bank with him.."

He was referring to the cash box that Black's group had been keeping secret from Hammel and the rest of the organisation. Black was nodding assent.

"So we've got to get rid of Brown and Erik before we get to Læsø the day after tomorrow. We can't just tie them up and put them ashore."

He said.

"And the best time to do it is while they're together. A surprise on the bridge when we have Læsø in sight would be the best, I think. Now none of us have tried this kind of thing before, so we're going to have to think about it. I think we should all get some sleep now. We can talk about it down below after breakfast."

The meeting broke up. Hansen and Mogensen stuffed their sports bags with their share of the weapons and left. When they'd gone, Black locked his door and pushed a chair in under the handle. He opened the top drawer under the bunk and stowed an AK74, two Czech copies of the Uzi, and half of the ammunition that was on the table, and closed it again. Then he loaded a Makarov, put on the safety, and put it under the rolled up blanket he was using as a pillow. A few seconds after he had rolled fully clothed onto the mattress and pulled the blanket over himself, he was fast asleep.

"Four slices of bacon, three fried eggs and four onion rings inside half a loaf of bread - Now that's what I call a sandwich!"

Robson's jaws gaped and when they were fully open, there was just exactly the amount of room required to slide one end of the sandwich in. Tony Lawson watched him in disbelief from across the table, over the top of the newspaper. Jack's jaws closed. There was a strange crunching noise. Lawson shook his head.

"From the looks of things you've had more than one of them!"

He mumbled and turned back to the newspaper. He was referring to the fact that Jack Robson's weight had passed the twenty stone mark ages ago...

"You're just jealous! You shrimp....!"

Jack laughed.

But Tony wasn't listening. On page three, directly opposite the nude that said nothing to him, there was a small article from a local politician. When he had read it, he folded the paper and threw it on the table.

"What do you think of that bastard Langley? You know, he'll not be satisfied until he shuts this place down!"

He said and grabbed the red and white striped mug on the table in front of him.

The tea was getting cold. He grimaced. Jack wiped his jaw with a paper serviette.

"Well, that's nothing new. He was against even setting up this place. And to tell you the truth, if I didn't work here I'd want it closed down as well. I mean, what's it all coming to if you can't walk down the street without somebody watching you on the one of them screens!"

He nodded in the general direction of the monitoring console. The wall above it was filled with screens, each showing a street corner, or a market square or a crossroads. Common to all, were the people who moved rapidly through the field of vision of the camera.

"What's wrong with that? When you walked around the town before, you could never be sure that you weren't being watched from a window, or a street corner, or a doorway somewhere. Anyway, most people don't mind being watched because they've got nothing to hide!"

Jack laughed.

"We've all got something to hide Tony. Mind you, we don't often peddle it on the street! But that's not the point, is it ? Let's take an example. Let's say you got off work and went back to your car to drive home. Let's say that when you got there, there was this bloke sitting on the bonnet waiting for you - a bloke you'd never seen before - nasty looking type. Anyway, when you ask him to get off, he stands up and pulls out a gun and puts the muzzle right against your forehead. You'd shit bricks, wouldn't you? Anyway, this bloke, he says, kind of like in a gangster film - I want you to do me a favour. If you do, I'll make it worth your while - big time. If you don't .... Then he cocks the revolver, and you're sure your time has come! But then he lets the hammer down again, careful like, and he says - I want you to keep an eye on the Midland Bank. I want to know who comes in and out and when. I want to know everything that happens there during the next week.....What would you do?"

"You've been watching too many late night movies, Jack. That's a stupid question."

"No it isn't. It's serious. What would you do? You've haven't got all that many options Tony. One, you can tell him what he wants to know, and if he keeps his promise, you'll get well paid and no body finds out. Mind you, next time he needs a favour he'll be all over you like flies on a piece of shit! Then again, you can tell him what he wants to know, after which he bumps you off because you're a witness to whatever he's got cooking! Or, you can tell him what he wants to know, then tell the cops - in which case him and his mates'll have a grudge against you....."

"Alright, that's enough - I get you're point. Whatever I do I'll be up the creek without a paddle. But that'll be too obvious. If anything happens to the bank, the cops'll be all over this place looking at the videos. If they find out I've been watching the bank more closely than I should be in the normal course of a normal day, they'll bust my ass as an accomplice, and this nasty bloke of yours knows that already!"

"True, but he could pay you to look the other way at the critical moment..Couldn't he?"

"I suppose so, but that would at most win him a few seconds."

"That may be enough."

"I still say you've been watching too many films! All right, I'll agree there is a risk that security guards like us can be forced or paid to do something that we wouldn't otherwise do. But on the other hand, think of that gang of muggers down in Grey Square last week. The cops would never have caught them in a month of Sundays' if it hadn't been for the video. Or what about that car thief they caught Monday night outside the Central Station? If Charlie hadn't noticed that the car he parked was on the list of stolen vehicles, they'd never have been waiting for him when he came back, would they?"

"That's true. On the other hand, what about Stan Briggs?"

"Yeah, well, Stan should never have been working here!"

Tony looked deep into the mug. Jack watched the bald patch on the top of Tony's head.

"I'll never understand what made him sell the video of that bloke topping himself in the lift to the TV."

"Money, Tony - money, or the lack of money. We've all got our price. Even model citizens like you and me!"

"Yeah, well. Anyway, let's get back to work before the boss comes back. We've already had ten minutes more than we should!"

Both men stood up and started clearing the remnants of lunch - the dirty mugs, knives and forks and crumbs off the spotty tablecloth. The office door opened. Both turned their heads to watch two strangers enter. The tall one was obviously a copper. The shorter, and younger one, looked like a dirty, tatty sailor that had just washed ashore.

Chapter Fourteen – Gunboat Diplomacy

For the first time since the Professor Petrov had put to sea from Klaipeda, the sun was shining from a clear, cloudless sky. Far off on the starboard aft quarter, it had just raised its lower limb above the horizon. The air was still cold. The temperature outside on the bridge wing was five below zero, but the chill factor made it feel even colder. Erik was huddled in a greatcoat, in the shelter of the windscreen, looking down at the deck below. His fingers felt like ice, although his hands were thrust deep into the pockets, and the heavy collar was turned up against the wind. His eyes were watering. The bridge wing door was closed. Inside, Brown was standing behind the chart table wielding a pair of dividers over the chart of the waters around Læsø. Only ten sea miles to go before the island came in sight. If what Britta had overheard turned out to be true, then it should be happening any minute now. He watched Erik, huddled on the other side of the bridge wing door. There was no sign of any unusual activity there. Erik was still looking ahead.

Brown stretched, holding one hand over his solar plexus. His shoulders and back were stiff. He stretched, and breathed in heavily. Then he turned around and put on the heavy parka that was hanging from the hook just beside the door to the pilots' resting room, where his gear was now stashed. This might be my last trip - he was thinking. Oh - what the hell, anything's better than dying of old age! Oh, I guess I'm just tired! It's been a long trip, but for some of us it's going to end soon. He said his prayers.

Brown wasn't a religious man in the normal sense of the word. But he was a spiritual man. What's the difference? The difference is that whereas a religious man can quote pages from the bible, and goes to church to worship, the spiritual man knows there's some kind of after life but isn't prepared to bet on how it looks. When Brown prayed, he didn't mutter dogmatic sentences. He just looked out through the Bridge window, both hands in the pockets of the parka, a pair of Zeiss binoculars hanging around his neck, and wondered what that last journey would be like, and whether he would miss anything in the life he was leaving.

He was momentarily so far away, that he almost didn't hear the bridge wing door slide open. It was the sudden cold draught that caught his attention. He turned his head toward the door. Erik had stepped inside and had his back to Brown. He was shutting the door again. Brown watched him without moving. When Erik turned around, Brown could see that he was blue in the face from the cold. Erik clapped his hands and blew on the fingers...Brown felt somehow very far away. Watching Erik walk across the bridge was like watching an actor cross the stage below. While Brown himself was sitting above, and away from the whole show, alone, on the balcony at the back of the theatre...The problem is, to quash the mutiny with as little damage in the wheelhouse as possible - he was thinking.

"Time for coffee." Erik said, without glancing at Brown, and left the stage through the door behind the chart table.

The stair well went into semidarkness when Erik closed the bridge door behind him. There was only one working bulb left to light the stairs down to the deck below the bridge. When he arrived at the galley, Erik found the others sitting around a table. He didn't bother to greet them - he was too cold. He made a beeline for the coffee, poured himself a mug, and stood caressing it for a long time, until his fingertips began to tingle in the heat, and he couldn't hold on much longer. He didn't notice the others watching him, but after a while it occurred to him that there was no talking, so he looked up. Their faces were expressionless. Erik sat down beside them and drank his coffee without saying a word.

Erik had half emptied the mug, when Black said,

"What's it going to be, Erik? Are you with us, or against us?"

Erik looked up. He had absolutely no idea what Black was talking about. The others noticed the surprised look on his face. Mogensen didn't like the fact that they'd kept Erik in the dark. You see he liked Erik. They went way back, back to school. They had been in the same class, played on the same football team, watched videos at Fatty Hansen's house on a Friday night when Fatty's parents were out playing the violin and harmonica at the social club. Erik had always played the game straight. But Black, on the other hand.... If it comes to a show down - Mogensen thought - I'm backing Erik.

"What's what going to be?"

Erik put the mug down on the table. There was a long, drawn-out silence. Black said blandly,

"We're taking over the boat - are you with us, or against us?"

Erik looked around. He was searching each of their faces for any hint of a smile or chuckle. There wasn't any. When his gaze turned back to Black, he said,

"You're serious aren't you?"

Black nodded.

"When?"

Black checked his watch.

"In ten minutes." As he was speaking, he put a Kalashnikov on the table. While Erik was still looking at that, Black added a Makarov pistol. The other two placed weapons on the table too. Erik looked up.

"Pick one - if you're on our side!"

Erik took a Kalashnikov.

"Why wouldn't I be?"

He asked, and checked the magazine. It was full. Mogensen smiled. Hansen looked relieved, and said

"Didn't I tell you he'd be with us?"

Black looked disappointed. Erik noticed that. Maybe it's time to start keeping a lookout for Black - he thought.

"What's the plan?" He asked.

"In a couple of hours we'll be off Læsø. We've got to take over the boat by then. What was Brown doing when you left the bridge?"

"Just standing. Looking through the front window. What are you going to do with him?

"What do you think..?"

Black answered, and demonstratively pulled back the cocking handle of the Uzi he was wielding. Erik shrugged and said nothing.

When Erik had been gone for a few minutes, Brown walked over to the starboard bridge wing door and opened it. A sudden, icy wind whipped around his ears and down the cleft of his shirt, which was open at the neck. He didn't mind, although his body shivered ever so gently for just a few seconds before becoming quite still again. Brown crossed to the port bridge wing door and opened it too. Another icy wind, this time stronger as the warmth in the wheelhouse was sucked out. He checked the door behind the chart table to make sure it was closed and unlocked, then went to stand behind the table, looking forward, again with both hands in his pockets. The stage was set. Only the other actors were missing.

In a while, there was a clinking sound, of metal on metal from one of the outside lighters. It was difficult to pinpoint which one from where Brown was standing. His heart missed a beat, then picked up again and accelerated. He stiffened involuntarily, made an effort of will, then relaxed again. But now the adrenaline was pouring into his bloodstream and the main spring was being wound.

The door behind Brown opened slightly, ever so gently. A moment later Mogensen peeked timidly through the gap. Brown was standing just three feet away to the left with his right side and back to the door.

When Mogensen kicked open the door and jumped inside, aiming the pistol at Brown, Hansen followed with a Kalashnikov. Brown didn't seem to notice at first. There was a long, painful silence. Then Mogensen shouted

"Don't move Brown!"

At that, Erik, armed with a Kalasknikov, stepped into the wheelhouse from the starboard side, and Black, armed with the Uzi, came in through the port door. All were pointing their weapons at Brown, who still hadn't moved an inch, but just stood, statue-like, looking ahead.

Black and Erik approached the chart table. Black was now sure that things were going according to plan. Actually, this had been a lot easier than he had suspected. Brown should have been putting up a fight by now. Bullets should have been whistling around the wheelhouse. But instead, Brown was quiet. He knew he was beaten! Black's back straightened just a little bit more. Now HE was in charge!

"What do you boys want?"

Brown asked. There was no sign of emotion in his voice. He looked around their faces. Hansen was scared stiff. Mogensen less so. Erik showed no sign of any emotion whatsoever. Black was supremely confident.

"We're taking over the boat, Brown - and we're putting you over the side where you can't get in the way! Take your hands out of your pockets - slowly - and put them above your head, where we can see them!"

Black watched Brown take his hands out of his pockets ever so slowly. There was no sign of a gun in his right hand - but what was that metal thing in his left? It took a second or so for it to dawn on Black. His expression changed. A handgrenade!

Brown said,

"Yes boys, a handgrenade - and as you can all see - "

He showed them the grey metal object clasped in his hand,

"- the pin is out!"

He let the message sink in.

" So I'm off on a one way trip? In that case - you're all coming along with me!"

He opened his fingers.

The cocking handle left the handgrenade and flew off across the wheelhouse. It seemed to everyone present to take forever to rattle against the hull somewhere. Black and Erik came alive first. They ducked down behind the chart table and began scrambling for the door. A second later, Mogensen and Hansen tried to get through the door to the stairwell at the same time. There was a very brief panic, then Mogensen pushed through, fell down the stairs, and Hansen followed him. Brown tossed the grenade into the hole behind Hansen and drew a pistol. By now, Erik had reached the starboard wing door and Black had reached the other. Brown wasn't about to cross in front of the door to the stairwell, so he just stood there, waiting for the blast that came a second later. Smoke and shrapnel belched through the open doorway. The front window cracked as something hit it, but didn't break. Then there was silence, a silence only broken by the sound of the engine thumping away, unconscious of the life and death struggle taking place above. Brown sprang through the door to the stairwell and pushed his way through the smoke that now just hung there, thick and black and with that unmistakable tang of pitric acid. The smoke moved as he passed through it, swirled in the square of sunlight behind him.

Brown found Hansen first. The body was lying head down on the stairs, with one arm under, and one leg crossing the other in a queer, disjointed fashion that no living human can do. There were bloodstains on the back of his leather waistcoat. A small, red, waterfall flowed down the stairs until it became just a drip, drip, drip. Brown stepped over the body, avoided the blood, and continued until he found Mogensen, flung in a corner further down. A piece of shrapnel had burrowed deep into his skull.

A few seconds after the explosion, and the shock, had subsided, Black decided to risk his neck, and raised his head to peer into the wheelhouse. He started to raise the gun when he saw a figure framed in the opposite doorway, but let it fall again. It was Erik. Black stood up and stepped into the wheelhouse. He expected to see blood and guts everywhere and got a surprise, because there was none. There was a heavy, pungent smell hanging in the air. Erik crossed to the chart table, weapon ready. He took a quick look behind. Black watched him. Erik straightened.

"He's gone!" He said.

"What do you mean - he's gone?"

Black said in disbelief and took several quick steps around the chart table. Erik was right, Brown had gone. There was only one place he could go to from here. They took up positions on opposite sides of the doorway and peered into the gloom. It was impossible to see down into the hole. The single, solitary bulb had gone out, and there was still some smoke obscuring the semidarkness. They looked at each other.

"He must have chucked the grenade down the stairs, waited until it went off and then gone that way!" Erik said.

"Steen! Michael!"

Black shouted into the hole. There was no reply. He tried again. Still no reply. He turned to Erik.

"We've got to find Brown. But we've also got to find Steen and Michael. One of us has to go down there and check it out!"

Erik shrugged

"If they're alive, then they're surely messed up so bad they can't move. Brown would have killed them otherwise, and we haven't heard any shooting!"

Black thought about that one for a moment.

"You're probably right. All right. We'll try something else. It's time to call reinforcements - you stand guard."

Black locked the door to the stairwell while Erik stood guard. Then Erik used the VHF to place a call to Bjarne, while Black took a look outside. When Erik got off the line, he went over to Black, who was standing in the port bridge wing door, and said,

"It'll take them four or five hours to get here. In the meantime we're going to have to go down to the engine room and stop the engine, then go out on deck and drop the anchor. You and Michael were down in the engine room. Can you stop the engine?"

Black nodded.

"No problem. But getting there and back isn't going to be easy. Our only hope is that Brown doesn't know we've called for reinforcements, or that we're going to anchor here. What worries me, is how he knew we would try and take over the boat!"

Erik shrugged.

"He's probably been wandering around with that thing in his pocket for just such an emergency. You know Brown...."

They locked the doors to the wheelhouse, and took out the keys. The windows in the doors were too small to crawl through, but they both knew that at the most, this could only delay Brown a few moments if he decided to enter the wheelhouse after they had gone. Still, they'd know he had been there on their return. Black took the first, tentative step through the door to the stair well. He stopped on the top step and turned to Erik.

"Keep a sharp eye out behind us, and let's hope we don't walk into an ambush!" He said, and turned away without waiting for an answer.

"I hope he's run out of grenades!" Erik said.

Black hesitated a moment with one foot in the stair then pressed on. Dispersed they would be an easy target for Brown. If they stayed together, inside the narrow confines of the corridors leading to the engine room, then at least they could keep a close watch. Erik followed, a couple of yards behind Black, and turned often to check behind. He checked even more often after they had passed Hansen and Mogensen's bodies....

The lights were lit on the deck below. Each time he passed a cabin door, Black kicked it open and jumped to one side, while Erik kneeled and pointed the Kalashnikov back up the corridor behind them. Black didn't bother going inside. He simply turned on the light, took a quick look, and went on. About ten seconds later, Erik followed. Nobody was there. The bulb in the last cabin was out. Black flicked the switch a couple more times. There was nothing. He put a foot inside, changed his mind, and went on down the lighter.

They reached the engine room without having run into Brown, and stopped in the entrance.

"He must be around somewhere!"

Said Black, and opened the hatch.

"Maybe he's waiting for us up on deck."

Said Erik, just as Black stepped in through the open hatch.

"Maybe he's right here!"

Said a third voice from the top of the lighter behind them. Erik turned on his heel. Brown's face was just visible from where he was lying flat on the deck at the top of the lighter. Erik started to back into the hatch opening. Brown pointed the pistol and squeezed the trigger. Two shots boomed out in quick succession in the narrow corridor of steel plate. The first hit Erik in the chest. As he was falling, the second hit him in the left eye. He was dead before he hit the floor, but the muscles of his right hand, contracting in the moment of death, sent a spray of bullets whining up the corridor. Brown rolled aside and into the darkened cabin.

A moment later, Erik's magazine was empty and his gun fell silent. Just as silent as Erik himself, who lay in an ever widening pool of thick, bright red liquid, on the deck, half in and half out of the engine room hatch.

Several long moments passed for Brown, who sat on the deck, his back to the wall on the right of the opening, expecting a barrage of fire from Black. It didn't come. Instead, there was silence, or what could pass for silence in the deafening noise from the engine room through the open hatch. After a few seconds, there was a clash and the noise died to a relative whisper immediately. Brown hit the floor and rolled out into the corridor, ready for action.

Black had pushed Erik's body out into the corridor and slammed the hatch. Brown could see the last of the hatch locks turning from where he lay. They stopped turning as he watched. Brown stood up and went down the lighter. When he got to where Erik lay, he walked through the pool that filled that end of the corridor, picked up the Kalashnikov, getting his hands bloody in the process, and stuffed it into the bottom hatch lock. Black wouldn't be getting out that way! A slight trickle of blood from his left ear told Brown that the sound of the gun going off in the narrow corridor had damaged the ear drum.

Britta was armed and nervous when Brown knocked and pushed the crumpled sheet of blank paper in through the gap at the bottom of the door. He entered without saying a word, but she noticed the bloodstained hands, the dark stains on the green parka, and the bloody footprints. Brown emptied the pockets of the parka, four magazines for the pistol, and two handgrenades, onto the bunk. Britta took a look out into the corridor, spotted Erik, and the Kalashnikov jammed into the hatch lock, and came back in, tearing down the grey blanket in the process.

"So they did try it then, just like they talked about!"

She exclaimed.

Brown nodded and started to take off the parka. A sudden jarring pain in the right arm made him shudder. He realised for the first time that he had been wounded. It came as a surprise. He hadn't felt anything at all. He flexed the fingers of his hand. They seemed to work. Britta noticed, and came across the cabin.

"Have you been hit?"

"I think so. Right arm somewhere. I can still move my fingers though. It must be a flesh wound. If I'd been hit in a bone I'd know it for sure. Give me a hand to get this off."

Britta stepped behind him and helped him take off the parka. When it came off, she threw it into a corner. It smelled of blood. It was difficult to see if there was a stain on Browns navy blue sweater. She helped him take it off, and threw it onto the bunk beside her book, the one she hadn't finished reading, and that had lain there for at least the last two hours, since the trouble began.

It was indeed just a flesh wound. The bullet had entered through the outer upper arm muscle, and exited lower down, just above the elbow joint. There was some blood, but not an extraordinary amount. The hole had begun to close.

"You were lucky there! It just missed both your shoulder and elbow joints. Strange angle of entry though. You must have been lying down at the time."

"I was - but I wasn't taking a nap!"

From somewhere outside, there was a strange, deep, bellowing noise. Five times it sounded. First one second, then one seconds' silence, and so on. Britta raised an eyebrow. Brown, who had by now turned to face her, suddenly got nervous.

"Christ, there's nobody on the bridge and we're steaming at full ahead! We'd better get up there, and fast!"

Brown picked up the pistol and the extra magazines in a hurry. He headed for the lighter and the bridge. Britta followed, leaving the cabin door gaping. She was surprised when she passed Mogensen; less surprised when she stepped over Hansen, but shocked when she reached the bridge!

A giant ferry was sailing straight towards them, and there was land not a whole lot away off the port bow. Brown was at the wheel, turning hard starboard. The ferry was blaring out a warning. It couldn't manoeuvre this close to land without endangering itself. The Professor Petrov's speed was unabated. Slowly she began to turn starboard. The seconds ticked by. She turned more. When she passed the ferry on its port side, there was no more than fifty yards between them. Brown righted the wheel. Britta went to the port side door and looked up at the vessel. There was a man on the port bridge wing. He was shaking his fist at them. Britta turned round and went back to Brown.

"We'd better get that wound fixed right away. I'll fetch the first aid kit."

Brown nodded. The first aid kit was screwed to the bulkhead behind the chart room table. A bright red box with a white cross in the middle of the tin lid...

When Britta had finished dressing the wound, she went to stand on the port bridge wing, to get some fresh air. The island looked lovely in the sunshine, although the trees, which were easily visible from this distance, were still bare. Spring was just around the corner. The ice had long since slipped its grip on the waters around Læsø, although when she looked down, she could almost feel their coldness.

While she was looking down, she noticed a pair of hands pushing a white cylinder overboard from somewhere on deck level. The white cylinder was attached to a rope, which was again attached to the ship. When it hit the water, the white cylinder cracked open, and an orange life raft carefully unfolded itself. When it had done so, and was alongside the ship, pressed there by the force of the water, and held in place by the thin rope, the hands reappeared further astern, just above the place where the life raft was. A rope ladder was pushed out over the side. Within a few moments, a young man, armed with a machine pistol, was climbing down the ladder into the life raft. Britta stepped back from the railing. If he saw her standing watching, he might begin shooting. A short while later, the life raft reappeared at a distance off the stern, tossing and turning in the wake of the ship. It was still afloat, and the young man was still in it. She went inside and shut the door.

"Now all we've got to worry about is Black! He's still locked in the engine room and might get up to no good down there..."

"You don't need to worry about him any longer, he's just left the ship in a life raft."

Britta said, blandly. Brown stared at her, amazed.

"Did you see him?"

She nodded.

"Why didn't you say so? I owe that bastard for Peter!"

Britta approached and stood right in front of him. She looked him straight in the eye, gripped his shoulders, and said –

"Hansen, Mogensen and Erik are dead - I think you've paid your debt - don't you? And anyway, unless you want to turn this thing around and steam straight back to where he got off, then you can't do anything about it. And even if you did turn the boat around, Black'll be ashore before you got half way back. You could of course go ashore yourself and chase him....."

"Alright, you've made your point..."

"Good!"

She said, and continued,

"And anyway, we have some cleaning up to do downstairs - God, how I hate scrubbing floors!"

"They're called decks."

Said Brown. She scowled.

"Floors, decks, specks, hecks, I don't care, I hate scrubbing them all!"

Brown laughed.

"Alright, I'll give you a hand to clean up the mess as soon as we're clear of danger and back in the sea lane again. We've still got three days sailing to go, and I've had enough close shaves for this trip, thank you very much!"

"Me too. And by the way, I think it's about time you told me your real name."

"Bill Lennox."

Brown said, and didn't care.

"What's it all about?"

Watkins asked, as he took off his woolly hat and threw it on the table. It was six in the morning and he should still have been in bed. His legs felt as heavy as lead, and when he'd taken off the jacket and thrown it on top of the hat, his shoulders felt like a great weight had been lifted off them. Wailes pointed to the coffee pot gurgling away by itself in the corner.

"Get yourself a mug and come over here - for as Sherlock Holmes used to say - the game's afoot Watson!"

Watkins crossed the room towards the coffee pot. He felt like he was ninety years old. When he got there, it was a trial to decide which mug to take. Wailes watched him, and shook his head.

"That's what you get for drinking too much Brown Ale!" He shouted. Watkins winced and waved Wailes' comment away. The first splash of coffee missed the mug, but the rest went the right place. When the mug was full, Watkins picked it up and dried the outside with the blue and green striped towel hanging on a nail in the wall. He went over to where Wailes was waiting with a cigarette in his mouth, his own mug, and his feet up on the desk. Watkins sat down heavily and sipped.

"The Sea Swan's been spotted." Wailes said.

"Where?" Watkins asked.

"Berwick. She put in to the harbour and took on fuel. The harbourmaster saw her arrive an hour ago. After she'd taken on fuel, she left again."

"What was he doing up that early?"

"She - the harbourmaster's a woman up there. I don't know. Anyway - we've got the Sea Swan localised now."

"What were you doing up that early?"

Wailes shook his head. Watkins was a sorry sight. His eyes were bloodshot, his skin grey, his shoulders slumped.

"Get it together John! I've called the Navy. They've sent a couple of SBS blokes out in a rubber boat to see if they can spot her. I've told them to keep their distance once they know where she is going. I don't want anything to happen until that coaster from Lithuania arrives!"

Wailes smiled. The job was coming to an end and at the moment, it was looking good.

"We'll wait here until the Navy calls - I've no intention of rushing up to Berwick, only to find that the Sea Swan has sailed back to Newcastle! You'd better get some more sleep - Christ! - you look like something the cat dragged in!"

Watkins said nothing. He put the mug down on the desk, got up, went over to where his jacket was lying, climbed onto the table, and put his head on the jacket. Before you could say the words "Jack Crawford", he was fast asleep....

Two hours later, when the rest of the crew was just beginning to turn up for work, the phone rang on Wailes' desk. He had been dozing uneasily, but the ringing brought him around. He picked up the handset.

"Wailes." He listened for a few moments.

"Thanks - I'll be there in about two hours. Good work!"

He put the phone down and stood up. His chair scraped on the bare floor. Wailes took a gulp of coffee and shuddered. It was cold, and acidic. He wiped his lips with the palm of his left hand, and went across to where three of the crew was deciding whether or not to play a prank on Watkins, who was curled up on the table in a deep sleep. When Wailes approached, they backed off and went to work. No one said anything to Wailes. He had been grumpy ever since their visit to the security company headquarters. He had been happy to find that the security camera at the north end of the bridge had spotted the missing boat, but was pissed off about them not having found it after two days....

Wailes shook Watkins, who awoke with a start.

"They've anchored the boat off the Farne Islands. Get yourself a couple of headache tablets and let's get going."

"What about breakfast?"

"The Navy'll give breakfast when we get there."

Watkins was sitting up now.

"Where's there?"

"We're meeting the Navy at Sea Houses in two hours - so come on, fill 'yer bjuts!"

Watkins smiled.. "I love it when you talk dirty!" He said, referring to Wailes' attempt at the local dialect, and got off the table.

Ten minutes, and three headache tablets later, they left the office, unnoticed.

The harbour was actually at North Sunderland, and is not normally visited by ships larger than fishing boats. The harbour is at the end of a channel through the rocks that stretch almost a kilometre out from the shore. The channel faces north-east, but there is a mole at the end, pointing north-west, protecting the boats laid up behind it from waves sweeping in from across the open reaches of the North Sea. Another mole stretches out across the rocks on the north side of the channel. Both moles have flashing lights mounted on short towers at the ends. The outer light flashes red, the inner green. The northern mole also has a shorter fishing boat quay sticking out from it in a south-easterly direction, with a dog-leg going south south-east in the middle. The harbour is too shallow for frigates like H.M.S. Battleaxe. She was lying at anchor in sixteen metres of cold, grey, quiet sea water, just by the red marker buoy one sea mile south-east of North Sunderland; hidden from the land by a heavy, rolling fog that trundled in over her from the east.

Wailes parked the car on the northern mole, at the end of the fishing boat jetty. He and Watkins got out, locking the doors behind them. They walked down the jetty to the end. The fog tasted of mussels and seaweed. It was low tide. Two men clad in diving suits were waiting in a RIB with two very big outboard engines attached. Both were armed with Heckler and Koch MP5 machine pistols. A third man, dressed in the uniform of a naval lieutenant, was waiting for them.

"Commander Wailes I presume.."

He said, and scowled at Watkins, who did not fit his image of an officer in counter-intelligence. Wailes took the hand he offered.

"Yes - and don't worry about my friend's appearance - he's got it where it counts."

The lieutenant embarrassed that his gaze had been observed by Wailes, turned and started to climb down into the rubber dinghy. The rungs were dirty and slippery, but he made it safely. First

Watkins, then Wailes, followed. When they were safely aboard and seated, the lieutenant signalled the man in the open cockpit. The second man slipped the moorings. The engines started immediately. The RIB sailed quietly out through the harbour entrance, past the fishing boats tied up at the jetty, and two eager sea fishermen who stood with mugs of hot something cupped in their hands at the end of the outer jetty. Once outside the harbour, the engines roared, suddenly violent. The fore end of the RIB raised itself out of the water, and the bow came around to a more southerly course. Ten minutes later, the RIB was tied up alongside the waiting frigate, and Wailes and Watkins were following the lieutenant up the lighter. The watch was silent. No piping aboard, just a stiff salute as Wailes and Watkins went by on their way to the bridge.

There were three men gathered around the chart laid out on the chart table, when Wailes and Watkins arrived. They looked up. The captain made the necessary introductions quickly and without the least little bit of ceremony.

"I'm Captain Andersen, this is my number one, Commander Payne, and this is Lieutenant Maynard, who will be leading the boarding party."

Each of the other two nodded as their names were mentioned.

"I'm Commander Wailes and this is my associate, Watkins - counter intelligence." Then to Captain Andersen, "Have you been briefed on the situation, Captain?"

"Yes, and no. The admiralty signal told me to place my ship entirely at your disposal. It was my boys who found the Sea Swan. Perhaps you can fill us in on what's going on?"

Wailes nodded.

"I can fill you in on some of it for sure. The rest will have to remain restricted I'm afraid. We're expecting the Sea Swan to meet with a coaster from Lithuania. We don't exactly know what will happen when the meeting occurs, but it is vital that we prevent both the coaster and the crew of the Sea Swan from escaping once they are in our grasp. The crew of the Sea Swan is mainly ex-soldiers. They are certainly armed, and you can bet the lives of every man in your boarding party that they are prepared to use their weapons. What the status is aboard the coaster is unknown. Do you mind showing me where the Sea Swan has dropped anchor?"

"They dropped anchor right here, in two metres of water just west of the Longstone lighthouse. It's pretty sheltered in there, at least as sheltered as any place can be out here in an easterly gale. You'll notice that the islands are pretty flat, just a collection of rocks really. You say the coaster is coming from Lithuania? - Well, then she'll be coming in from the north east. She can choose two courses of action, north of the islands, or south. If she goes north around Whirl Rocks and Longstone, she'll be able to get within a couple of hundred yards of where the Sea Swan in anchored. There's around twelve meters of water there. On the other hand, if they go south around Longstone and stop around Craford Gut, here between Longstone and Clove Car rocks, they'll have sixteen meters of water and still have only a couple of hundred yards to the Sea Swan. I guess they could choose either direction."

Wailes was thoughtful.

"Any chance of covering both sides?"

"Might be a problem if the people on the Sea Swan are as well armed as you say. I certainly couldn't get the Battleaxe close enough without being spotted. The forecast says this fog is here for the rest of the day, so if the coaster arrives before the fog lifts, I wouldn't be able to provide the covering force with precise fire support. We might end up blowing both the Sea Swan and the coaster out of the water, leaving no survivors - which isn't actually the point, as far as I can see."

Wailes nodded.

"No, it isn't. And you'd risking hitting your own covering force too."

"Precisely.... I think too, that this position is as close as we can get without revealing ourselves as a warship if the fog starts to lift. If they're watching their radar, all they'll see is a blob. We could just as easily be a freighter laying at anchor for some reason or another."

"Might I suggest something, Captain?" Commander Payne interjected.

"Go ahead Charles.." Andersen replied.

"We could send a fire support team armed with a heavy machine gun and a brace of stinger missiles up the west side of Brownsman Island, through the gap, here, and land them on Big Harcar. The top of Big Harcar is five meters above sea level, so a rubber boat shouldn't be noticed if it moves quietly."

"Yes, not a bad idea. A fire support team could cover both the north and south approaches from there, and the ranges in both directions are so short that they would be able to provide adequate backup for the boarding party. I like that. We'll do it...Now all we have to do is to find out where and how to place the boarding party. North and South Wamses are the answer I think. The boarding party can travel along with the fire support team until they reach the Wamses'. They can stay under cover of the islands until the fire support team radios the approach path of the coaster. Lieutenant Maynard, your task will be to circumvent the coaster when she arrives. Get her between you and the islands and approach from seaward. Most likely the coaster crew will be engaged watching the islands. If you are fired upon, call for support and the fire support team will back you up."

They reached a consensus. Watkins, standing watching, turned his back to the chart table and went out onto the bridge wing. Wailes arrived a few seconds later.

"This is it, John. Let's hope everything goes well."

Watkins nodded. He was feeling a little bit queezy in the stomach, even though the ship wasn't moving at all.....

Wailes noticed, but chose to ignore what he saw. Instead, he slapped Watkins on the back and said,

"Come on - they're getting the launch ready - let's go down on deck."

"Why?"

"Because we're going along with the boarding party. I want to be among the first to get on that coaster when she arrives. Are you carrying?"

Watkins opened his jacket. He had a snub-nose thirty-eight tucked under his left armpit in a leather holster. Wailes nodded in approval. Watkins closed his jacket, breathed in deeply, righted his woolly hat and followed Wailes down the lighter to the deck, where some sailors were man-handling the launch over the side with the aid of a derrick.

Dougy shut the fridge door and looked around the saloon of the Sea Swan.

"No beer left!" His tone was sombre. Well, it was a bit like being at a funeral with no body wasn't it? Bob wasn't listening; he was on his side on one of the bunks, facing the hull, with a blanket pulled up over his head - asleep. Brian was messing about with the radio. He was calling the coaster at regular intervals on a little-used channel on the VHF.

"Professor Petrov - this is C Four - come in"

He spoke into the mike while Doug stood behind him, watching. When he released the mike button, there was a brief scratch of noise, then silence. There was no answer.

"You've been at that for two hours now, why not give it a rest?"

Brian turned in his seat and looked up.

"I'm going to keep it up until I've heard them answer. Why not go ashore and get something for us to drink? When they get here we've got something to celebrate. And even if they do come up on the radio before you get back it'll still be a couple of hours before we can go and meet them!"

Doug nodded. He climbed the lighter to the wheelhouse. The port door was open. Billy was just outside, scanning the fog with the binoculars. He looked around when Doug approached.

"I'm going ashore to pick up some booze, Bill - anything you want?

Billy shook his head, then pointed in the direction of the walkie-talkie that was lying on the table.

"Take that with you. If anything starts to happen out here, get back as quick as you can. Er, by the way, you can get me a pack of Woodbines."

Dougy climbed over the side into the rubber dinghy. He turned on the petrol tap just under the outboard motor and pumped the rubber bulb to prime it. It took a couple of pulls to start the engine.

When it came to life, he sat down and pulled the hood of the donkey jacket over his head. It was cold, and damp and he couldn't see more than a couple of hundred yards ahead. But that wouldn't be the worst part of the trip. The current was the worst. He would have to sail in big a half circle north of Brownman Island to avoid hitting any rocks, and that would put at least another half-hour on the trip. Still, at least the sea was calm. He turned up the engine when Billy had untied the line and thrown it into the dinghy, and headed away from the Sea Swan.

After a while, Billy checked his wristwatch. It was almost eleven, time to wake Bob to take over the watch and have some tea. He went inside, hung the binoculars on a wheel spoke, slid the wheelhouse door shut, and went down into the saloon.

Thirty minutes out from the Sea Swan, Dougy lit a cigarette and relaxed. The outboard sputtered away merrily to itself. Being alone in a rubber dinghy in the fog is a strange feeling. It's like you're boxed in, in a tiny world that's only as big as your range of vision. It a way it feels comfortable, because you can encompass the whole of this microcosm with just a few glances here and there. In another way it is tense - because your head knows that the world is bigger than this, and that danger can loom at any time from the grey shroud around you. After a while, you start to imagine sounds and shapes among the fog. Dougy put this down to the fog moving around. That was partially true. On the other hand, there were in fact shapes in the fog. They were sitting quite still, with their engines silent, drifting on the current with guns sticking out in all directions, like the quills of a porcupine, while the little engine in Dougy's dinghy gurgled to itself ahead in the fog as he passed them by.

Bob yawned and rolled over onto his back. The blanket fell partially onto the deck. He got a sudden chill and pulled it over him again. This time though, he didn't cover his head, but put his hands under it and looked around. His body felt heavy. What time was it? Eleven?

"I must have been asleep before my head hit the pillow!"

He muttered. At any rate, he couldn't remember having fallen asleep, and he had been away for seven hours! After a few moments of looking at the deck head, he rolled over onto his left side and propped his head up on one hand. Billy was making the tea on the gas. Brian was on the radio. Billy turned around as Bob sat up and scratched his sleepy head.

"Tea'll be ready in a minute."

"How long have you been up?"

"Just a couple of hours."

Bob looked around the saloon. Something was missing.

"Where's Dougy?"

"Gone to pick up some booze for tonight - he left about half an hour ago. Here."

Billy put a cup of tea on the table. Bob threw the blanket to one side and got up. He only had underpants on, and started to get dressed immediately the chill in the air hit his warm, naked skin.

"I hope he gets some ciggies - I ran out last night!"

A woman's voice came out of the loudspeaker just above the radio. Brian stiffened. Bob and Billy stopped what they were doing and looked in Brian's direction.

"C four - This is the Professor Petrov. Receiving you loud and clear."

A scratch of noise - and silence.

"She's here!"

Brian shouted. Billy turned to face Bob. They looked at each other in silence for a few long moments. Billy was thinking that this was the moment they had all been waiting for. Bob was hoping that Dougy would bring whiskey - because he intended to party until he fell down later on! Neither could guess what the other was thinking.

"Professor Petrov - my position is - fifty-four degrees thirty-eight point five North, zero degrees thirty-seven point one west. I repeat fifty-four degrees thirty-eight point five north, zero degrees thirty-seven point one west. Over."

A long moment passed, then the voice returned.

"Roger - we'll be in position within approximately three hours. We'll call you again then. Over and out."

Another long moment. Then they all started yelling and dancing about. After a while, Billy went back up to the wheelhouse. This is great - he was thinking - what a breakthrough! He turned on the radio. It was tuned to the local radio FM station. The news had just finished and the announcer was reading the weather report. It looked like the fog was beginning to move inland, away from the islands. The next program started while Billy was training the binoculars to the north east. They played "Smoke on the water - Fire in the sky". Billy didn't notice.....

Stephen Maynard was on his knees in the prow of the launch. A navy blue sweater now hid the white shirt. The lapels stuck out through the neck hole, and the knot in his black tie was visible just under his chin. He was wearing a bulletproof vest and a chest rig with eight pockets. Six of them were long and slim and held spare magazines for the Heckler and Koch MP5 he was cradling in his left hand. The other two carried hand grenades. Not the old fashioned Mills bomb type, but the flash-bang ones which are ideal for close quarter combat. He didn't feel the cold and damp. He was sweating.

In the launch behind him, nine men were crouching as low as they could. A tenth man was sitting in the rear, guiding the boat towards its destination, the port stern quarter of the Professor Petrov, just a hundred metres away. Wailes and Watkins were there too, seated on the floor of the launch, on each side of the control cockpit, out of the way. Their weapons were not drawn. The four men on the starboard side of the launch were pointing their weapons at the accommodation block of the coaster, which had not changed either speed or course since it had been intercepted by the launch. Maynard had taken this as meaning that the crew of the coaster had not suspected anything yet. The coasters' propeller was kicking up white foam that disappeared into the fog behind her.

The launch entered the coasters' bow wave, and was jostled violently. Maynard hung on to the knotted rope tied to the ring at the tip of the launch. This lasted for a few seconds, until the launch reached the relatively calm waters close to the hull, where the grey water seethed and bubbled as the rusty metal cut through them like a dull knife. There was a slight bump as the two vessels met. Their speeds were matched perfectly. The oarsman knew his job well. Maynard dropped the knotted rope, picked up the grappling hook.

282

This is the tricky part - he was thinking. A couple of twirls with the hook, a last heave-ho, and it left his hand, flying straight upwards.

The grappling hook curved in over the railing of the Professor Petrov. The sound of its contact on metal disappeared in the noise of the coasters' engine, which thudded monotonously away without change. Maynard took up the slack. When he met resistance, he tied the knotted rope to the launch and started climbing it. The man just in front of Wailes stood up and threw another grappling hook up over the railing. Within seconds, while Maynard was climbing the rope under the watchful eye of the men on the starboard side, four grappling hooks had secured the launch to the side of the coaster. The men on the starboard side started to climb to the deck. Nobody appeared on the coaster to hinder them.

When Maynard reached the deck, he took a quick look around. He noticed immediately that one of the life raft holders was empty. The wires, which had held it in place, dangled from the eyes. The bottle screws at the ends of the wires lay on the deck. He scanned the accommodation block for any sign of activity. The vessel seemed deserted. But appearances can be deceptive, so Maynard kept the machine pistol at the ready and crouched in the cover of the stern capstan, until his men started to arrive over the railing.

When his men were assembled on deck, Maynard assembled a little group of three just beside the engine room escape hatch. There was no talking. Each man knew precisely what had to be done.

Sergeant Thompson opened the escape hatch carefully. It was rusty, so that was difficult. The lights were on in the engine room. There was a short ladder going down to a catwalk just a couple of meters below. When the hatch was open, he dropped into the hole, landed on both feet, then slipped on an oily patch and fell on his stomach, with his torso protruding through the railing, looking straight down. He drew a quick, anxious breath and slid backwards onto the catwalk before bringing his machine pistol into position to cover himself. Nothing moved below.

The other two men in Thompson's party climbed through the hole. When Maynard was sure that there was no sound of gunfire, he sent three men into the accommodation block through the door into the galley, two men to the lighter on the starboard side, and started up the port side lighter to the bridge with the rest. Wailes and Watkins were just climbing over the railing. Wailes said,

"We'll follow Maynard up to the bridge, John. Keep your weapon cocked, and guard our ass but don't fire on anything until it fires on you first, or looks like it's going to."

Wailes drew his revolver and started up the ladder after the last man in Maynard's party. Watkins followed without a word.

When Maynard got to the bridge, he crouched down below the window to avoid being seen by anyone inside. The wing door was closed. He crept forward until his back was against the windbreak, and waited. The others crouched and huddled against the steel plate, like a big, fat worm, stretched out down the lighter. After a short wait, that seemed like forever, the engine pitch dropped, and the vibration stopped. Just like a jack-in-the-box, Maynard jumped up, pushed the wing door open and stepped inside, machine pistol at the ready.

There were only two people on the bridge. A man in a parka stood facing the door behind the chart table. He had one hand on the handle, and the other in his right pocket. He looked surprised. The other occupant of the bridge was a blonde woman in a heavy sweater who was standing beside the radio, with the handset in one hand and a pencil in the other. Maynard pointed the machine pistol at the man and signalled him to take his hand out of his pocket. The man straightened, and did so. Maynard pointed at the woman. She dropped the handset and raised her hands.

Maynard didn't say anything. He stepped sideways, away from the door, keeping his eye on both, and felt a lot more comfortable when the men behind him came inside, weapons at the ready. The man and the woman stayed frozen in their places, hands resting on top of their heads. Maynard crossed the bridge to the starboard side, and slid the door open. He stepped outside, and was faced by the weapon of one of the two men he had sent that way. The other was pointing his weapon back down the lighter. They relaxed. Maynard went inside, just as Wailes entered the port side door.

Wailes started to laugh. It was the first sound anyone had made in ages. It rang out like thunder in the confines of the bridge. Maynard looked at him.

"Well - Blow me down! Bill Lennox, you old bugger!....What are you doing here?"

The man in the parka let his hands fall slowly, and said, in a heavy Geordie accent that blew Maynard and Watkins away.

"Well, well, if it isn't my old mate Avon Wailes! Still got that Colt I see. Isn't it about time you changed it for a Smith and Wesson?"

Wailes looked down at the revolver, then looked up again.

"You know, I do believe you're right Bill!"

He turned around and threw the Colt through the door with all of his might. It was disappearing over the side at about the same time as Lennox and Wailes were giving each other a big, brotherly hug of welcome.

The sound of the outboard motor came closer. Brian turned the binoculars in the general direction of the noise, which was difficult to pinpoint in the fog. After a while, the rubber dinghy appeared. The shape by the engine was huddled in its duffle coat, with the hood pulled up over its head. There were four boxes in front.

Brian turned around and stuck his head in through the open door.

"Dougy's back!" He said loudly enough for Bob and Billy to hear.

They were sitting around the table down in the saloon, checking the weapons that were lying there. Bob had just finished loading the pump gun, and laid it on the couch beside him. Billy looked up.

"About bloody time - It took him long enough! - Hey Brian! You'd better come down and stand by the radio, the Petrov's due to come on at any minute!"

Brian stepped inside and backed down the short lighter. He took off the parka and hung it on the hook to the left of the entrance. Billy turned his attention to the pistol in his hand and began dripping oil on the breach. Brian sat on the lighter, facing the saloon, and lit a cigarette. At the sound of the flint striking, Bob turned his head.

"What about a ciggy Brian?"

Brian tossed him the pack. Bob caught it in one hand, pulled out a cigarette and began to search for his matches, which were somewhere among the rags and iron on the table. The outboard engine in the rubber dinghy stopped just outside. There was a slight bump. Bob found the matches and struck a light to the cigarette. Brian reached over to the radio table and took the pistol that was lying there. The magazine was out. It lay where the pistol had been. Billy had his head down under the table. He had dropped a bullet on the floor and was rummaging around to see if he could find it. There were footsteps behind Brian.

"It's about time you got back Dougy! Where the hell have you been?"

He stated sharply, and half-turned.

The man in Dougy's donkey jacket saw the pistol in Brian's hand, pulled his own pistol, and fired at Brian from point blank range, twice in rapid succession. Brian collapsed in a heap on the deck. The two bullets buried themselves in the thick deck planking.

Billy forgot about the bullet on the deck, and being in the unhappy position of sitting, while his torso was under the table, he chose to let the rest of his body hit the deck under the table. The cigarette dropped from Bob's mouth at the sound of the first shot, but being the professional he was, and having the shotgun handy, he had it in his hand a moment after the sound of the last shot reverberated around the saloon. Click, clack. The first round went into the chamber. Boom! The gun went off in the direction of the lighter, and a rapid click, clack later went off again. Billy crawled out from under the table and rammed the magazine home in the pistol. Bob stood up, jumped into the centre of the saloon with the shotgun pointed at the lighter and fired again. It was unnecessary. The man was lying in the wheelhouse, dead.

"What the fucks' going on - where's Dougy? Who the hell is that?" Bob shouted.

Billy didn't answer. They looked at each other. Both wondered what was going on. Billy acted first. He pushed past Bob, jumped over Brian's lifeless body, and ran up the lighter into the wheelhouse, holding the pistol in front of him. Bob could see Billy in a crouched posture, pointing the gun first in one direction, then in another, and again in a third, before he stood upright and let the gun fall to his side. Bob hurried up the lighter. There was nobody else in sight. Billy went across to the man that Bob had shot. He was lying face up on the floor, arms played out and a whole lot of blood on the deck around him. Billy opened the duffle coat and straightened.

"A fuckin' marine! Shit! You know what that means?"

"Navy's here!" Said Bob, and continued "Got a ciggy? I lost the other one downstairs!"

Billy took the packet out of his breast pocket and handed them over. Bob took one and handed the pack back to Billy, who also took one, put the packet back into the pocket, and lit both. Neither said a word, but looked around outside. There was no sign of activity to be seen anywhere.

"Wonder what happened to Dougy?"

Bob asked himself aloud.

"Either arrested or dead. In any case, we've got to get out of here, and now!"

"What about the coaster?"

Billy thought about that one for a second then seemed to make up his mind.

"Forget them - If the Navy's here, the coaster will be their first target, it's certainly easy to spot. Let's get the anchor up. The current'll take the boat north. When we get a little bit away, we'll start the engine and bugger off."

"Got a better idea." Said Bob. "We pull up the anchor, start the engine, set the auto pilot to take her north, and bugger off in the dinghy in the other direction." Billy laughed.

"Nice one, Cyril! I like that one. Let's do it now!"

Bob reached into the saloon and took the parka from the hook where Brian had hung it. He went on deck and climbed overboard into the rubber dinghy. It was a shame to have to do it, but there was no other way. He heaved the four crates of beer Dougy had bought overboard. Billy disappeared into the saloon and brought up a jerry can of extra fuel. He stopped on the way back just long enough to prise the empty pistol from Brian's dead hand and take the magazine from where it still lay on the table under the radio. He went outside. Bob had just heaved the last crate overboard and was standing waiting in the dinghy. Billy threw him a pistol. Bob put it in one of the pockets. He kissed the shotgun goodbye and dropped it over the side. It would be too obvious once they got ashore - if they ever did...! He took the jerry can Billy handed to him, set it in the bottom of the dinghy and sat down to wait for Billy.

Billy started the Sea Swan's engine. Then he came out. Bob watched him walk uneasily forward with the capstan handle in his hand.

Billy bent down, pushed the square end of the handle into the top of the capstan, and wound. He wound, and he wound. Bob couldn't hear the ratchet click in the noise from the engine, but he could clearly see the links on the chain moving upwards, and feel both the boat and the dinghy already begin to drift sideways in the current. The tip of the anchor appeared above the water line and stopped. Billy left the capstan handle in place and hurried aft to the wheelhouse.

Bob held on tightly to the wooden slat he was sitting on as the dinghy followed the hull of the boat around, clasped tightly to its side by the current. The engine increased in speed, then dropped again in tone as the gearbox was engaged to send the boat forward. It was at that point that the first salvo of heavy machinegun fire arrived. It ripped up the water on the port side, falling short of the boat by a hundred metres or so. There was no sound at all, but Bob recognised the crackling splashes that went as suddenly as they came.

"Come on Billy! Get a move on - they're firing at us!"

There was no reply. The Sea Swan gained momentum. The glass in the wheelhouse shattered as the next salvo arrived out of nowhere. Billy ducked out through the open door and clattered over the side into the dinghy. He dropped the mooring.

"Hit the deck!" He shouted above the noise of the engine.

Both threw themselves flat in the bottom of the dinghy, raising only the tops of their heads to look over the side.

For a while, the dinghy, having a momentum of its own, followed the Sea Swan as she picked up speed. But then it began to lag behind, coming into the wake of the receding boat, and bobbing like a cork in the troubled waters left by her propeller.   A short burst of fire fell not far away from the dinghy, and for a moment it looked like they would be hit. But the gunner must have changed his mind, because the next salvo, a long one, raked the Sea Swan from stem to stern. She didn't stop.

"Use the oars!" Billy exclaimed, "But don't sit up!"

Each took an oar. While lying on their backs in the bottom of the dinghy, they began to row, ever so still, towards the south east. More salvoes of gunfire. Still no reaction from the Sea Swan, which was by now almost invisible in the fog, that had thinned considerably within the last hour. Then there was a huge, sudden blink of fire and flame on an island to the south west of the dinghy's position. Both Bob and Billy saw it, and the ball of flame that shot towards the Sea Swan. The ball of flame hit the boat. She exploded instantly, lighting up the fog with a blinding white light.

At that instant, Bob shouted,

"Them bastards have got missiles! Let's get out of here now!"

With that, he jumped up and started the outboard. Billy stayed in the bottom of the dinghy and pulled in his oar. Bob had dropped the other one over the side.

It took long minutes for the dinghy to slip through Craffords Gut and turn north east into the cover of Longstone. Bob kept looking over his shoulder to see if anyone was following, and to check that the island from where they had seen the missile fired was out of sight. When they had rounded the southern tip of Longstone, Billy sat up. He lit two cigarettes and handed one to Bob.

"What now?" Said Bob.

"I don't know." Said Billy. Both fell silent.

When the fog finally drifted inland, H.M.S Battleaxe arrived on the scene. She manoeuvred within range of the Professor Petrov and prepared to take the launch on board. The fire support crew had returned. With them they brought a piece of the stern of the Sea Swan that they had found floating in the area. They had searched for more than two hours and had found no survivors, and only one body among the wreckage, that of Brian.

Captain Andersen stood on the bridge wing, watching, until the launch was safely in its cradle on deck and the men had begun strapping it in place. The other launch, the one which had been used by the boarding party which was still aboard the Professor Petrov, had already been taken aboard. Andersen went inside the wheelhouse and took the radio handset off its hook.

"Professor Petrov this is H.M.S. Battleaxe. Over."

On the Professor Petrov, Bill Lennox put down his mug of tea and picked up the handset.

"Professor Petrov here. Over."

"H.M.S.Battleaxe here. I'm heading south for Newcastle. Follow me at a safe distance. Over."

"Professor Petrov here. Roger. Willco. Over and out!"

A short while later, the Professor Petrov turned south in the wake of H.M.S. Battleaxe. Only elusively thin wisps of grey remained to block out the warmth of the sun.

www.ingramcontent.com/pod-product-compliance
Lightning Source LLC
Chambersburg PA
CBHW030409030726
47497CB00002B/546